D1624455

KING
KILL

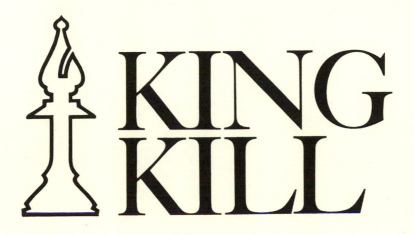

KING KILL

a novel by

THOMAS GAVIN

RANDOM HOUSE · New York

Copyright © 1977 by Thomas Gavin

All rights reserved under International and Pan-American Copyright Conventions.
Published in the United States by Random House, Inc., New York, and simultaneously
in Canada by Random House of Canada Limited, Toronto.

Library of Congress Cataloging in Publication Data

Gavin, Thomas.
    Kingkill.
    1. Schlumberger, William—Fiction. 2. Maelzel,
Johann Nepomuk, 1772-1838—Fiction. I. Title.
PZ4.G284Ki   [PS3557.A955]   813'.5'4   76-53455
ISBN 0-394-49827-5

Manufactured in the United States of America

98765432

Designed by Anita Karl

First Edition

For Claire

For you see, ladies and gentlemen, and above all, your Imperial Majesty, with a real Nightingale one can never calculate what is coming, but in this artificial bird everything is settled. It is this way, and no other! One can explain it; one can open it and show how it's almost human; show where the records are, and how they play and how one thing depends on another—!

Hans Christian Andersen in
"The Emperor's Nightingale"

Certain Arabian chess authorities believed that the term "checkmate" derives from the Persian "Shah-maat," which they translated as "The king is dead."

Contents

PART I

1 | False Facts

WILLIAM SCHLUMBERGER was a hunchback chess genius who reportedly died of yellow fever in 1838. The story of his death is a footnote in several American newspaper accounts detailing the death a few days later of his employer, Johann Nepomuk Maelzel. That death, wrongly described as natural, occurred on the brig *Otis* bound from Havana for Philadelphia.

Schlumberger's deformity—the result of a childhood fall from a swing—did not make him a cousin of M. Hugo's simian gargoyle. In the words of one observer, a journalist known for his acute and merciless eye, Schlumberger was a man of average height who had "a remarkable stoop in the shoulders." In their last years together, when Schlumberger's hump weighed more each day, each hour, he still topped Maelzel by at least three inches. But against Maelzel, stature had no more advantage than virtue. His bellow drowned Schlumberger's deferential whisper, the flash of his gold-flecked eyetooth dazzled Schlumberger blind, left him tottering, hesitant, easily drawn into the wake of Maelzel's hard-clopped stride. It was to be expected that Maelzel, a man of considerable renown—inventor, entrepreneur, canny businessman—would overshadow Schlumberger even in death. That, like so much else, was inevitable. Though the automaton chess player had been exposed as a hoax, it was not yet generally known, after all, that the deformed Alsatian identified in the obituaries as Maelzel's "associate" had been for twelve years the unacknowledged chess master of the United States. And no one knew the man who claimed he saw Schlumberger's corpse lied.

Since I have destroyed Schlumberger's journal, no evidence disproves that lie. No record exists to explain how, in the years following his alleged death, the passion contained no more by chess fed on arson, murder, solitude. No record but these pages, which I shall perhaps never finish. Or finishing, never publish. Publishing, disguise as fiction.

Let it be fiction, then—or biography, what you will—when I begin the true story of Schlumberger with the assertion that on the night Johann Nepomuk Maelzel left him for dead in a Havana hotel room, he had his first fire dream.

2 | The Fire Dream

IN THE DREAM the Turk's eyelids remain lowered, his eyes locked on the chessboard, even when the ceiling starts to blister and hiss. Schlumberger stands on the other side of the velvet rope that keeps back spectators—ten feet away from the Turk. The room is steeply shadowed, but Schlumberger makes out aisles of glass cases. Stuffed birds on branches planted in cement. The wired bones of a mastodon. Beside him, a still companion: a statue of Lot's wife, eyes starkly empty, struck blind by dread knowledge. In a distant corner a serpent of flame uncoils down the fringe gilding a drape. By its gently pulsing glow, Schlumberger gazes steadily at the Turk, gazes at his stiff left arm, extending with arrogant familiarity along the flank of the board, its fingertips deep inside enemy terrain, almost to his opponent's king row. Curiously, no part of his weight leans on the arm. His body is balanced rigidly erect. And the weight of the arm itself is supported entirely by the fingertips. The sole purpose of this pose is rhetorical.

A histrionic air is also implicit in the right arm, held at nearly a right angle from the body, bent at the elbow. As if offering escort to a lady. The forearm, appearing to have just completed a sweeping gesture, is poised, potent with menace, over the chessboard, the hand arcing down from the wrist to fingers that are straight, tapered, touching one another. Their tips form the base of a cone. The fingers cup a chesspiece so delicately their purpose might be a caress. The piece itself is concealed from view, but a survey of those remaining on the board and those out of play on the sidelines indicates it is the white queen. White queen to king's knight four would check the black king.

Smoke weaves across the board, a sinuous tendril, dispersing among embattled pawns. Puffballs from the Wagram cannonade. Schlumberger coughs. More smoke, thicker. He is not surprised. For some time now he has been aware of the serpent in the room, slithering along the floor. Perhaps he should cry out, run, but he may not, must not interrupt the Turk's next move—the one which will check Schlumberger's king. Now, however, the serpent's breath searing his cheek, Schlumberger knows the fire means to kill them. The game is no longer important; the Turk will realize that, surely. Once he realizes the danger, the Turk will rescue him. But how to get his attention? Slip under the rope, seize the Turk's shoulders, shake him out of his concentration. But when Schlumberger tries to step forward, his legs won't budge. His feet might as well be cast in iron, locked in place by a magnet under the floor. At first this startles Schlumberger. Then he remembers: I am in check.

He tries to resign himself, wants this explanation to be a reassurance. Why then is he trembling? It is as if an opponent were offering a queen sacrifice; he cannot see the trap, but it must be there. He reviews the logic of his position, searching for the flaw through which the flame will strike.

As he thinks he watches the chessboard, squints against the smoke which wavers and passes, obscuring it, coming more densely now, its hue thickened from white to yellow. In a far corner of the long room the ceiling belches, buckles, suddenly gravid. Plaster rains merrily onto a glass case under which ivory figurines pose and grimace, their Oriental concentration undisturbed. A concentration deep as sleep. Deep as that of the Turk, whose hand still lingers over the white queen, though the move before him is obvious and final. Can it be that the Turk himself is wary of a trap? Or can he possibly be taking pleasure in drawing out interminably Schlumberger's humiliation? It occurs to Schlumberger that hesitation itself may be a part of the Turk's strategy.

Now the smoke hovers among the hairs of the silver fur fringing the Turk's jacket at elbows and collar. He shows no alarm. When smoke swirls past his turbaned head, his expression remains placid, cheeks sucked in with ascetic calm, lips retaining their slightly voluptuous pout. Nor is he startled by a flaming roof beam that gives way with a groan and swipes down upon one of the glass cases, batting it off its feet. The glass shatters, spraying ivory figurines.

The Fire Dream

Despite these distractions, Schlumberger is still thinking. He is in check. Therefore he cannot move his legs. It is, in any case, not his move at all, but the Turk's. The Turk, then, must be the rescuer. But the Turk. . . . Just as Schlumberger is about to penetrate the lie sugaring the dream's secret truth, the smoke congeals in the shape of yet another plan. It is only necessary to shout. The Turk's attention will be drawn from the chessmen. And once he recognizes the danger, surely that mind capable of releasing fantastic possibilities for mobility in rooks and knights will be able to devise a stratagem to compensate for Schlumberger's temporary paralysis. Thus encouraged, Schlumberger shrieks, "Fire! Fire! The building is burning!" An explosion of flame pairs his shadow with the Turk's against the high wall. As he muses on the frenzied dance his cries lose urgency, settle into a chant. "The building is burning," he chants. "We both will burn, both will die." And he works melodic variations on these phrases like an operatic tragedian until he is giggling so hard he can no longer speak. Smoke tears his eyes; heat dries the tears.

His throat tightens on the laughter, chokes it to a cough; and coughing smoke, gasping, sucking it deep into his lungs, enveloped in thick billows that surge and spill as they break in lazy waves, he wonders uneasily how he could have been coughing so long without noticing the smoke. Coughing? Wasn't he, just a moment ago, laughing? Not him, no. Who, then, could have mocked this danger, mocked the Turk? An uncomfortable suspicion hovers in the smoke, which parts in a sudden display of candor, releasing for inspection this fact: no amount of screaming will ever distract the Turk. Schlumberger knows this. With beads of sweat trickling through his eyebrows, making him blink, he knows that only one thing ever made the Turk raise his eyes—a false move on the board. Then you would hear the gears in his chest sputter as if the human error had filled him with speechless outrage, and the lids would snap up hard against the roof of the carved eye sockets, unshielding those two ice-grey circles of glass. Schlumberger never knew a man that didn't look away.

The dream offers a final ruse. Move out of turn, it whispers, take one of the Turk's rooks with a pawn, using a knight's move, forcing the Turk to surrender his attention. Impatient at last, Schlumberger rips aside this lie. He confronts the truth he has always known—the Turk's legs are useless as his own.

KINGKILL

The Turk's legs are in fact the only purely decorative part of his anatomy. Schlumberger has often remarked on the contempt for them shown by the Turk's artificer, who did not even provide the cabinet with a niche where they might rest comfortably, but wrenched them sideways from the torso to dangle over the edge of a stool hinged to the cabinet. Schlumberger knows they are nothing more than a pair of balloon trousers stuffed with rags, ending in pointed slippers sewn to cotton stockings that are sewn to the ankle-fitting trousers.

Now Schlumberger is laughing again. He turns on his heel and strides to the door, his legs miraculously restored. It was never he who was in check, but the Turk. For Schlumberger there was never the slightest danger. Turning in the doorway for a gloating final look, he feels a rush of giddy ecstasy as he pierces the dream's last secret—it was he himself who set the fire.

At this moment a glowing woodchip lands on the Turk's fur collar. It puffs into life, locking the Turk's head in a flaming vise. As fire strokes the well-oiled cheeks, Schlumberger screams and wakes.

3 | The Impossible Machine

NOT AN ECHO but a memory of sound fills Schlumberger's ears as he wakes. He has just opened his eyes to find himself alone in his hotel room. The door closed too softly to produce an echo, though in a room sparsely furnished as this, carpetless and high ceilinged, the echoes might have been expected to breed like the mosquito larvae in the ditches and rain barrels outside the hotel.

The sounds made by the closing door repeat themselves endlessly in Schlumberger's mind. The scrape of the bolt against the doorjamb, followed by the click as it shoots into the slot, seems to fill the room with syncopation. The rhythm a sluggish machine might produce. First the almost inaudible grating the bolt made as the hand on the other side of the door pulled it slowly, carefully into the doorjamb against the resistance of the hidden spring. Then a sharp betraying tick when the spring snapped the bolt into the hollow in the doorjamb. And Schlumberger opened his eyes.

And the sound repeats itself in his mind. The snap is like a rifle report in Schlumberger's ears, made sensitive by the fever. Each time the spring begins its forlorn resistance, yielding by fractions to the hand steadily pulling on the outer doorknob, Schlumberger braces for the climax, breathes freely only after its charge of pain has exploded in his ears, and breathing, hears again the first scrape of the reluctantly yielding bolt.

Lying on the sweat-drenched pillow with his head turned in the direction of the door, Schlumberger is aware, despite the delirium

[9]

which has abstracted the sound in his mind from its cause, that the door has recently been closed. Woven in the interstices of his auditory memory is a visual image which may also be a memory; or, since he has the impression that his eyes were closed until the first crack of the snapping bolt, perhaps the image is merely an imagined reconstruction of sounds and silences that penetrated his sleep and were interpreted by some level of his mind other than that creating the fire dream. A level perhaps not fully apart, however, for the image Schlumberger remembers or imagines is a figure standing in the open doorway, a figure that has turned, in the act of leaving the hotel room, to regard him. And its face is that of the Turk, his eyes grey circles of glass, glaring their disdain for some awful error. Sometimes the Turk's cheeks and turban are on fire as they were in the dream. Sometimes the flames pale and crystalize into the frosty crown and full sidewhiskers of Johann Nepomuk Maelzel, frowning at the pocket watch in his palm, then at the still figure of Schlumberger lying on the bed.

This, at any rate, is how Schlumberger will re-create him many years later in his journal—that leatherbound volume of nearly three hundred quarto pages, his companion in lonely hotel rooms and stagecoaches and steamships. His last entry left only four pages blank. Most events were recorded on the night of the day they occurred; occasionally, however, a long entry recollected something that happened weeks or even years earlier, such as the fire dream, the escape from Havana, the haunted voyage of the brig *Otis*. In those hectic days Pepysian tranquility eluded him.

Maelzel, then, had just returned his watch to its waistcoat pocket. The frown that crossed his brow as he tried to read its dial by the flickering lamplight did not disappear when he raised his eyes for a last hasty glance at the bed. From beneath the sheet a writhe and a restive moan cautioned him to close the door with care.

Throughout the preceding days, while Maelzel was waiting to see whether Schlumberger would die, he had been tinkering with some gears and bolts the desk clerk had lugged up to the hotel room in a carpet bag. Schlumberger had taken the extra blanket the clerk had brought along with Maelzel's bag, and crawled back into bed with it, where he shivered and watched Maelzel through the gauze curtains draped from the bedposts to serve as mosquito netting.

"What am I doing in your bed?" Schlumberger asked.

The Impossible Machine

"That's what I was going to ask you," Maelzel said. "Why can't you flop in your own room if you're going to get sick?"

Schlumberger remembered there was a reason why he was in Maelzel's room, and it had to be concealed until he could stand without getting dizzy. There would be no trouble concealing it: he couldn't remember it himself.

He recognized by the way Maelzel attacked the buttons of his waistcoat that he was in a mood to tinker. He knew it was only when the tinkering fit was on him that he snapped his cravat in the air as he drew it away from his neck. *Now he'll take off his cuffs and roll back his sleeves,* Schlumberger was thinking as he watched. *Then he'll sit himself at that table as if he had a roast duck on it and pick up that wrench like a fork.* But after Maelzel took off his cuffs and collar he undid his shirt buttons with the same rapid, confident, economical finger motions he had used on the waistcoat; and he took off the shirt and hung it on top of the waistcoat over the back of the chair before pulling out the chair and seating himself the way Schlumberger had expected, as if to a feast.

"Why are you getting undressed?" Schlumberger had croaked. He was disturbed to see Maelzel naked as a turtle out of its shell. His torso was a driftwood white, protected only by a thick grey fleece that spread across the upper back and curled like wooly suspenders down past the bald shoulder knobs onto his chest. It made decorative sworls round the nipples of his sagging womanish dugs.

At first Maelzel had ignored the question, his quick hands pulling gears and wheels and bolts from the bag and arranging them on the table according to some esoteric pattern. Then he had chuckled with a malice Schlumberger couldn't account for and said, "You're the one who's always complaining about the heat. Remember last week, how you, quote, fainted from the heat inside the box, unquote?"

"It's not just heat this time. It's fever. God, I'm sick. My muscles hurt. And my bones: did you ever have an ache in your joints, so when you move it feels like one bone is grinding against the other?"

Maelzel gave a refined snort and tucked his lower lip under the other like a man who refrains from saying the obvious. Then, when his tactful silence had been played for all its rhetorical value, he said the obvious anyway. "First it's heat. Now fever's your excuse. Me, I'd call it fire. Fire*water*."

"I told you I wouldn't drink before games any more and I didn't,'' said Schlumberger, practically whimpering. "God dammit, I'm sick!'' At this point Maelzel paused in his tinkering and looked over at Schlumberger.

"Maybe you are at that,'' he said. "I didn't notice you all rolled up in that blanket. My God, boy, don't you know it's not even noon yet and a horse can get a lather out on that street without even trotting.''

"I got the chills,'' muttered Schlumberger, beginning to drift away from the conversation.

Maelzel peered at him through the gauze netting, then said with a wry smile, "It's a pity I can't just oil you up the way I do the Turk.''

Schlumberger was thinking about this as he fell asleep. Cool oil squirting into his knee joints, his elbows, arm sockets, balming the pain. But the pain came back, the oil turned into his own clammy sweat soaking the sheets. He awoke in the afternoon needing water. Maelzel had gone out, probably to eat. The table was still full of machine parts. Some of them had been connected to one another. There were rods connecting wheels to other wheels that turned nothing. There were gears with their teeth set against the teeth of other gears that were attached to wires strung through pulleys and dangling over the side of the table. It looked as if somebody had been skinning a mechanical rabbit.

Schlumberger swung one leg over the side of the bed, catching his toe in a hole in the mosquito netting. He was planning to go down to the dining room for water. He hoisted himself gingerly onto an elbow, but as soon as he tried to sit up, he got so dizzy he could barely organize the muscle coordination to flop himself back onto the mattress rather than the floor. He slid back into sleep wondering how to get water.

Somewhere in the room there was water dripping. A steady *toc-toc* of water slapping into a puddle. *It's raining,* Schlumberger thought. *All I'll have to do is find the hole in the roof where it's leaking through.* His eyes were still closed. He could feel his lips crack like caked mud when he tried to smile. *I can open my mouth and drink it fresh from the pump.* He opened his eyes and the rain went away and there was Maelzel glaring at a contraption of spinning gears that lifted a rod at each revolution and dropped it back with a *toc-toc-toc*.

"I need water,'' Schlumberger whispered.

A spring somewhere deep in the guts of the machine relaxed and

[1 2]

the wheels slowed and the *toc-toc* of the rod slowed and stopped. Maelzel cursed. Then he said, "Later, Willy. I'm busy now."

Schlumberger moaned and tried to scream, but only managed a hoarse cough. He trembled furiously.

"Now. God. Damn. You," he whispered. "I need. Water *now!*"

"I think you're delirious," Maelzel replied. "I suppose you know I had to cancel tonight's performance."

The window was dark. A lantern burned unsteadily on the table, making the shadow of Maelzel's contraption undulate on the wall beside him. Maelzel wiped his oily fingertips with a rag and came to the bed. He pulled back the gauze curtain to get a better look at Schlumberger. He squinted down at him through his spectacles with the same shrewd appraisal he had a moment before fixed on the machine.

"Yes, there's no doubt of it," he said. "You're delirious. Christ. As if you weren't enough trouble. Drunk half the time."

"Please," croaked Schlumberger. "Please, *now*. Water *now*." And he made dry sobs like a man scratching flint.

By the time Maelzel returned with a pitcher and a cup, Schlumberger had produced his own water. He was leaking a thin mucus from his nostrils and his eyes were red-rimmed and puffy. He drank a quart of water with his head cradled in Maelzel's arm. Then he vomited most of it onto the floor and fell back exhausted, asleep immediately. That had been on the first day of the fever.

BY THE THIRD NIGHT, with Schlumberger dropping out of delirium only a few times a day, Maelzel must have been thoroughly frightened. If not for Schlumberger, then for loss of the skills only a man of Schlumberger's genius could provide; and also, most probably, for his own skin. He may not have been certain Schlumberger had yellow fever, but by now he would have been fairly positive it wasn't a cold or a mild grippe. There was no money for doctors, just as there was no money for another hotel room where he could breathe air that hadn't passed through Schlumberger's wet, hot lungs.

During the past week the heat and humidity had become intolerable. Maelzel had abandoned his tinkering and now spent his time pacing the room in a wide arc around the bed where Schlumberger sniffled and moaned and gargled phlegm with every breath. It must have been fear as much as the heat that sent the moisture trickling through the thinning hair on Maelzel's scalp and down his armpits along his rib cage. Fear coated him with a swampy film from Schlumberger's lungs.

His pendulous dugs had been soaked and dried so many times they were chafed raw where they swung against his rib cage, and when Schlumberger opened his eyes, Maelzel was pacing with his arms folded and a breast resting in the crook of each arm. The hairs sprouting from the nipples were plastered to the skin. Schlumberger tried to make his eyes look somewhere else. A lewd old whore in Paris used to offer her wares the same way, leaning her elbows on a window sill and singing out to the men that passed below her in the street.

"Am I going to die?"

Maelzel stopped pacing.

"That's the first lucid remark you've made in three days," he said. He pulled back the gauze curtain strung from the bedposts. The spectacles clamped on Maelzel's beaky nose did a good job of disguising what went on behind them, but Schlumberger caught something in a glint over their rims that frightened him. It was the look Maelzel gave to a gear worn past repair.

"I was joking," Schlumberger whispered, forcing his lips into a grimace. "Why aren't you at work?" he croaked. He was proving he was lucid. "What is it?" He made a twitch that was supposed to be a nod in the direction of the machinery on the table. "Another trumpet player?"

Maelzel seemed relieved at the switch of focus. He dropped the netting and backed away from Schlumberger, turning to the table on which the gears and rods had been organized into a complex maze.

"It's something to show that damned writer."

"Writer? Who?" Schlumberger was trying to stay interested, but with each breath he took, he felt his mind casting ballast. He was like a balloonist rising, the car swirling with the currents the clouds followed.

"Poe," said Maelzel. "You ought to remember Poe and his filthy article."

Schlumberger was floating, buffeted by a stiff wind, but he managed one more question.

"Poe? A writer?"

"Yes, Poe," replied Maelzel irritably. "The one who said it was impossible to make a machine that could play chess."

Those were the last words Schlumberger heard. The wind was

gone now; he was in a dead calm, cloudless and hushed. A white blur hovered at the edge of his vision. *A patch of cloud,* he thought, but turning toward it he saw standing beside him in the car the statue of Lot's wife, staring with sad blind eyes. And before he could wonder how this might be, he found himself waiting behind the velvet rope, his king desperately at bay before the Turk's queen.

He was beginning his first fire dream. He would wake to the scrape and snap the bolt made as Maelzel closed the door.

4 | Schlumberger Subdues the Flesh

SCHLUMBERGER'S CAR hit earth with a bump. The fever was gone. He smiled.

Within an hour he was in the hotel dining room sipping soup with a trembling hand. He got so little from the bowl to his lips that he put his face down to the table to narrow the distance his spoon had to travel. By the time the soup was finished his trembling had been brought under control. He was still smiling. He ate four pieces of buttered bread and drank half a bottle of wine. Then he walked smiling among the waiters and tables of the dining room, nodding to strangers who were smiling at him, and up the stairs with his hand prudently sliding along the banister, congratulating himself at every step. On the last few steps his hand was gripping the banister tightly, making short leaps from grip to grip. He saw himself in the hall mirror at the landing. His smile was clamped to his teeth and his lips were white against the teeth, white as the tips of his fingers clutching the banister post. It was thinking of Maelzel that made him smile, thinking how surprised he would be to see Schlumberger alive. It was thinking how he would kill Maelzel.

Somewhere between the onset of his illness and his apparent recovery, which was actually the remission period preceding the development of the truly lethal symptoms, Schlumberger had decided he must kill Maelzel. If there was ever a moment when he subjected the impulse to the scrutiny of logic before letting it harden into purpose, he was not aware of it. At some moment the reasons why Maelzel had to die must have been hard little pebbles strung on a chain that Schlumberger fingered like an old woman at her beads. But the beads had come

[16]

unstrung and rattled off to hide in the chinks and fissures of Schlumberger's brain. He could no longer recite the words of the prayer. But he had the faith.

Without it, he probably would have died. Religious people are sometimes able to call upon tremendous reserves of energy, and Schlumberger had undergone a conversion. So when his body began to do unspeakable things to him, he tightened his smile and thought about his mission.

The first thing his body did to him was to reject everything he had eaten. After the first few upheavals, it was no longer the horrible gut-wrenching nausea he occasionally experienced when he was drunk. The vomit came smooth as a baby's. The only problem was that it wouldn't stop coming. With his stomach scoured of its contents, the vomit became watery. Then Schlumberger noticed his body was producing a thick blackish substance along with the water. He decided it was blood. Soon his body was also leaking blood into the chamber pot from his anus and penis. His insides felt as if they were being ripped apart the way a quick impatient woman might rip out a crooked hem.

The attitude of the hotel management to Schlumberger's illness must be deduced from the description of the ordeal later entered in his journal, particularly from his record of a pleading monologue the room clerk delivered from the other side of a closed door. The attitude was more businesslike than compassionate. The manager would have known the probable cause of the fever—that it was spawned in poisonous fumes emanating from decaying sewage and that it spread by contagion. The garbage and human waste rotting in the streets had given Havana a world-wide reputation as a pesthole. Augmenting this reputation was the fever itself. Introduced in 1761, probably by way of Vera Cruz, it claimed three to four hundred lives a year. After more than two generations the local inhabitants had developed immunity. A disproportionately large number of its victims were therefore strangers to Havana—immigrants and visitors like Schlumberger. The fever was a constant threat to the solvency of the hotelkeepers who lodged the visitors. The fear of contagion could empty a hotel within half an hour.

The manager of the large harbor-front hotel on the Passeo de Paulo made up his mind to evict the sick man in room 211. The decision was not particularly humane, but when his clerk mentioned that the sick man's skin seemed to have turned lemon-yellow, the manager knew it was the fever and Schlumberger was sure to die anyway. The manager didn't see why it had to be in his hotel. Particularly since Maelzel had departed without offering any payment on account.

He sent his clerk upstairs to notify Schlumberger. The clerk stood outside the door repeating, "You'll have to leave, Mr. Schlumberger, did you hear me? I am very sorry, Mr. Schlumberger, but the management requires the room by noon today." The only answer he got was the thin trickle of Schlumberger's large intestine bleeding itself into the chamber pot. The clerk went back downstairs and informed the manager that he had notified the gentleman in room 211 that the room must be vacated by noon. At 3 P.M. the manager told the desk clerk to use his master key to enter room 211 and remove the luggage and tell Mr. Schlumberger that if he did not vacate the room immediately he would be forcibly evicted. The clerk went upstairs slowly and was gone nearly half an hour. He whispered to Schlumberger through the door. He started out whispering very formally, and when no answer came from the occupant of the room, but only the horrifying trickle and groans and once a curse that the clerk was not even sure was directed at him, he began to whisper almost like a lover, telling Schlumberger with a voice that occasionally broke or choked, suspending phrases in long pauses while he groped for the precise and tactful word, how he needed his job, how he mustn't get fired again, and, without ever actually calling Schlumberger a dead man, taking great care not to refer even obliquely to Schlumberger's illness, how dear life was to the clerk, how totally dependent on him were his wife and five children.

Just when the manager's impatience was beginning to veer into alarm, he saw his clerk coming down the stairs, walking stiffly. The manager knew by the way his clerk walked what they had both guessed without saying it before the clerk was sent up—that he wasn't going to be able to make Schlumberger leave. The clerk was wearing the sweat beading his upper lip like a battle scar. He hesitated a little before speaking to the manager, then said he hoped the manager would understand—he was a family man with five children. Then he explained that he had spoken most emphatically to Mr. Schlumberger through the door, but he did not and, being a family man, would not enter the room of a man with the fever. The clerk did not whisper this speech, but said it with a firmness tempered by respect, and with only a slight tremor. Then he stood still expecting to be dismissed.

Schlumberger Subdues the Flesh

The manager was a man of compassion and understanding. He understood about the five children, and in fact (though he would not mention this to the clerk) he was not at all surprised that the clerk balked at his instructions, which he was never convinced would have achieved the desired result in any case. He also understood that the clerk, in all respects save those touching on yellow fever, was diligent and courteous, and knew how to keep an accurate balance sheet. Therefore the clerk was not dismissed. For the rest of the day the manager dealt with the problem of Schlumberger by worrying about it.

The next day a guest informed the manager that there appeared to be someone calling for help in room 211. The manager gave a competent smile and said the problem was being dealt with. The guest took the arm of his wife and went away quite satisfied, but the manager must have realized that he needed to make a plan. There was a doctor the manager knew, a man who used to come into the hotel bar frequently until he ran up a startling bill and was told he would not be welcome again until he paid it. The manager probably found out the doctor's address from the bartender. He may have gone there personally in the buckboard Schlumberger often had seen him driving around town; more likely, he sent for the doctor and took him into his private office, where the conversation would have turned first to the doctor's liquor bill, about which the manager would be very understanding, and then to the manager's problem, the sick man in room 211. Depending on how far the manager figured he could trust the doctor's discretion, he may even have admitted that the sick man probably had yellow fever, which the doctor could see would be very bad for business unless it were handled with the utmost delicacy. If the doctor had not raised an eyebrow by this time, the manager might even have pointed out that since the sick man was sure to die anyhow, a potion of laudanum that would end his agony a few hours earlier would be a mercy, and—this in a rush, knowing he was in it beyond backing out now—those few hours would mean a great deal to the manager as well, would mean the body could be carried out that night, by way of a back stairway while the guests were sleeping, and found perhaps in an alley or maybe even washing against the pilings down on the docks.

The doctor's liquor bill must have been very high and he must have run out of credit all over town because that night he was creaking up the back stairs of the hotel along with the manager and his clerk, who had been put on the night shift especially so he could come along. The manager must have wondered for a long time what to do about the clerk. If Schlumberger just disappeared, the clerk might be able to put the manager in an awkward position, even a dangerous one. Better to have him along, all the way in, since he knew so much already. That was how the manager would have reasoned it.

The clerk resented being made party to something that was not supposed to be part of a hotel clerk's regular duties, but while he was able to refuse in the name of his five children to do something the manager himself was unwilling to do, he was unable to refuse to follow where he would not go alone. The sounds from Schlumberger's room had stopped altogether. When they had heard nothing but silence from the room for ten minutes, the manager gestured the clerk to the door lock. The doctor was still breathing heavily from his climb, filling the dark hallway with a tart smell. The clerk swung the door open. The doctor's whiskey smell was immediately overpowered by another odor, a sweet stink that made the manager and the clerk gasp. The doctor rocked back on his heels and looked professionally profound. Then the clerk stepped aside to allow the manager to pass. The manager glanced at the doctor, who passed the glance glassily back. Then the manager went just inside the doorway and turned viciously to the clerk, gesturing him to the bed.

"Pull back the blanket," he ordered.

The clerk started to protest, but the hard edge to the manager's voice had told him this was not the proper moment to discuss his familial responsibilities. He approached the bed, where a blanket concealed what looked like the contours of a man's body. He pulled back the blanket. On Schlumberger's face was a rictuslike smile, and in his hands were a pair of cocked dueling pistols. He asked for food.

Schlumberger kept one pistol trained on the manager and one on the doctor while the clerk scurried down to the kitchen. Though Schlumberger was not in a mood to cultivate conversational arts, he managed to inquire after the whereabouts of his companion, Johann Maelzel. The manager told him Maelzel had probably left Havana, since the local town hall had canceled all remaining performances of the automaton chess player and the other mechanical inventions that were part of the act. Being a man of principle even with a gun pointed at his chest, the manager went so far as to remind Schlumberger that Maelzel

[20]

had neglected to ask for a bill before his departure, and he hoped Schlumberger would be kind enough to settle their account. Schlumberger ignored this remark. Then for a few minutes everybody waited for the clerk in an uncomfortable silence, broken at last by the doctor, who began to reproach the manager, saying he had not expected to find such a healthy patient. The manager shushed the doctor savagely and tried to tell Schlumberger he had brought the doctor to treat Schlumberger. But the doctor was annoyed by the manager's rudeness, and before he was done telling the manager what he thought of him, occasionally soliciting sympathy from Schlumberger himself, who had imperceptibly shifted into the role of the doctor's ally and fellow victim, Schlumberger had pieced together enough of the manager's original plan to make his rictus tighten a little wider across his face. Once there was a tray of food in front of him Schlumberger lost interest in the manager, who slipped out of the room unnoticed along with the clerk and even the doctor. The manager returned some twenty minutes later with a police officer, but Schlumberger had heard them coming and disappeared.

Schlumberger's determination to kill Maelzel had protected him not only from death, but from the idea of death. Death came like a rapist to his body, forcing submission to its obscenities. But Schlumberger had that impregnable recourse of whores and saints: he could put his mind somewhere else while his body was being ravished. It was no more possible for death to force upon him a consciousness of his vulnerability to total extinction, which is the idea of death, than a man could truly violate a woman who is calculating her bank account or the immensity of God's love. He had been penetrated, but he never made that spasmic flinch that is the mind's orgasm at the thought of its annihilation. He was innocent of death's carnality. And this virgin myth of immortality was shielded from doubt and ambiguity by the purity of his decision to murder Maelzel.

THAT NIGHT a gentleman of quality with an unfortunate habit of frequenting the sailors' saloons along the Havana waterfront reported to the police that someone had stepped out of an alley and robbed him at gunpoint. The press, doubtless quoting the gentleman's statement to the police, noted a peculiar fact: when, in fear of his life at the "wild and desperate appearance of the bandit," the gentleman offered his gold watch as well as his money, the bandit snatched it so viciously that the victim's vest was torn, but instead of stealing the watch the bandit dashed it to the cobbles and ran away. The gentleman described his assailant as tall, but extremely stoop-shouldered, perhaps even a hunchback.

It was never clearly established that Schlumberger was the hunchback in question. His journal makes no mention of it. But there is no doubt that he required money and succeeded in obtaining it in short order. Though he was not by nature a robber, he had acquired that sense of expedient justification characteristic of persons living in service to a self-transcending idea. His central article of faith, that Maelzel must die, was by now developing a theology to explain its revelation. Maelzel had to die, Schlumberger had decided, because this was the only way to prevent him from building a machine that could play chess.

5 | The King and the Drummer Boy

AT THE CAFÉ DE LA RÉGENCE, where Maelzel had gone thirteen years earlier looking for someone who knew end games, the tables were full of chessboards and the walls were full of mirrors. The mirrored chessplayers reflected in opposing mirrors replicated infinitely each move of the solemn, glaring, pipe-smoking, immobile chess players. To Schlumberger this meant that each time he drawled *"Échec,"* his final gesture was simultaneously recorded by a universe in his image. To Maelzel, poised like a retriever in the doorway, a decisive man momentarily undecided, prodded by debt, lawsuits and rage, the mirrors were a bafflement camouflaging his quarry among what seemed at giddy first glance to be several thousand rather than a few dozen men.

Schlumberger was as young as the century in 1825, but in the past three years he had developed the predictable routines of an old man, dislodging himself only by necessity from the corner armchair at the Régence round which the diminishing moons of his reflections orbited. Maelzel had forayed into all the courts of Western Europe without finding a place where he could sit down before glancing over his shoulder for a process server. Having exhausted the patience of a continent, he was now preparing his retreat in characteristic fashion— by planning another invasion. This time his target was the vastness and enthusiasm and credulous wealth of the United States, where his penchant for living off the land might be dissembled. He was counting on America's remoteness from the Napoleonic Wars to provide a climate innocent of the knowledge that a campaigning army has a ravenous appetite but plants no grain. He could not, however, launch his campaign without a good captain of artillery. For this he required Schlumberger.

Unfortunately for Maelzel, Schlumberger required practically nothing. At his corner table in the Régence he earned the few francs he needed for board and lodging by giving chess lessons. He lacked the teacher's passion to share his knowledge, and once his pupils had mastered the idiosyncratic hops and glides by which the various pieces moved and captured, they progressed further only if they could turn to account the one truth Schlumberger did care to impart, which was the infinite power of Schlumberger to thwart and humble them. The few with the resilience to absorb along with this truth a feeling for the versatility of the instruments through which it was conveyed became quite good chess players against people other than Schlumberger. One of his pupils was Fournié de St. Amant, known in later years as the "Viceroy" of Schlumberger's sole rival, Louis Charles Mahé de la Bourdonnais. From 1820 to 1840 La Bourdonnais was acknowledged as the greatest chess player of the Régence and therefore of the world. When news of Schlumberger's "death" in Havana reached St. Amant, he paid tribute to his former master for "initiating him into the great combinations of the game."

After his workday was done Schlumberger vacated his chair to stroll for an hour along the Rue St. Honoré and returned to the café for an evening of relaxation, which consisted in teaching all challengers free of charge the same lesson his pupils paid to learn. He was defeated only when intoxicated, but this happened frequently enough against crucial opponents to bar him from a secure place in the very top rank of players. Despite its drawbacks Schlumberger's fondness for wine served his reputation well. In the first place he often won against formidable players even while he was accumulating empty saucers on his table nearly as fast as captured pieces. Secondly, though some could boast of having beaten Schlumberger, anyone (with the sole exception of La Bourdonnais) who asserted himself a better player was met with a shrug: "Ah, but you know that night Schlumberger could hardly lift a pawn."

Thus did Schlumberger evade check. The defensive nature of this strategy was essentially foreign to his board game, which in middle and end games at least was rapacious. Only once had a threatening coun-

The King and the Drummer Boy

terploy been invoked, when an emissary from the Frankfurt chess club refused obstinately to engage forces until Schlumberger was thoroughly sober. Schlumberger taunted and raged, but so many wagers had been made on the match that he was forced to comply. The match was rescheduled for the following evening. All the next day his usual chair was vacant. At the appointed time he appeared, pale and sweating but sober. The spectators who were accustomed to his habit of scooping up a piece and flicking it dartlike at the desired square gasped when his hand trembled over a bishop's gambit. With contemptuous rapidity he defeated the Frankfurter four times in a row and left the café without speaking to anyone. When he returned two days later to his accustomed seat, he explained that he had taken ill with fever on the night of the match. A few with sufficient cleverness and malice whispered that he would have said the same thing if he had lost. The fact remained that the upper limit of his powers was still a vexing mystery.

Seldom did anyone broadcast his annoyance with Schlumberger's drinking; away from the board he had developed an attack that employed a hearty male charm and an acrid wit to much the same effect as Bonaparte used cannon and cavalry. His technique was first to isolate his victim, then reduce all witnesses to the status of accomplices in the attack that followed. "And then we have D—," he would begin, pausing with dagger poised at his enemy's jugular. And in the pause he had a way of casting round the table a bright innocent smile which coaxed from even the least bloodthirsty members of his audience an anticipatory grin that broke, as he thrust home, into wicked robust laughter. Never addressing his victim, speaking of him in the third person as if he were not present, Schlumberger would assume the droll tones of a lecturer and confide to the waiting smiles that D—'s bishop had been too busy hearing the knight's confession to defend his king; or that Captain von K— offered his queen like a pander. If anyone bridled under this attack or attempted a retort, Schlumberger would immediately sing out, "No harm done, think nothing of it!" with such good nature that he had a nearly universal reputation as a jolly companion. When he had clearly carried the day, he would settle into his armchair and turn upon himself what appeared to be the same tartness of phrase he used on others. Then by some alchemy the mocking tones that made buffoons of others delineated a character with, to be sure, its eccentricities, but on the whole brilliant and captivating.

He liked to conjure for his friends the child Schlumberger masquerading as a dolt, only to make a sputtering fool of the adult who had condescended, with a wink to his cronies, to give the boy a lesson in chess. Variations of this drama appeared so often in Schlumberger's reminiscences that the few who withheld their admiration sometimes muttered that the small Alsatian village where he spent his youth must have been populated by more players of master quality than had passed through the doors of the Régence in a generation. Each seemed to have been unbeaten until he met Schlumberger, and no matter how eminent the reputation or reverberant the shock waves from its collapse, the next opponent always drew his chair to the board in a magical chuckling ignorance of the drubbing in store for him.

The one point on which Schlumberger's reminiscences departed from the mythic formula for chess geniuses to be found in the published boastings of Philidor and Ruy Lopez was his assertion that it had been his father who taught him the game. Schlumberger, then eleven years old, had forcibly been enlisted to relieve his father's boredom during an illness that confined him to bed. Schlumberger delighted to report that he had hated the long incarcerations in the sickroom with the bristly, smelly old man, learned the rules of chess only under threat of a beating, and played only when he was brought up short by a command as he tiptoed past the sickroom door or when his mother bribed him with sweets.

"A marvelous teacher," Schlumberger would say. "He used to crack me across the knuckles with a stick for a stupid move, and once when I deliberately gave up my queen on the fifth move because I wanted to watch one of the emperor's regiments march through town, he leaped from his bed and chased me all the way down the hall before he collapsed. I lost on purpose until I discovered an even better revenge."

The better revenge, of course, was to win, but his cultivation of this new tactic was short-lived. On the night he discovered he could outplay his father and did so four games running, the old man abruptly died. "If he had known proper pawn play," Schlumberger would add to round off the tale, "he could have died undefeated." The laughter would bathe him like waves breaking against a rock. He was thinking of something else.

The King and the Drummer Boy

AMID HIS CLAQUE of admirers, surrounded by buzzing huddles of important but relatively impotent enemies, Schlumberger was to all appearances comfortably wedged for life. It is little wonder that when Maelzel at last located the hunchback who had been described to him, he was unprepared for the proprietorial air with which Schlumberger dangled a leg from one arm of his throne while lodging his elbow on the other. Maelzel had asked not only for a good chess player but an impoverished one.

He hesitated a moment longer. Placing his right hand in the pocket of his frock coat, he clasped his left hand over the pocket to steady something that bulged there, then twisted several times the wrist of the concealed hand. Each twist was accompanied by a faint clacking. Then he set himself in motion, zigzagging among the tables toward Schlumberger.

Just then Schlumberger was alone. The night before he had lost a game to La Bourdonnais, and the hangover had made him cross. In the two games he had played so far this evening he had humbled his opponents with insulting haste, making each move a gesture of contempt. The word traveled around the mirrored room that Schlumberger was out of sorts, and his usual challengers left him to sulk.

He had open on the table the *Analyse de Joue d'échecs* of Philidor, the great eighteenth-century master, and the board was arranged in the pattern of one of Philidor's end games with Philip Stamma. He had gone a long while without making a move. Anyone watching might have guessed he was not contemplating the problem at all, but merely admiring the intricate carving of the black king, which was fashioned to a likeness of General Bonaparte.

The anonymous artist had found hidden in the ivory an image quite unlike the prancing Caesar fantasized on canvas by David. About the pose itself there was nothing unique: head at an arrogant tilt; hands clasped behind the back; one leg forward, slightly bent at the knee, balancing, while the other rooted the trunk on a smooth line through calf-length boot and tight breeches to crotch. But the slight hunch to the shoulders this posture produced had been grotesquely emphasized. The artist had called up a wind to shape the long military overcoat to the contours of the figure's back, rounding it, weighting it with a buzzard's stoop. Schlumberger's own stoop was scarcely more pronounced.

People often thought he had a stoop rather than a deformity, until they saw him drunk. Only then did they know his body wanted to curl upon itself the way fingers want to become a fist.

But nobody who saw him that night, alone amid the host of Schlumbergers gliding on the mirrored walls, knew that for the past half hour he had thought of nothing but the weight of Napoleon's back. Gazing at the figure, he felt the rolled collar rising high against his own neck; the coat's draping fall from shoulders and back made him feel the back's heaviness, the ache of it sweetened by a bearing of authority and arrogance that seemed to twist deformity into a new fashion in elegance. The carved face hypnotized him. The delicate lines and planes of the ivory worked changes in his own face. His jaw angled to a perceptible thrust. His brow tightened to mirror the carved brow. Beneath it the twin miniature pocks counterfeiting irises bored into Schlumberger's own eyes a living reflection of sorrow and horror. To Schlumberger the eyes were glaring not from the stepped and grooved pedestal of a chesspiece but from some hillock above the battlesmoke at Austerlitz or Jena. Schlumberger was there too, gazing down at the surge and writhe of his Grande Armée, watching it carve the flesh on the field and the map of Europe to a pattern born in his mind.

His lips mimicking the triumphant puff and curl of the ivory lips, Schlumberger reached a hand to interpose a bishop between his king and Philidor's queen. At that moment, however, the thump of cannon was displaced in his ears by the clackety-clack of a tin drummer boy with a key in its back who came waddling like a tipsy Goliath across the black and red squares. With stiffly pumping arms it broke through a phalanx of pawns and sent Bonaparte spinning onto his back.

"Ingenious, isn't it?" chuckled Maelzel. "My own invention."

Schlumberger regarded the beaming face.

"Ahhh," cried Maelzel, "the little corporal himself!" And, returning the black king to the square from which it had been toppled, "Not a bad likeness either. A very indifferent chess player, by the way, at the time I met him—that was in 1809, the Wagram campaign, you know. I daresay he had time to sharpen his end game those last six years, marooned out on that damned English rock." And then, since Schlumberger through this had not unfrozen a single muscle from the mask of seething outrage his face had assumed after the first startlement, "Oh, pardon the interruption, I merely wished to introduce myself by presenting you with a sample—'' here plucking up the drummer boy and depositing it directly before Schlumberger on the table, where it stood with drumsticks raised, poised, threatening cacophony; while Schlumberger, not breaking contact even for a moment to glance at it, kept his eyes pinned to Maelzel, who at last, like his drummer boy, wound down, stuttered, and had to take a breath before stretching a new smile and continuing, "—a sample of my artistry. I am Johann Nepomuk Maelzel. Court mechanician of the Austrian Empire.''

"You will remove that toy from my board," said Schlumberger.

6 | The Goddess from the Machine

"PLEASE ACCEPT IT with my compliments," replied Maelzel, adding a generous wave of the arm. These opening gambits completed, he seated himself and quickly brought his queen to the center: "I have a machine that plays chess."

Schlumberger counterattacked briskly: "I have no interest in machines."

"This machine plays chess like a master."

"Artists play chess. Philosophers, scientists play chess. Machines do not play chess."

"It has never been defeated."

A pawn-dainty smirk from Schlumberger.

"It can beat you." This almost a whisper: "Even you."

A pause, full of lazy fury, then: "For twenty francs I will do you the honor of being proved a liar by William Schlumberger."

Maelzel's grin spread his whiskers. The inhabitants of the Régence watched a proprietorial palm fall on Schlumberger's rounded shoulder as he was led to the door. Check and mate in four moves.

AS SCHLUMBERGER followed Maelzel down the dark aisle of his Rue St. Honoré exhibit hall, he made out on the stage someone sitting at a table, someone with a hideously bulbous head. When they clattered up the rehearsal steps toward it, the figure did not rise to greet them, did not wave or nod. On stage Maelzel disappeared into the wings for a moment, leaving Schlumberger alone with the still figure. *Could he be wearing a hat?* he wondered, peering sidelong through the gloom. He felt uncomfortably ignored. Once the lamp Maelzel had been fumbling puffed into life, the bloated head became a turban of yellow silk, the table a finely molded cabinet.

Maelzel set the lamp on the cabinet beside a chessboard, saying, "Monsieur Schlumberger, meet the Turk, the world's first and only automaton chess player."

The Turk wore a fur-trimmed jacket of regal purple with sleeves cut off at its elbows. A puff-sleeved shirt that matched the turban bloomed from the jacket sleeves. One smooth hairless hand held a pipe. The other stretched alongside the chessboard, supporting the entire weight of the left arm on the tip of its little finger. Despite the unlined poreless shine of nose and brow, the face was not just a block of polished wood. The downcast eyes, the horsehair moustache drooping round the lower lip, conveyed a pure intensity of concentration. Schlumberger was momentarily embarrassed to hear Maelzel talking in its presence as though it couldn't hear. He described its accomplishments like a boastful parent, telling how it moved its head, raised and lowered its eyelids, moved its arms and hands to manipulate chessmen, and said *"Échec"* at the end of games.

"This is the one thing in my show I don't claim credit for inventing myself," Maelzel said. In the shadowed corners Schlumberger noticed a spangle-chested soldier with a trumpet to his lips; a shell as high as a stagecoach, cupping a three-step platform on which a score of miniature musicians brandished instruments; and, hanging by their hands from a rope stretched the length of the stage, two limber-jointed marionettes with impossibly cheery identical smirks. Maelzel stood behind the Turk with a palm on each of its shoulders.

"Royal mechanic for the Empress Maria Theresa put him together in 1770," he said. "An amusement, if you will, for the Viennese court. Von Kempelen was his name, Baron Wolfgang von Kempelen, one of the greatest mechanical geniuses who ever lived. I acquired it in 1804, bought it from his estate. Paid 15,000 francs and people laughed at me: 15,000 francs for a toy! Ha! This little toy's been putting meat on my table ever since."

By this time Schlumberger was no longer bothering to listen. He waited impatiently while Maelzel opened the various doors and drawers of the cabinet to prove there could not be a chess player hiding inside. Shadows swirled and dodged, fleeing the lamp in Maelzel's hand as he illuminated the crannies inside the cabinet and pointed out each gear and shaft with a mystifying explanation. The lamplight did not penetrate past the third row of auditorium seats where Maelzel's prattle echoed in dust and darkness. The double doors at the front of the hall had been left ajar when they entered and Maelzel had also opened a stage door leading to an alley, but no breeze stirred. Both men had removed their jackets against the heat.

Despite the dense crochetwork of gears and wheels with which the cabinet appeared to be filled, Schlumberger was quite positive it contained a human being, and not the least concerned to puzzle out how someone might be concealed there. His conviction was based not on knowledge, though one or two of the *professeurs d'échec* with whom he consorted at the Café de la Régence might have been in a position to explain the secret. He simply considered the idea of a chess-playing machine an absurdity. The mechanical chess player must have been occasionally mentioned in the circle of Schlumberger's acquaintances, but it was to him a curious toy, beneath the notice of the professional chess player. What did concern him was whether the person hidden inside the box could play better chess than he could.

On this point he quickly assured himself. Within ten moves he not only controlled the center, but had managed to wedge the machine's queen into the back row behind one of its own pawns. Schlumberger would have felt extremely annoyed at the waste of his time if he had not recalled that the twenty francs Maelzel would owe him was equivalent to what he could earn in five days of lessons.

Maelzel was taken aback when his ritual prelude—the opening of cabinet doors, the accompanying science-chatter of gears and spring tensions and counterweights, scrupulously obfuscatory—failed to impress. He had hoped to overwhelm Schlumberger with showmanship before broaching his true subject. But in Schlumberger he found a man not simply skeptical, since that state of mind admits of doubt, but one who took for granted the very fact—the impossibility of a machine playing chess—that all the illusions of the machine were coaxing him to question; took it for granted so thoroughly he did not even bother to refuse to be fooled. He was a man interested solely in chess. Which was not one of the machine's accomplishments.

As the rapid middle game became end game Maelzel read Schlumberger's impatience. He was tapping his thumbnail against his front teeth. Sometimes he worked his mouth to produce different tones like a man mouthing a jewsharp. Meanwhile the machine ground its gears with agony as his traps tightened their jaws.

During one of the long intervals in which the machine plotted its feeble counterattacks, Maelzel abandoned the head-cocked frowns that were part of his role as expert mechanic listening for the tiniest dissonance in the orchestrated cacophony of the machine's gears. Schlumberger was obviously unimpressed with these finer points of showmanship anyway, so Maelzel wandered into the wings for a moment and returned pushing a stuffed chair, which he positioned beside the chest facing Schlumberger. He sat down with a sigh that punctuated what had gone before and promised a fresh approach for what would follow. He coughed, a little peroration. Repeated, since Schlumberger, bored with the game from his own side of the board, was busy devising a strategy by which the machine could beat him. On the third cough Schlumberger looked up to find them sitting almost side by side, man and machine— the man trying on smiles as if he weren't sure which size would fit, fidgeting, sweat racing from hairline to eyebrows across the undulant terrain of his brow; the brow of the machine fixed in a pure mahogany calm of contemplation beyond desire.

"You must admit," Maelzel began, "the illusion is extremely convincing. Though you appear to be an unsuceptible subject."

"Illusion?" Schlumberger said, his faint trace of surprise suggesting he had been unaware of any attempt to deceive him. "Machines do not play chess."

"I see." This in a tone brittle but still amiable, followed by the dignified nod of a gentleman acknowledging to another that he has been scored against. "One of my former assistants, no doubt, has got his tongue oiled and spoken about confidential matters." Then, raising a hand to forestall objection, "You needn't confirm it, I think I know which one. Some men offer a promise with a little core of poison—like one of your pawn sacrifices."

"Pardon," Schlumberger raised his hand. "It is my move at last."

A moment later Maelzel resumed. "Having, shall we say, guessed the machine has a human agent, you will perceive my problem."

Schlumberger's mouth opened in stupid puzzlement, directed not at the board but at Maelzel's question. His eyes narrowed into a look you could direct without insult only at someone who was not looking

[3 3]

back. Maelzel, looking back, looked away. It was no good trying to make Schlumberger draw it out of him. He was going to have to spell it out.

"I am about to embark on a lucrative tour of the American states. Most lucrative, for *all* concerned. My problem, as you have demonstrated, is that I have not got the services of a *premier* chess player."

The machine labored through a move. Without waiting for the arm to return to rest position, Schlumberger palmed a rook and settled in its place his queen.

"*Échec*," he said; then in a louder voice, "*Échec*. Can I be heard above those grinding teeth?"

"Yes, quite well," Maelzel replied; and then hurriedly, "What I wish is to give you the opportunity of joining my entourage. And sharing in its spoils. May I count on you?" Schlumberger ignored the hand Maelzel extended toward him, concentrating instead on the mechanical fingers closing around the Turk's king, advancing it haltingly into the shadow of the remaining rook.

"This is too absurd," he said, sweeping a bishop from the sidelines to a square on a diagonal with the machine's king. "*Échec et mate*. This game was over fifteen minutes ago." He rose, holding out his hand to Maelzel not for the expected bargain-sealing clasp, but palm upward. "I believe you owe me twenty francs."

"Of course, Monsieur Schlumberger, but you're not, not going *yet*. This twenty francs—here you are—is nothing compared to what, please listen for a moment, compared to what I can offer you." This, somewhat breathlessly, brought them to the stage apron. Schlumberger had one foot on the rehearsal steps. "You haven't even seen, asked, how the machine works."

Schlumberger, taking in the controlled smile, admiring the tightness of the mask, the determined affability, persuasive without risking coercion, decided he could effect another twitch in Maelzel's right eyelid if he condescended to explain: "What you are offering me is an opportunity to leave the Café de la Régence—to leave the chess capital of the world—in order to pit my talents against Red Indians and coonskinned frontiersmen on the outposts of North America. I decline."

"But the United States are full of enthusiasm for scientific progress. Such a machine would fascinate them. They would make us rich."

The Goddess from the Machine

"Do you want to be rich, Monsieur Maelzel?"

Maelzel could not make up his mind whether the raised eyebrows and politely gaping jaw were only feigning surprise.

If at that moment Schlumberger had turned on his heel and left Maelzel sputtering, he would most probably have returned to the Régence in time to resettle himself in his armchair, play a final match before closing time, concocting for his cronies a quaint anecdote about his brush with the famous chess machine, and live out a satisfying lifetime orbiting from the Régence to his modest *pension* and back. But while he was hovering at the door the moment when it was still possible for Maelzel to be just an anecdote in his life winked out like the final ray of light from a star dying centuries away.

Later, in the same way he would replay the moves of a losing match, he will segment the next few minutes into a series of images cued by a knocking from the box: the swell of Maelzel's cheeks getting out of the way of his most potent smile; the "one moment please" bob-and-skip that sets in motion his stride to the chess automaton; the scoop of his palm toppling chessmen into a tray to clear the board; the simultaneous movement of Schlumberger's hand to his own forearm to reclaim the territory shocked by Maelzel's departing clutch and release, his hasty brand, which had conveyed with subtle menace the same thing the smile had said obsequiously—"Our business isn't finished yet." The next image is Maelzel bent low over the cabinet, his arms outstretched; his hands grip the top of the cabinet at either side; he appears for a moment in intimate communion with the Turk; then his back and shoulders tense—there is a moment when Schlumberger is thinking of a priest muttering the Latin prayer of consecration over the Host—and the entire top of the cabinet comes away in Maelzel's hands. He grunts, holding it clumsily, yet manipulates it with a distinct flourish as he sidesteps to reveal:

> *hooking over the side of the box*
> *four fingers*
> *almond-white against the mahogany*
> *then with a*
> *grunt*
> *like the pop*
> *of a bubble surfacing*
> *a white figure*

surfaces
rising waist deep from the hole, her shoulders
glistening, the sweat
streaming into the V of her cotton shift
 (plastered wet under her breast as she swipes
   an arm across her brow),
thrusting at Maelzel with the other hand
 a small oil lamp
saying, "take this goddam furnace."

For a moment Schlumberger thought she would keep on rising—a machine-born Aphrodite. Instead, after hiking one leg over the side of the box, with her elbows locked, hands joined at the rim of the box to make a pivot over which to swing her crotch, she leaned for the swing, exposing two meaty globes, and noticed Schlumberger in time to say, "I thought he was gone," before completing the swing and heisting the other leg over the box rim to land barefoot on the carpeted floor. Then, with effortless contempt, she locked his eyes onto hers so he could look only there while she approached and glided past him through a doorway to the dressing rooms, lapping over him a wake of salty bodysmell that pinched his nostrils.

AT THIS POINT Maelzel must have made some apology for her immodesty, pleading the heat of the night, the stifling confinement of the box; pleading, probably, his own astonishment that his assistant had disrobed to endure them. But Schlumberger will remember only that he must have been somehow drawn to the side of the automaton, for he will recall himself peering deeply into the shadowed cavity, his fingertips smoothing its red felt lining.

After a long moment he turned to Maelzel. At first he felt as if a chock had been jammed between his jaws. Then he said, "A woman. I've been playing a woman."

"As you have seen," Maelzel shrugged, "chess is a man's game."

"And you want me to take her place inside there? Tell me, Maelzel, with all the players at the Régence, what made you approach me with this proposition?"

"I asked for the best chess player in the club. They told me Schlumberger."

"A lie. They told you La Bourdonnais. He can be beaten, he shall be, but I have not yet done it, and I despise flattery."

"They told me La Bourdonnais, and I said, no, he is too rich. Give me the name of a man as good as La Bourdonnais, who is also hungry."

"Now you are telling me the truth," said Schlumberger, gazing again so intently into the box he might have been examining his reflection there. Barely audible to Maelzel, he said, "And you want me to stuff myself inside this machine, be its guts, its brain—"

"You would still be Schlumberger," said Maelzel, letting his whisper glide unobtrusively into the current of Schlumberger's musings, "only with a full belly."

"I play better on an empty stomach," snapped Schlumberger. "Good night, Mr. Maelzel. Let me remind you I correctly maintained that no machine could play chess."

7 | The Artist at Work

ON HIS WAY HOME Schlumberger was accosted by a prostitute for the first time since he came to Paris. Usually he walked like a man with a destination rather than a quest. That night, however, he had paused outside Maelzel's door, turned first up the street in the direction of the Café de la Régence, then with a gesture of impatience, the kind of exaggerated headshake and fingersnap used to disguise confusion as remembered intention for the benefit of anyone watching, he turned back toward his *pension* on the Rue St. Honoré. As he drifted through the darkness between islands of lamplight, a piano was rolling and thumping, and someone in an upstairs window called plaintively into the busy street and was answered by an obscene bark that struck the accent of the music like a lyric.

When a hand slipped through his arm, he swung toward the woman in a motion so like the start of an embrace that she completed it, pressed herself against him with a delighted laugh, whispering, "I've been waiting for you."

A disturbing familiarity in the eyes raised intimately to his own snagged him. He said, "But I don't know you," half convinced it was a lie.

"Sure you do," she purred. "We're old friends."

Under the thin silk of her dress a thigh nuzzled like a puppy between his legs, and abruptly he shoved her. She staggered back yipping.

"Don't touch me," he said, and hurried away. A horror of venereal disease had helped to keep him virgin at the age of twenty-five.

The Artist at Work

Stepping rapidly along, he couldn't outdistance the cheap scent the woman's brief contact had transferred to his clothing, nor her eyes, with their bold claim of intimacy. *It was ridiculous,* he was thinking. *They weren't even the same color as the other's, that damned Aphrodite's*—when he realized that a few moments before the streetwalker had accosted him he had passed her standing in a lighted doorway and looked at her, particularly at her eyes, with no more thought that he was being regarded in turn than he would have given to a horse at an auction. He must have appeared to invite her attention, he realized, sorry now as he recalled how his push had stripped from her eyes their experienced lewdness, exposing a fear that showed her surprisingly young. Too late to apologize now. Anyhow there was no way he could explain that he had wanted to taste her eyes for the same reason a thirsty man drinks salt water.

Before he was a hundred yards along the street, his pace settled again to a stroll. The first thing he did when he reached his apartment was to throw wide the casement window, flush out the noonday heat that had baked through the garret roof; but before he removed his frock coat, he crooked his forearm and buried his nose in the sleeve, inhaling deeply the lingering perfume.

The image it called up was not the streetwalker, but the woman in Maelzel's chess machine. As he undressed for bed her presence haunted the darkness of his room. Sleep was a long time coming, and for the first time that he could remember, it took an effort of concentration to analyze the moves in the game he had lost earlier in the café. Halfway through the night he awoke, plunging like a stallion against the mattress.

He had been dreaming that when he checkmated the mechanical Turk, it rose to its feet and removed its turban, shaking loose a tumble of curls as it said, "I've been waiting for you. We're old friends." Schlumberger fumbled at his bedside table for a tinder box and struck a light. The lamp sucked ghosts from the room like a vacuum pump. The familiar objects it revealed calmed him, restored him to a world where his responses could be calculated on squares of red and black.

To anybody but Schlumberger himself, his sleeping quarters would have had the personality of a museum showroom. The bed, the chamber pot, and the washstand had been elbowed aside by four large tables. On each were crowded two or three chessboards with ivory-carved chessmen poised in attitudes of threat and counterthreat. They would have appeared to be on display, but for the artless way the pieces not on the boards clumped and sprawled. Schlumberger kept games in progress on all the boards, and during his waking hours seldom went more than five minutes without making a move on one or the other.

He had acquired the chess sets, some of them quite valuable, four years earlier when his mother and his paternal uncle had blessed him off to Paris, armed with funds to make his way in trade. After a brief apprenticeship under his elder brother in the Paris outlet for the family manufacturing firm, Schlumberger invested in a harness shop owned by an acquaintance of his uncle. He would have had a greater capital outlay if he had not already spent a substantial portion of his patrimony on every quaintly carved chess set that struck his fancy, and on countless expensive volumes of chess literature. After a series of financial tragedies patiently and sympathetically explained to him by his uncle's acquaintance, he was made to understand that he no longer owned any bridles or saddles, and it appeared for a time as if he might have to sell his chess collection as well. Faced with this possibility, he discovered that during the hours he had left the ramparts of the harness shop unguarded, he had been acquiring the skill which would rescue him from collapse. By giving chess lessons and by retreating from his plush apartment to a small *pension* kept by a portly widow, he could maintain himself not simply in solvency but luxury, surrounded and possessed by his possessions.

Against a wall at a corner of the room stood a bookcase stacked haphazardly with the quarto and folio volumes of his chess library, all within easy reach of his seat before an ornate mahogany writing table facing the other wall. On the wall above this table hung a folio-size engraving of Philidor excised from one of Schlumberger's books, and directly beside it, at eye level to one seated at the table, a mirror. The table itself held a brass inkstand and penholder, three or four quills and a penknife, and a bound volume of quarto pages already nearly a quarter filled with Schlumberger's backslanted miniscule handwriting. Here during the cool morning hours of each day he religiously made journal entries, at this time usually consisting of notes and analyses of games played the night before. Interspersed with purely technical data and fragmentary paragraphs toward an essay on center control were notations of a more personal character. The record of his own state of mind was usually a brisk single word: "Ecstasy" and "Desolation" were used most commonly, occurring with about equal frequency, followed by multiple exclamation points.

Notes on the personal and tactical oddities of his opponents, however, were lovingly detailed, suggesting that his reputation as a wit was at least in part the result of a spontaneity rather carefully rehearsed. Another favorite genre was the description of an opponent at the moment of defeat, a phenomenon Schlumberger recorded with the clinical passion of a natural historian. "As he seated himself for the ninth game," began a description of the final round in a victorious match, "he was constantly swallowing, and the nervous cough I first noticed in the sixth game had become so pronounced I thought he would retch up his dinner. It was then I knew I had totally *crushed* his will." On another occasion he wrote, ". . . and I brought forward my knight, cutting off his king's retreat. His sharp intake of breath was quite audible to me. Before he exhaled he made a sucking noise with his tongue against the inside of his upper teeth. I saw his eye rapidly trace over the board as he realized it had been not he but I who had authored his last seven moves—as surely as if I had passed across the board to him written instructions for each!" It was to this volume that Schlumberger turned for solace and inspiration in the early morning hours of August 1, 1825. Here he made the first in a series of entries which, in the course of time, would infringe more and more on its character as a chess manual, eventually transforming it into the intimate record of his mind.

Tallow spots blotting the page corroborated the agitation the words recorded. After noting the time, 3:30 A.M., he writes in uncharacteristically heavy quill strokes, "For women chess is a drawing-room entertainment. They mix their moves with green tea and gossip. And Maelzel is worse—he would make the game a tent-show attraction, with people paying to see not the conflict of logic and genius operating on a field unsullied by emotion, but only a *machine*. And if he wanted to pervert nature, he might better have trained a dog to walk on its hind legs than a woman to make chess moves. When I realized it had been her I was playing, I felt *violated*." Then, after an inkless scratch which indicated the quill had dried during an interval of meditation, these words, occupying a line by themselves: "She has left me no place to hide."

Aside from the strain of misogynism in these lines, their slightly hysterical tone reflects the idiosyncratic role chess played in Schlumberger's psychology. From brief notes scattered through the diaries, it is possible to deduce that for Schlumberger chess must have been akin to an act of creation. Each problem was the primal chaos, from which he wrought a universe that achieved stability the moment his opponent's king became locked in check. To be creator, however, was not to be *primum mobile*.

Opening moves, with their infinitude of possibilities, filled him with terror. In the face of such random potential, he was often nearly paralysed. In his younger days, before he disciplined himself to play the first few moves by rote, he had once agonized so long over his response to an opening that his opponent stalked away in disgust. His panic was particularly acute when he played the white pieces. Then the responsibility to stretch forth the hand that shattered the initial symmetrical balance of the pieces was his. He had to use his passivity as a prod, driving his opponent to declare a personality. Then the horror of chaos became a problem in form. He swung into his middle game, usually from a defensive position, with his efficiency uninhibited and deadly. His opponents would sense the energy rising in him like a swollen river seething against their defenses, pressing ever harder, thrusting ruthless tongues into the secret places where the mortar had been hastily applied. The breach would start perhaps as a trickle, a pawn in a surprisingly potent position, then a hitherto well-pinned bishop become miraculously sinister. Then, as Schlumberger intuited the game's perfect economy of moves, the breach became a flood. His moves in end games were precise and rapid, each giving shape and clarity to the order declaring itself under his hands. The feeble ploys of his opponents were but the clay's rebellion against the swift shaping fingers of the Maker, and when Schlumberger breathed *"Échec!"* Time was born. Pawns could return to their rank; rooks, knights, and bishops once more could take their accustomed positions, flanking and guarding the king's tranquility, the queen's aweful power.

On the few occasions when Schlumberger lost, he punished himself by drinking until the law of gravity fled him like an exorcised demon. He would spend hours barging around his room, concocting absurd games as the tables caromed off his thighs; and when he had won all the games or despaired of them or the tilting floor had spilled the pieces, he would stand still to let the walls stop whirling so he could find the one on which the mirror hung, and he would take it in his hands to watch himself weeping as he talked to his dead father until his tongue dissolved into a paste that clung to his palate. At last, closing his eyes, he would yield his clutch on the spinning world and cartwheel off into black space. His first act when he awoke was to replay the losing game in his mind. He imposed upon each of his errors a dozen different corrections. He had to convince himself that defeat was an aberrant trifle in a universe dominated by order. Then he allowed himself to rest, eat, and return to the game.

But on the night Schlumberger first encountered the automaton chess player, no application of chess strategy could cure his insomnia. Manipulating words was not nearly so thorough a balm to his mind as manipulating chessmen. Where a chess combination could exactly reflect his intention, his words seemed to be saying both more and less than he intended. No structure revealed itself through them; no order. The phrase "no place to hide," for example, affected him so powerfully that he unconsciously repeated it as the opening statement of his next paragraph. Rather than develop whatever idea it suggested, though, he continued the paragraph with a description of the dream that had wakened him.

After throwing aside the turban she lay back across the table like a sacrifice, opening her arms. Embracing her, he heard the rustling of skirts, which became, as he pulled down her bodice and cupped her breast, rubbing his lips across the nipple, a constant faintly grating purr, a stroked kitten purr, and when he lowered himself upon her, the thrust of her pelvis against him had no sway, no inclination to linger or tease, but only a piston precision, relentless and hard. The purr by this time had become loud enough to be the unmistakable whirr of gears. "Automaton," he whispered, and looked up to see Maelzel nodding and grinning.

Here the dream either ended or Schlumberger lost fortitude to continue his description. What follows in his journal is the classic item by item paean to the charms of her face and form, starting with "raven's breast" for hair and working its way down, methodical as an anatomy lesson and perfumed with heady clichés. Perhaps he could only bring his feelings under control by pickling them in the language of sentimental novelists. Perhaps for him the words throbbed with life. In any event the attempt breaks off before he is obliged to grapple with any organ below the collarbone. At this point he rose to answer a knock at the door, steeling himself to another flutter of cryptic hints about late hours from his concierge. With his brain secreting tropes of almond, ruby and alabaster, it must have seemed like opening a door upon his own dream to find her standing breathlessly in the shadowed hallway.

8 | A Masque for Marionettes

It was 8 A.M. He had been writing FOUR and a half hours. Building a cage of words to trap the ghost that roused his body had done its work, exorcised his body from his mind; but now it resumed its accustomed place. Pain seeped into his spine, starting low and rising as water fills a glass. He wondered how long his shoulder muscles had been taut. When he saw her, his hand dropped limp from the door handle. He stood dumb, emptied of words. Like a magician's dupe, he had wrapped her in words, bound them tight and labored over the knots, only to find her triumphantly free in an eyeblink. His control over the words had given him the illusion that he also controlled the actions they recorded. Her appearance robbed him abruptly of this sense of power. He abdicated, for the moment at least, any attempt to shape what would follow.

"Please explain to your concierge that Monsieur Maelzel requires me to see you on urgent business," she said, stepping past him into the room. The motion of her passage turned him inward as if her skirt ruffles brushing his thigh had been gearteeth that caught and spun him like a wheel. Before the momentum was spent a hand hooked his forearm and jerked him back toward the open door.

The concierge was shaking her jowls like weapons and whispering with a shocking lack of ambiguity, "Forbidden, Monsieur Schlumberger! Strictly forbidden. It is not allowed to entertain ladies in this house."

"Urgent business," he stammered, remembering his instructions.

[4 5]

"She is from Monsieur Maelzel. It's quite proper, I assure you." And he closed the door.

The woman from Maelzel's automaton stood in the center of Schlumberger's room. Like an enemy queen that had slipped past his guard to menace an unprotected king, she unsettled the balance of each piece of furniture. It was impossible that sweat had ever beaded her powdered brow, pale now as a gull's wing. The breasts that had swung heavily toward him as she climbed from the Turk's box were tamed by the snug ring of an empire waist. They were wrapped in pale blue silk dappled with yellow marigolds. Her clothes and her bearing were a disguise he was forbidden to remind her he had already penetrated. The hand she extended to him exuded a discreet perfume.

When she said, "I am Madame Rouault," he was startled to realize he had not until this moment known her name. With his lips to the cheek of his pillow, he had already addressed her with the intimate pronoun.

"Monsieur Maelzel would like to engage you to teach me end games," she explained.

Schlumberger sensed immediately that she was lying. She was an ambassador sent to persuade him to reconsider his decision. Her story was plausible, he could not denounce it out of hand, but the conviction that he was being toyed with gave him a resentment that cleared his brain. As he watched her speaking he pared the troubling entity of his dreams to the familiar shape of an opponent, with whom he entered into his customary relationship.

She was not sufficiently gifted in the techniques of chess, she explained, to be a player of the premier rank. Schlumberger was faintly shocked that this admission cost her no apparent discomfort. On the contrary, he noted, she dismissed her shortcomings with an impatient shrug. Maelzel had decided, she continued, to advertise that the Turk would play end games only, rather than tax the patience of audiences through the less dramatic opening and middle games. Here Schlumberger had an eerie feeling that he was being addressed by Maelzel himself, somehow controlling Madame Rouault's jaw. The phrasing was his, Schlumberger felt certain, and the woman hurried through her lines with an absense of hesitation not likely in spontaneous speech. She sounded like a bored actress in a rehearsal. The real purpose of playing only end games, she rattled on, was that it would enable her to memorize a repertoire of winning combinations, which would reduce the possibility of losses that might—and here she paused, perhaps only for breath, but continuing with a note of genuine feeling— "that might damage the Turk's reputation." The feeling she injected was contempt.

Schlumberger said, "Does Monsieur Maelzel think he can devise a table of logarithms for winning chess?"

But the woman, not waiting for response, had cast a rapid glance around the room and seated herself at his writing table as if she had been dropped there. Her hands found a perch on her lap, almost by accident. If one of them had dropped to her side, Schlumberger felt sure she would have been content to let the arm dangle from its socket. Her lethargy was so complete that he was about to ask if she felt ill. She drew a long breath, however, and apologized for her exhaustion in a more natural tone. Maelzel had kept her awake all night, she said, devising a way to deal with the crisis in their American tour plans. Since Schlumberger refused to join the company, her proficiency in end games was essential to the tour's success. Without expert training, she had no chance of competing successfully, and the tour might as well be canceled. Nobody, not even in America, would pay money to watch a chess automaton lose games.

"If he cancels the tour," she concluded, "I will lose my job."

The quick pathetic look with which she punctuated these words made Schlumberger laugh outright.

"Are you aware that you are no better an actress than you are a chess player?" he said. "I can do nothing to help your stage career, but I will give you an elementary chess lesson free of charge: never allow your opponent to convince you that he has fewer options on the board than are in fact available. For example: your job. I must teach you end games, because if I don't you will have no job. But what would have happened to your job if I had accepted Maelzel's offer to replace you in the machine?"

"Then I would have stayed on as the tour's business manager. But if there is no tour at all, I have no job at all."

"That sounds believable," Schlumberger conceded. "But it does not begin to exhaust the available options. Why does my refusal stop all the wheels from turning? All Maelzel has to do is ask somebody else to run his damned machine."

"You don't understand how important secrecy is to the Turk's

[4 7]

reputation. Monsieur Maelzel can't take out an advertisement in the evening paper to fill this job. And every time he approaches someone who refuses him, there's another person who knows the secret of the machine. He bit his nails for three days before talking to you."

"Excellent!" Schlumberger crowed. "I am beginning to think you would make quite an apt pupil. But let us consider still another option. A lowly pawn play, perhaps, but one learns never to underestimate the importance of the pawn. Since I have already turned down Maelzel's primary request of me, what makes him think I will involve myself in his swindle in this secondary way?"

Madame Rouault shrugged. Schlumberger noted a hint of hesitation before her reply. "There is no mystery. Monsieur Maelzel wanted the best operator available; he also wants the best tutor."

"Maelzel himself attempted flattery. A gambit that does not succeed with me."

"Why must it be a trick?" she replied impatiently. "You are a tutor, are you not? Your reputation as a master is well established? Can you be so unconvinced of your own worth?"

This last question stung like a bite on an abcessed tooth. She accompanied it with a direct stare. Up till now her most earnest speeches had been directed to his hairline or the mole under his lower lip. Schlumberger turned from her curious eyes and let the moment grow into a pause.

"I assure you," the woman added in a low voice, "Monsieur Maelzel does not need to be convinced of your genius. He is prepared to triple your usual fee if you will tutor me."

"Now I see it," said Schlumberger returning smartly to the offensive. "He has made himself vulnerable by revealing his plans to me. He is buying my silence."

"Precisely," she shrugged. "And you must add that he is also guarding his secret, since consulting another chess master would risk spreading the suspicious fact that his business manager requires instruction in chess as well as accounting. To be really thorough, we might just mention that my acquaintance with the game extends barely to three months, and if I attempt to meet serious competition without help, I shall completely swamp the Turk's reputation. But we've been over that already, and besides, it is a notion so lacking in subtlety that I'm sure you'll disregard it."

A Masque for Marionettes

"Your sarcasm is not persuasive, Madame," Schlumberger said. "But perhaps I am being too subtle. Perhaps I should tell you plainly that I find Monsieur Maelzel's offer insulting and repulsive. He mocks the game of chess, Madame, first by making it a carnival entertainment; then by perpetrating the lie that a machine could supplant the creative intellect of man; and finally by making it the occupation of a woman, who would be better employed tending her children."

She rose to her feet.

"My only child, Monsieur Schlumberger," she said, "is dead. I shall have no more."

In chess Schlumberger sometimes experienced moments of intoxicating sensuality. They came at the turning point of a hard-contested game, after his opponent had been harried from one defense to the next, shucking each illusion of power and pride until he stood trembling and naked under Schlumberger's eyes. Then Schlumberger's breath would come in shallow pants. His heart would pound in his ears as he awaited what would come next; waited with the cold passion of a scientist on the verge of wrenching a secret from the heart of nature; waited for the final bit of evidence that would confirm his theory: that moment when his victim would topple his own king to signal defeat and raise his eyes from the board to the eyes of Schlumberger, mutely confessing the single truth that gave order to Schlumberger's universe. For these occasions Schlumberger reserved a special smile.

It was this smile which faded from his lips at Madame Rouault's rejoinder to his last speech. Her eyes blinked angrily to abort a tear threatening to spill onto her cheek, but she refused to be shamed in her nakedness. As in their last encounter, Schlumberger watched her walk to the door. Each step fascinated him; it seemed as if each of her steps was the product of a unique decision that must be renewed at every moment. Yet it was not a hesitant walk, only slow, meditative almost. Schlumberger found himself thinking, *This is how she must walk away from the grave where her son is buried.* And as her hand reached the door he was creating the scene: fresh flowers, he could see them, and her standing over the grave, taking only a few moments from a day filled with other errands; gazing at the headstone, bewildered more than grieved at the chiseled dates bracketing so small a segment of eternity; then turning away, walking back in that same deliberate pace that had got her to his door, where she had turned and was now giving him a look that told him there was no way he could ever hurt her.

That was what her voice told him too as she said, "I will inform Monsieur Maelzel that you have declined his offer."

The knowledge that he was powerless before her flooded him unexpectedly with relief. Robbed of the pleasures of triumph, he stammered his way into the sweet pleasures of yielding. He had been very crude, he said. He had not imagined . . . certainly if he had known he would not have . . . and his objection to Maelzel's offer was only that . . . She took her hand from the door handle, but made no attempt to ease his confusion. He offered to teach her end games—not for Maelzel's sake, but for hers. She took that statement and weighed it a moment and returned it. "I am not to be pitied," she said, and he quickly said, "No, of course not," and claimed it would have been foolish of him to refuse so much money, he'd actually had no intention of doing so and only had the idea that by not immediately agreeing he might have driven his price up still further.

An entry in his journal indicates he must have found it quite marvelous that the breasts which had excited him once suckled a child. Around this image he fantasized a mystical tableau—a crèche with no room for a Joseph.

9 | Schlumberger as Homer

SCHLUMBERGER'S APPRENTICESHIP in the art of poetry was served in conversation with his concierge, lullabying her moral vigilance with stories explaining Madame Rouault's daily morning visits to his apartment. Schlumberger himself had at first balked at making a classroom of his apartment, but Madame Rouault had convinced him that for Schlumberger to instruct her publicly at the Régence where he met his other pupils would compromise the neutrality of her association with the chess automaton.

The same threat dictated that Schlumberger create for the concierge a legend with an intricate body of lore. He planted the grain of sand in the oyster almost immediately, for Madame Grandit's marching, moral footsteps treaded up the stairwell directly on the echoes of Madame Rouault's departure. Her appetite for confrontation was at first baffled. Schlumberger told her that his visitor had been his sister from Alsace. She would be visiting him regularly for a time on business connected with the settlement of his late father's estate. This information settled in Madame Grandit's mind as a constant irritant. She rolled it on her mental palate. For the next five days she formed around it layers of suspicion and indignation.

Slowly the wariness with which she saluted Schlumberger's entrances and departures stiffened into a trembling rigidity. Schlumberger took note. He summoned his full powers of imagination and knocked on her door.

"I have a confession to make," he began, fumbling his hat like a penitent schoolboy. "My father has been dead four years. My sister's business does not concern his estate. It is far more serious." Then, drawing on his own experience in the world of trade, he created for his sister a husband: a capricious gambling popinjay husband whose financial irresponsibility had brought his interest in a harness shop to ruin, threatening the family with eviction, himself with debtor's prison. Naturally at this moment of crisis, Schlumberger must console and advise his distraught relation, frantic with worry over the fate of her six children.

At this point Madame Grandit's jaw gaped. Her jowls wagged like a turkey's wattle. She exclaimed, "And she so young!" When Schlumberger, in an inspired stroke, added that the husband was given to frequent drinking bouts, Madame Grandit's eyes brimmed. She made the convert's leap into faith. Schlumberger was the successful shaman who tames the elements by naming them, brings coherence to the mysteries of the universe. Henceforward, Madame Grandit accepted the daily apparition of a young and voluptuous woman for consultations in her lodger's quarters with benign complacency. Her head cocked to one side as she swept open the door to admit Madame Rouault. She emitted little mews of sympathy that followed the visitor to the second turning of the stairwell. Schlumberger found that the lie he planted had been transformed into a milky pearl of kindness. It thrived quite well on tiny but regular tidbits. One day he reported that the children were sick with fever. For a few days thereafter he deftly built to the infection's crisis. He broke the fever and the tension at once with a miraculous recovery that occurred a few hours after Madame Grandit offered the beleaguered family her services as nurse. The very next day he sighed and hinted that his sister's husband was a wife beater. As the weeks progressed Madame Grandit, who suffered mightily from lumbago and arthritis, noticed that she had not felt so spritely since she was a girl. She attributed it to a new mineral water one of her neighbors had persuaded her to drink each night before retiring.

While Schlumberger unfolded this domestic drama for the ear of his concierge, he was simultaneously weaving into his chess instructions with Madame Rouault a tale of more epic dimensions. Once in a small Alsatian Troy there lived a hero denied his birthright by a twist of fate. Though the youth's origins were shrouded in mystery, his prowess in battle marked him a prince in disguise, and after slaying a giant that had terrorized the countryside, he set out to find his true homeland and claim his rightful place in the world. Narrowly escaping shipwreck among the Scyllas and Charybdises of the Parisian financial seas, he arrived home at last in the Café de la Régence, where he was daily slaying rival suitors to the hand of his Penelope, the title of supreme master in the world of chess.

Each day as Madame Rouault's eyes grew wide with wonder he saw reflected in them a more flattering image of himself. He began to discover there a Schlumberger he had never before acknowledged, a man wounded in his contact with life, whose heroism was as much a matter of stoic resilience in the face of repeated injustice as it was the more spectacular courage of the battlefield. Other virtues blossomed under her gaze: he became patient in his explanations, not just with her, but even to his other students, whom he continued to instruct at the café. The reproofs that used to make his protégés quail became gentle, good-natured, more articulate.

Since her eyes, her words, her actions all had a tantalizing ambiguity, he made her casual gestures into signals he might interpret as caresses. Every comment that passed her lips was fired in the furnace of his mind till it yielded a precious metal of secret significance. Each glance of hers revealed everything by saying nothing; her twin orbs were ciphers; placed behind some fantastic integer of his mind, they multiplied to a number approaching infinity.

As Schlumberger re-created himself to match the image reflected in Madame Rouault's eye, he was also using the impenetrable black of her pupil as a primal gneiss in creating his idea of a woman. His fidelity was to nature rather than life—his own nature. The woman's ideal configuration of planes and curves—the angular skull over which flesh stretched tight as a drumskin, the full lips and breasts and hips, the delicious tongue-tip hollow above her breastbone that deepened when excitement made her neck cords stand out—these were a mold into which he poured the woman in himself.

Playing chess with her he felt his identity seesawing back and forth across the board. He maintained sufficient stability to control the game, but when he observed her lips tighten against the pressure of his attack, or saw the sudden breeze of insight rippling the surface of her brow, his sense of himself was seized with vertigo. He went spinning dizzily not to annihilation but to complete repossession of himself in the body of the woman. He inhabited her motions: the closing arc made by her arms as she removed her hat, the dip of her shoulder while she caught the folds of her gown to glide into the chair opposite him, the sweep of her forefinger from her gently nipping teeth to the queen's pawn with which she opened every game. As a gloating flush drew up the corners of her lips, he experienced total participation in her triumphant strategy, even while he knew the movement which had captured his rook also surrendered her queen.

And when she hesitated at the portals of one of his traps, her fingers playing delicately as the forelegs of a spider over the grooved surface of the chesspiece, his gaze would lift, I know, from her hands to her languid smile, and from there, I made no apology for knowing, to the almost translucent web of veins and flesh cupping the tender meat of her eye, which would—which *did*—make him hardly able to keep from gasping like a swimmer just bobbed up from the bottom of the lake.

10 | Commentary on Two Epistles

SHE SAILED FOR AMERICA on the twentieth of December. With her were Maelzel and her husband. Schlumberger had to wait nearly five months for her first letter. When it finally arrived, it was a fat one, seventeen sheets filled on both sides, continued under nearly a dozen dates throughout the crossing. It had been posted the day she landed in New York harbor.

There is little reason to doubt the general sincerity of her complaints. The ritual, perfunctory agonies of seasickness settle after a few days into long rolling swells of boredom. She found herself bracketed between the two men like a piece of loosely stowed cargo. Maelzel seemed to spend all his waking moments in the dining room at cards. Her husband is mentioned only four times, always with reference to the stink of his pipesmoke in the close confines of their cabin. All this is, of course, preparation and counterpoint for numerous paragraphs of timid nostalgia for her morning chess lessons with Schlumberger. Her coquetry permits her only the most oblique reference to their last meeting, no mention at all of their parting kiss. Schlumberger's rendering of that kiss occupied nearly four hundred words of a journal entry dated November 29. That much for the kiss itself, in an entry running to nearly two thousand words.

His report of the incident had a fever dream clarity of detail, but his points of emphasis were oddly displaced. He begins, for example, not with her entrance, but with the waddle and purr of two pigeons sheltering on his window ledge from a slushy rain. He makes me see their grey chubby bodies, the rainbow necks shimmering apprehensively as he approaches their perch. When Madame Rouault finally appears, he seems less conscious of her than of the shower resonating on his attic roof, as if the musical score were so hauntingly pure it overshadowed the entrance of the prima ballerina.

He choreographs each step in her attempt to dispose of her umbrella, which was reopened and shaken in the hallway, partially closed to allow passage through the door of his apartment, fully opened and set upon the floor to dry, snatched up and planted in Schlumberger's hands while she spread a newspaper, then redeposited so hastily that almost a quarter of its circumference was left dripping onto the carpet, watering a sunflower parched to its threads. Watching her fussily shuffling hands as she bent over the papers, he thought she must be upset by something more than the strand of hair that was flopping onto her brow. When the door first opened her eyes had skittered away from his. Her hands might have been mittened and numb with cold the way they fumbled. When at last she rose and turned to him, he had to ask her to repeat her first words, drowned by the staccato raindrops and the fluting spill from a clogged eaves trough. She murmured at a pitch with the cooing pigeons, raised her skirt a few inches, extended a soggily toed shoe. He saw her lips say, ''. . . into a puddle.''

The sight of her bare ankles resting on the footstool before the stove where her shoes were drying gave him a mnemonic shock. It jarred to the center of his consciousness an August evening three months earlier, the night he had first seen Maelzel's chess automaton. The memory of the panic her nakedness had then aroused surprised him. It seemed an intrusion on the relaxed intimacy he now felt as he watched the firelight glowing on her shins, warmly wrapping halfway round her calf. He wanted to find something to say to her that would show how much he had changed in the past three months and how good he felt about it. He wanted a way to put into words the intimacy he felt they shared. He couldn't be sure it was really there unless they talked about it. And he wanted to say something to hurry the future, to hurry away from even the memory of the panic that had suddenly bobbed to the surface of his mind.

''In another month,'' he said, ''you will be good enough to play La Bourdonnais.''

Then she told him she would be leaving for America in three

weeks. This was their last meeting; she would depart on a packet for Le Havre the following day.

He walked over to the window, he says. There was a hysterical slapping of pigeon wings, muted by the intervening glass. He watched the birds circling the rooftops in the rain. Their first impulse as he had approached was to drop toward the street, but they had quickly flapped out of the narrow canyon and away out of sight behind the gable opposite his window.

They came into sight on the other side of the gable, returning, and he looked again at the woman sitting by the fire, her back rigid, her gaze not toward the flames but sharply away, falling perhaps on the wet umbrella. She had not moved since she spoke. Save for the change in his own perspective, he might have been regarding a statue frozen in the instant she told him she was leaving. All Schlumberger could see of her face was a crescent of brow and cheek. The knob of her jawbone under the ear made a jutting line that said, I am cruel. It connected to a porcelain-white neck that said, I am soft. A moment ago that softness had made the cruelty unbearable. But now, without the slightest altera-tion in her pose, the cruelty melted under his eyes into a pathetic determination. He noticed that the hands on her lap were clasped tightly as if restraining one another. Her hands spreading the papers had been clumsy. When she entered she had not been able to meet his eye. Her voice a moment ago had been brittle with tension, clearly audible for the first time since she entered. When he grasped her by the shoulders and commanded, "Look at me," he must have needed only a glance to see what he hoped to find in her eyes, because the next sentence of the journal tells that while the pigeons chortled on the window ledge he was kissing her for a long time.

Even if it were possible, there would be no point in quoting the passage in which he renders the kiss itself. A glance at the appropriate scene in almost any novel of the period will suffice to illustrate the absurd cataract of words his culture prescribed for the account of any contact between the mucous membranes of a man's and a woman's mouths. Beneath the rhapsodic prose, almost like a code message imbedded in a deliberately banal text, one point is clear. Following the initial ferocity with which he pressed his lips upon hers, as her tongue slipping past his teeth transformed his theft into her gift, a gift he discovered himself able not only to accept but return, Schlumberger experienced for the first time a sensuality that breached the solitude of his fantasies.

11 | Schlumberger in Time and Eternity

DURING THE MONTH of December, 1825, the chess analysts at the Café de la Régence began to notice that Schlumberger's game was suffering a strange degeneration. Each of his moves had once been the aesthetically perfect coevel of his opponent's thrusts. Now they were a series of graceless lurches. He made mistakes. The masters murmured astonishment. He compounded the mistakes into blunders. The masters snorted. They did not try to muffle their snickers. Everyone who had ever lost a game to him, which meant everyone, enjoyed seeing the merciless Schlumberger kneading his hands together to keep them from trembling. They enjoyed watching as desperation heated him up, reddened his cheeks, made sweat pop out on his brow. Then the strange thing would happen. He would be in a position where everybody agreed he had no choice but to resign. Then he would stretch a hand to make a move and—an explosion. It was spontaneous combustion. His inner temperature would reach a certain peak and there would be a flash, and by the time people had blinked and were ready to look at the board again, the heat of Schlumberger's imagination had taken the stereotyped personality of a knight or a rook or a pawn and melted it into a new shape.

The first time it happened the few who saw it never believed it could happen again. But he repeated it. Schlumberger couldn't seem to play any other way. Each night he had an audience. Not just the usual few onlookers, but an audience. They would gather around his table like astronomers watching the convulsions of a dying sun. It was clear that his games throughout that winter and into the summer of 1826 were

[5 9]

making chess history. It was equally clear that they were being played by a man for whom the game had become an agony.

None of them had any way of connecting what was happening to Schlumberger with the departure on the twentieth of that month of the packet ship *Howard* from the harbor at Le Havre, some 220 miles down river at the mouth of the Seine. None were aware that among the portmanteaus and trunks in the *Howard'* s cargo hold were five carefully wadded crates that cradled the several parts of the world's only automaton chess player. None knew its passenger list included the mechanical entrepreneur Johann Nepomuk Maelzel, his burly assistant Rouault, who kept to his cabin throughout most of the voyage, and Rouault's wife, raven-haired and sullen and seasick.

SCHLUMBERGER'S first attack of melancholia held off till nearly a week after Louise Rouault's last visit. It took that long for him to recognize that what had taken place between himself and Louise Rouault was already part of his past. There must have been a moment when her lips had slid away from his for the last time, a moment when her hands were tucking at her hair, smoothing her gown, and she was collecting her hat, her bag, the cumbersome umbrella. But all these actions that might have fixed the temporal contours of his experience were no more visible than stars at noon. The eternal instant of the kiss blinded him with its glare.

From his journal entries throughout that week it would be impossible to discover that he was still eating and walking to the Régence and playing chess. Maybe he wasn't. Maybe he stayed in his room and wrote the whole time. What he wrote was a series of footnotes and appendixes to his last meeting with Louise Rouault. He would pounce on a memory, maybe even something he had already mentioned in the November twenty-ninth entry, and wring its neck. He would gut its vitals and strew them on the page—the pressure of her lips, the fine meshed veins of her closed eyelids, the sudden twist that locked her hips against his. What he produced in the end was a carcass stiffened with a peculiarly convoluted syntactical wire and stuffed full of adjectives.

These exercises in emotional taxidermy postponed the onset of the terrors that would transform Schlumberger's chess game. By making the events of November 29 exist in an artificial present tense, he could isolate them from an uncertain future. He hadn't been able to clip

Louise Rouault in his arms tight enough or long enough on that twenty-ninth of November to prevent her from floating away down the Seine to Le Havre on the thirtieth. Already his little mounted specimen of eternity was being nibbled by moths. He was only dimly aware that he would have to stop embalming his past long enough to take action in the present if he wished to preserve his specimen from corruption.

The most logical step would have been to follow her and either bring her back or accompany her to America. This could have been done by simply accepting Maelzel's offer to join his entourage as the director of the chess automaton. But Schlumberger made no inquiries about sailing schedules. He bought no tickets. He contented himself instead with the hope that she might simply return. The only one of his faculties this decision strained was his imagination. For two nights, returning from the Régence in a fall of sticky snow, his pace and his heartbeat would quicken as he neared his apartment, building to a momentum that shot him up the steps three at a time. And he would burst open his door, breathless, convinced that he would find her standing by the fire, seeing her there already in his mind, seeing her turn to him, startled rigid, raptly gazing, her gaze surrendering her soul to the last crumb. He could see her dashing to his arms with a cry. And each night when the door banged against the inner wall the concierge would caw from downstairs and Schlumberger, after groping in the dark for a candle, would listen to his teeth chattering until he had poked some life into the cold grate. On the third night and thereafter, Madame Grandit's sleep was undisturbed.

It was not until the sixth day after she left that he became fully convinced she was not coming back. When that happened he didn't even have to think in order to know what to do next. He went to the Régence to play chess. His one unassailable refuge in timelessness had always been chess, where the relationship of a lusty knight to his queen is frozen in feudal hierarchy. All strife is played out according to rules not subject to change and decay. The field of black and white squares always numbers sixty-four. They always greet the eye in the same comfortable pattern.

I think Schlumberger's first impulse had been to make his passion a part of this ideal world that he controlled with his mind. That was what all the words in his notebook were—a way of gaining control. But when Louise Rouault escaped from the page and escaped from the eight by eight square board where his mind was at home, chess lost its vitality. The only way he could continue to play at all was by making his chess game subject to all the terrifying laws of time and chance into which she had strayed.

IT HAPPENED in the early evening. The waiters at the Café de la Régence were lighting candles on the huge chandelier at the hub of the main playing room. Schlumberger was midway through a game with a retired *drapier* named Chalot, who had become a frequent habitué of the café. The old man brought to the tables with him the same authority and assurance that had served him well in the days when he was advising the fine ladies of Paris on the proper cut of material for a bay window. He would contemplate the board with a lordly frown and munch on his lips, then extend his arm for a move like a monarch about to sign a treaty. He could usually be counted on to mount a spectacular attack with the pieces that were inadvertently guarding his king. Schlumberger occasionally played him—he liked hearing the bewildered painful grunt Chalot produced each time he was checkmated.

At the moment, however, his mind was on Louise Rouault. His reverie was beginning to titillate his body as well as his mind. To restore a certain aesthetic distance to his meditations, he directed his attention to the board. Chalot was in a position to place him in check on the next move. Schlumberger cast a quick glance at the old man's face. Chalot was yanking at his beard, looking vexed and important, but oblivious to his opportunity. With elbows on the table and both hands working busily, he had tugged his whiskers into a pair of tusks.

Schlumberger slowly became aware that Chalot's hands were disgusting. He was fascinated by his own revulsion. He watched the too-long nails becoming shiny with grease from repeated strokes through the beard. A brown mole made a kidney-shaped stain from the knuckle of Chalot's right forefinger to the first joint of his thumb. Suddenly a thrill of nausea shot through Schlumberger's bowels as he imagined this hand with its greedy springy fingers kneading one of Louise Rouault's breasts. The next instant he found himself wondering for the first time what sort of man her husband was.

Schlumberger had known Louise Rouault was married the way you know the distance to the nearest star. It was a fact too large to assimilate and too insignificant to matter. She was one of those women who don't *smell* married. The way she walked, slipping loosely in her joints, filled each motion with her flesh, seemed to grind between her hips a perfume with a hungry reek. Yet a tension, a nervousness checking her grace, interrupting its flow, kept from it any suggestion of parody. Rather than using her body, advertising with it, she was betrayed by it, her secret revealed. And her nervousness—sensed by Schlumberger in the flick of a glance, a gesture broken, disguised, completed in response to another intention—was not naïve, not virgin. Which made it easy for Schlumberger, in the first weeks he knew her, to think of her as a widow. That provided his dreams the stimulation of a fairy-tale impediment: to win the princess, there was a glass mountain to climb, a spell to break; a ghost to lay.

Then, in the course of conversation little remarks fell: Henri's socks needed darning; Henri will ask Maelzel for more money. Quick strokes, the kind a seashore artist has memorized, used to construct not a portrait, a study, but an abstraction of the subject's most salient characteristic: youth, hope, confidence. Schlumberger eventually had to recognize that the husband she sketched for him really existed. But Henri Rouault was less alive to Schlumberger's imagination than the ghost he replaced. Since the existence of a husband complicated Louise Rouault's identity beyond Schlumberger's powers of assimilation, he chose not to think of him at all.

Until a voice across the table from him said, *"Échec!"* and Schlumberger raised his eyes to find the ghost made flesh.

IT WAS A HAUNTING. And the worst of it was that the ghost assumed the flesh not just of old Chalot, but of everyone Schlumberger played. Into each game, no matter how hard he guarded against it, would come thoughts of Louise Rouault. And the thought of her absence led inevitably to anxious speculation about the unknown husband who possessed her, enslaved her, made her body writhe to the rhythm of unspeakable brutalities. Schlumberger felt the force of his own love shrivel. With it went his sense of mastery on the chessboard. Looking with secret horror into the faces of his opponents, he would discover there the lines of cruelty and lust; whenever he became sensitive to the virility of a smile or a thickly corded neck, he grew sick with dread that by such a smile, such a concourse of muscle, Louise Rouault could be enthralled.

[6 3]

Once joined, the connection between Schlumberger's chess opponents and Louise Rouault's husband made an unbreakable weld in Schlumberger's mind. Pathetic journal entries show how he fought the obsession: one entry begins with a prayer remembered from childhood, breaks into a litany of past triumphs, and ends with a feeble boast. But the obsession fed on the strength of his resolution to ward it off. His opponents became invested with a magical potency.

The sweats and the trembling hands noticed by the chess connoisseurs of the Régence, then, were the public symptoms of a compulsive jealousy. But this did not concern them. Tranced in the hush that accompanied Schlumberger's every move, they would have been hard to convince that the conflict on the board was less dramatic than the one taking place in Schlumberger's mind, where the fear that shattered his concentration fueled in him a saving hatred. In this hatred, fanned white-hot, he forged the strokes of fitful brilliance that rescued his game from disaster.

12 | Forth to the Promised Land

WITH THE ARRIVAL in mid-May of Louise Rouault's first letter from America, Schlumberger's imagination erupted in a spectacular display. One memorable victory involved a queen sacrifice on the twenty-third move. Thereafter the arrival of her letters, regular as the transatlantic packet boat, had a barometric correspondence to his most intense creative flashes. They restored to bearable intensity his fear of her phantom husband. They cuckolded Henri Rouault. They described Maelzel's efforts to organize the chess automaton's debut in New York, the inadequacy of her own attempts to sustain the Turk's reputation for perfection, and the roaches infesting the hotel where they slept. To Schlumberger all this was intimate and wicked.

As the spring of 1826 blossomed into a steamy summer the ghost haunting Schlumberger lost some of its protean dexterity and incarnated itself more and more often in the sneering hauteur of Louis Charles de la Bourdonnais, the supreme chess master of the Café de la Régence and the world.

From about the end of May through the middle of August the name of Schlumberger was mentioned with increasing frequency as the principal threat to the eminence of La Bourdonnais. For what follows, however, I have only the uncorroborated word of Schlumberger's journal. In unofficial play during the late morning and afternoon of August 15, he says, he played a series of three games with La Bourdonnais, accepting the customary advantage of pawn and first move in each. He granted La Bourdonnais' request for a draw in the first game and won the second and third before the thirtieth move. At this point

Schlumberger, supported unanimously by those club members in attendance, demanded the right to combat La Bourdonnais on even terms. La Bourdonnais agreed only after much dispute, for the pawn-move handicap had become as much a vanity to him as it had been to his teacher, who had retired permanently from the game when La Bourdonnais became powerful enough to make the advantage decisive. The contest was adjourned until evening. Schlumberger went home in a state of high excitement. He tried unsuccessfully to sleep.

What went through his mind as he lay sweating in his garret was not the strengths and weaknesses of La Bourdonnais' chess strategy. It was the timbre of La Bourdonnais' voice, its effortless resonance, its insolence. He had a way of inflecting the most commonplace statements to give them an edge that made you watch his eyes to learn whether you ought to smile at the joke lurking just out of range. Nothing was too insignificant for Schlumberger's inventory: the fitted waist of La Bourdonnais' frock coat, his spade-pointed, black, tough whiskers, his casual stance, one foot turned out and thumb hooked in the pocket of his waistcoat, elegant and heroic as a statue.

All these things Schlumberger had watched secretly and admired, copied until he almost forgot they belonged to someone else. Now he suddenly felt like a child caught posing in front of a mirror with one of his father's hats down around his ears. He realized everyone must have chuckled behind his back to see him aping the manners of La Bourdonnais. Those manners he now recognized as the authentic expressions of a man who knows he can command the soul of any woman he fancies; hopeless to counterfeit.

Schlumberger had listened avidly to gossip about La Bourdonnais' conquests. On the boulevards he had craned his neck to spot the women pointed out to him as La Bourdonnais' current lovers or former lovers. He had always planned that one day he would learn this secret of La Bourdonnais as well as he had learned how to dress, how to suck his lips as he pondered a move. Now, however, he could think only of the poor cuckolds waddling beside those coolly silken-swathed ladies, and he knew himself ridiculous and impotent as they. It did no good to tell himself La Bourdonnais could not possibly be the husband of Louise Rouault. He knew that with his mind, but his body knew a more profound truth that acted on it like three cups of coffee before breakfast.

Now with his bowels spitting a watery shit and his nerves strung to the pitch of a scream, he had recourse to his favorite defensive ploy. He poured himself a glass of whiskey. He vomited into his washbasin at the first swallow. Shortly after 8 P.M. he dressed and prepared to return to the café. He was met on the stairs by his concierge, who gave him a thick envelope from Louise Rouault. Hastily slipping it into his waistcoat pocket, he proceeded to the café. He took his usual seat and, since La Bourdonnais had not yet arrived, opened the letter. He had expected to find many pages. Instead there was a single leaf covered with the familiar sloping hand, and a sheaf of American currency.

In his journal he quotes from her last paragraph: "In short, he (Maelzel) claims—with what justice you have seen—that my disastrous play has jeopardized the entire tour. He is threatening to abandon us and return alone to France. Last night Henri blackened my eye, he has been drinking for a week and is no use to me or himself. Please come, *mon cher,* I am surely lost without you."

The American notes were passage money.

Schlumberger offers no explanation for his next move, apparently considering it self-evident. His knack for pertinent detail does not entirely leave him, however; he mentions that it was La Bourdonnais with whom he collided in his stride to the door. He is uncertain whether it was La Bourdonnais or someone else who called after him, "Where are you going?"

It was with delight, he says, and a feeling of liberation that made his ears sing, that he whirled about at the door to look down the mirrored walls of the Café de la Régence for the last time. Then, "To America!" he shouted, and turned his back on their astonishment—leaving behind the chance to overcome the greatest chess player in Europe; leaving behind, perhaps, a defeat he may have known he would force upon himself; leaving behind, in any case, whatever knowledge of himself would have come out of either victory or defeat; and most certainly leaving behind a world that had until that moment symbolised all his hopes and ambition.

Like so many dream-struck pilgrims before him.

PART II

13 | Schlumberger's Sleep Is Interrupted

SCHLUMBERGER HAD his first look at the man he was hoping to cuckold on the evening of October 1, 1826. During the six-week crossing he had lain churning like a piece of ill-digested meat in the belly of the transatlantic packet. The magnified ticks and creaks of the beams straining against the ocean's crushing bear hug startled him from his sleep; the submarine gurgling he could hear each time he pressed his ear to the wall of his berth terrified him. He occupied his time in making up different versions of what would happen when he came face to face with Henri Rouault.

A newspaper detailing the barbaric practices of the American frontier gave Schlumberger a source of inspiration for his meditations. It contained an illustration captioned DISCOVERED IN SIN, showing a woman who had sunk to her knees amid billowing petticoats; her hands were joined in supplication before a man hoisting a meat cleaver. It was a poor enough drawing full of vaguely suspect anatomical details. The artist had made the cleaver-wielding arm ape-length, then disguised the other in the folds of a cloak to escape comparison; he had clearly never seen a woman's calf. He had no idea what laws determined how it joined the thigh—but here the petticoat rescued her from obvious deformity as the cloak had her assailant. These deficiencies inspired Schlumberger's participation in completing an intention that had been beyond the artist's technique. In the hands of a more skilled draftsman the man would have had too precise an identity to invite refinement; Schlumberger needed only a glance at the face, all eyebrows and moustaches and menace under its top hat, to know what was required to make it live—he donated to it the features of La Bourdonnais. It glowered at its victim with the complex ruthlessness of a Borgia cardinal. The artist had cartooned his one expression of dreamy calm into the woman's gaze at the descending blade. Schlumberger took this hint and transposed it into the face of Louise Rouault, suffering with love. From there it was only a question of making the rectangular frame boxing the sketch into a doorway at which Schlumberger himself stood, the witness, taking the place of the artist who had forgotten to draw in his own drawing hand and the corner of the sketching pad to complete the triangular balance of his study in domestic intimacy.

Then the scene came alive: La Bourdonnais, drunk and insolent, standing over the trembling Louise, abusing her in some undefined way (Schlumberger edited out the melodramatic cleaver), then leaving off his curses and turning with a look of puzzled vexation as he became aware of Schlumberger at the doorway, and Schlumberger cool and vicious saying, *Get out. She's not taking that from you any more.* And the insolent La Bourdonnais, lips curling back in a rage that was always, in every version of the drama Schlumberger could imagine, doomed to ignominy, was helpless before the power Schlumberger drew from the knowledge that the eyes of Louise were on him, brimming with love and despair.

The image of her grateful adoring eyes made bearable the agonies of Schlumberger's seasickness, which lasted the entire voyage with brief remissions during calm weather. He achieved a detachment from the flutters of his stomach by imagining that Louise, as some mystical by-product of their mutual love, had been gifted with a second sight that enabled her to watch over his every move like the guardian angel his mother had invented to calm his night terrors. She hovered up near the shadowed corner of his windowless, moldy, stale-aired cabin, biting her lovely lip each time he moaned. Soon he found himself arranging his head and arms more decorously on the pillow. He experimented with his moans to try which of them might make the tears glistening in the eyes that glowed down at him brim over onto the cheeks. In this way he ceased to suffer his miseries and began to perform them.

Schlumberger's ship docked in New York harbor amid a forest of masts. By that time, he was experiencing everything that happened to him both as actor and observer. In the persona of his angel he looked on as Schlumberger wrangled for a seat on the Boston stagecoach. Though he spoke English well, his ear for the Yankee dialect was poorly tuned, and it had taken him a long time to learn that the automaton chess player had departed New York two weeks ago. During the two-day coach journey he superimposed the beloved face over the grizzled leathery countenance of the Yankee peddlar who sat opposite him. He noticed only after half a day on the road that his right cheek and sideburn had been dewed with a fine spray of tobacco juice which entered Schlumberger's rear window a moment after the peddlar spat it from the front window. A relentless thumping recorded on his flesh every rut and rock below. The face blessed him with a tired smile as he shifted from one buttock to the other. The peddlar had to rap his knuckles on Schlumberger's knee to get his attention, though Schlumberger was looking directly at him. Schlumberger greeted with astonishment his suggestion that they sleep together. The peddlar cackled ribaldly and explained the custom of American innkeepers, who often bundled two and sometimes three guests into the same bed.

"You ain't in Europe, no more, Frenchy," he chortled. "Ain't no fancy hotels where you get a bed all by yourself, 'cept in the big cities. You bed down with me, otherwise some galoot come rollin' in on you drunker'n a skunk in the middle of the night. Keep you awake the rest of the goddam night."

"Galoot?" asked Schlumberger, trying to look alert.

It was a good idea to be acquainted with your bedpartner if possible, the peddlar added, just to be sure you didn't get stuck with somebody who had bugs. Schlumberger found out what bugs were, thanked the peddler for his advice, and accepted the offer. Almost immediately he regretted his cordiality. Once the peddlar had identified him as a pliable foreigner, Schlumberger became the victim of an informal lecture on the virtues of the infant nation. Soon the image of Louise was exorcized by the peddlar's twangy drone. Schlumberger feigned interest in the old man's anecdotes and admired the saleable items in his knapsack, which ranged from scissors to boot hooks, buttons, hair brushes, razors, and snuff boxes.

Schlumberger had been living with a dream creature whose responses he could manipulate with a thought. He winced at contact with the unmalleable crudities of a real human being. He longed to be alone so that he might put himself once again in communion with the pale spirit whose eyes approved his every breath. He hurried through his supper at the coach inn and went upstairs to his bedroom, leaving the peddlar in the bar, sitting around the fireplace with a crowd of local customers. On his way into the dining room half an hour earlier Schlumberger had passed the same group of men pensively resting the bowls of their clay pipes on their knees and sucking at the long curving stems or tapping them against their teeth as they succumbed to the hypnotic lethargy produced by fire. The peddlar had broken the trance, or rather changed its focus and quality. He had supplanted the darting flames with his own voice, mellow and vulgar and seductive. He piped his audience from farmer's daughter jokes to a pitch for hand mirrors and harmonicas. The carpet bag at his feet was already open.

Just as Schlumberger reached the top of the stairs, the peddlar finished a joke. Schlumberger shut the raucous shrieks of appreciation behind an oak door. He stretched himself on the straw ticking, expecting the ministrations of his angel. Then he felt a cockroach crawling on his throat. He leaped to his feet with a muted cry and spent the next half hour exterminating the tenants of his bed. When he lay down again his flesh was quivering with disgust. Each time he shifted his weight the straw beneath him made scuttling noises. He shrank from the imaginary touch of insect or rodent. His angel made no appearance.

After an hour of tension he began to relax. It no longer mattered whether an insect crawled on his body, so long, he added sleepily, as they didn't touch his lips. Then, just as he was dropping off to sleep, he made out, hovering in the darkness, a luminous familiar face. The yearning eyes and melancholy smile of Louise Rouault did not leave him when he closed his eyes.

She did leave less than an hour later when the Yankee peddlar lurched into the room. He pitched himself onto the mattress beside Schlumberger. At first Schlumberger thought he would be able to sleep again once the peddlar's snores settled into a rhythmic pattern. But he underestimated the sleeper's versatility. Sometimes the snores would chatter like a stick up and down a picket fence. Then they would engage in a dialogue of fitful wheezes. A snore of rising inflection would end in a question mark, answered by a long declarative drone. It was a somnambulist's catechism. Then for a while the snores would stop altogether, and wait until Schlumberger was almost convinced they were gone before galloping off with a lusty whinny. He fell asleep again at about 4 A.M., half an hour before the coach was due to load up for another day on the road.

The coach broke an axle on a stretch of corduroy road ten minutes after the start of the day's journey. Corduroy was the name the Americans had for a pavement made of logs. Since trees were abundant it was natural they should be put to as many uses as possible, but in the typical haste and impatience Schlumberger was beginning to recognize as a native American characteristic, the logs had not been planed into even planks. They were simply stripped of branches and dragged out over the road. The spaces between logs were packed with earth, which washed away in the first thunderstorm. The advantage of such roads was that vehicles which traveled them would not sink up to the axles in mud during the damp season. The disadvantage was that riding them in a coach without springs was like having your buttocks slapped with a barrel stave every other second for as many hours as you were on the road.

Another disadvantage was the kind of breakdown that had afflicted Schlumberger's coach. The driver, his cheek bulbous with chew, threw his hat in the road. He squatted to look at the axle and cursed it, despite the interfering chew. One of the passengers said his language was enough to char the weed. Another said he sounded like he was preaching a revival. Then he explained to the passengers that the tools he might have used to repair the axle had been stolen on his last run. To forestall any grumbles against his competence, he used a tone of high righteousness. None of the passengers challenged him. His righteous tone quivered close to the brink of his raging one. All the passengers sensed that the man who nudged him into a stream of curses like the ones he had directed at the axle would have to fight or die of humiliation. Once he was certain no one would dare berate him, the driver became calm and businesslike, dispatching a youth who had been riding on the box with him to the inn where they had slept. The plan was for the youth to use one of the saddle horses from the inn to ride to the coach station in Hartford for a vehicle that could pick up the stranded passengers.

After this was arranged the passengers, six in all and all men, stood around the coach for a while, exchanging jovial curses and spitting in the dust. The driver's style had proved infectious. Each man seemed to be trying out how closely he could approximate the driver's swagger without becoming so boisterous he called down the driver's attentions on himself. When the sun got high and hot, they retired to a clump of trees by the roadside. Soon the peddlar Schlumberger had slept with had organized a poker game. Someone began passing a bottle. Schlumberger neither played nor drank. The only game he knew or cared to know was chess, and he was drunk on love. He planted his back against the rough bark of an oak and closed his eyes. "Queen, goddammit," the peddlar was saying in his Yankee twang. "Gimme the fuckin' queen." But Schlumberger had tuned his ears to hear only the first faint breeze of some faraway turbulence rustling the leaves arched over him. As he fell asleep it became the whispered voice of Louise Rouault.

The coach arrived in mid-afternoon. It was the latest American development in elegant transportation—the Concord coach. It had a profile like an egg that had been windowed and fringed with red paint and set on wheels. At first the new coach seemed to ride more smoothly, but Schlumberger had been on the road only a few minutes when he felt a familiar nausea. He looked round himself like a man who wonders where a bad smell is coming from. Then he realized the coach was swaying. The movement was like the rolling wave motion he had lived with the past six weeks, except that on shipboard he had been at least alone. Here his stomach turned over and again over to the drone of the peddlar's commentary. "Goddam, thet were a dilly," he would say as a wheel dunked into a bone-jarring rut. "Thet's what we calls a dilly, Frenchy." And the other passengers would chuckle at the peddlar explaining American slang to the foreigner.

The coach made Schlumberger seasick because its body was not cushioned by springs, but hung suspended on multi-ply leather straps nailed to the frame. When the driver first flicked his reins and hollered, "Hi!", the horses exploded with a vehemence that jerked the coach back to the full elasticity of the straps, then flung its weight forward into the building momentum of the horses, which responded to the suddenly lightened load with another thrust that flung the coach back again. From then on the passengers experienced a steady seesaw. One moment Schlumberger would be flattened against the wall in a dip that tilted the passengers opposite into a throne above him, the next he would be bracing himself with his hands on the bench to prevent himself from being catapulted into their laps.

To take his mind off his stomach, Schlumberger tried to fix his attention on the painted door panels inside the coach. The one closest to him on his right depicted Lot's wife looking at the burning city. The flesh of her face and chest was still warm. She didn't seem aware that her feet, her gown up to the waist, and her left arm, which extended down along her side, had all become hard white salt. Her right arm had not yet crystalized because she had raised it above her brow to shield herself from the glare of turrets wrapped in cones of flame. In the turret windows black silhouettes of the damned writhed in burning rooms. Her concentration on the spectacle appeared so great the artist must have intended to suggest she would never know what was happening to her. In one instant her blood would freeze in the tubes of her heart; in the next, just as she began to miss the warmth it pumped, her mind would harden like ice over a pond. She would have not a moment to regret that no grief nor rage, no wisdom could ever crack the hard smooth innocence of her brow to stroke their sweet furrows in her flesh.

The other panel showed Orpheus rising through a coiling path out of a red pit. He had just taken the flute from his lips, his corded neck and sidelong eyes told that his head was turning back toward his shoulder to see whether Euridice was following. She was there, but he would never know it. Already her body had a ghostly translucence. By the time her lover's head was fully turned, she would have disappeared. Her last act before returning to the underworld was to wildly throw up her arms. It was not possible to say whether she was making a vain attempt to warn him or simply despairing at his lack of faith.

Schlumberger decided the two panels had a message for him. At first he thought the idea was that you shouldn't look back. He must not pine for the comforts of his old Paris apartment and the pleasures of chess. He had not played chess, except in his mind against himself, for six weeks. Then he thought he saw in the panels a lesson about curiosity, but he couldn't see how he was guilty of any curiosity, so the lesson didn't seem to apply. He was superimposing the face of Louise Rouault on the features of the agonized Euridice when the rain began splatting on the baggage tied to the roof of the coach. The passengers reached outside to fumble with the snaps on the leather shades rolled above the windows like eyelids. When the shades had been unfurled and resnapped against the box, Schlumberger found himself inside a shadowy echoing womb where he could dream his dreams in peace. The darkness inside the coach seemed to inhibit the conviviality of the other passengers as well. Conversations tapered into silence. A meditative calm settled over the buffeted box, broken only by the tobacco-chewing peddlar's occasional spitting. Now that the window was closed, he spat on the coach floor. He could see just well enough to aim between Schlumberger's boots and not well enough to be a hundred percent accurate.

Again that night Schlumberger slept poorly. He found himself— with the foreigner's defensive politeness—nodding and grinning when he should have said a vehement no. He wound up with the peddlar as a bedpartner once more. Since the broken axle had added hours to their travel time, they were forced to put up at a small inn some fifty miles from the usual stop at Uxbridge or Mendon.

The rain had become a drizzle so light it was almost a fog by the time Schlumberger stepped down from the coach. After his supper he retired immediately to his room as before, spread one of his extra shirts over a damp spot in the mattress and fell asleep. He awoke with a thunderclap. The rain was vollying against the roof. Above the place he had covered with his shirt a drip nearly as steady as a trickle was falling on his thigh. The peddlar was snoring beside him. He hunched to a sitting position with his back against the headboard and his arms circling his legs. He tried to get back to sleep resting his forehead on his knees. An hour and a half later he began to doze.

In his first dream of the night Louise Rouault was standing over the corpse of her husband, who had the features of La Bourdonnais and a round dark hole between his eyes. "There is the cleaver on the floor beside him," she was telling Schlumberger. "I had to do it." "Of course," Schlumberger heard himself reply. "He was a monster." And taking the smoking pistol from her hand, he flung it to the floor, where it landed with an unnaturally loud thump. Her face shone with gratitude. He was about to take her in his arms when he realized that somehow the pistol was still in his hand. He threw it from him again, violently, and heard a repetition of the thumping noise, which continued and became a thumping on the door of his bedroom.

The door opened briskly just as he opened his eyes, and a face poked inside, whiskered, nightcapped, materializing like spectral ectoplasm from behind shadows that danced across it in correspondence with flickers from the candle in the landlord's hand. "Coach in the yard," he barked. "Board in ten minutes."

Schlumberger's Sleep Is Interrupted

With his mind on the strange dream Schlumberger left his bedroom in darkness, made a wrong turn, using a back staircase rather than the one he had entered by. The door he opened admitted him to the yard of the inn, but the coach was pulled up at another door. Above the pattering the raindrops made in the cobbled courtyard he heard one of the coach horses sneeze and shake itself in the traces. He stood in the doorway trying to decide whether it would be easier to cut across the court to the coach or turn back and thread the labyrinth to the other door. The running lights of the coach reflected in the puddles, defining the perimeters of a path by which he thought he could cross without getting his feet soaked. He tucked his bag under his arm and sprinted for the coach. A sudden gust doused the coachlights. Running in darkness he splashed through puddles. He reached the coach soaked to the knees. Once inside he settled into a corner seat where he would best be able to brace himself against road shocks. He was becoming an expert traveler, fussy as an old man about his comfort. He groped about in his mind for the dream, but it was gone.

The coach had been bobbing along not more than a quarter of an hour when Schlumberger noticed a sudden diminution in the noise of the carriage wheels. A list brought the weight of the other two passengers on his bench heavily upon him. From the driver's box hoarse bellows brought the horses to a halt. Schlumberger, nearest the window, pushed out the snaps that held its leather curtain and looked out. The running lights winked in a sea of mud looming uncomfortably close to his eyes. As he watched, the horses apparently relaxed their tension on the traces. The coach tilted another two inches. Then Schlumberger heard the driver sloshing toward them. The driver grunted, fighting the door open, gouging away the mud with his boot heel to make the bottom edge swing further out.

"That'll do," he said. "You can squeeze through there. Everybody climb down."

Through the window Schlumberger saw the driver's legs to the knees. Below the knees they were lost in mud. None of the passengers moved. One of them, Schlumberger couldn't tell who, asked, "What's happened?"

The driver told them two of the coach wheels had gone off the edge of the log road and got stuck in a mudhole. By way of apology, he allowed that the rain made it "hard seein'."

There was still no movement from the passengers except a few minor adjustments of position. Schlumberger felt a weight lift from his shoulders, which had been squeezed between the wall of the coach and the press of the man next to him. He breathed easier. Everyone was afraid to move any more for fear the coach would fall on its side in the mud. Somebody muttered, "I ain't goin' out in that swamp." Others murmured assent. The mutiny had found its leader. Then the same passenger shouted, "Let the horses pull us out! If we'd wanted to wade in that mud, we wouldn't be payin' you to drive us to Boston."

The driver made no answer to this, but Schlumberger heard above the pelting rain the sucks and splashes of footsteps. He was relieved. The thought of the mud and stinging rain made him feel as though a layer of skin had been peeled off his body, leaving its surfaces raw as they would be in a high fever. He expected the tug of the horses directly. Five minutes passed. Then the leader of the mutineers, who had the window seat opposite Schlumberger's, lifted back the leather curtain and gave an outraged shriek.

"What in thunder you doin' over thar?" he bellowed.

Peering through the curtain that was now hanging perpendicularly from the top of his own window, Schlumberger saw the driver squatting under an oak tree by the roadside, his bottom perched on an exposed root. When the driver had finished tearing a chew of tobacco off his plug, he made his answer, talking just loud enough to be heard above the rain.

"If them horses coulda pulled that coach outa the mud by themselves" he explained, and stopped to develop saliva for his chew, "I hadn'a asked you to do it. But since you-uns don't wanta git yer feet wet, I'm fixin' to sit right here till that mudhole dries up."

Schlumberger felt a cold rush of water down his ankles as his boots sank over their tops in the mud. The tragically mourning eyes of Louise Rouault hovered in the darkness outside the radius of the lamplight. He joined the other passengers and laid his hunched back against the side of the coach with a heroic grimace.

THE STAGE PULLED into Boston early that evening, nearly twelve hours late. Cracked mud fell away from Schlumberger's legs as he swung down into the yard of Lamphear's general stage office in Hanover Street. Once out on the street he forgot the directions he had asked in the livery stable. The attendant had been quick and aggressive and looked ready to be impatient with a foreign accent. When he found himself for the second time confusing the direction of the fourth and fifth turns, Schlumberger didn't have the courage to request a repetition. Despite the man's calloused hands and Yankee twang, his air of contemptuous authority made Schlumberger think of La Bourdonnais. When the man's hand swung inward to illustrate the direction of a curve in a street leading up from the harbor, Schlumberger was thinking of the way the aristocratic wrist of La Bourdonnais would slip his queen behind your guard. His eyes had the same air of remote mockery, as if they read in each of your gestures a complicated joke you had not intended.

As he stepped into the Boston streets, a predictable train of associations led his mind from La Bourdonnais to his approaching confrontation with the husband of Louise Rouault. All the rich fantasies that the past few days of hardship had bludgeoned below the surface of his consciousness bobbed up more buoyant than ever. Her face rose before his eyes like a harvest moon. Her voice cried, "Save me, save me, oh hurry!" in tones he had never heard her use. They could not have quickened his blood more if they had been the cries of her coming orgasm. He glanced anxiously at each likely building, expecting the sheer force of his will to make Julian Hall appear around each of a dozen next corners. Nobody watching his brisk determined pace would have believed he had not the slightest notion where his destination lay.

Some time later Schlumberger stopped a lamplighter trudging his rounds in the early dusk. By this time it was raining again, not heavily but with a monotonous pocking in the puddled streets. The lamplighter was puzzled by Schlumberger's inquiries about Maelzel, but instantly recognized a description of the automaton. "You just keep on down Congress Street till you get to Milk Street," he said. "You'll find Julian's Restorator right there on the corner."

Crossing Water Street, Schlumberger got some protection from the rain as he passed beneath the overhanging branches of the elm trees on the grounds of the Dalton mansion. On the other side of the white board fence along which he walked, a warm orange light glowed in one of the upstairs windows. Soon, Schlumberger was thinking, he would be able to stretch his feet before a fire and make a long accounting of his ordeal for Louise. His boots were heavy with mud and water. With each footfall tickling water oozed between his toes. As the branches above him thinned he made out through the mist the steeple of the Old South Church, a block over. The spire was a sentinal guarding the respectability of the neighborhood, watching his progress past the Dalton house stable. It was eclipsed at last by the Tucker house, whose front wall was set flush with the sidewalk so that he was momentarily bathed in gaslight as he passed below the parlor window. The steeple was well behind Schlumberger's right shoulder as he drew abreast of the last house on the block, which faced Milk Street.

The side yard of this house was littered with uprooted bushes. The trunks of two small evergreens had been hacked off at stump level to expose the side wall of the house. Over that wall a length of canvas had been nailed. Even in the gathering darkness Schlumberger could make out the crimson lettering: MAELZEL'S MANSION OF MECHANICAL MARVELS. Another sign, bearing the same inscription in gold capitals against a red field, hung over the main door. It swung out over the entrance like the blade of an ax, its frame bolted into the lettering of an older, faded sign against the wall. That sign read simply, JULIAN. Across the lower story wall along the whole length of the building a billboard notice had been repeated in every unwindowed space. Two had been plastered side by side onto the oak door. Schlumberger climbed the steps to the door, passing into the potential arc of the hovering sign. It creaked menacingly as he read for the third time the four alliterative M's, this time in black headline type. The ORIGINAL AND CELEBRATED AUTOMATON CHESS PLAYER, in letters not quite as thick as those containing Maelzel's name, headed a list of mechanical marvels that included THE AUTOMATON TRUMPETER AND THE MECHANICAL THEATRE, PURPOSELY INTRODUCED FOR THE GRATIFICATION OF JUVENILE VISITORS. Schlumberger swung his portmanteau down from his shoulder where it had rested against his humped back, and placed it on the stoop while he read, "He moves his head, eyes, lips and hands with the greatest facility, and distinctly pronounces the word '*Échec*' . . . when necessary." A parenthetical statement informed Schlumberger that "*Échec*" was "the French word signifying 'Check.' " Momentarily Schlumberger experienced the grotesque thought that it was himself he was reading about. This, then, was how they saw him. That word, "*Échec*," which embodied so much of the triumph and meaning his life had possessed, required translation. For the first time Schlumberger could not call up the worshipful image of Louise Rouault to calm him. He jerked his face away from the poster as if it had been an open furnace, searing and blinding him. He tried to find her face in the moving shadows of the trees down the block, the settling fog, the lone star glimpsed through an opening in the cloud ceiling above him. But for the moment he had quite forgotten what she looked like.

When his repeated knocks brought no answer, he tried the door and admitted himself into what had once been the dining room of a restaurant. The smell of mildew permeated the room like a rich incense. The tables had been replaced by rows of straight-backed chairs, all facing a stage at the other end of the room where a headless man sat before a cabinet. One of its hands rested alongside the chessboard on the cabinet. The other was raised, suspended, as if about to give a blessing to the reverently attending chairbacks. To the right of the figure stood a deal table on which an oil lamp burned like a sanctuary light. By its glow Schlumberger saw that the stage framing the headless god had been concocted with garish shabbiness. A purple curtain had been nailed from floor to ceiling along the flanking walls, but there was not enough of the flimsy material to be drawn closed even if there had been a pulley on which it might have traveled. A strip of the same material had been nailed across the ceiling to create the effect of a proscenium arch. About two feet before it reached the stage-left curtain the material had run out. A length of white sheet completed the intention. A velvet-wrapped rope hung on wooden posts stretched from curtain to curtain, marking the border of holy ground. Schlumberger was not certain whether the trappings were meant to suggest a church or a theatre.

Then from a door in the back wall entered a man. He shuffled down to the deal table. The lamplight glinted on his spectacles as he scraped a chair away from the table. Seated, he gave Schlumberger his profile. He was facing the headless figure in the center of the stage, but he seemed to be looking at a polished ball on the table before him. After a few moments he picked up the ball and juggled it in his hands until Schlumberger recognized it as the automaton's head, unturbaned and hairless. It was quite easy to recognize once the man turned its face to his own so that the man and the Turk's head regarded one another. The man's hand was under the base of its skull. He stared at it with what might have been resignation or puzzlement or awe. With the skull of Yorick awaiting its epitaph, he was a mute Hamlet who could only stare and stare at the cheekless, lipless smiling teeth.

The man shifted the automaton's skull to his left hand and thumbed down the jaw with the other hand. He inserted an oilcan into the Turk's mouth. After a few squirts he worked the jaw shut and open until its bite was no longer accompanied by a squeak. Then he poked the needlepoint spout of the oilcan delicately into the corners of the Turk's eyes. He wiped oil from the Turk's cheeks with his handkerchief, patient and tender as a parent soothing away a child's grief. Schlumberger came down the aisle toward him. The man squinted in his direction and tipped his spectacles from his nose up onto his crown.

Schlumberger's journal records that he felt a peculiar shock at the encounter which followed. The man, uncertain of Schlumberger's identity, rose to meet him, shuffled forward a few steps. He was broad in the chest and belly, but he carried his weight as if it were a natural fullness rather than the distended flab of overindulgence. Though he was not yet forty, his thick body and flat-footed, resigned stance and walk suggested an older generation. As he approached, Schlumberger put on his face the tight efficient smile of a man about to address a stranger. He shifted his bag to the left hand so that the right was free to be extended briskly when he was within grasping distance.

"Could you tell me where I might find Monsieur Maelzel," he said. "I am William Schlumberger."

As he pronounced his own name he looked for the first time into the eyes of the other man. A sensation as tantalizingly subtle as a rich perfume wafted through Schlumberger's memory, but the recognition was not immediate. Before he could interpret the meaning the eyes had for him, he had to dissociate them from the heavy wedge of brow tangling over the nosebridge and from the tobacco-brown hollows scooped into their sockets. What he saw, however, when his mind had filtered out these irrelevancies and isolated the brown heavy-lidded eyes flecked with autumnal gold, was the same gaze of nobility and suffering love that he had conjured into his memory of Louise Rouault's face to be his talisman and guardian angel throughout the privations of his six-week odyssey.

Schlumberger's Sleep Is Interrupted

The man looked Schlumberger up and down like a peasant girl confronting the power and sinful nakedness of Michelangelo's David. Then, offering his hand to be squeezed, he said with terrible dignity, "I'm Henri Rouault. I believe you are acquainted with my wife."

14 | Morning Ablutions of Rouault

WEDGED IN THE PAGES of Schlumberger's journal I discovered a manuscript in another hand. Both sides of some twenty pages were covered by an erratic script. Loops and slashes asserted ideas qualified in tortuous miniscule scratches. The left side of each page had an inch-wide margin, or once had. Afterthoughts and corrections of the main text obliterated it. Sentences, sometimes whole paragraphs, were scored out. Some thoughts were not merely corrected, but suppressed, inked over in thick black bars. The first few words of each line held steady. Then a magnet seemed to bend the line toward the lower right corner of the page. The edge of the page clipped the line off. I got the feeling that if it had been left unchecked, the line would have dropped into a spiral following the author's thought, trailing him into his labyrinth. The manuscript broke off in mid-sentence two-thirds of the way down the last page. Its author could be identified without a signature. It was the love letter Henri Rouault wrote his wife to justify the murder he planned to commit.

The logic of homicide began with church bells. The morning after he met the man his wife had lured across an ocean Rouault awoke to the sound of church bells. Lying awake behind his closed eyelids he heard them chanting their daily imperative: Love the Cross of Christ, Love the Cross of Christ. The tone on which he placed the word, *Love,* was sometimes oddly muffled, irresonant, like the sudden chirp of a pubescent boy. Reading Rouault's yellowed pages I can feel the sun warming his face, making the darkness behind his closed eyelids the color of blood. I can feel it drying the mucus in the corners of his lips. His one dream all night, it seemed, was of Louise lying beside him. Now he was holding his own breath to listen for hers. He calculated the specific gravity of the mattress to determine if it still supported her body. But he was not ready just yet to reach out or to open his eyes and find out for sure. His nose detected a randy incense of dung.

The bells were pealing in the accents of a taunting child. *Nyaa*-na, *nyaa*-na, *nyaa*-yaa, *Love* the, *Cross* of, *Chri*-ist. It occurred to him that perhaps this meant loving the hunchback chess player as well. The letter elaborates this notion of Love with the authority of a theology text. But the manuscript page can be read like the face of a bad poker player. He exposes his resistance to the idea in the crabbed hand, the involuted syntax. The capitalized abstractions ("Atonement . . . Divine Retribution . . .") plug the gaps in conviction. On the other hand, it was impossible for him thoroughly to hate anyone as miserable as Schlumberger had appeared that night. You might hate him just a little for the pity that had flickered behind his eyes when Rouault identified himself as Louise's husband. Yes, you could fan that into a nice hate if you worked at it. But the hunchback's moment of compassion had rapidly given way to his more typical mood—a self-absorbed anxiety. Too strong a resentment of such anguish struck Rouault as absurd. On the whole it was more comfortable, as well as more in keeping with the injunction of the bells, to return pity to pity. An eye for an eye.

What could you do but pity him, standing there dripping and shivering at the thought of seeing his angel again? Wet as a dog splashed by a cartwheel. Rouault's father once threw an old collie from a punt to see if it would swim. A minute had gone by before the dog broke water, its ears drooping in shame and terror, frantically whirling its paws. It was odd to notice that even before the hunchback knew what kind of reception he would get from Louise, his face had the look of a dog thrown by its master into deep water.

It was Maelzel that Schlumberger asked for, Rouault recalled, but that hadn't fooled Rouault. There was the slightest hesitation before Schlumberger pronounced Maelzel's name, as if another intention had been quickly censored. And the eyes, the hunchback's eyes were darting over Rouault's shoulder, sliding off toward doorways, corners. *Well, let him simmer,* Rouault thought.

And when he said, "I believe you are acquainted with my wife," he got what he wanted from the hunchback's reaction: a quick surge of eagerness, checked almost immediately by caution; then, after the briefest calculation, a realization slipped smooth as a cloud-shadow across the hunchback's face—if the proper tone were used, he might even feed his hunger with a casual question. But before Schlumberger could use the moment so tantalizingly offered, Rouault withdrew it, saying, "Mr. Maelzel will return in a few minutes. He is meeting with a newspaper editor. You'd be surprised how much the success of our tour depends on the press." Leaving Schlumberger no recourse but to enter the conversation on this current. Rouault soon bore him into shoals and eddies far from his intended course. *For a chess player,* Rouault thought, *he's easy enough to read.*

He invited Schlumberger to watch him reattach the Turk's head, and continued reading him in glances as he worked and chattered. "You'll be pulling his strings soon enough," he said, indicating the rods inside the automaton's trunk that connected to its neck swivel, its jaw, its polished eyelids. "You might as well see how it works." And as Schlumberger bent to see the intricate connections, Rouault speculated on the dark comma of hair tacked to his brow. Was it an accident of wind and rain, or was the resemblance to David's Napoleon intended? The lips were Napoleon's, too; full, almost pretty. That of course was nature, but the little pout he gave the underlip could be art. "It's done on the pantograph principle," he said. "You pull this rod inside the chest, and he blinks his eyes." The beard was wrong for Napoleon. What was it saying? Not full, not the aspiring patriarch style; he was too young to want that anyhow. Still in his rebel stage. Wiggling a pair of fingers behind your head. What, then? Just a fringe really, as if he didn't really want it at all, except for the tuft at the chin. Ah! he'd got it now: when the hunchback's hovering face eclipsed the lamp on the table beyond him, Rouault saw how the beard firmed out the profile of a weak chin. That explained it. Ha, wonder if the hump was real? Pillow strapped on there? Little sympathy bid? No, he tried too hard to hide it, squared his shoulders. Hardly know it was there if you didn't want to. Stroke it for luck sometime. What, though, did it say about him? Have to consult a professional bumpreader for that. "It will be a relief," Rouault said aloud, "to turn this machine over to a professional chess player." No, phrenologists didn't do back bumps, only heads. What about nose bumps, he wondered. That's a beaut. Look at it on one side, the nose ran smooth and straight, dull as a virgin. From the other angle: that nice thick knob at the bridge, just enough to put his whole face in order. Give him a history.

"There, that should hold him." Then, pitying the wilted points of Schlumberger's collar, he added, "Now I'll bet you'd like a chance to get into some fresh linen. Follow me and I'll show you to your room."

As they passed single file along the upstairs hallway Rouault nodded to indicate Maelzel's bedroom and paused at his own room long enough to give Schlumberger a glance at the twin pillows lying side by side above the scarlet counterpane. "I wonder if I left my . . . ," he muttered, laying his hand on the knob to swing the door wide, while Schlumberger craned to see over his shoulder. Poised in the doorway Rouault flicked his gaze back from the room. He caught the brief struggle as the hunchback mastered his curiosity. He bestowed on that curiosity and upon the control which so quickly masked it his rueful smile of recognition. "No, I guess I left it downstairs," he said, and closed the door upon further inspection. Then, speaking directly to Schlumberger this time, he said, "We're quite cozy in here, as you can see. Quite at home. Your room is down here. Have you any objection to yellow curtains?"

WHEN THE BELLS stopped pealing Rouault opened his eyes a slit, just enough to see through his lashes the crucifix hanging on the wall beyond the foot of his bed. *Love the Cross,* he prayed. *It's a sin to hate him anyway.* It had been much easier to not hate him after the others got back. That was half an hour later. Schlumberger had changed clothes and found his way back downstairs to the sitting room. He and Rouault sat drinking tea and unenthusiastically exchanging impressions of America. "I recall the day we landed, I . . ." one would say, and the other's immediate, "Ah yes, I, too," would flatten whatever effervescence the anecdote promised, leaving the raconteur to hasten through a few highpoints: " . . . the coach . . . the innkeeper . . ." Then he could drop into silence again and suck the coppery taste of futility from his mouth while the other manufactured words a while. During one of their intervals of silence the rainpatter surged and through the outer door-way wafted a damp draft. Murmurs in the hall burst into a duet of laughter. A moment later they entered, breathless and beaming, brushing water from their shoulders and stamping it out of their shoes. The wood floor made their stamping sound like the barks of a welcoming dog.

"Ah, Monsieur Schlumberger has arrived," cried Maelzel. "Perhaps we can afford to eat this week after all."

Rouault saw the hunchback's vexation as Maelzel's bulk loomed toward him, blocking his view of Louise. She was still in the doorway, panting and ruddy. A lock of hair had escaped from its tuck beneath her broad-brimmed American bonnet. It lay along her cheek. By the time Schlumberger's eyes could discreetly disengage from Maelzel and seek their true pole, she had crossed to Rouault. She planted a wet puppy-nose kiss on his cheek and stood with her arm linked through her husband's.

"How was your journey, Monsieur Schlumberger?" she said demurely. Without waiting for a reply she brought her lips to Rouault's ear. She began whispering in his ear. She had shocked Maelzel, she whispered, by skipping across a puddle on Congress Street. She spoke with an uncharacteristically girlish giggle. She was leaning nearly her whole weight on Rouault's arm.

THE MEMORY of her body's weight returned to him now. He sensed that he was quite alone in bed. He opened his eyes fully, renouncing sleep. The smell in the room made him think of a barn where he once found a swallow's nest. Another room, too; at first, before he was fully awake, he half thought to find himself in the room they had slept in when they were first married. His palm slid hopefully across the sheet beside him, but not even the memory of her body warmth remained. Only a morning coolness on the sheet where the sun had not been able to reach it. The sun, already high and warm, reminded his stomach of the time. The previous night, too, he had been hungry, with a fretful ache in his gut that didn't make the actual chewing and swallowing of food any less forced.

The four of them, or rather the two pairs, Rouault claimed by Louise and Schlumberger borne away by Maelzel, had decided to celebrate Schlumberger's arrival in a restaurant on Milk Street. Rouault at first declined the champagne Maelzel ordered. His wife chattered in his ear, punctuating her talk with little pats and caresses and squeezes that made his forearm tingle. He began to understand the role for which he had been cast. When Maelzel, with a mock flourish, poured the first refill, he offered his glass with the others.

"It was actually Rouault's idea to have Louise write you," Maelzel was telling Schlumberger. "He was certain that once you knew from a direct report how successful the enterprise could be—with the right operator for the automaton, of course—you would be unable to resist the offer."

Rouault beamed and nodded at Schlumberger's verifying glance. Under the table Louise's fingertips were lightly stroking his thigh. Schlumberger's eyes flicked to Louise and rested there. Then she must have given him a sign, a smile, a wink. Rouault saw the hardness melt from his astonishment. Schlumberger's face blossomed into a smirk of childish guile. He turned his attention back to Maelzel, who was saying, ". . . find that American chess players are a match for your European subtlety. You must be on your guard. To survive in America you must be direct and vigorous and powerful."

"In chess," Schlumberger shrugged, "there can be no power without thought. It is absurd to pit subtlety against power as if they were two different—"

"You will see, Willie. You have not yet played any Americans. That handicaps you in discussing their merits."

"My name, sir, is William. If you question my ability to compete with American chess players, why did you summon me? What made you pay my passage across an ocean to take over the controls of your mechanical puppet?"

"We mustn't be surprised at this display of temper," Maelzel said. He addressed Rouault and Louise with a smile that tightened his lips without showing any teeth. His lips thinned as they pulled wide. At their corners they curled and sliced a thin wedge into his full, red, dimly freckled cheeks. A straight line across his face from the tip of each wedge would have passed through the base of his nose.

"We are forgetting how exhausted we were directly after we landed. It makes one . . . snappish, even with one's friends." Turning to Schlumberger, he continued, "And surely you must admit it is unfair, Willie, to insist that I am responsible for your presence here. Assuming you were a man who knew his own mind, I took your refusal in Paris as final. It was, as you well know, Madame Rouault who 'summoned' you, as you put it. And you reconsidered your refusal for reasons of your own." Was there, Rouault had speculated, an edge of mockery in that phrase: *reasons of your own*. "You mustn't be quick to take offense. The last thing I wished to suggest is that I lack confidence in you. If I had not the greatest respect for your powers, I would not have offered you the opportunity to join us in the first place. And I am certain you will be a match for whatever talent the United States have to offer. I only wished to prepare you for . . ."

And he talked on, stroking, smoothing, shaping, prodding once again, while the hunchback winced and resettled himself and his cheeks began to glow like coals under the steady pump of a bellows.

But all this, Rouault realized, was a part of the plan, merely a way of clearing a few pawns to open the board for important pieces. Throughout dinner Maelzel darted from one subject to another, easing rooks and knights into position, setting up combinations. Before the hunchback had a hint that he was involved in something more than filling his stomach in the presence of the woman he had crossed an ocean for, Maelzel had control of the center.

"You must take our advice in adjusting to American customs," he said, clamping a fatherly palm over Schlumberger's forearm. "We shall lead you in everything."

When they were back at Julian Hall having tea in the sitting room, Maelzel opened his attack in earnest. He had slipped away while Louise was lighting a fire under the kettle and Rouault and Schlumberger were lighting fires in their pipe bowls. Just as the three of them were settling into easy chairs, they heard Maelzel clattering down from the second-floor bedrooms. He stopped in the hallway to let them admire him. He was wearing a different vest. The gold of his watch chain embroidered his rich purple paunch. His cravat was freshly fluffed and shaped. His grey sideburns were combed to points below the ears. His smile spread broad enough to expose a glint of gold at the root of an eyetooth. He was going out, he announced. Business, he said in a tone that let you know he thought it was amusing to call whatever it was he was going out for business. Then, as he was walking from the sitting room doorway down the hall to the front door, he called back, "Schlumberger, I expect you to have your fuck-hole in that box by eight o'clock tomorrow morning, and don't get out till you know how to play chess in it."

The door slammed. Maelzel's voice had been as casual as his footsteps. He had even taken the time to affect the Yankee drawl that colored his speech these past few weeks in moments when he was being particularly American. But Schlumberger didn't have a chance to get to his feet, let alone formulate a rebuttal, or even a curse. If you had been deaf, Rouault thought, you would have concluded simply that his first sip of tea had scalded his mouth. If you had been deaf, you wouldn't have heard the way the cup rattled as he replaced it in the china saucer.

It was to Louise he had turned then, using for the first time a tone that claimed an intimacy beyond formal politeness. Rouault had been expecting that tone of voice all evening, especially since they had ordered the second bottle of champagne. Rouault had been dreading to hear it, because he did not know how he would react to it. He found that, like Schlumberger, he stayed seated and made no reply.

What Schlumberger said was, "Does he think I am a stable boy he has hired?"

Rouault saw his wife's exquisite shrug. "That's his way," she said. "You will get used to it." When Schlumberger replied that he would not, did not intend to "get used to it," she repeated the shrug. Rouault was familiar with the gesture. They sat for a while listening to Schlumberger breathing as if he couldn't decide between rage or tears. Then Louise put down her knitting and sat on the arm of Rouault's chair and leaned her bosom against his cheek. He felt the sharp nail of her forefinger slide along the back of his neck, tracing the crown of his collar till it found his right ear, which she tugged as she murmured, "It's late. Take me to bed, *mon cher*."

As they were walking to the door, Rouault realized that his wife intended to leave Schlumberger alone in the sitting room. "Wouldn't you like to go to bed also, Monsieur Schlumberger," he called. "You've had a long journey." And Louise, with a laugh, added, "Remember: you have to be up early in the morning."

Now WHILE HE DRESSED, the dung smell pinching his nostrils, Rouault wondered whether Schlumberger had been on time his first day on the job. *I'll find out at breakfast,* he thought. *It will be a way to gauge his capacity for defiance. No; the truth: it will be a chance to watch how he squirms on the hook. Oh Christ, I don't want to hate.* He pressed his lips to the feet of the crucifix on the wall. *Teach me to have no enemies. To have no desire. To love without desiring. Teach me to love her as you do.* His palms were pressed flat to the wall on either side of the crucifix.

He laid his cheek against the wall and extended his arms until his pose mirrored the Christ's. His arms tingled with the strength of acceptance. Four minutes, perhaps nearly five passed before the ache in his shoulders penetrated his meditation. He let his body relax. His head bowed, his forehead rested against the wall. He held himself still, listening for final instructions from the carved figure writhing in its private eternal agony.

Then he got the chamber pot from its place at the foot of the bed. *All these years,* he thought with wry pleasure, *she still hasn't learned to cover the pot when she shits in the night.* Three coffee-brown lumps neat and reeking. An island in a yellow sea. He gazed into the porcelain bowl as if reading an augury. Then crossed with it to the open window, flung the sun an offering. Molten amber flashed a moment in the sunlight, *Beautiful, even that!* then splashed in the yard below. A sparrow fled with a squeak. "It's still piss," he said firmly, turning away from the window, but his eyes were smarting from the brilliance.

And last night it had been only candlelight, but as it had glowed on her white skin when she pulled her shift over her head, his heart had pumped his organ thick in seconds, till he had to turn away from her to concentrate on the thorny crown pressing his savior's brow. Agony had melted the savior's face, drawn down the eyecorners, gaped the jaw. Her shadow pouring along the wall eclipsed the face before its lips could repeat their seductive promises. She had stepped between the wall and the candle as she buttoned her nightgown. Her face was still turned away from him, just as it had been during her moment of nakedness. When it accidentally came under his scrutiny, the downcast eyes effectively insulated her from his yearning. Even when they heard the gentle tapping at the door, she would not have met his eyes if he had given any inclination he might answer it. His immobility succeeded in drawing from her the briefest glance of querying vexation, which he met with a stare that said, *That was your cue, not mine.* She opened the door only a few inches.

On the other side of it Schlumberger's murmur was just loud enough—intentionally, Rouault was certain—for him to hear a request for a candle. Schlumberger had barked his shin groping in the dark. So he said.

"You'll find them in the top drawer of the bureau," Louise

replied, "on the left side towards the back." Was there, Rouault had wondered, a whisper in the pause that followed before the hunchback's footsteps creaked away down the hall? Or had a look been sufficient for whatever promise or agreement they needed?

Apparently Schlumberger at least had found the communication unsatisfactory. When the second knock came Louise was already in bed. Rouault thought he detected a tremolo in the voice they heard through the door. "Henri, see what he wants," Louise said, dramatizing a yawn. Rouault was determined to possess the courage of his obstinacy if nothing else. Sitting on the bed to take off his boots, he said, "It is not with me that he wishes to speak." The knock sounded again, indeterminate—half between command and plea. Rouault felt rather than heard the furious hiss as his wife whipped back the bedclothes and went for a second time to the door. He lay back on the mattress and turned onto his side so he wouldn't have to look at the door. "I can't seem to locate them," he heard Schlumberger saying. *Why does he have to whine,* Rouault thought. *Why is it always her in control?* "Perhaps you could bring a candle and show me."

"Certainly, Monsieur Schlumberger," she said in a tone of cheerful formality. "It was rude of us not to have thought of that before." Three light steps brought her back to the bed, but instead of simply taking the candle from the night stand, she was sitting on the mattress, her weight depressing it as she leaned over him, and to keep his back to her, he had to stiffen his body against the new center of gravity which was opening him toward her like a flower to the sun. He felt her breath a moment before her lips touched his neck just below the earlobe. "Henri, darling, I'm so tired," she cooed. "Won't you find a candle for Monsieur Schlumberger." The tip of her tongue made a nuzzling thrust into the whorl of his ear. She lay back, leaving him to realize she had drawn the sheet over her body, settled herself quite finally into bed, while Schlumberger was still standing in the open doorway. He rolled out of bed and fetched the candle in a small panic of outraged privacy, as if the stranger's eyes on the two of them in bed would have compromised his modesty. He was halfway down the hall before he realized that only his obstinacy had been compromised. He comforted himself with the thought that it had not been for her, but for Schlumberger he was going, to save him another intolerable moment of looking on from the doorway. If his wrath were forged in righteousness he might slaughter the hunchback, but he was incapable of calculated rudeness. And she, of course, had counted on that.

He had gone straight for Schlumberger's bureau without a word. He clapped the candle he was carrying onto the bureau top, opened the first drawer, pulled out a candle without hesitation and plugged it into the cup of the empty holder on the dresser with a quick twist to screw it down onto the prickit. Then he straightened the wick with thumb and forefinger, tilted it into the flame of his own candle and presented it to Schlumberger with a gesture of maximum eloquence. Schlumberger stopped him on the way to the door with, "I was not familiar with the room. It all seems quite obvious now, in the candlelight, that the bureau is—"

"Yes, of course."

"I had only been here for a moment, you know, when I came up to change clothes, and I never troubled to notice—"

"You will excuse me," Rouault had said. "It's been a long day and I wish to get back to bed," and catching the opportunity he added, "with my wife."

He left Schlumberger standing in the middle of the bare room. Stripped of his cutaway coat and waistcoat, with his cravat unwrapped and the high collar open, Schlumberger's shoulders narrowed up to a slender, almost serpentine neck. His frame seemed too frail to bear the huge knot of bone in the middle of his back. Rouault had thought only children showed pain so artlessly on their faces. The sight gave him no pleasure. It was too much like looking into a mirror. Rouault knew the moods of his own face well. He was a man who could not shave without examining his features for fresh scar tissue.

When he returned to his bedroom, his wife was lying with her eyes closed and her mouth open. She breathed deeply. Asleep? So soon? If she wasn't then she wanted to appear so. It came to the same thing.

He had hesitated with his hand cupped behind the candle flame. Its soft light made an amber glow on his wife's brow. He thought of the same amber tint radiating from the vulnerable undercurve of her breast as he had glimpsed it when her arms were raised to draw the shift. He blew out the candle, but not the image. He sat gingerly on the bed and managed to stretch his weight onto it so evenly the springs barely creaked, and fell asleep in the middle of his *Pater Noster*.

Morning Ablutions of Rouault

HE MUST HAVE returned the chamber pot to its place at the foot of the bed, but he couldn't recall doing it. Nor did he remember sitting on the bed and taking the candle from the night table. He must have been picking tallow drippings from the candle and the iron holder. They were strewn on his lap and on the floor between his legs. He had rolled a piece of tallow between his thumb and forefinger till it was warm enough for him to knead his thumbprint into it. He was meditating now on something that had flashed momentarily through his mind last night as he was lighting Schlumberger's candle. Finding the candle so readily where the hunchback had professed bafflement had given him the righteous anger of one who exposes a lie. It had been a good feeling, confident, assertive. Tipping the two candleheads together, he had congratulated himself that his hand was steady, not a drop of wax would be spilled on the bureau top. Then, as the dry wick flowered from the other's flame, there kindled in him, throughout his body so that he could feel it warming his belly and informing the poise of his fingertips and the solidness of his stance all at the same time, a sense of grace, of power, and for a moment, as he would try to explain it in the letter to Louise, the mob was surging behind him again, lifting him, sweeping him on its crest through the August night toward the textile mill, its brick walls reared in his memory like the battlements of a besieged castle.

These days were charged with an heroic nimbus, apparently, which he thought it important for his wife to appreciate. Nearly two and a half pages of the letter were devoted to facts that must have been more than familiar to Louise Rouault. Their relevance to the murderous project he was outlining was obscure but somehow essential. Luddites the press called them, after a Leicestershire half-wit named Ned Ludd who had chased a teasing village boy into a house, and when the boy proved slippery, he had mounted a grand annihilating rage upon a pair of frames used in stocking manufacture. And the textile craftsmen threatened by mechanical looms, who had also found their tormentors elusive, adopted the name, turned its jeer into their own potent charm, and marched with a hundred torches on a Nottingham mill.

The first surge of the battering ram had produced only a feeble knock on the oak door. It had been Rouault who started the chant which harmonized the mens' wills. His cry was not eloquent nor unique, but fierce as their resentment. "Burn the machines!" he had shouted, and the mob took it up while he marked the strophes with his torch waving like a baton; with each cry of "Burn!" the men on the ram struck home, each time more powerfully, the torchlight glistening in the sweat on their shoulders till the oaken boards began to split and yield at last with an almost human shrieking of metal on wood, as if the men had burst the hymen of some terrible virgin. And Rouault had been the first man inside, leaping over the rent timbers no longer a door with that superhuman grace which now descended upon him only in dreams. And when they had stacked their hay bales upon the giant looms, his had been the first torch to touch them into life. He remembered his ecstasy as the fire poured not just from the torch but from the arm itself that had hurled the torch, from the heart pumping blood to the arm. He saw the fire, his fire, explode and shoot crackling spurts up the pyramid of straw to envelop the machine that had robbed them of their jobs.

Eventually of course the well-drilled, stolid redcoats routed them. Rouault fled England under threat of death, crossed the Channel with the smell of smoke still clinging to his clothing like an aura of heroism, and while the heat still singed his cheeks he married a distant cousin from a branch of the family which had remained in France when his own Huguenot ancestors had escaped to England a century before.

"I married," he wrote, "and found there was nothing for my torch to burn, and I would be wiser to douse it, and survive longer." In short, arsonists had less stable occupations than weavers. He married, and the memory of that youth sprinting up the factory aisle toward the huge, cloth-webbed scaffold returned to him only at odd moments, like last night as he had lit Schlumberger's candle.

THE BRITTLE TALLOW DRIPPINGS rained onto the floor as Rouault stood up. He made the sign of the cross and went downstairs to see whether his wife had left him any cheese for breakfast. He thought he had convinced himself that loving was the best revenge.

15 | A Question of Timing

ROUAULT'S DETERMINATION to "love" Schlumberger collapsed after slightly more than two weeks—on the evening following Schlumberger's second defeat as the automaton's director. So long as Schlumberger remained pitiable, Rouault was faithful to his resolve. It was not difficult to offer *Pater Nosters* for his soul while Louise was making him suffer. She continued as she had begun that first night. She fenced herself demurely inside a white-picket politeness, met his laboriously contrived occasions for private conversation with naïve oblivion, and nuzzled Rouault like a fond and wanton wife at every public opportunity. Under this regime Schlumberger developed white knuckles and a spastic muscle in his left cheek that were almost endearing.

Neither was Rouault's spiritual equilibrium disturbed by what he overheard from the storeroom where Maelzel was training Schlumberger to operate the automaton. Every day Rouault worked in the shop area, assembling a gigantic music box called a panharmonicon which Maelzlel claimed he had invented. Every day he listened to dialogues like this: "No, before you make the Turk's move, you *must* duplicate your opponent's move on the board inside your box. Is that understood?" Silence. Audible sigh. "Is that understood?" Silence. Grunt. "Now again!" And after an interval, *"Nein, du Arschloch!"* Followed by a salad of French and German curses, garnished with a smattering of American obscenities Maelzel had acquired listening to stage drivers on the trip to Boston.

Schlumberger's docility under these barrages surprised Rouault.

His difficulties in learning the mechanics of the automaton were puzzling. Often while Maelzel was explaining an important step, he would apparently drift into lethargic daydreams. Even when he was listening, or making sounds that indicated he was listening, the simplest mechanical sequence required three or four explanations. Maelzel, who had begun his demonstration of what he considered an ingenious marvel with an enthusiasm he felt any reasonable man would share, was by the afternoon of the first day speaking in a dogged, frequently quivering snarl: "This is the pantograph. No, forget that, call it just the rod. The rod. Now to make the Turk open his hand, you twist the pan—the rod, twist it counterclo—twist it this way. Do you understand that? Do you, God damn you, understand?"

Once the lid of the box was clamped down on Schlumberger and Maelzel began playing games with the automaton, simulating performance conditions, the strange lethargy continued. After waiting an unconscionable time for the automaton to make a move, coaxing with arguments like, "You must remember your audience, Willie, you cannot take as long over a move here as you could in the Café de la Régence," Maelzel would erupt with a piercing obscenity and bang on the cabinet with fist and foot. Whereupon the automaton would immediately come alive and make a move so quickly it was impossible to avoid the suspicion it might have been made fifteen minutes sooner. Maelzel made no secret of his opinion that Schlumberger was falling asleep inside the automaton, and Schlumberger made no effort to deny it and no apology for it.

Maelzel's irritation with Schlumberger's apparent lack of aptitude was compounded by a public challenge from a highly reputed New York chess player known as Greco. Maelzel foresaw a match which could make or ruin the Turk's American reputation, but he had been forced repeatedly to postpone it with a plea of "mechanical difficulties." At the end of the first week he increased the rehearsal hours of the mechanical difficulty from eight per day to twelve, and announced a firm promise to begin public performances on the sixteenth of October. In the intervening week Schlumberger's performance continued disturbingly erratic. On the opening night the automaton functioned with the reassuring predictability of a machine for two games. Then, just as Maelzel's tight pacing began to break into his customary strut, the automaton lost the third game to a novice. The following evening it lost the first game, and Maelzel offered a half-hearted repeat performance of the "mechanical rope dancers" and closed the performance.

That night Schlumberger ceased altogether being pitiable.

As he lay alone in bed Rouault was concentrating not on the performance just ended, but on the scene that had followed the previous evening's performance. Perhaps it was his efforts to synchronize the complex mechanism of the panharmonicon that led him to conceive his problem as a question of timing. Thinking as a way of not thinking while he tried not to listen to the noises on the other side of the wall, the murmurs and harsh sibilants that were seeping through the wall like a slow-pouring syrup, he tried to wonder why Schlumberger's wild tantrum after that first performance had struck him with the sensation he might get from a poorly balanced clock, as of something jarring in the rhythm.

The moment on which Rouault was trying to focus had been postponed by the strict adherence to one of Maelzel's rules: the automaton's director must not be released from the box until well after the last patron had departed from the exhibit hall. Hardly any time at all had elapsed from the last spatter of applause, which Maelzel took beaming at stage center, till Rouault spied him at the exit door in the front of the hall, shaking hands and receiving congratulations like a minister after a fist-pounding sermon. Rouault smiled as he collected spittoons from the aisles, thinking what Maelzel must have looked like with his coattails in the air skipping from the side door around the hedgerow to the street door in time to miss not a single accolade with his starchy bow and solemn frown. The importance of any compliment Maelzel received was magnified a hundredfold, Rouault had noticed, by the air of judicious discrimination with which he savored it, the head gravely nodding, the lips pursed, sometimes almost parted as if about to contradict the speaker if he should utter the slightest hyperbole. Though Rouault had never known him to do anything but bow and nod no matter what was said.

When Maelzel said goodnight to the last customer, Rouault was turning down the wicks on the stage lights. Maelzel slammed the bar over the street doors and stalked up the aisle humming fiercely. His footsteps clopped in time with the tense vibrations of his humming. The tune escaped through the spaces in his clenched teeth. He hummed a martial air with an obsessively regular beat. Rouault knew that tune as the one Maelzel hummed when he was about to make money or an enemy.

They entered the property room together, but only accidentally so, since Maelzel had not unfixed his gaze to nod or glance at Rouault. Louise had just finished putting away the puppet rope dancers. The automaton stood in the center of the room. The Turk's lowered eyelids suggested that somewhere under the velvet turban a brain was still calculating the combination which had defeated it. Maelzel's heels drummed like pistol shots on the floor as he stalked to the automaton. He snapped back the two bolts concealed by the overhang of the box lid and lifted it off with a grunt. Schlumberger blinked up at Maelzel and made no immediate effort to rise. The twitching corners of his lips might have been awaiting permission to smile. His wary eyes danced eagerly up at Maelzel, as if they were fearing something they wanted. Rouault, waiting for the bark of Maelzel's obscenities, had an impulse to slam the lid back onto the box. Once he had watched his father pitchfork a rodent after the plowshare lifted the roof off its burrow. But Maelzel condensed the full range of his customary litany into three words. "The chess genius," he sneered, and turned on his heel.

Maelzel's words hit Schlumberger like heavy breath on a window-pane. After a surprised blink, rage fogged the eyes and made them opaque. But here was where the clock missed a tick, Rouault was thinking, because that rage, which seemed real enough, should have brought him to his feet before Maelzel had gone half the six steps to the door, yet Schlumberger was only gripping his hands on the sides of the box to pull himself up when Maelzel's hand yanked the doorknob, and Rouault realized with amazement that for the second time in two weeks Schlumberger was about to allow Maelzel to slam a door on him.

The voices on the other side of Rouault's bedroom wall fell silent. He listened to the straw ticking of a mattress crackling like dry kindling into flame. The creaking of bedropes settled into a rhythm as he forced himself to think of Schlumberger standing waist-deep in the automaton's cabinet like a livid jack-in-the-box, saying, "What does he mean by that!" at the just-slammed door.

Lying in the dark room Rouault repeated the doorslam in his mind until it drove out the sound of creaking bed ropes. He played the sequence again and again, starting with Maelzel's parting words because that was where the timing had gone wrong. Six quick steps to the door, but surely enough time for Schlumberger to leap out of that box and snatch him by the collar, wrench him back for a confrontation. "Or, if he doesn't think with his body," he wrote in his letter to Louise, "he could have used his tongue in even less time. If he'd wanted to." But while Maelzel's boot heels were rapping out their staccato, Schlumberger was languidly figuring out how to stand up in the box. And before he could quite collect a lungful of air the door slammed. This time when it slammed it jarred awake in Rouault's mind an understanding, as he told Louise, of "just how dangerous a chess player could be."

This time he heard not just the slam, but its echo. No, that's not right, he corrected himself, because this scene last night *was* the echo, and the noise that produced it was that other slamming door the night Schlumberger arrived, when Maelzel had walked out after telling him to be inside the box by eight in the morning. That night, too, Schlumberger had let him go and fumed at Louise instead. As if she were an ambassador through whom he addressed a senile and petulant monarch, venting thoughts he would not dare in the exalted presence. Except that his words hadn't been for Maelzel at all. Even at the time, he had known the anger directed at the monarch concealed a message to the ambassador herself. It had been one of the few times when she had permitted him to address her as something more than an acquaintance who was the wife of a business associate. And that incident must have been the inspiration for last night's scene. What had before occurred spontaneously had been, Rouault realized it now, deliberately arranged last night, and the only evidence of artifice was that slight break in synchronization, that six beat pause—no, seven if he counted the door slam itself following the footsteps.

Rouault turned onto his side in bed, facing away from the wall, and made himself appreciate the artistry of it. He had always supposed chess players were gifted with a superior analytic faculty. With this hunchback, though, it might just as easily be a genius for improvisation. Because there must have been only an eyeblink between Maelzel's parting jab and Schlumberger's decision to control his rage, delay it until Maelzel got out of the room. Thinking of it made Rouault tuck the blanket closer around his neck. He felt a shiver of cold-blooded admiration. Somewhere in the genuine sense of outrage Schlumberger had felt, there had been a hurricane eye so calm he found there leisure to recognize, in the space of an eyeblink, a potential parallel between the scene Maelzel was thrusting upon him and something which took place two weeks earlier. And in that same eyeblink, in the midst of his hurricane fury at Maelzel, he had calmly tacked and drawn in just enough sail to make a quite convincing—at the moment anyway— seven beat pause before he let the wind catch it and run. Why? Because, and this too he must have decided in that languid eyeblink, he could use that fury to force a channel through the placid swamp of formalities Louise had enforced to prevent him from reminding her that he had crossed an ocean for her.

Then the storm had broken, with him standing in the box bracketed by the stiff raised arms of the automaton.

Glaring at the door still vibrant with the energy of Maelzel's slam, but addressing Louise, he had said, "Does he think I will allow myself to be insulted?" The register of his voice threatened to rise into a shriek so uncontrolled that both Rouault and Louise were horrified into an immediate effort to calm him. "Let him find another chess player then! If he can!" And they were grasping his arms, helping him over the rim of the box, clucking, "No, no, you mustn't think that, it's only his manner, he means nothing by it." And Schlumberger in that almost-shriek saying, "And when he does, I'll challenge him. Play his goddam machine everywhere it goes. I'll beat it, I'll beat whoever plays in it. Then where will its precious reputation be?"

The Turk's arms, Rouault recalled, had been outstretched as if in blessing. Its eyes remained modestly downcast. The rigid lips made a line that suggested beatific tranquility. While Schlumberger ranted Rouault found himself thinking that in a church, garbed in biblical robes, the automaton would have been a source of inspiration. Perhaps virtue was only the ability to stand still no matter what happened. Louise was holding Schlumberger's forearm close to her body with both hands, as if to restrain him from following Maelzel. Schlumberger attempted feebly to break past her to the door. One of her hands released his arm and gripped his lapel.

"You must know how much we need you," she was saying.

"We?" Schlumberger choked out a laugh to underscore his irony.

"Of course," Rouault said. "We don't want to starve." His voice was louder than he had expected it to be, and more steady. "Without a first-rate chess player inside the automaton, we don't eat. Surely you must understand how my wife and I need you.'' Both Schlumberger and Louise were staring in surprise. Rouault was nearly as astonished as they were by his intrusion, but he continued. ''What about the letter my wife sent you from New York? I thought it explained our situation very well.''

Louise dropped her arms to her sides. At the same instant she and Schlumberger took a step back from each other. Schlumberger could not decide which foot to rest his weight on. Louise clasped her skirt as if to lift the hem from a puddle and released it, spreading her fingers. Then Schlumberger's eyes narrowed on Louise, and he said coldly, ''I see.'' He told Rouault, ''I'm sorry for your financial difficulty, but I've made up my mind. You can tell Maelzel to start looking for another chess player.'' Starting toward the door he addressed Louise, saying, ''I can see I never should have left Paris.''

''You'll be returning then?'' Rouault snapped. ''I'm surprised.''

Schlumberger stopped with his hand on the door handle.

''Will you earn your passage giving chess exhibitions?'' Rouault asked softly. He was ignoring his wife's eyes. ''Do you really think that's what they paid money to see tonight? Chess?''

He crossed to his wife's side and locked his fingers in hers.

''Back in Paris,'' he said, ''you could have told Maelzel to go to hell. Here you have to tame yourself. My wife was being tactful when she said we need you. That was only half the truth.''

At last Rouault had got Schlumberger's full attention. *That was something anyhow,* he thought, covering with his forearm the ear that was not buried in the pillow. *With her in the same room, I might as well have been trying to get the Turk to look at me.*

''I would rather beg,'' Schlumberger said, ''than spend another night here. You tell Maelzel that.''

He slammed the door louder than Maelzel had, as Rouault was replying, ''I don't think so. You're not proud enough to beg.''

Louise yanked free her hand and slapped Rouault hard across the cheek.

''Now look what you've done,'' she cried. ''I was handling him without any help. Why couldn't you be still?''

Rouault glanced at the immobile holiness of the Turk and said, ''I'm not a statue, Louise. Sometimes a man gets tired of being still.''

''And that business about the letter. I won't even ask how you dared to read it, but how did you think it would help to mention it?''

''I didn't—'' Rouault started, then took a breath. ''I didn't want to help. I wanted him to go away.''

''But you agreed to . . .'' she fumed. ''You promised you would . . .''

''I promised I would stay with you,'' he shrugged. ''That wasn't even a promise, really. You have to will a promise. I was just telling you a fact.''

''You're very clever, aren't you,'' she said. ''But not clever enough to learn how to play chess yourself. And not clever enough to have a slit between your legs. And who do you suppose that leaves to fix up your cleverness?''

Rouault's head jerked sideways as if he had been hit again.

''You don't have to tell me what happens next,'' he said. ''I knew I hadn't really driven him away when he left a message for Maelzel.''

As she was leaving Rouault called, ''Louise.'' She stopped impatiently in the doorway. Rouault did not want it to slam again that night. ''Louise. I thought you wanted me to read the letter. I thought that's why you left it out on the dresser. I thought you must have decided it would be easier to tell me that way.''

After a moment she said, ''Maybe I did.''

She closed the door softly.

My little rebellion, Rouault thought. *Not much like Nottingham.* He had hurled his torch in an arc that scattered shadows to the corners of the high factory ceiling, and when it had plummetted like a shooting star into the heart of the weaving machine, he had raised again the cry of ''Burn! Burn the machines!'' that filled the air with a rain of fire and a hundred chorusing voices. But the factories were still there, saved by the Redcoats' rifles, so even that hadn't been much of a revolt—not nearly so effective as Schlumberger this evening, after the automaton's second loss in as many nights, heisting himself to a standing position in the box under the hail of Maelzel's curses, and keeping on his lips that suggestion of a smile, not even needing to broaden it into a sneer while Maelzel described what he did with sheep and his mother and what he ate and sucked and slept in and with. And this time it had been Schlumberger striding nonchalantly to the door as Maelzel shrieked, ''What about Greco, then, you shitsmear, if you can't even handle these bumpkins, what will you do when we have to play Greco?'' The first faint curling of the lips was still on Schlumberger's face when he said, "Do you think I can't handle Greco or any other chess player in America—if I want to?" and left, not even caring, this time, to punctuate his exit by slamming the door.

In the silence that followed Rouault had waited for what he knew would happen, for Maelzel's eyes to fasten on Louise, and for her answering look of hatred and submission.

He was beginning to notice a scorching pain in his neck and shoulders. The muscles of his neck and shoulders were drawn into taut wires that held him motionless. He was breathing shallowly. He had not shifted his position on the bed since he rolled onto his side. His stiff legs wanted to be drawn toward his body, but he could not move them. He felt like a tin soldier that must still lie at attention after it has been knocked over. While his mind was crowding out the noises, his body had been straining to hear, and even when he could not keep from hearing, it had at first been easy to ignore the predictable bass moans he had prepared himself for, but then something began to happen that he hadn't prepared himself for, another sound, a slight tentative mewing, like a kitten buried under a heavy darkness, frightened, hardly daring to plead for release, then suffocating, clawing, urgent, and the cries grew urgent beyond any demand Rouault had imagined could be there before they broke into a gasp, a sob, a long purr that writhed like a cat between his legs and slowly diminished into silence. But long before the silence came Rouault had stopped needing to listen. There was nothing more he could have wanted to know.

He continued holding himself rigidly until his muscles began to tremble. When the trembling passed he found he could roll onto his back. He lay with his legs outstretched, his hands crossed on his breast, like a carving on a medieval coffin lid, but his stillness was no longer strained. After a long time he brought three fingers of his left hand to his lips and kissed their tips and stretched them through the darkness with unwavering instinct to touch the feet nailed in agony one over the other to the cross that hung from the wall.

Then he whispered, "Hail, Rabbi."

16 | A Summer Idyll

"BECAUSE AS SOON as my hand touched the foot of the cross," he wrote, "I knew it was a lie. And to let Him know I knew it, or maybe just to let myself know, I said, 'Hail, Rabbi.' Because I hated Him then. Even while I was submitting. For expecting me to endure something that can't be endured. Hated Him most of all because He wouldn't let me go, even then, wouldn't let me stop loving. That's when I understood why it had been with a kiss. Not from cheap irony. But because he couldn't stop loving Him either, no matter how much he hated Him. And when He asked, Will you betray the Son of Man with a kiss? Luke doesn't record any answer, but I know there's only one thing he could have said: No other way, Master. In love, no other way."

Here, in words and phrases scored and rewritten and rescored, Rouault's thought squeezed like saxifrage through the fissures of a mind clenched in the habit of secrecy. The calligraphy revealed what the words of the confession only hinted, disguised from himself as much as from Louise—that here was when he decided to murder Schlumberger. Later in the same manuscript he would make much of the fact that the plan, fully crystalized, presented itself to him during the eight o'clock Mass on the twentieth of October. But here, three days earlier, he had already taken the crucial step in his decision. It was by the will that he would be judged. Once it had yielded to hatred, in the very moment of yielding, he was damned. The act which gave his hatred form was almost superfluous. He could not be more damned than damned. And yet, his theology balanced its ruthlessness with a mercy that was unbearably seductive: if a thought could damn him, the movement of the soul by which he repented it could also be accomplished in a moment. The only moment that counted was the last one. The final moment decided the meaning of a lifetime. Until he was dead, nothing was irrevocable. So he was damned—for the moment—and he prolonged his moment, trembling, stretching out his hands like a man in total darkness to explore the dimensions of his new freedom.

But for the moment no act suggested itself.

Getting out of bed, dressing in the dark room, walking silently down the hall and down the stairs and through the shop area and out onto Congress Street—these were not acts. They were only a way of recognizing that he could no longer lie still. He made no mention in the letter of how he passed the balance of the night: walking the streets of Boston, most probably, while stars rose and wheeled through their arcs and set obedient to plan, and he alone careened lawless through the sky.

What finally drove him back to Julian Hall was the presence of other people. At sunrise they appeared on the streets, the lamplighter snuffing wicks, the vendors selling milk for breakfasts. The very triviality of their errands further isolated him in his aweful specialness. Only those living in grace could so prodigally squander their time. The damned, who purchased each moment with eternity, had to be careful to make its value worth the price. The slightest glance from a stranger seemed to scrape his flesh. He was climbing the hall steps, returning to his room with the desperate weariness of an animal harried to ground after a long chase, when he heard footsteps in the hall above him.

"When you didn't answer his knock directly," he wrote, "I thought at first it was because the hunchback was still with you. That was stupid, of course, because he wouldn't be knocking unless he knew you were alone. And when he had to keep on knocking, I knew you were having the dream again."

It was always the same dream, and she had detailed it to Rouault a dozen times. She heard the knocking but couldn't wake up, because she was pinned under a crafty weight that recentered itself to counter each of her squirms. An unbreakable grip locked her hands wrist to wrist above her head. Another more playful grip squeezed her breast to a swell and teased the nipple. Knees between her knees kept them spread, while a bellows breath in her ear hissed in time to the searing jabs. Each jab rooted a new secret of agony from her core, unexplored until now except by her own intimate and sympathetic finger. When she tried to scream another mouth swallowed her voice.

With her ribs flattened under the bucking weight, the mouth glued over hers like a leech, she knew she would smother in another few moments, and when the moments passed with her hysteria still mounting she knew even more surely that the weight would keep on pressing forever, for all the time she had, for all the air she had left in her lungs. Yet another part of her mind, the part that heard the knocking through the dream and struggled feebly toward it, had been here many times before and knew that after a final grunt the weight would roll off and she would be in her own bed, washed and wrapped in soft linen, sobbing regularly but comfortably while her mother crooned, *Hush my baby, your daddy's coming right up,* and then his quick steps on the stair and the door opening and him standing there as she raised her arms to him and gave a wail she had been saving that froze in her throat when she saw the ruthless calm of his eyes. *I told you to stay by the house,* he said, and at last she filled her lungs and loosed a shriek that tore the fabric of her dream with a convulsive mew. Her eyes opened just as another knock shook the door.

"Just a minute," she said thickly, the powerlessness of the dream still weighting her tongue. She had tossed back the sheet and risen onto one elbow when the door opened. Maelzel stepped inside, freshly combed with his sidewhiskers curled to points like the feelers of an old and crafty catfish just lumbered up from a mudbottom flat, crisply collared and cuffed and wearing a brocade vest and new-laundered trousers carefully rolled to erase the crease characteristic of cheap store-bought goods that had lain on the shelf.

"Ah, you're looking tousled enough," he said.

"Get out of here," she said, all trace of sleep gone from her voice. She did not draw the sheet back across her body, or even pull the cotton nightgown over her exposed thigh. "What gives you the right to—"

He closed the door behind him.

"Feisty in the morning, aren't you," he said. "Have a hard night?"

"I have not asked you to come in here."

"I'd have waked you more gently," he said with a shrug that

might have been apologetic and a leer that cancelled the apology, "if I'd known the door was unlocked. All that banging around, no wonder you're in a foul humor."

He pulled a chair away from the wall and heisted one foot onto the window ledge with a grunt. He took a long draw on his cigar, rolling it between his pursed lips and breathing smoke that roiled in heaving dragons that the window breeze caught by their tails and taffystretched and sucked away.

"I'd like to dress in private."

Maelzel pursed his lips and gave a sympathetic *moue,* but did not stand.

"At least put out that goddam cigar," she said. "You're smothering me."

Maelzel estimated the remaining potential of the cigar, judged it sufficiently exhausted and sailed it past his foot out the window. He confronted her with an expression that suggested he had made every reasonable concession.

"Bad dreams?" he asked.

For a moment her anger was clouded by another feeling, and she lay back on the pillow with a sigh.

"Most people dream what could never happen," she said. "Why do I only dream what's real?"

Maelzel stood abruptly and said, "Listen, Delila—" Then, containing his impatience, he sat on the edge of the bed and took her foot in his hand. With her foot resting in his lap he slid his palm along the instep, using the same firm stroke with which he would have soothed the neck of a skittish horse.

"Listen, Delila," he began more softly, but with the impatience not completely smoothed from his voice, "I'll tell you what's real. What's real is that we've got a formal challenge from Greco, you hear me? What's real is that I have to answer him today. So I need to know whether our machine is in working order, or do I tell them we're still having mechanical difficulties. I need to know whether you cut our Samson's hair last night."

"Christ," she laughed; a sharp monosyllable like the bark of a fox. "I used to think you only talked that way in front of an audience."

"All right then," he said. His hand was no longer stroking her foot. His grip on it had a deliberation and containment that had become menacing. "I need to know whether Schlumberger is well and truly fucked, and is he going to do what we tell him."

She jerked her foot from his grasp and swung her legs off the bed. Her feet padded quickly across the floor as she crossed to the dresser. Dust motes that had been floating aimlessly in the bar of sunlight from the window whirlpooled in her wake, then spun from orbit back into their ceaseless meander.

"What would you say if I told you I enjoyed it?" she asked.

"I would say, Is he well and truly fucked, and will he do what we tell him."

She looked at her image in an oval mirror on the dresser, curling a strand of hair around her forefinger and pulling it behind her ear. The mirror had been Rouault's gift on their first wedding anniversary, chosen with a fine instinct for her need to satisfy not vanity but what he sensed obscurely as a desire to know herself. She noticed that Rouault's shaving brush was damp, but the basin before the mirror was clean, still glistening with a few drops of water. The pitcher beside the basin was full of fresh water and the towel he had left for her was not damp.

"Where is Rouault?" she asked.

"I think he's gone to Mass. He passed me in the hall looking very pious. You don't want to tell me about it, do you?"

"Don't talk about him like that."

"Nothing I say will please you today, is that it," he answered. He was no longer bothering to disguise the fury in his voice. "How shall I talk for you? Shall I say, When I passed your husband on the stairs he said he was on his way to fill his nostrils with incense because he couldn't stand the stink of Schlumberger's semen in your cunt? Is that what you want to hear?"

Her hand darted to the pitcher as if she meant to hurl it at him. Once her fingers closed around the handle, the pitcher itself seemed to resist her intention. Not calmly but with deliberation she raised the pitcher, poured from it into the basin with a formality and concentration she might have acquired from Rouault, who ritualized every act, pouring from a pitcher as if it were important to fill the basin not overfull or scantly but just so. She dipped her hands in the water and raised them to her eyes. She kept her fingers pressed over her eyes a few moments, then withdrew them, blinking water from her eyes, and regarded her face. She examined her face with the trancelike detachment of a woman telling the time by her body. She raised her eyebrows to stretch the skin at the corners of her eyes. Maelzel's jaw and his thin lips appeared at the mirror's upper curve.

"You don't want to tell me," he said. "Look at me."

She brushed a drop of water from the end of her nose and picked up the soap.

"You won't look in my eyes," he said. "You don't want to talk. But I know how to make you, don't I?"

A shudder stiffened her back. He placed one hand on her shoulder. Held loosely in his fist was a tangle of leather thongs that dangled over her right breast.

"No," she said. "No, I told you once was all I could take. I mean it, *no.*"

As she lunged for the door, the thongs whipped in the air and he hooked an arm around her waist that jerked her feet off the floor. She grunted, breathless, and began to rasp for air. He shot the bolt on the door easily, with her still gasping, inert as a sack of potatoes in his arm, but she was fighting him again as he dragged her to the bed. He dumped her on the bed face down. Holding her down with a knee on her back, he jerked a thong free from the tangle and wrapped it around one of her wrists. He chased the other wrist and caught it.

He bound the two wrists together, then looped the free end of the thong between them while she was saying, "I don't want this, truly I don't, Johann, not now, I don't want this." He propped her against the headboard and raised her arms till he could loop the thong around one of the posts, hanging her by the wrists. For a moment they looked at one another, panting. Her elbows hung forward, cowling her face. "The pillow," she gasped. Her back was only half supported by the headboard. He stuffed a pillow between her back and the headboard. The vertical line between her brows faded as the pain eased, and with it her will unclenched like a fist, opening her to another influence that emanated from the man who was muttering, almost crooning to himself as he spread her unresisting legs and lashed each of her ankles to the posts on the footboard. When the quick whistling gasps of her struggle began to subside they were overtaken by a deeper, more rhythmic and no less urgent breathing that made her chest rise and fall in counterpoint to the regular flaring of Maelzel's nostrils as he sucked and pumped, sometimes almost snorted, humming deep in his throat. She arched her body off the mattress to help him as he hitched her nightgown up her thighs to expose her pubis. He sat on the edge of the bed. She felt his hand clamp with vicious potential on her inner thigh but that was happening far away to somebody else.

"Now tell me about Schlumberger," he said

The quick shake of her head signaled not refusal but irritation.

"Don't you want something else first?"

Maelzel frowned as if he were puzzling out the solution to a riddle. Then he roughly, quickly manipulated the buttons on the breast of her nightgown, opening a V that forked from the cleft between her breasts.

"That's not enough" she whispered.

He hesitated, scowled impatiently.

"Tear it, then," she whispered. She was like an actress, cueing an understudy in a role she had played with another leading man.

He hooked his fingers inside the cotton gown and ripped it to the waist. Her breasts gave a frantic twitch like a pair of sunblind animals flinching in the sudden light. Tears brightened her eyes.

"Oh please, no," she said. "He didn't do anything to me."

"Now tell me what happened."

"What am I. What am I comes first."

"That's easy," he said, relaxing. He was smiling, for the first time. He made a wry mouth at her hanging breasts. He weighed one of them in his palm like a fruit of dubious freshness.

"Slut," he said, smiling into her eyes. His eyes brought her into their sights like a disinterested marksman aiming at an unmoving target, while his voice began squeezing off shots with flat, precise regularity. Occasionally, he would interrupt a string of monosyllables, *bitch, whore, cunt,* to strive for some more imaginative insult. "Fuck-machine," he said once with speculative calm. "Put a penny in its palm and it spreads its legs. I could make one like you in the shop. Simple job. Customers come for miles to see it work. No trouble with break-downs either. Just stick it in a corner. Little oil between the legs, keep it from squeaking." But Louise Rouault accepted everything he said with no special accord for his stylistic frills, her head hanging penitently between her arms, nodding slow agreement at every word, tears squeez-ing from her closed eyelids, her lips writhing against her teeth. She never noticed that as Maelzel continued his voice broke occasionally as if some agony of his own were trying to wedge through his detachment. "Now," he said. "Tell me about it."

She began lazily, her eyes slitted, as if recalling for a lover a curious dream from which she had not fully awakened: "I was calling, all the while my mother and sisters were washing me I kept calling for—"

"Not that one," he broke in. "I know that one by heart. I want last night."

Her eyes came fully open, unglazed, fixing him with imperious clarity.

"I didn't want this, I told you," she hissed. "But now I'm in it, and I want it *all*."

"Fucking sow," he said. "Have it all then," jamming his finger into her vagina.

She tricked a semblance of life into his blunt, hard, predictable thrusts by churning them between her hips, and in a few moments her eyelids fluttered, beating like the braking wings of a bird as she settled to roost in her dream, saying, "—calling for him. And when they found him . . ."

She heard his rapid footfalls on the stairs, thinking of his arms, the dark hair growing heavy down to the first knuckles of his hand like a fingerless glove, the weight of them circling her when she sat on his lap by the fire, the serpent flex of muscle as he lifted her or made his forearm a chinning bar. They had reached up to her where she stood in the crotch of the apple tree laughing and terrified at him coaxing, "Jump," he laughing too at her hesitation, and even in the moment of irreversible letting go and the giddy rush in her ears she knew already the arms were catching her.

"One look," she was saying, "standing in the bedroom door, and he gave me one look. And I knew all that washing. Momma washing me, my sisters wringing the towels. All that washing. It didn't make any difference. Not to him . . ."

And when she stretched out her arms for his arms, she had seen how his eyes went to her shift tightening under her breasts, and he said, "Cover yourself."

" 'Cover yourself,' you said."

She was whispering, telling it like a long penance at the altar rail after Saturday confession, where the buoyant flood of the absolution

could drown the shame of yielding secrets to the priest, yielding them as
she did now, as she felt herself beginning to yield an ultimate privacy to
the insistently poking finger, and resisted it, saying, " 'Why weren't
you in the house,' you said. 'You belonged in the house, your sisters
were in the house—' "

And she broke off, listening to another voice, as if he had hauled
himself hand over hand up through the years into her present by the
same chain that anchored her in their past. After only a few moments
she began shaking her head vigorously, and burst out: "But I was a
child! What did I know about the soldiers!"

*Because the night before he had said, "I saw campfires in the
woods on the way in." Which meant troops passing through again, and
they had learned it made no difference whose they were, their own when
they weren't marching in files under the bright tricolor were as bad as
Germans or Redcoats. "So tomorrow you stay close to home." But in
her life there had always been armies. Cavalry and infantry, they
pumped through the main street of their village like a slashed artery
spurting blood. Once when she was nine the emperor himself had
passed on a dancing white stallion, with his eagles soaring above him,
looking much more fresh in the noon sun than the lines of horsemen
clopping in his trail, and by some instinct for a kindred mind, she later
thought, he had singled her out from the waving throng and raised a
gloved forefinger to his brow and tipped it toward her, possessing her
so completely in the single glance they exchanged before he jogged past
that until the day she began letting Rouault do all the praying for both of
them she had only to close her eyes as she closed her mouth around the
communion Host to know the color of God's eyes.*

*And since there had always been soldiers, the campfires she saw
from her bedroom window that night, winking in the woods at the edge
of the pasture, were unimportant, and the next day cottonwood
puffballs filled the air like summer snow, and when she was sent out to
stake the cow the trees were swaying and the puffballs floating in the
blue sky, and she never even glanced back toward the house. Lying in
the long grass under the oak tree at the edge of the woods, she forgot
about soldiers. She had seen none, she told herself, they had broken
camp at dawn and were miles away. She concentrated on hearing above
the noise of rustling leaves the gurgle of the stream in the gully dipping
away from her, but she must only have imagined actually hearing it*

A Summer Idyll

because she never heard the feet that must have come sloshing through the water.

The mound of earth that puckered round the oakroots pillowed her head. The trunk rose above her until it wedged in the tossing foliage. Down through the leaves drifted the puffballs, churned by the madly rocking branches as she slipped her hand inside the waist of her skirt, thinking Father Pierre would say it was wrong when she confessed on Saturday, but on this day nothing could not be forgiven. When her eyes focused again she realized she was no longer alone.

Or still alone, since she had lapsed from speech, discarding the illusion of addressing Maelzel as she strained deeper toward the blend of memory and fantasy she hoped would release her. But in another moment she gasped and hissed, "Stop, oh God, it hurts, God."

Maelzel had been regarding with curiosity the thickening of a blue vein that shot her forehead from hairline to nose. He removed his hand, and reached instinctively for a handkerchief. As chess was Schlumberger's passion, Maelzel's was tinkering with machinery, but he was fastidious about engine grease.

Louise slumped against the headboard, holding her sobs against a lip whitened by the clamp of her teeth.

"There now," Maelzel crooned. "I told you it would be fun. Pushed you into a sweet little frenzy that time, didn't we?"

"Fun," she whimpered. "Don't you know what pain looks like?"

Maelzel shrugged. "You went dry," he said. "I could feel you dry up. Next time—"

"Never!" She shot at him. "Not even for Henri."

"What's happened to the concerned wife? It would kill him to lose another job, wouldn't it? Isn't that what we decided?"

"He'll have to take care of himself."

"Just as I thought: you did it for you. Why don't you admit it?"

She was beyond weeping, even beyond rage, as she gazed up at him through tangled strands of hair and said, "I was wrong. Whatever I hoped, whatever I thought I could learn by pretending to be who you think I am—I was wrong. Now untie me."

"Not yet," he said. "Tell me about Schlumberger."

"Untie my wrists."

"About Schlumberger," he insisted, folding and pocketing his handkerchief.

"Pig," she said, then, "Shy, but I rubbed him up. Rode him like a horse. Almost bucked me off at the last. But I broke him."

"You talk like a man," he chuckled.

"I wonder how well you'd like *really* being a woman. Being nailed to the ground. Can't move or breathe. Maybe you would. But I hated it."

Maelzel glanced at her bound wrists.

"Sure you did," he said.

"Don't just look at them, damn it, untie me."

"So he's well fucked. But will he play chess?"

"You can set up your match with Greco."

He nodded briskly as he rose, deftly flicked the thong from the bedpost and left her to finish the job. On the hall steps he confronted Rouault, who looked unable to decide whether he was going upstairs or down. "Come with me, Rouault," he said. "I want to show you how to get at the joint that makes the Turk's arm jerk on the return. It needs oiling." And, as Rouault hesitated, stammered, Maelzel turned him firmly with a hand on his bicep.

"Come on," he urged. "She doesn't need you."

17 | The Burning Bush

ROUAULT SPENT most of that day in the workshop valeting the machines. In addition to lubricating the Turk, he resynchronized the string section of the panharmonicon orchestra and trudged through a dozen other minor tasks Maelzel had assigned. He wondered momentarily if Maelzel suspected that he had overheard his conversation with Louise and designed the list of chores to occupy his mind. Such compassion would be unusual for Maelzel. Perhaps it was prudence that motivated him. In any case, it didn't succeed: Rouault's hands were trained to perform automatically. They didn't need a mind guiding their actions any more than the panharmonicon orchestra needed a live conductor. That left his mind free to sleep if it could, or pace off the walls of its prison. He tried to make it sleep, but before long it was trying to escape through his eye sockets.

The pain behind his eyeballs apparently forced him to stop work shortly before noon. He did not join Louise and Schlumberger for lunch; they assumed he had chosen to cut himself a few slices of cheese and bread and eat alone in the workshop, as he often did. After washing the dishes Louise went to her room, where she found Rouault lying in bed with a damp cloth over his eyes. He had just come upstairs for a minute, he explained, to search for his spectacles. She told him he knew he got headaches when he did close work without his spectacles, and helped him rummage in his linen drawer and under pillows for a few minutes. In the afternoon he went back to work without them.

Early that evening the throbbing pain drove him to the Catholic church on Congress Street, where he knelt in the dark box and confessed his sins. The examination of conscience in his Missal had given him little help in describing them. When he whispered about bearing hatred against a fellow man and questioning God's mercy, he felt as if he were talking about the doings of a stranger. The lonely celibate on the other side of the grill asked, "How many times?" and sighed his absolution in a Latin from which time had eroded more than a few syllables.

While he recited his penance at the altar rail, Rouault's eyes were drawn to the sanctuary lamp flickering inside its red glass bowl. Though the light was a single candle, it irritated his eyes. He closed them, but the afterimage did not fade. The light seemed to loom, he wrote, until it enveloped him in a white brilliance that shimmered with the throbbing of the pain behind his eyes. The pain and the brilliance grew more intense over a time which may have been fifteen seconds or as many minutes, and at last "exploded with an unbearable white flash in which I could hear a sound like cymbals vibrating." Then a diffuse circle of red light appeared amid the white like the sun through a fog. He took it at first for the red flame of the sanctuary lamp. Then he realized it was "not light at all but blood," and for perhaps the length of a minute he saw with intense clarity the bodies spurting blood, spinning and tumbling in a dance so beautiful it brought him, apparently, to something like an aesthetic ecstasy. His hold on the vision receded gradually, and with it went the pain behind his eyes. He returned to the workshop in time to prepare for the evening's performance, and found his spectacles lying on the automaton's cabinet, cupped and covered by its left hand, as if the Turk had performed a sleight of hand with them.

Rouault had always dealt with his rage as if it were a temptation, something that horrified the brain and tingled the loins. Knowing it was evil gave him the strength to wrestle it down. It wasn't always easy. It took a three-day fast to scour from his mind the image of silk-hugged flesh that once had beckoned from a whorehouse doorway. And *this* image, this writhing flesh and spurting blood, rose up solid as a pagan statue whenever his mind idled. It did not return with the same visionary clarity, but it was at least as vivid as his memories of early childhood. Frequently Rouault's temptations had come to him in the form of mental pictures, but always before they had crumbled to dust in the vibrations set up by his whispered prayers. For the next two days he prayed for the Virgin to cast her veil over the disturbing images, wash his mind from

The Burning Bush

horizon to horizon in her sacred blue. Smothered in *Aves* no image could retain its power to corrupt.

The day he bought the pistols he had attended Mass. Whenever the bloodthoughts quickened his pulse and breathing, he forced himself to contemplate the redemptive blood Christ shed for his sins, the blood of salvation. *"Hic est enim Calix Sanguinis mei,"* the priest was saying,—This is the Chalice of My Blood—raising as he spoke the wineblood-bearing chalice to the brooding crucifix above the altar. And even as Rouault whispered with him the sacred words, the new thought stopped him: *What if it's the only way to save her?* He sucked in his breath, sucked the words of consecration back from his mouth. The blue veil of calm that had been settling over his mind was snatched away like a silk handkerchief. Now roiling clouds covered the sky, each struggling into the image of his desire. He fought to give them flesh. He and the priest completed their transubstantiations together. *But it would damn you,* he thought, knowing even as he conjured the words the irrefutable response: *Wouldn't you accept even that if it is the only way to save her?* That made it real. When the others filed up to the communion rail to receive the sacrament, he remained kneeling in his pew, trembling with the joy of his damnation.

It was so real he could smell the mold on the stair landing. The window in the hall above him diffused a pale early morning light onto the ceiling, but it couldn't reach him deep in the stairwell. He was a shark fathoms deep in darkness, circling patiently, eyeing the surface for swimmers. When the door opened the east light from her bedroom haloed Maelzel before it closed again. He lumbered toward the stairs, groped for the rail, humming through his teeth as he always did till he heard the hammer cocking, toneless as a tongue snapping the floor of his mouth. Then he would stop, one foot already taking his weight on the first step, and maybe there would be just enough light to see that thin-lipped smile dissolve into confusion, then as Rouault brought his arm up steady, what? What would he like to see beyond the cocked hammer—disbelief? Panic? No. Annoyance. Ah, yes. Then, as the barrel spurted flame, Maelzel's face, drenched with pure horror, then blackness, the blood-spurting weight pitched into his arms, shrugged off to thump down the stairs, the pistol clattering after it as he yanked its mate from his belt, rushing three at a time the remaining steps to greet Schlumberger in the open door, yes, they would both have been with her together, that's how it would be, and Schlumberger naked, frantic as a monkey scampering the other way down the hall while he calmly brought the second pistol level, cocked and placed the shot just below and to the left of the hump that rode the monkey's shoulders.

Turning on his heel he found himself jolted nearly off his feet by a stranger who had been pacing a few steps behind him in the street. For a moment their arms tangled in something resembling an embrace. Then, cringing at the thought of blood, Rouault pushed violently. He didn't even hear the man's curse. He was striding back in the direction he had come, back to the shopwindow he had passed three times already that morning. The case that occupied a central position in the window display was lined in scarlet. Between its open jaws the velvet was soft as the inside of a mouth. Bedded snugly on the tongue the two pistols offered themselves one under the other, barrel to butt. The irrefutable barrel of one asserted an intention that was upside down parodied and precisely cancelled by the opposite-pointing barrel of its twin. She would be clutching the bedcovers to her throat as he entered, but she would know immediately what he meant when he said, "It was the only way I could save you." The sheet would fall away from her body as her arms opened.

The bell above the shop door shrilled like a vulture claiming its feast. The gunsmith, selecting a hunting rifle from a rack, stroked a hand along its barrel as he handed it across the counter to a customer.

"This is a sure kill," he crooned. The customer accepted it into his grasp as Rouault had seen a day-old infant passed from one pair of maternal arms to another, with the same instinct of care, the same sense of being in the service of a sacred mystery.

Because she will know that it would have been no good telling her. Moses coming down from the mountain didn't use sweet words. No, you smash the golden calf. Smash them both.

"What can I interest you in, mister?"

The gunsmith finger-combed a strand of hair onto his sweat-shiny dome. From the damp stain in his shirt's armpit Rouault whiffed a perfume like a mixture of rubbed copper and machine oil.

"Those pistols," Rouault said, "in the window."

The gunsmith's smile included Rouault in a common secret, as if he had discovered they shared the same vice. He nodded wisely and started for the display case.

The Burning Bush

"How much are they?" Rouault called after him.

He carried them home thinking of flames. Torchlight lunging up the mill walls. He carried them under his arm wrapped in brown stiff paper that crackled like kindling. Kneeling to place the package in a back corner of his dresser's bottom drawer, he remembered his torch soaring toward the ceiling, diving like a hawk of flame into the huge wooden loom, nesting there, almost winking out, puffing awake in the lace stretched between beams like the branches of some hideous angular tree, then snapping ravenously at the branches themselves, while men with sledges set to work on the boiler plates with a clangor of Easter church bells, and more torches filled the air.

He remembered the look of raptorial hunger that rounded her eyes when he used to tell about it, telling her father, his cousin, how in Nottingham the weavers and spinners refused to sell themselves to the mills where the machines had been built to rob men of work, and when the mill owners hired paupers from the workhouse to tend the machines, how the craftsmen came at night with torches. Sitting over the dinner table with his cousin and his husky sons, he told of the Luddite riots, and the Redcoats sent by Lord Liverpool to quell them, and the search that went out for Rouault in particular while the ink was still damp on his broadside against machines, signed not "General Ludd" as the others were but with his own name. He boasted the story to remind them it was not a common beggar eating their bread, but an exile. Still planning at that time to return to England, he boasted the way you tell of something you think is yet a part of you.

He remembered how he felt when he became aware that she always contrived to be there, listening. Clearing dishes from the table or fetching cheese and more wine, she lingered and listened, while he pounded his fist as he described the poor quality weaves done by machine, and sometimes, sidling into a corner behind her father so he couldn't see her and tell her to leave, she looked at him as she listened. Fourteen years old and seven months pregnant by a rapist, but not even that thick waist and lumbrous walk could make him think of anything but a hawk fierce with starvation when she fixed her eyes on him. A caged hawk, pleading with those round mad eyes not simply for a morsel of attention, he realized with awe, but for deliverance.

Now in his room at Julian Hall brooding over the crackle and dance and blossom of flames, he traced the progress of the past dozen years.

He had extended his wrist to receive the raptor's searing grip, dousing one torch for another. Then the revolutionary begat the lover, who begat the husband who begat the cuckold. It had been a long time since she had looked at him with anything but a dull languor that did not even flare into contempt.

The husband in him had so thoroughly tamed the revolutionary that he hadn't realized he missed that look until a night about a year and a half ago, shortly after he went to work as Maelzel's assistant. During a tour of Austrian commerce centers the panharmonicon had broken down in the middle of a performance. Along with the automaton chess player the panharmonicon was a prime attraction in Maelzel's mechanical theatre. It operated on the principle of the player piano to simulate the sounds of a forty-piece orchestra. It was scored to produce something that might be recognized as the "Wellington's Victory" section from Beethoven's Battle Symphony commemorating the defeat of Napoleon. It was Maelzel's pride, and a constant source of vexation to him that the chauvinism of the French deprived him of the opportunity to display his masterwork in his Paris exhibit hall. He never failed to introduce it with the information that Beethoven himself, acting on an inspiration provided by Maelzel himself, had written the march expressly for the panharmonicon. He didn't elaborate on the lawsuit Beethoven had brought against him over ownership of the music. That night just as the French horns were about to be overwhelmed by "God Save the King" signifying the British triumph over the French, the panharmonicon had ground to a halt with a cacophony like a drunkard stumbling around in a closet full of bagpipes. After the performance Maelzel had furiously blamed the failure on Rouault's incompetence. All the spools needed to be resynchronized. The weights that made them turn needed to be rebalanced. The broken gears had to be replaced. Maelzel stripped off his coat and attacked the machine. At three o'clock that morning he growled from the machine's innards, "Get that wife of yours down here and have her make strong coffee."

For the rest of the night Louise was with them, passing Maelzel tools and coffee through a crevice in the panharmonicon machinery as if he were a trapped miner. She cooed with mock horror at his obscenities, which made Maelzel laugh while he was still cursing. When he needed to adjust a gear in a high corner of the machine, she held the lantern tirelessly, and Rouault saw by its light that she was watching him work in a way he recognized with envy. "The wrench, no, the big one, damn you," Maelzel would rasp, and she would hand him the wrench he wanted with that round hawk-mad stare, predatory and yearning and worshipful. Rouault saw Maelzel reading her look.

The machine was fixed in time for the next performance. Shortly after that Maelzel began taking Louise to his room for chess lessons while Rouault oiled the machinery in the automaton chess player and bugle player and the panharmonicon. They were employing a fairly good chess player at the time, but Maelzel claimed it was always wise to have someone in reserve in case of illness.

Until recently the affectionate rituals Rouault and Louise had developed in their first year together had lubricated the squeaky joints of their married life as courtesy lubricates social life. The undercurrent of boredom in the ritual kiss, the ritual endearments, the ritual intercourse he thought of as a new phase of their love. After the passionate splash, the mighty river's rolling calm. So long as her boredom remained placid his did.

Her dissatisfaction with the jobs he took to support them stirred occasional white water on the placid river. Every night she would tell him that the work he did was an insult to his abilities. At first he would argue against this, but soon he began treating his employers as if they were insulting him. He changed jobs frequently. First he gave up weaving because a man who had organized the torching of a textile mill could not be expected to fuss over a snippy customer's specifications in a weave pattern. For a while after that he was a journeyman printer, which was as near as he could get to the kind of pamphleteering that had made him famous and hunted in Nottingham; his poor command of French idiom had doomed his fantasy of a career in journalism. Then he was a cab driver, an interim job that he kept five years. Then a lamp lighter in Montmartre. When he got back from his rounds he would try to persuade Louise to let him use their savings to buy a loom. Weaving was after all a skilled trade. He had learned patience. Louise begged him to try once more to better himself, and he became apprentice mechanic to Maelzel. When you have given up everything for a woman she acquires the value of all you have forsaken, which makes her too precious to contradict.

Also Rouault had learned that Louise interpreted confrontations with shouting and tears as weakness. Shortly after the chess lessons in Schlumberger's room began, he had risked one such confrontation. It resolved nothing. He had not accused Louise of infidelity. Judging by Maelzel's occasional habit of dining out and spending late evenings with affected young men, he was not certain there was any infidelity. If there wasn't, the charge would have enraged Louise more than he could tolerate. Instead he accused her of not trusting him with full responsibility as the family breadwinner. She suggested he make Maelzel teach *him* chess, in that case, and fell silent. Rouault carried too much bulk to be even passably comfortable in the automaton box and he was not adept at chess. Since she would not end her silence and he could not endure it, he began talking to God.

God was also silent, but He listened well. Occasionally one of Rouault's prayers coincided with an event that might embody a cryptic consolation or directive. Louise returned from her first chess lesson with Schlumberger humming contentedly, which she never did when she was content. She flicked the knot under her chin and deposited her bonnet in a hatbox with a near perfect imitation of the way she customarily disposed of it. When he asked, "How did it go?" her shrug signified an obligation dutifully met and already forgotten. Then, because it would not have been customary for her to continue avoiding his direct gaze, she turned on him a face smoothed bland as a death mask. Behind the malleable flesh the raptor eyes danced undisguisably. With something like simultaneity Rouault experienced: jealousy of the chess player; the sweet knowledge that the look not exclusively for himself was also not exclusively for Maelzel; and disappointment in Louise. Her infidelity (if such it was, considering his reservation about Maelzel's sexuality) had left him tragically abandoned; her promiscuous infidelity rendered him absurd.

She rummaged the closet shelf for the box containing her knitting and settled in the chair by the window. The sweater, planned for his birthday seven months ago, was half finished. She had scarcely touched it in seven months. Rouault decided not to say, "Only four months till Christmas," and focused on his newspaper. The needles clicked not half an hour. She stuffed the knitting back in the box and the box back on the shelf. She swooped toward the window as if to plunge through it.

One hand ripped and nibbled at her nails. The insane eyes sought a perch. Finaly she clamped her hands over the back of a rocking chair and allowed him to overhear her say, "He's almost funny."

"Who? The chess player?" Rouault asked softly. He didn't wish to wake her. He wanted to find out all he could before she returned to herself.

"He would be the funniest man alive if he weren't so . . ."

"If he weren't . . ."

"So ruthless."

The delight of her shiver made Rouault wish she were more practiced at deception. She told how during the lesson Schlumberger's hand locked around her wrist, and he'd said, "Move it." She hadn't realized she'd even touched the piece, she explained; she was pondering her next move.

"And when he said, 'You touch it, you move it,' he was trembling. I almost laughed. I was about to say, 'This is only a lesson.' And I saw him trembling."

She sat on the bed and threw herself back in a sinuous stretch and said, "I always thought chess was a game."

As he watched her, Rouault began for the first time to experience her eyes as something that happened not to him but to her. He had not realized how his shoulders must have ached under the weight of his hatred for her until this new compassion buoyed him dizzily toward God. That night God spoke to him from a burning bush, and thereafter he dreamed often of fires.

Now, with the pistols waiting snugly in a corner of the drawer, he thought of the orange flame that would explode the darkness of the stairwell. It had the righteous logic of Moses hurling the golden calf into the fire: the god I can destroy did not deserve your worship. *Damning my soul to save hers,* he thought, breathlessly joyful at the identity between God's will and his own. With the pistol smoking in his hand he will bellow from the doorway Moses' words, *Who is on the Lord's side? Let him come unto me.* As she opens her arms to him her awareness that she is seeing him for the first time will make her lidless eyes naked with love.

Perhaps if he had wholly trusted this vision, no further preparation would have seemed necessary, but in the days that followed the purchase of the pistols he would work many hours on the letter which he intended Louise to read after his arrest and study during his trial and cherish after his execution like the knucklebone of a sainted martyr. He toiled over phrases with the passion of a legalistic Evangelist schematizing the insights of revelation.

18 | The Man Who Wasn't There

ANY EXPLANATION of an historical puzzle that accounts for all the known facts and provides a certain economy of causes for the given effects and explains human motives without too frequently contradicting itself has a good chance of being considered the truth. Which is why Rouault's letter is so persuasive; it takes the second most puzzling fact of Schlumberger's chess career (the first being why he would consent to play chess inside the automaton at all)—namely, that he lost two games in his first week of play as the automaton's director, and scarcely any thereafter for twelve years—and not only explains it in a way that seems to make any further explanation superfluous, but does it without even intending to, as an accidental secretion of a grief and passion that were focused on someone else entirely. Which of course makes it all the more convincing.

Schlumberger was after all a chess player, a man with an instinct for sizing up complex power vectors and manipulating them to his advantage. What could be a more logical extension of that faculty than for Schlumberger, realizing the letter which lured him to America had been a calculated ploy, to respond in kind, to hold Louise Rouault to a promise he felt she had reneged on by employing the most potent weapon at hand: refusal to work. It presumes a certain callousness in him, a certain practicality inconsistent with romantic tradition. But it might as easily be construed as a passion so grand that it could rationalize the most ruthless tactic as an incidental expedient.

It might even be true. The only mistake would be to think of it as the only truth. To think that if the effect—Louise coming to Schlumberger's bed—was one that he might reasonably be supposed to have desired, then the cause—the two games unaccountably botched, lost to amateurs by a man who had found only one person in all Europe qualified to meet him over a chessboard without boring him—must have been calculated to produce it.

There is no reason to believe Rouault didn't observe Schlumberger accurately, but there was only one Schlumberger he needed to know. He wasn't concerned about the Schlumberger who played chess surrounded by the mirrors of the Café de la Régence and the applause of the most sophisticated devotees of the game in the world, or about what happened to Schlumberger when he spent his first two weeks in America learning how to disappear. His disappearance wasn't just a question of learning to shuffle around inside a wooden cabinet so that an audience would be unaware of his presence. If he had stopped playing chess altogether, turned his whole mind to racing horses or carpentry or even to loving Louise Rouault, there would have been more of him left to recognize as William Schlumberger than there was on the October night when he crouched inside that cabinet for the first time. Once the lid closed him inside the machine, he disappeared not just from the eyes of his audience, but from his own as well. Whoever was making the Turk's moves inside that cabinet, it was no longer Schlumberger. It was a creation of Johann Nepomuk Maelzel, who had already fashioned so many machines that as the moment to test this one before an audience for the first time approached, he didn't have a thought to spare for the miracle he had accomplished.

Maelzel thought he had spotted the one he was looking for leaning against a pillar near the back of the hall. Too far away to see him in any detail, but Maelzel didn't even have a description of him so that didn't matter. He just looked for the one who would be in the audience, but not part of it, and the man by the pillar drew his eyes almost immediately. Amid the holiday crowd, eager, bumptious, elbow nudging, conversing across one another along the aisles, heads bobbing for a better view of the automaton, eyes wine-bright, it wasn't hard to pick out the man who was there on business. He was short, beefy and bald, appearing perhaps more solidly planted by contrast with a lanky giant bobbing at his shoulder.

All right, then, Maelzel was thinking, *Look your fill.* He directed a polite but challenging smile to the man by the pillar. It produced no response. The man remained silent and motionless, observing the milling crowd and Maelzel strutting back and forth before it, observing with an air of detached and condescending boredom, his thumbs hooked in the pockets of his waistcoat, occasionally drawing from one of the waistcoat pockets a gold watch which he regarded briefly and clapped shut with a thumb flick that communicated to Maelzel a sense of ruthless impatience.

The message had come just after supper that night, delivered by a young chimneysweep who disappeared into the early dusk as soon as it had passed into Maelzel's hands. "Guard well the reputation of your automaton," it read. "Greco will be present tonight." That was why Maelzel had been so edgy when he went upstairs to tell Schlumberger to get in the box well before the audience arrived. It was not, he reasoned to himself, that he hadn't confidence in Schlumberger as a player. *But what a dolt he is inside the box! Everything has to be explained half a dozen times and sometimes he seems in a trance. That woman must have him crazy. Just so he gets it straight tonight. The chess game will be all right, you goddam Greco back there with your smirk, this boy can wipe that smile off you quick enough, if it's simply a question of chess. But just so I don't open that goddam cabinet in a minute and have him tumble out snoring on the floor, that's all that bothers me.*

And thinking of that unpleasant possiblity, Maelzel swung into his routine speech, so well practiced in his crisp buoyancy that no one noted, except possibly the man standing by the pillar, the strain that he put on the windup line—". . . beyond shadow of doubt that what you behold is a pure machine!"

Thinking, *I hope to God he heard it,* Maelzel extended his arms as if he were about to cue a symphony, shooting his lace cuffs another millimeter down from the end of his jacket sleeves. The bend he had to make as he swung open the door flowed into a low bow, directed not at the audience but at the box itself, as if he were presenting a crowd of eager courtiers to royalty.

Ahh. The audience noted with satisfaction, and a few with scepticism, that the portion of the box's innards which had been revealed, occupying the left-hand third of the rectangle facing the house, offered no place of concealment for a man. *Well, at least he got that part right,* Maelzel thought, knowing that Schlumberger was hunched forward into the middle and right sections of the box, separated by a partition from the portion he had just exposed. The opening was packed deep as the eye could see with machinery. Behind a wide grillwork two interconnecting flywheels hung in the upper left corner like a pair of suns. From them radiated rods that connected to other rods and to a smaller satellite wheel below and to the right of the suns and to the shadows deep in the mysterious core of the box. These constellations hung above a horizontal tube spiked like the roller of a player piano. All this was an intricate brass doily that made no mechanical sense whatever. It made a nicely balanced composition in brass. Its rampant tentacles extended barely two inches deep. Beyond that depth went only a few metal rays cast by the cold suns. They traversed a distance less deep than the reaches of space between stars, but no less hollow.

With a brisk pivot Maelzel walked behind the automaton and lifted the bottom edge of its fur-fringed coat. Addressing the automaton with exaggerated deference, he said, "I'm sure Your Grace won't mind if I hold your train?" Then he flipped the garment over the automaton's head. The audience laughed, throaty bass from the men, soprano fillips from the few women. "He's very shy," Maelzel said, building on the laughter. Lifting an edge of the cloth, he peered underneath and said, "Peek." Just as the laughter from this remark had diminished enough for him to be audible, he gave a mock start and said, "Keep those hands on the table, now, I'm sure insanity would hurt your concentration." This time the masculine bellow went uncounterpointed, while youths blushed and maidens pursed their lips.

Then, showing by the return of military precision to his movements that the interval of levity was past, Maelzel took two steps to the right of the automaton and snapped his fingers. Louise Rouault brought a candle from the wings. The gown she wore, carefully selected by Maelzel, was a part of the spectacle. It was cut and scooped and cinched to make the men whistle, which they did. Maelzel accepted the candle with a choppy nod. He opened another door at the rear of the box and passed the candle back and forth. The audience saw it winking between the interstices of gearteeth. The few skeptics peered closely to detect the silhouette of a man. But Schlumberger was not there.

As he handed the candle back to Louise Rouault, Maelzel nudged the rear door shut with his knee. Then he restored the automaton's dignity, fussing over the draping of its folds like a professional manservant. Each of his gestures was like a hypnotic pass over the audience,

[1 3 2]

smoothing the last ripples of its frivolity into a bland seriousness. He had made it forget that a moment ago he had been treating this delicate mechanism as a Punch-and-Judy puppet. The room was still with anticipation as he stepped once more to the front of the automaton. The stillness of the audience told Maelzel just as surely as its laughter had how thoroughly he was in control. He cast a glance over the house, saw that the man by the pillar was again looking at his watch. He hungered jealously for that man's eyes, the only ones in the room which were not at that moment riveted on himself. He kneeled on one knee to draw out a drawer that stretched across the lower six inches of the chest's entire front. He pulled it almost to its full extent to demonstrate his willingness to account for even the most trivial space in which a man might secrete himself. The audience saw that it contained only a loosely rattling set of chessmen and a box of six miniature chess sets composed into a repertoire of the Turk's favorite end games. The few who were working hard at playing the game Maelzel was leading them through also noticed that he had pulled the drawer far enough to dispel any suspicion that it might have been shallow. They did not notice the springs pressed against the drawer's floating back, or know that when the drawer was shot back into its slot the back would return only halfway, telescoping the depth of the drawer, leaving room behind it for Schlumberger to stretch his legs comfortably.

The audience was now satisfied it had thoroughly scrutinized all but the large compartment to the right of the still-open front door. This occupied two-thirds of the chest's area, and was surely the logical place for a man to hide. Maelzel allowed a pause before opening the double doors. No verbal preamble could have been as eloquent as his smile. Winking a trace of gold from his left eyetooth, the smile compounded a transparently childish guile, a smugness that would have milked hatred from a saint, and for those acute enough to sense it, not a little contempt.

Maelzel knew his gloat infuriated the audience. It was his most cleverly polished contribution to the illusion. *I am so confident in the truth of what I'm showing you,* the smile was saying to the audience, *that I don't even need your good will.* What Maelzel did need at that point in his demonstration was time. This was where Schlumberger always got confused during the rehearsals. The inside wall of the compartment which Maelzel had not yet opened had two doors in its back half. One hinged against the back wall of the cabinet and swung out toward Schlumberger. The other, which covered the same space, hinged against the inside wall itself, and swung inward, neatly partition- ing the small compartment which the audience believed was full of machinery. Once Schlumberger opened these doors it should be a simple maneuver for him to back into the smaller compartment, sliding noiselessly on a runnered stool along a pair of well-oiled rails.

This much Schlumberger usually got right. The problem came with the floor. The back part of the compartment floor was hinged against the outside wall and in its center so that when Schlumberger brought his knees up under it, the floor buckled into an inverted L, making a small table on which he could rest a chess set. Again and again during rehearsals, however, when Schlumberger retreated into the small compartment, he would forget that he had to unhinge the floor and let it drop over his legs and smooth the felt lining over the floor before drawing the partition closed. Maelzel was holding his breath as he leaned forward to open the outer doors of the large compartment. He half expected to see a pair of partially flexed knees, stupidly confident of their invisibility.

The cabinet doors swung open at his touch. He stepped back. Schlumberger was not there. Screwed against the back wall was a pair of horizontal quadrants. A few spring barrels and wheels were tacked into a decorative arrangement that suggested mysterious functions. In addition a small cushion lay beside a shoebox-sized casket of polished mahogany. Without actually saying anything about these artifacts, Maelzel left the audience with the impression that they had an essential function in the rite it was about to witness.

He could relax now, at least until the game itself started. He gave a smile to the one he had identified as Greco and began the next stage of his demonstration with an apology to those for whom further proof of the automaton's purely mechanical nature was unnecessary. An openly cynical chuckle rippled through the crowd as he reproached "those few whose faith in the veracity of human nature has been undermined, perhaps by a knowledge of the duplicity in their own hearts." He managed to flatter each of his auditors that he was among the minority whose worldly wisdom would insist on his putting the machine to its full test. His true opinion, expressed frequently to Schlumberger during their rehearsal sessions, was that the American audience would prove particularly gullible. Not that it had any great naïveté about the human potential for duplicity, he would explain. But the Americans had a passion for new ideas. Having just made a new nation, the Americans welcomed every new idea out of a sense of patriotism.

With a mock sigh to his audience Maelzel quickly disposed of the possibility that the large compartment might contain a false back. He opened a small door at the rear of the cabinet and made passes with a candle similar to those he had employed at the other rear door (now closed).

Then he swung the entire structure around so the automaton's back was to the audience, flung its robes once more over its head, and opened doors in the thigh and back. The Turk's thigh was a hollow tube containing wires strung on a wheel. His backbone was a metal rod.

His demonstration completed, Maelzel pushed the machine down the center aisle. Its doors swung wide and the audience applauded enthusiastically. Maelzel did not fail to notice that the one he had identified as Greco kept his thumbs hooked in his waistcoat pockets throughout the triumphal parade. But for the moment, with the applause not yet beginning its diminuendo, he refused to worry.

He had proven Schlumberger did not exist.

19 | Mechanical Difficulties

To UNDERSTAND what chess became for Schlumberger on the night of October 16, 1826, it is necessary first to recall what it had been. Because the walls of the Café de la Régence were mirrored, there were, in effect, no walls at all, only a glittering horizon on which the figures of chess players glided through an infinite multiplicity of gambits without suffering the least suggestion that the mind of man aspired to any function other than chess. No matter where on that horizon Schlumberger gazed, he could locate himself. Extending his arm over the board to position a rook on a file with his opponent's king, he would confirm the reality of his act with a glance at Schlumberger's hawkish profile; casting his eyes over the shoulder of his opponent, he would often model the pose and expression that this man should see when he raised his eyes; with a hasty check of the mirror reflecting the mirror that stood behind him he would arch his back to correct the stoop that might be bunching the collar of his greatcoat. Playing chess in the Café de la Régence, therefore, Schlumberger both discovered and created himself in its mirrors. Among these mirrors the most important had been not on any of the walls, but in the eyes of his several opponents. There he found proof beyond doubt that an entity which he experienced disjointedly as a bowel, a bladder, a precociously rheumatic back and a complex of secretions and hungers could marshal these tickles and itches sufficiently to induce in the person sitting opposite him feelings Schlumberger could name: puzzlement, awe, fear, jealousy. Naming them he learned to know himself.

Now imagine Schlumberger in Maelzel's box. The mirrors have

disappeared, the illusion of infinity they suggested has contracted to an area scarcely more roomy than his coffin one day will be. What will confirm his existence? The oil lamp? It hangs from a hook on the wall thickening his air; when he moves his first pawn the shadow of his arm and hand falls across the board. The shadow's sycophantic eagerness to touch his fingertips with its own explains nothing.

Only one mirror remains for Schlumberger. He turns to it with the instinct of a blind man offering his face to the sun. After wielding the pantograph to complete the automaton's first move as a copy of his own—he scracely hears the gasp and purr from the audience that greets the regal sweep of the machine's arc—he cranes back his head. On the ceiling above him, framed in a square gouged deep in the wood to make the board wafer thin, is a chessboard diagram that precisely copies the size and position of the polished board above, where the Turk's wooden hand has just completed its miraculous simulation of life and intelligence. Each square is numbered to correspond with numbers on the board in Schlumberger's lap. In the center of each square is a hinged metal flap. On all but the last two rows parallel to the front of the cabinet the flaps hang at a forty-five degree angle from slender wires. The flaps of the last two rows, corresponding to the positions of the black pieces on the board above, are clamped against their squares, held by magnets concealed in the base of the black pieces. Schlumberger concentrates on this diagram, waiting an answering tap on the wall of his dungeon. His mouth falls reflexively open, the base of his skull almost touches the hump erupting from his left shoulder blade. After a few moments a flap beneath the black queen's pawn square drops like an unhinged jaw. An instant later the black queen's pawn-four flap slides up the wire with a barely audible *toc*. This alone must serve as a reply to Schlumberger's declaration that he exists. Whatever passion his attack rouses he will divine not in the living eyes of his opponent but in the patterns of counterattack and retreat transmitted by the machine's sliding flaps. With all the game's seductive impurities thus refined out of existence, perhaps the one discovery available to Schlumberger is whether it was ever chess that he loved.

He copied the move of the black queen's pawn in the board on his lap. Then he made his own move, advancing the white king's pawn a single square, and tilted his head back again to the diagram above. Three minutes passed. His concentration was interrupted by a rapping on the wall next to his ear. Maelzel's apologetic voice told the audience that perhaps the automaton's delicate machinery had been damaged by the stage journey. Schlumberger realized he had not recorded his move on the Turk's board. As Maelzel's knock sounded urgently again Schlumberger lifted the pointed end of the pantograph lever out of its resting place in a hole to his left on the board. Above him the arm of the Turk lifted from the pillow on which it rested between moves. As Schlumberger directed the lever point along the pawn's file and plugged its tipped end into a hole in the square where his king's pawn had been, the automaton's arm glided to the corresponding square and descended, its hand covering the white king's pawn. Schlumberger gave the handle of the lever a twist. The automaton's wooden fingers drew together, gripping the piece. Schlumberger lifted the handle out of its hole and inserted it in a hole next to the one currently occupied by his king's pawn and untwisted the lever. Above him the arm of the Turk, having perfectly mocked Schlumberger's motions, released its pawn, glided back to its pillow, held itself suspended over the pillow, then lowered gently onto the pillow.

Thus the game proceeded, Schlumberger diligently translating a sequence of dropping flaps and plugs and twists of the pantograph into a semblance of the game which had once satisfied his every hunger. After his sixteenth move he squeezed the bellows that made the automaton's voicebox rasp the one word it knew: *"Échec!"* By the tenth move in his second game he had sufficiently mastered the mechanics of this new game to wonder wistfully what his opponent looked like. As he captured the black queen's knight and manipulated the pantograph to remove it to the side of the board, he tried to imagine a flicker of surprise and fear crossing a human face. What human face? His mind cast about, touched momentarily on La Bourdonnais, withdrew as if it had touched flame, called up Henri Rouault, withdrew even more decisively, tried Maelzel, could conjure no expression on his features but a scornful grin; at last no face would rise before his mind, but only the polished inscrutable features of the Turk himself. The flap on square forty-two dropped, bland and speechless as the tongue of a communicant. *His queen,* Schlumberger exclaimed and glanced to confirm the identity of the piece on his own board; *what can he possibly intend to do with his queen?* He waited for the board to speak. Louise Rouault's thumb and forefinger closing upon a chesspiece, he recalled, always gripped so firmly he could see white under her fingernail. On square fifty-seven there was a minute tremor of the flap, as if the player hesitated over his intended move. Then the flap under square sixty shot up, and the voice of Maelzel announced in a tone solemn with fear or rage, "Ladies and gentlemen, the automaton is in check."

After another three moves the automaton was forced to resign. The Turk's arm glided across the board and stopped over its king. The fingers which usually drew together to grip a piece clamped shut, their tips touching, while the arm still hovered above the white king. The arm came down slightly right of center on the square, nudging the piece, then jerked petulantly to the left. The king sprawled into a black rook. Both fell. Two other pieces were jarred from their squares. The audience fell silent, as if it had witnessed a breach of decorum. The Turk's solemn mien, the formality of its squared shoulders, the flowing grace of its other moves, allowed no suggestion of the potential for a gross gesture. The automaton had not been designed to lose gracefully.

Before wheeling the automaton into the hall's makeshift property room Maelzel gave a brief speech. The delicate balance of the machinery had been damaged during the stage journey to Boston, he explained. Sometimes months of tuning were required . . . adjustments of infinite complexity . . . to restore the automaton's capacity to calculate . . . the correct response . . . for a subtle challenge. Here Maelzel nodded respectfully to the subtle challenger, an apothecary's assistant who had cheerfully cast himself as the machine's foil and was unpleasantly surprised by his triumph, convinced he had somehow blundered and spoiled an excellent entertainment. Nothing in Maelzel's words, but an odd resonance, perhaps, or the hint of a brutal clip to his phrases, made this speech a stylistic blend with the Turk's resignation gesture. It scarcely mattered. The majority of his audience had come to marvel. It would not deny itself the pleasure.

A few minutes later the lid of Schlumberger's hiding place was raised and he found himself gazing up at Maelzel's nostrils, which pinched in a delicate snort as if he were inhaling a minute particle of snuff.

"The chess genius," Maelzel drawled.

20 | Reprise, The Man Who Wasn't There

IF IT HAD NOT BEEN for the ubiquitous presence of Louise Rouault, haunting in its separate ways each of the three men, it might have been possible for Rouault and Maelzel to accept that Schlumberger could have lost those two games at least partly because he was confused and disoriented during his first week inside the automaton. Rouault, with his instinct to make all suffering his own, might even have figured out how the automaton threatened Schlumberger's relation with the game itself. Neither of them paid much attention to what Maelzel called Schlumberger's "sleeping sickness." Maelzel assumed it was a stall, the irritating but ultimately ineffectual rebellion of a man who knew he was trapped and wanted to salvage a fragment of autonomy. Rouault was perhaps more conscious of it than Maelzel as a way of hinting at what could happen if Louise remained aloof. Neither one would have guessed that the box was not just a threat, but a seduction.

For a long time Schlumberger didn't realize it himself. Eventually he uncovered, or perhaps admitted, the link between his grotesque scramble inside the dark box and the sleeping sickness, which in turn concealed—with a craft more subtle than the intricate mechanical hoaxing of the automaton itself—a further secret. But in his postmortem journal entry after that first night's play, the only impression he was aware of was panic.

He describes his absurd groping for the lamp. The darkness inside the cabinet was nearly total. A dim luminosity from the air slits between the rims and the lid of his box outlined his roof, but not the floor where the small oil lamp was. It would have been impossible to lose a lamp inside a two-by-four foot box unless he was in a panic. The lamp was kept in a compartment in the back wall of the cabinet. The cabinet opened into the Turk's crotch area. Schlumberger had dropped the lamp as he was removing it from the compartment, then got twisted around groping for it, and lost his bearings inside the box. The second-ranking chess wizard of the Café de la Régence was scuttling like a furtive rodent from one corner to another of a dark box.

A moment ago Maelzel had inserted a large key in a hole between the automaton's shoulder blades. The sound of the ratchet wheel slowly tensing from a resonant clack to a ticking was Schlumberger's cue to prepare for the automaton's opening move. Before he could make that move, Schlumberger had to find the lamp, strike sparks from a tinder-box flint to light it, brace the hinges on his peg-in chessboard, insert two sets of chessmen in the proper positions for the start of a game, and attach a jointed lever to the lower end of a vertical rod hanging like a metal esophagus from the Turk's thorax. The ticking stopped. Maelzel had wound the ratchet tight as it would go. Now Schlumberger should be guiding the lever, which had the same general shape and versatility of movement as a dentist's drill, towards the square occupied by the white queen's pawn. He should be palming the pawn with one hand while he pegged the pointed end of the lever in its place. But he was still groping for the lamp.

Whenever he moved, a sharpness, probably a geartooth, scraped the tip of his hump. His hump was higher than his head. His head was jammed forward between his knees. His rib cage squeezed his lungs. His rib cage in this position was like a hand clamped around a damp sponge, squeezing out water. The water was the air he breathed. He began gasping, still groping, and whimpered as his gropes, becoming frantic now, scraped his knucles against other sharpnesses inside the machine. Outside Maelzel was explaining that sometimes when the machinery was too tightly wound, it needed a thump to start it moving. He knocked sharply on the cabinet wall next to Schlumberger's ear.

He shifted his weight to search with his left hand the corner where his right couldn't reach. A fang sank into his hump. His legs trembled, resisting the temptation to mule-kick. His arms wanted to flail. In another moment he would have to use the last remaining air in his lungs to scream. His mind was thinking, *No, you mustn't,* but his lungs were paying no attention. They were sucking together the air he needed for a scream. His fingers, the left-hand fingers, touched a smoothness, closed around the lamp. He pouched it inside his shirt next to his sweat-streaming belly, while he opened a tinderbox that hung from a cord around his neck and struck sparks with the flint and steel. At first the smouldering rag seemed to be eating the last air in the box, the air he needed to survive five seconds longer there. Then it ignited the sulfur-tipped splinter he had dipped in the smouldering cotton, and he touched the flame to the wick of the lamp. It burned with a steady spearpoint of flame that showed him where he could stretch his legs. He filled up with air at last like an expanding accordion. Against his ear another knock sounded, imperative, desperate. He found the handle of the pantograph device that controlled the automaton's movements, screwed it onto the connecting rod inside the Turk's thorax. He barely heard the murmur of admiration that swept through the audience as the Turk launched a regal arm over the chessboard, closed its fingers upon the white queen's pawn, and arced it two squares forward.

The dropped lamp does not fully account for Schlumberger's panic on the night of his first game. More significant details can be found in a journal entry written years later—one of many entries in which he returns to the events of his first month in America. There he confesses in a tone of puzzled horror that he simply did not want to light the lamp. A despairing reluctance that brought him almost to tears enveloped him as, in response to Maelzel's cue, he opened the cubbyhole where the lamp was kept. His account of the incident suggests that he more than half-guessed that his fingers let the lamp slip on purpose. He marvels with ironic self-suspicion that he could have spent so long (it must have been close to five minutes) searching an area that measured barely two feet by four. "All I wanted," he says, "all I desired in the world throughout the whole evening was to drop off to sleep. I was like a hibernating bear inside my cave. The darkness was my blanket. Can it have been the closeness of the air inside?"

His unnatural desire for sleep at a time when he would normally be keyed to the highest pitch for the coming encounter could not have surprised Schlumberger quite so much if he had taken the time to leaf back through his journal entries in the two-week period of his apprenticeship inside the automaton. Buried under details about his infrequent meetings with Louise Rouault and his efforts to master the mechanics of the automaton are recurrent complaints of a strange torpor that saps his powers of concentration. It began the morning after his arrival in Boston, the first day of his initiation.

"Well," Maelzel had said, "get in the box."

There had been a casual arrogance in his smile. He gestured foppishly toward the open cabinet. Schlumberger felt a prick of outrage, then shock as he realized he was about to ignore the trace of contempt in Maelzel's command. The narrow box into which he stared repulsed him. His decision to direct the automaton must have been taken in some purely theoretical part of his mind. The thought of climbing inside that awful coffin surprised him. Knowing he was going to do it frightened him.

Maelzel waited, still smiling, one hand resting on the cabinet edge. He had raised his eyelids just far enough for a gunmetal glint to tell Schlumberger he was being observed. The eyebrows, dark wedges honed to points at the temples, were raised, too. The amusement they wrote on his face was italicised by two deep lines in his forehead. Frown lines starting from either side of his nosebridge chopped upward through the horizontal lines, canceling the amusement with a scowl. He could be amused or scowling, depending on whether Schlumberger read him across or up and down. When he tried to see both expressions together, they made an unreadable grid. Maelzel's smile, too, was a double entendre. It pulled his lips toward his whiskers, but it didn't say, *Let's try to get along,* or *This business is absurd but necessary.* All it said was that the mind peering out from beneath the drooping eyelids was tickled by a tiny but constant source of pleasure that it was sharing with nobody. In profile the chin below the smile and the nose above it were both cut to jutting points that menaced like a pair of vertical horns. "I said get in," he rasped, tossing the horns.

Schlumberger, grunting, hiked a leg over the edge of the cabinet. Lowering himself inside, he experienced a vague sensual thrill, succeeded almost immediately by an unmistakable intimation that he was about to penetrate a secret far more significant than the workings of an automaton. He felt breathless and naked. He tried to disguise the sensation from Maelzel, who peered at him over the rim of the cabinet. He felt as if he were being watched through the crescent of a jakes door.

KINGKILL

"Comfy?" Maelzel crooned, and Schlumberger caught enough breath to answer, "Well enough," as he stifled a yawn that made him shiver.

Schlumberger's mind had a knack for creating feast days and shrines. As Maelzel impatiently watched him settling his back against the wall, Schlumberger was thinking, *The first night I saw her she lay just as I am now.* (Actually both he and Louise Rouault squatted on a low stool. The journal contains more than one such minute discrepancy.) *Her flesh was held in by these same walls.*

"I said you're not paying attention," Maelzel said, and something that had been just looming into Schlumberger's consciousness skittered like a frightened minnow back into the depths.

"What? Yes, I am. You said the stool slides on . . . on . . . ."

"On runners. And you have to lock these hinges under the chessboard to keep it out of your lap. Now, we'll go through it again . . . ."

The box was filled with echoes. A voice just at the threshold of his hearing murmured and sighed, telling him the box's secret meaning, but Maelzel's rasping baritone rattled through the crucial revelation. He slipped deeper into the box to better concentrate on the whispering voice, but a sudden giddiness frightened him, made him grasp for one of the sharp geometrical edges cut according to Maelzel's directives. Running his fingertips along the scarlet lining of the cabinet, he shook his head clear and did as Maelzel instructed.

His strange yearning to allow the ghostly voice inhabiting the box to lull him asleep was no serious problem during the rehearsal period. Even after the lid was closed upon him, sealing him into a cozy isolation, the walls were not sufficiently thick to cool the singe of Maelzel's exasperated voice. "You have to *twist* the handle," he would growl, and on the accented word the growl would break through its crust and erupt in a quivering shriek that sprayed a sizzling lava over selected syllables in the next comment as well: "You *just* swept *half* a dozen pieces *off* the board." And Schlumberger would summon all his concentration to determine what was meant by the handle, in which direction it twisted, and how this action found a logical context among a chain of other foreign and arbitrary requirements. Each day while a part of his attention focused on Maelzel's instructions, he would be drawing long breaths through his nose until he imagined he had captured a lingering tang of the sweet sweat-smell that had aureoled Louise Rouault the night he watched her climb out of the box. When he felt he had found that current, he would let himself sink on its drafts into the oracular trance in which he sensed the machine's ultimate secret would be revealed. But each day, just at the moment of discovery, Maelzel's harsh Germanic obscenities would scald him back into the world of twisting handles and hinges.

Not until forty-five minutes before the start of the autmaton's first Boston performance did Maelzel allow Schlumberger to spend a minute alone with his own mind while he was inside the cabinet. On that evening he rapped on Schlumberger's door at five minutes after seven. He demanded to know why Schlumberger was not yet in the box. Schlumberger opened the door to him with a mixture of astonishment and vexation. He had been in the midst of a nap, sleeping off his dinner-wine lethargy. He remained Maelzel that the performance was not scheduled until eight o'clock.

"Need I remind you," Maelzel replied, "of the long-standing rule that the automaton's director must be inside the cabinet well before the arrival of the audience? All we need to turn our fortune into the biggest joke of two continents is for some stray cat prowling behind the scenes to see you lowering your tail into that box."

Schlumberger bellowed that he had not been informed of this precautionary tradition, but by the time he got the words out, Maelzel's head was already sinking below the edge of the top stair at the end of the hall. Schlumberger spat furiously into his chamber pot and lingered in his room for five rebellious minutes, but by a quarter past the hour he was securely tucked inside the cabinet. His docility is not wholly remarkable. He had earlier in the day spent nearly ten minutes in private conversation with Louise Rouault.

The journal reveals that her conduct toward him during this interval was elusive to the point of insult, but she apparently struck a fine balance, stroking his ruffled pride just enough to assure his cooperation. Only three days previously Schlumberger had devoted an entire journal entry to an analysis of a smile she had bestowed on him as they passed on the stairs. From it he deduced that there were mysterious reasons why they must continue, for the time, to conceal their love, but that she would come to him at the first opportunity. His talk with Louise on the day of the first performance had been no more conclusive than any other that had passed between them in the two weeks since he had arrived. Her words were cryptic, spoken as if the conversation were being overheard. Her influence was so great over him that Schlumberger, too, spoke in hints. Whenever he threatened to grow impatient, she would cast a glance over her shoulder at the kitchen door. (All their rendezvous took place in this room or the parlor, both of which were also frequented by Maelzel and Henri Rouault.) Then she would fix him with mute imploring eyes, and make a remark about the weather. These moments of semi-intimacy satisfied Schlumberger sufficiently to make him discount the coldness with which she treated him in the presence of the other men.

Thus, on the night of his first performance, Schlumberger found himself spending a longish interval inside the automaton cabinet with no duties to perform and no voice to disturb him but the eerie undersea lullaby which inhabited his darkness.

For a brief period after the lid was lowered into place, the darkness inside the box was total. He had the sense of having disappeared even to himself. When he waggled his fingers in front of his eyes, he saw nothing. The darkness acted like a chemical solution, dissolving the flesh that contained him. He felt himself expanding to fill the entire box, rising up the metal spinal column of the automaton to look out upon the world through its glass unblinking meditative eyes.

But soon his ceiling became suffused with a faint glow outlining the rectangular confines of the box. It was like the original act of creation, separating light from the primal darkness. In each wall, he noticed, were two narrow slits, just at the place where the wall met the ceiling. Concessions to his humanity, he realized, his need to breathe air, concealed from external view by the overhang of the lid. He reached a hand to the wall, drew back sharply when he felt a pulse. Convinced himself somewhat shakily it had been his own blood pumping to his fingertips.

He listened to his own respirations as his breathing grew regular again, fell gradually into a steady powerful rhythm lapping at the shores of consciousness. Then he heard the ghostly voice calling his name and closed his eyes, then lazily reopened them on the red felt lining above, which became—had always been, he realized—*her* color, the color in which she was bathed in any image of her he could recall. It tinted her the way sunlight diffused beneath a parasol takes on the color of the silk material. Only it hadn't been a parasol, he was thinking, no, not a parasol, but a petticoat, and he beneath it, wrapped in it, hiding from *Maman*. He had been lying on his back amid the cast clothing of a laundry hamper, burrowed into one of his aunt's petticoats, his arms arching above him so the sunlight from the bedroom window tinted his body—he had shucked his clothes before climbing into the hamper. Tinted it the same color the stained glass did when he sat with his family at ten-thirty Mass in the pew under the window showing Magdalene washing the Savior's feet with her hair. As soon as he squatted inside the cabinet that image of himself making a cathedral arch of his arms to see the sunlight through the silk had flicked into his mind. Though he had never consciously thought of it before, he knew instinctively it belonged to him, was part of his history; he felt no more surprise with it than he would feel slipping his feet into a well-scuffed boot creased and molded to the shape of his own stride. He had lived with it all his life, heard the whispered rustling of that silk each time he was tossed half-awake by a dream in the star-silent morning hours, and felt the same silk whisked away just as he opened his eyes upon the sun.

But he couldn't anchor the image in time. He must have been very young to fit inside the laundry basket—yes! the one that always sat by the bed in his mother's room. But it wasn't his mother's, no—his aunt's petticoat, the one who came visiting from Crécy, Papa's sister who had glided always with a faint rustling from under her skirts that he had never noticed in women before and who the first time he saw her had shown the tan arcs of her nipples above the crescent of her Empire bodice as she leaned to embrace him, saying to his mother, "And this is your little man?" Now it was coming, unfolding itself to him, and he thought, *It was naptime and I was in Maman's room, because my cousin, Leon, was sleeping in my bed, and, yes, I fell asleep there in the hamper.* Now the dream was coming back to him, too, a dream within the dream his memory had become. And he recalled that as he grew drowsy after a long time squirming bare among the silks, he had pretended his aunt was whispering to him, "It will be our secret, you hiding like a tiny mouse under my gown wherever I go." And her imagined voice had lullabied him smoothly from fantasy into dream, and in the dream he felt his loins churning in a sinuous feminine wiggle, his hands palping at his meatless breasts, stroking down his shivering torso which was not his but the body of his dead aunt and Louise

Rouault, yet still his, his since he had discovered with no effort or surprise that she was not another, but himself, and his hands moved confidently to the swelling curve he knew they would find in place of his own narrow, bony hips.

As Maelzel, with an initial lurch, began pushing the automaton from its backstage storage room to the exhibit hall where the audience was waiting, Schlumberger stirred in his dream and whimpered, just as he had blinked half-awake and whimpered when he had been yanked painfully by the forearm out of the hamper, brought dangling up to his mother's fierce plum-flushed face that shrieked, ". . . and *this* is where you've been all this time while we searched and called and . . ."

Then Schlumberger heard Maelzel say, ". . . beyond shadow of a doubt that what you behold is a pure machine," and knowing the door of the first compartment in which he must not be found was about to be opened, he began struggling upward though fathoms of sleep, rising more buoyantly each time he relinquished another dream-image, so that by the time he surfaced, moments later, he had salvaged nothing of its secret but a few puzzling spars and keg splinters that drifted out of his brain as he thought how he must now slide from the large compartment into the small one and close the partition after him before Maelzel opened the cabinet doors to prove Schlumberger was not there.

BUT YEARS LATER, after he heard that she was dead, he prolonged his mourning with the hopeless fancy, sustained over many months, that her spirit might contact him in a dream. And eventually the only detail he was unable to recollect in the candlelight journal entries, which he secreted during that experiment the way a snail adds chambers to its shell, was a clear image of the aunt herself, who always had the face of Louise Rouault.

21 | An Epistemology of Language

WHAT FINALLY GAVE Schlumberger as much as he was ever to know about Louise Rouault—more than he got from all his questions, more than he could plumb in his deepest thrust inside her body—was the visit to Professor Sophman, the phrenologist. It began as a joke on a night when he had almost given up believing he could ever learn anything about her but how she made him feel. The joke soured, but he would ruminate on what followed and spin it into his journal for years to come.

In the two weeks after the night Louise came to his bed, Schlumberger's performance inside the metal entrails of the automaton was a flawless impersonation of a dependable, efficient machine. His difficulties with the mechanics of the box evaporated. Even more puzzling—though Schlumberger did not then bother to puzzle over it—the strange lethargy, which he attributed to the stale air inside the box and which Maelzel contemptuously dubbed "sleeping sickness," evaporated as well. But he won games by habit, since his mind was always on Louise. He won without caring, simply because he had spent more time learning the game than any of his opponents. Nobody who had other interests in life—like raising a family or learning a profession or working at a job—could hope to compete with a man who had been playing chess and reading its literature and brooding over its combinations and doing little else for fourteen years. While his opponents fumbled through their calculations like children manipulating the buttons on a waistcoat, he thought about Louise and rubbed the cramps out of his legs. When he heard the faint *toc* that told him the lifting of a chesspiece on the automaton's board had broken its magnetic connection with one of the sixty-four metal disks hinged to his ceiling, he glanced up to confirm that the move would be completed as he expected, then sliced his bishop to the queen's throat.

Loving a woman, Schlumberger desired more than possession. He wanted to inhabit her. She must contain him wholly since chess no longer did. He studied her as he once studied the grammar of chess, with the passion of a man who needs rules to keep from melting like tallow.

He started by making her talk to him, but in her voice words took on a melody that distracted him from what they signified. Then he gave himself over to his body until he learned its limit. He tasted her flesh. He became a connoisseur of her odors. His eyes mastered the syntax of flesh. The hollow that dipped away from her cheekbone taught him tenderness. The motion of her hips taught him new possibilities in walking. He studied the endless moods of breasts: their modesty behind a blouse; their eagerness pushing over the border of a shift; their coyness exposing a nipple above her bodice when she bent to remove a stocking; their tumbling, jouncing, swingsong playfulness and mockery and daring; their laziness as they evaporated when she lay on her back; their shyness in the week before period, eased by his tongue learning smoothness under the nipple; their voracity as his tongue and then his lips coaxed the nipples erect. With his hands he explored another definition of smoothness on the inside of a thigh, the harmony of curves with a palm under each buttock, warmth and moisture as his finger probed and stroked. When he had eased a space for his penis to follow, he learned a touch that he imagined was a language in itself, in which sigh answered thrust and writhe answered grind unambiguously until dialogue seemed to become duet and all language to fuse into one meaning.

But in the ebb that followed orgasm he would find himself once more only himself. The uncoupling made hypothetical what had min-utes before been certitude. And when she moved her hand to scratch her nose or turned on her side, he recognized with confusion and regret that it was no longer an impulse from his brain that controlled her body. Then he felt himself pulled under, filled and surrounded by his own body, like a swimmer caught in an undertow, and as the chill walls of his skin closed around him, he returned to the language of convicts tapping out messages on the walls of their cells.

"What are you thinking?" he would ask, leaning on an elbow to look down at her face.

"It's late," she would answer, or "Tomorrow is laundry day," or "Haven't you got all you want for now?"

"I was only wondering," he would say, and sulk until he got tired of waiting for her to tease him into conversation, and begin again with, "Tell me more about when you were a child."

She would toss her head on the pillow and say, "I used to stake the cow in the field," or "My father had strong arms."

And once, when he said, "That's not what I mean. You're not really telling me anything," she threw off the sheet and stamped to the middle of the room and turned naked to face him and hissed, "After your prick shrinks I can get my body back. But what I tell you no longer belongs to me at all. Do you understand that?"

"Of course," he said, not understanding. "Come back to bed."

That was how far Schlumberger's linguistic scholarship had progressed the day Maelzel discovered why the receipts for the previous two performances had dropped to half their previous level.

"It's a goddam bumpologist!" he announced, raking his chair in to the supper table. Schlumberger, Louise, and Rouault had begun eating without him. "The bastard's been feeling skulls for two nights now, telling people everything but what dolts they are to pay him money."

Maelzel pushed at Louise an arm with an empty glass at the end of it. She filled it with claret. The last fly of the summer had just completed an intricate dance and lighted in the butter dish. Maelzel's fork could not resist feinting at it on the way to spear a pork chop.

"Goddam *what?*" asked Schlumberger. With an envelope he marked his page in the book beside his plate. The book was a life of Napoleon. He retained many of the habits of his solitude.

"Phrenologist," said Rouault.

"Bumpologist," corrected Maelzel. He jammed his mouth with pork. Its bulge in his left cheek shrank as he chewed. Then he jammed his hand into his frock-coat pocket. It withdrew fisted around a piece of paper which he slapped onto the table beside Schlumberger's book. "Here. Read," he commanded. "A boy shoved it under my nose on Milk Street. Be instructed. Be edified." He slapped viciously at the fly, which had fallen in love with his lower lip.

KINGKILL

On the paper Schlumberger saw a cartoon profile of a bald head crawling with tattoos. After a moment he decided he had misread the drawing. The pictures he had seen on the skull were meant to be inside it. The skull was really a transparent bee hive sectioned into dozens of compartments. Something different was happening in each compartment. In one a man was tipping his hat to a lady. In another two men were trying to budge a mule. On the forehead a man cocked his head at an apple falling from a tree. Behind the ear a boy had knocked another down while a rooster watched from a hill. Where the sideburns should be a paunchy man gulped from a glass and across the table from him a man was bringing to his mouth a forkful of food about twice the size of his jaw. Schlumberger thought it was unrealistic for the face to wear such a placid expression with all those thoughts careering at once through the brain.

Type that curved with the contour of the skull informed him that Self-Knowledge was the Key to Success in Business and Love. The writing beneath the head claimed that Professor Sophman had revolutionized Phrenology by applying its principles to the Practical Problems of Living. He promised to help Schlumberger choose a career and select a mate. He would use character analysis to tell Schlumberger which of his virtues required assiduous cultivation and what vices imperiled his immortal soul. The lecture that night at the Liberty Tavern was free and would be followed by private consultations at twelve and a half cents a head.

Rouault poked at a boiled potato and said, "I thought you were a champion of advanced ideas."

"So I am," said Maelzel through a bulging crawful of pork. He raised a hand to indicate that he was not yielding the floor yet, and continued chewing. His jaw muscles worked rapidly. He chewed like a dog, with total concentration. His mind withdrew all its tentacles from their grips in the past and the future, and knotted them around the present moment, the act of mastication. He imposed on his canine snaps a methodical rhythm, as if he were counting his chews.

He gulped and gulped again and said, "The true phrenologist is a man of science. Dr. Gall's researches are the essence of scientific observation. He opened his house to the lower classes. Coachmen and street vendors gathered in droves. He took each man aside to quiz him on the striking characteristics of his fellows, and made copious notes on—''

''How did he win the assistance of all these 'lower classes'?'' asked Louise.

''With a little honey, the way you''—clamping his hand on empty air—''gather flies. He stocked his wine cellar with cheap gin and gave them the key. Pass that claret again, if you please. He even gave them money. And with the information he got from his notes he divided them into types: courageous and cowardly, combative and peaceable. Then he began measuring skulls. He used meticulous accuracy. The results were astounding. In all the feisty men the head was much broader *here*—'' (he placed his index fingers behind the tops of his ears) ''—than among the docile ones. *Voilà!* The discovery of the Organ of Combativeness.''

''But what is wrong with this Professor Sophman at the Liberty Tavern?'' asked Rouault.

''You mean besides the fact that he's causing us to lose fifty dollars a night?''

''Yes,'' said Louise. ''Besides that.''

''The cheat comes in the last line here,'' he said, jabbing a finger at the leaflet beside Schlumberger's plate. ''He claims you can develop virtues and eliminate vices, which is *bunkum*. If I build an automaton to stick its right index finger in its left nostril, you are *never* going to find that finger up its asshole. And if the organ of combativeness is highly developed in your brain, Rouault, you are going to double up your fist and strike whether you will or no. Which is why I say this Sophman is no scientist. He's a fucking preacher.''

Rouault had stopped eating. His eyes bulged. His lips pursed tightly. Just below his hairline beads of sweat crowned his brow.

He said, ''I'll tell you what your fine theory forgets.''

''It's not my theory, Rouault. It's a fact, discovered by Franz Joseph Gall.''

''It forgets *grace*.''

''What?''

''Divine grace. The redemptive grace of Christ's death on the cross.''

Maelzel smiled and sighed and sipped his claret. His rhetorical springs were tightly wound. Perhaps the fly that his hand kept waving away from his plate and his face had nothing to do with his decision that Rouault needed a lesson in theology. Perhaps that lesson was not required to prompt the decision Rouault took later that night. Perhaps only in retrospect, in the distorting prism of Schlumberger's journal, would the fly ever acquire the slightest importance.

"My dear Rouault," Maelzel began. "If you really wish to understand the mind of God, you should put aside the whinings of Hebrew doomsayers and study—"(Maelzel made the most delicate of pauses)"—the science of mechanics."

Schlumberger laughed, choking on his pork. Louise laughed. Maelzel accepted their appreciation by flashing the gold fleck in his eyetooth. Rouault sat still.

"I am quite serious," Maelzel continued. "Sometimes your ignorance of modern philosophy astonishes me. Read La Mettrie's masterpiece, *Man a Machine*. You'll find out that your 'soul' is only as large as your organ of acquisitiveness. 'Beings without wants are also without mind.' Read Diderot. The universe is a gigantic clock, set in motion by a master mechanic—not unlike myself." (Here he paused again for laughter.) "God set our world ticking in the ether, but he has no desire to hear the complaints of its little cogs and screws. Would I die to redeem a single bolt in my panharmonicon?"

"I think there is nothing you would die for," said Rouault. "There is nothing sacred to you. But I know this: you will die."

"Don't point your finger at me, Rouault. Graveyards don't terrify me. How would you like me to prove to you that this Sophman is nothing but a diddler, prove it scientifically?"

This time Rouault laughed, the scornful bark of the unbeliever.

"Here's what we do," Maelzel said. "We dress you in rags. Lace your head with straw. Make you up like the village idiot. Then we trot you down to Professor Sophman's lecture tonight and let him read your bumps. He's bound to use some audience volunteers in his little demonstration. Once he has described you as a thorough dunce, you stand and triumphantly prove your vasty wisdom by reciting the Book of Job verbatim."

This time Schlumberger did not laugh. Without his counterpoint, Louise's chortle sounded lonely and gauche. She clipped it off. The fly came to rest on the edge of Maelzel's plate and bathed its delicate feelers in a pool of pork grease. Maelzel, sensing he had ridden his joke as far as it would carry him, turned irritable and began restoking the rage he had sat down with.

"It wouldn't be a bad idea at all," he grumbled," *if* you were game for it. Showing that bumpologist up for a fool would be a good way to get back our audience."

Rouault had retreated from the encounter. With lowered eyelids and the pale martyr's smile, he was cutting himself a piece of bread as if he were alone in the room. Even he looked up, however, when Schlumberger said, "I'll do it then. I'll play village idiot."

Then, while they watched he warped like a leaf touched by flame. He clattered his fork onto his plate with a hand grown clumsy. The hand hung limp from the wrist, and from the palm hung limp splayed fingers. The arm carried it with a simian cock of the elbow to the top of his head, where the fingers plowed up a cowlick and reversed the slant of his forelock. Passing roughly down his face the hand squeezed the eyebrows into a perplexed frown, puzzled the eyes and left a loose lip hanging from the jaw. He rose to a crouch, his head dangling between his shoulders heavy as his hands on his wrists. Now he was truly a hunchback. Under the thick brows the eyes scuttled like rats at the mouth of a cave, stupid and shrewd. He sprang onto the chair at which he had been sitting. His tongue lolled in the grin that spread his face and did not manage to get out of the way as he croaked, "Doter Sobman: reab my bumps an' say who gonna marry me!"

22 | Schlumberger Unmasked

THE SIGN ON THE DOOR of Julian Hall told patrons that the evening's performance had been canceled due to mechanical difficulties with the automaton chess player. Mr. Maelzel promised that the regular schedule of play would be resumed at the noon performance tomorrow. Many of the disappointed customers strolled along Milk Street to the Liberty Tavern, where three shrill boys harangued passers-by and thrust handbills at them.

Schlumberger lurched down Milk Street bawling syllables. "Gaam!" he crowed. "Ee-mowb!" Maelzel paced him on his right with a hand gripping Schlumberger's bicep. Louise tried to hang on to his left arm, holding it like a tool she didn't know how to use. Whenever he shrieked or staggered violently, she would whisper with her mouth close to his ear as his bobbing head would allow, "What's got into you? Have you gone insane?" And Schlumberger would glare at her half-frightened and admiring eyes and explain, "Mubforg. Snog. Poom," until she felt Maelzel's cackles churning bubbles of hysteria that broke from her throat like laughter. Half a pace behind her Rouault marched.

Strollers on the boardwalk parted to let them pass. They stared or looked away with the awkward respect people accord a mind or body locked by deformity into an isolation more dismal than their own. Schlumberger filled their pitying silence with lewd brays. The success of his disguise intoxicated him. The joke was on everybody. The crowd did not know the head lolling between his curled shoulders could be held stiff and dignified; his three companions did not know what joy he felt in accepting, for once in his life, the weight of the hump between his shoulders, bowing to its pressure, wagging it above him like an obscene gesture. Freed from the necessity to keep his shoulders rigidly squared, his back straight as a plumb line, he discovered the true grace of his body. His hump might have been a balloon, buoying him as he cavorted nimbly along with Louise and Maelzel dancing clumsily out of step.

Still another secret delighted him: the gibberish language that completed his disguise revealed to him thoughts he did not know his mind held. A minute ago, as people first began staring at them, Maelzel had said through gritted teeth, "Don't overdo it," and Schlumberger answered him with "Nemtess woof!" The syllables had shaped his lips to a snarl he had not enjoyed since the night he first looked across a chessboard into the surprised, outraged eyes of his father and said, *"Échec. . . et mate!"* Later that night he woke from sleep to the sound of the old man gargling his last curses. From that time he had feared certain thoughts, knowing his words had the power to kill. Now he was using the power without remorse.

The versatility of his new language was unlimited. Just before they left Julian Hall he had spent a moment in the parlor alone with Louise. She had come upon him practicing his shuffle and stoop among the chairs and hassocks. "Why are you doing this?" she asked. "What is it you want?" And he lurched up to her, joining her in the twilight by the window. "Jub," he croaked. "Shibnol," his voice throaty with emotion. And finally, "Baaa," he breathed, telling her the last secret, the one he kept even from himself. His stoop had brought their eyes level. He raised his hands to her face and tenderly clamped her cheeks between his palms, his thumbs at the wings of her nostrils. He felt her neck tense to resist his will, but he drew her eyes close to his, so close the face mask could not distort communication. She was breathing quickly. Once she tried to twist away. His fingers gripped tighter. Crescents of white appeared under his thumbnails. He forced her to look until her eyes began to blink tears. "Don't," she whispered. "Don't make me love you." He could feel her trembling. He drew her closer, this time without resistance, and pressed their lips together. While he nuzzled her lips she gave a strange moan, as if she were breaking into a secret language of her own to answer his, and then they heard Rouault's footsteps on the stairs.

The Liberty Tavern was only half filled when they arrived. Maelzel strode up to a table near the fireplace and politely informed the two men seated there that they would have to sit elsewhere, the table was reserved for people who were participating in a scientific test of Professor Sophman's theories. The men looked at Maelzel and then at one another with affected languor, but when Schlumberger cawed at them they snatched their hats and gloves and made a dignified bolt to a table farther back. Schlumberger sat between Louise and Maelzel. The remaining chair would have left Rouault with his back to the lecturer. He drew it away from the table and planted himself to the right of Louise like a weary chaperone.

He's a castled king back there, Schlumberger thought. He was watching Professor Sophman pacing between the hearth and two long tables that barricaded him from his audience. He was pacing aggressively, like a man with someplace to go. He never went beyond the two tables. Now and then he shot a glance at the crowd to see how fast the hall was filling. Then he would flick a pocket watch from his waistcoat pocket and shoot a glance at it, keeping it tight to his vest and pushing a judicious lower lip at it as if it had been a mediocre poker hand, that didn't quite deserve folding. *A king in trouble,* Schlumberger thought, with relish. *Only pawns and a queen to keep me back. I'll destroy him.* The pawns were seven or eight plaster busts of famous men spread across the tables to regard the audience with blank eyes. All the faces were smooth and guileless as baby flesh and looked almost alike, though Schlumberger guessed that one was meant to be Napoleon and another George Washington. The queen sat portly and nervous behind one of the tables. She spent her time sharpening quills and adjusting the wick on a smoking lamp and squaring the corners of papers stacked beside a laurel-crowned bust that might have been Caesar. Her livid cheeks and quivering jowls looked artificial among the still, bone-white sentries. After every three or four turns the king interrupted his pacing to bestow a remark upon his queen, which she received in the stylized attitude of a stage actress, keeping her body toward the audience while she inclined her head attentively up and toward her shoulder, but not really looking at him. Crowd murmurs drowned their words. Ten paces away, Schlumberger watched Sophman's moving lips and shrugs and fluid gestures and the woman's deferentially nodding head. He suspected their conversation was a babble designed to prove how unconcerned they were that three hundred people were sizing them up.

Schlumberger Unmasked

The hall was nearly full now, and Sophman's chest seemed to expand a little more every time he cast his measuring eye over the crowd. Some of the men had cigars cocked in their teeth. Others sucked on longstem pipes. A haze silvered the nimbus around the recently installed gas lamps spaced along the walls. Those not smoking chewed. The hall resounded with the cocky ping of plugged spittoons. On the sea of grey and brown and black frock coats bobbed a flotsom of escorted females in yellow and pale blue gowns. Once Sophman's eyes fell directly on Schlumberger and lingered. Schlumberger gaped back, choosing that moment to drool the saliva he had allowed to collect in the pocket between his lower jaw and loose lip. It excited Schlumberger to see Sophman resume pacing, his curiosity calcified into pity and disgust. It excited him to know that behind the slackness and bobbing idiocy that had repulsed Sophman lurked the firm cruelty and cunning and strength of the real Schlumberger, and Sophman would soon know his mistake.

All the chairs filled with people. The last couple dozen customers pushed a horseshoe line along three walls. Sophman waited until the waiters had got their drink orders, then stopped pacing and stared the hubbub of the crowd to a murmur. He was a prophet calming turbulent waters. This display of power thrilled Schlumberger to admiration in spite of himself. Soon even the murmur died. Spittoons rang in the silence like altar bells. Schlumberger was even more impressed when Sophman turned his back on the silence he had won. He stepped up to rest one arm on the mantle and contemplated a large canvas nailed to the wall beside the fireplace. The canvas bore a head diagram similar to the one Schlumberger had examined on the leaflet. This head, too, was sectioned like a stained-glass window, but in place of pictures only numbers filled the spaces. Sophman's steady attention made the diagram radiate mysterious significance. He might have been addressing a prayer to a patron saint. Then he turned, sweeping off the mantle an object Schlumberger had not noticed, and confronted the audience with a stiff-armed salute. In place of a hand at the end of his arm was a human skull.

"Ladies and gentlemen," he announced, "the skull of Man." His voice was an invitation to reverence.

Slowly he lowered his arm and took the skull in his other hand. He addressed it like an elderly Hamlet, saying, "The casing, the sacred temple housing man's most noble faculty—" (unhooding his eyes at last to the audience) "—his intelligence."

Sophman's voice had a trick of pitch or cadence that made Schlumberger feel he alone was being spoken to. Its conviction poured like thick syrup over his skepticism. He would pause before strange words like "philoprogenitiveness" and articulate them precisely, sometimes stretching his lips against his white evenly set teeth. Often he would repeat the word, separating its syllables as if he expected the audience to be memorizing it. Sometimes he would cut off an idea by clamping his jaws on it with a clack like an audible period. When he made a claim that was particularly difficult to believe he would show the teeth in a benign smile and close his eyes momentarily, showing patience with jeers that never came.

He cupped the skull in his palm and extended it to the audience like an empty bowl, saying that the frail shell before their eyes once housed the most secret yearnings and passions and sorrows of a human spirit. Now the skull's owner was long dead and his secrets gone to dust. But, he said, it has no secrets from the phrenologist. He smiled and closed his eyes. Then he played his fingers over its surface, pausing now and then with forefinger pressed on a particular spot. "Philo-pro-genitiveness," he said and repeated the word. "Poorly developed. The man either had no family or cared little for its comfort." The finger stopped on other places which revealed the skull's owner had been cautious and boastful and miserly.

Then he took up a pointer and gave the audience a name for all the numbers on the head chart. The chart identified the precise location of the various organs which controlled human behavior. He turned to the busts on the table before him. He showed the large bumps of ambition and pride in Napoleon's skull. He pointed out Voltaire's bump of causality, proper to one of superior intellect. He was challenged as he pointed to a hanged murderer's bump of destructiveness. A man who identified himself as Doctor Rush said that a cast taken of a hanged man would have no scientific validity because the blood would congeal in the man's head when the rope cut off his circulation, producing swellings in the skull unrelated to the contours of the brain. While this point was being made Professor Sophman smiled and closed his eyes, nodding his head patiently. Then he said he had been careful to wait a sufficient time after the criminal had been cut down before taking his cast. Schlumberger learned that the bust he had taken for George Washington was actually cast from the head of a madwoman in a Philadelphia asylum who had drowned her three children and run naked in the streets. She had a highly developed bump of combativeness and scarcely any philoprogenitiveness at all.

At last Professor Sophman called for a volunteer from the audience. Schlumberger hesitated, his confidence in his disguise momentarily shaken. He was worried that he might not have remembered to keep up his bobbing and drooling during the speech. He was just rising to his feet when Maelzel pulled him down. "Wait," Maelzel whispered. "Give him a chance to make some converts before we prove he's duping them. The more they trust him now, the more they'll hate him then."

Professor Sophman had come out from behind his barricade of tables to greet a stocky gentleman who wiped his hands on his paunch as though he were stroking a rare vase. He took the chair Professor Sophman offered him with a grin directed to four or five enthusiastic claquers at the table where he had been sitting. He heisted one leg over the other and folded his hands below the knee. Jewels winked from a finger on each hand. As Professor Sophman stepped behind him, his neck craned in anticipation, stretching away his double chin. The tolerant frown he assumed when the phrenologist began massaging his scalp insisted that his position in the community would not be jeopardized by a bit of levity, and the occasional mock scowl to his claqueurs told them the joke, if there was any, would not be on him.

Oblivious to the hum of amusement his volunteer inspired, Professor Sophman produced a pair of large three-legged calipers and planted it ceremoniously on the head below him as if he were crowning it. The crown looked like the replica of a deformed insect. At the sight of this instrument the crowd lapsed into a hush of scientific reverence. Professor Sophman tightened the screw on the calipers and began calling off numbers, walking the caliper legs over the skull and baring his teeth to enunciate the numbers with ponderous precision. The brisk officious quill of the woman at the table recorded each number. At first Schlumberger thought the numbers corresponded to the numbered organs of the brain on the chart against the wall, but when the same numbers began recurring and Sophman never called a number above seven, he realized they designated the size of the organ measured. Once the professor pronounced, "Eight," and his secretary suspended her quill halfway from inkwell to paper. She cocked her head to a sharp interrogative tilt.

"Eight!" confirmed the professor, and she dutifully wrote.

"Pure theatrics," hissed Maelzel. Throughout the professor's analysis of the measurements he had taken, Maelzel's comments sizzled in Schlumberger's ear like the periodic eruptions of a steam valve under intolerable pressure. After a ritual compliment to his subject's Firmness and Benevolence, both measuring four on a scale of seven, the professor issued a stern paternal warning on the need to curb the organ of Acquisitiveness, which was a dangerous six and a half. "A cheap guess," Maelzel said, poking Schlumberger's ribs. "See the rings." The professor hastened to assure the subject that his Acquisitiveness was in no serious danger of menacing the populace, since the most outstanding feature of his brain, which measured an unheard of *eight*, was Adhesiveness, the organ which made him a model of friendship incapable of exploiting his fellow man for gain. Maelzel nodded viciously in the direction of the table where the man's adhesive cronies beamed approvingly. Finally, the professor counseled his subject on his Alimentiveness, an organ developed prominently only in gourmands of discriminating taste. "You don't need a calipers to tell how that hog got his gut," rumbled Maelzel. "Bah! No more science than you'd get from a weight guesser at a county fair."

Applause crackled mightily as the portly gentleman rose and pumped the professor's hand, radiating Adhesiveness. From various parts of the hall half a dozen persons demanded the privilege of baring their brains to Professor Sophman's omniscient calipers. "We've got to stop this before it gets out of hand," Maelzel said, and Schlumberger found himself yanked to his feet and propelled by an insistent hand in the small of his back toward the recently vacated chair. Vaguely, his sensibilities swamped by stage fright, he heard Maelzel's powerful voice hammering down the applause, introducing Schlumberger as a man afflicted since birth with a disorder of the brain, and offering him as a subject of study that could yield fascinating data to the science of phrenology.

For an instant Professor Sophman's brows contracted but he apparently realized that the upstart with the foreign accent had deftly refocused the attention of the audience, and he knew the rules of showmanship well enough to sense that he dare not disappoint its expectations. He bowed Schlumberger to his seat with a resigned, courtly grace. Schlumberger forced himself to keep his back hunched and screeched briefly to establish his character and rediscover his courage. The chill points of the calipers stilled his lolling head. He held his breath while the professor announced the numbers that told his fate. A minute bead of perspiration erupted from the topmost peak of his skull, and Schlumberger traced its erratic path through the jungle of his hair to his left ear, where a sonorous bell chimed relentlessly. Then with more surprise than fear Schlumberger realized that the professor had substituted a razor for the calipers and circumnavigated his skull in one quick slice that cut bone like butter. He glanced anxiously at Louise and Maelzel and Rouault, whose bland, concentrated faces assured him that this technique of brain exploration was customary among phrenologists, and relaxed into a pleasant giddiness while Professor Sophman lifted away the top of his skull as if it were an iron helmet he had been wearing so long he had forgotten its weight. Then the razor must have been delicately probing his raw brain, for he felt a localized tingling that stirred from its slumber an unbearably vivid image of his aunt Estelle stroking a fallen strand of golden hair away from her cheek. The razor sank again and up bobbed the lifeless white belly of a thumbnail-sized frog still bearing the vestige of a trail from its former life, which he had once trapped in a jar full of ditchwater and forgotten to feed. Then he saw a familiar gnarled forefinger and thumb closing over the black queen, his own queen, and his father's smug, triumphant voice rasped, "Never be in a hurry to bring out your queen, boy."

Schlumberger tensed his nostrils against the musty sickroom smell and glared with hatred at his father's pillow-framed face, then blinked and looked into the eyes of Professor Sophman which were studying his own carefully.

" . . . most curious formation," Sophman was saying, and Schlumberger caught at the words as if they were pages of a valuable manuscript caught up by a whirlwind and blowing, blowing one by one away, and he snatched from the swirl, ". . . none of the characteristic signs of . . . ," wondering why the professor was imitating his father's voice, why his tone was so remote and sad, and as his father's hand came to rest on his brow the whirlwind slowed into "reflective faculties of Comparison and Causality . . . only among men of extraordinary intellectual . . ." and the whirlwind abruptly died. In the stillness that followed, Professor Sophman said, "In addition, I detect pronounced development in the areas of—" (The regular toc-toc of his footsteps on the wooden floor ceased as he reached the far end of the table, pacing in front of it now rather than behind it, and turned back to Schlumberger to say—the constant effort of perfect articulation pulling the upper lip tight against the even line of his teeth as he pronounced the "Deee . . ." with a long drawl) "—Destructiveness . . . Wit . . ." (Pacing back now, stopping beside the chair where Schlumberger sat, speaking in a meditative but carrying voice as if to him alone, saying . . .) ". . . and Imitation—that disposition to mimicry which was measured at *eight* in the death mask of Mr. Burbage. The great British actor."

It took a moment for the audience to recognize the challenge in Sophman's words. It drew breath, a massive anticipatory gasp, held it—hushed, then exhaled a corrosive wind that stung Schlumberger's face, flaking the lines of the mask that had released him, freed him. His slack jaw ached. He wanted to wipe the drool from his lips. Sophman's eyes gazed down at him, slid like a knife edge between the cracks, under the paint, peeling away the mask. Schlumberger's mouth closed. He realized dreamily that he was on his feet, drawing himself up to his full height, squaring away the hump on his shoulders. He felt his hand caught and pumped in Sophman's. The burst of cheers from the audience nearly drowned his voice to his own ears as he heard himself saying, "Thank you." The applause swelled, the audience delighted at the falling away of the last artifice, leering at what it supposed was a man stripped of pretense, naked to its stare. Even through the cacophony Schlumberger heard the scalding, percussive snap of Maelzel's curses, but he paid them no attention. He was struggling with a claustrophobic panic. As he resumed his typical manner, he felt lock around him the granite brow and cheeks and chin of the mask he could not escape.

23 | The Professor's Teeth

"GODDAMMIT, WERA, get my teeph," a voice mouthed wetly.

The knock sounded again as his toes scuttled for their burrows in his boots and his fingers stitched rapidly down his waistcoat. Vera lifted his upper plate between thumb and forefinger from the washbowl and shook it once vigorously. She carried it by the palate arch, held away from her body as if she feared it might grow a ghostly lower jaw and nip her hand. The porcelain counterfeits dripped and glistened in their gold setting like pearls in a garish piece of jewelry. He snatched it from her and was already moving toward the door, cupping it to his mouth like a yawn, when she cried, "Wait." Her unpinned hair sprang out around her head in a stiff grey bush. She was groping at a knot tangled in the hair on top of her head. It fastened a cloth sling that firmed her sagging jowl while she slept. She barely had time to turn her back to the wall as Professor Sophman opened the door, sucking his plate into place with a moist smack.

It was only years later, when he had become an archeologist obsessed with deciphering the secret meanings of his own past, that Schlumberger constructed a narrative sequence for the scrapes and whispers his knock had startled to life. At the time he scarcely noticed that the door halted midway through a flourishing swing; the smile on Professor Sophman's face stiffened, and the teeth lengthened an audible quarter inch without any movement of the upper lip, revealing a thin rim of gold in place of gum; while over the phrenologist's shoulder his portly secretary was yielding to inspection only a humiliated back as she

[1 6 5]

vainly smoothed her plumage. He made no effort to receive or store these impressions. They simply clung to the magnetic field generated by Louise Rouault. Later in his journal he would gather them like a man who has lost something at a fair recapitulating the minutiae of what had been an aimless pleasurable meander, saying, *I stood by this gate during the horse show, and strolled past the cold-meat seller along the shadow of this tent, which fell then just here across my knees, and before that . . .* all the while scanning the ground for the bright familiar flash of a coin, a ring, something infinitely precious. For Schlumberger there was never any question of restoring what was lost. He might only hope to account for the loss itself. Assuming his own culpability as a first premise, he set up mirrors in his past by which he might trap himself in the act that had betrayed him. His mirrors were the eyes of other people. A property of mirror-eyes which he discovered after many trials was that they yielded a true reflection only after he had rendered in his journal their exact shade, counted each wrinkle and blink, and learned them so well he could have told what a sleeping mirror dreamt by watching the microscopic twitches of closed lids. Thus the practice of his narcissism forced him to cultivate the virtues that negate it.

His effort, then, was not simply to find himself mirrored in Professor Sophman's eyes, but to peer through them at himself. Once he could do that, he threw open Sophman's door and recognized that the man standing in the hall gripping the wrist of a reluctant woman was the same one who had tried to destroy Sophman's evening performance. Then Schlumberger knew that Sophman's first impulse had been to suspect another trick. He had learned to expect the tricks which are the lot of any man dedicated to uplifting his fellows. He had begun his career as a schoolmaster in upstate New York, where one evening as he strolled full of moony thoughts down a moon-bright path a gang of youths, his students, flipped a grain sack over his head and dragged him into the wood. Three days later a farmer passing on the road heard his hoarse sobbing and found him lashed to an oak, exhausted by hunger and rage. The community was looking for a new schoolmaster before the October frost. Master Sophman had taken to the open road with a knapsack full of cheap Bibles. He peddled them to farmers' wives, promoting the Word so eloquently it only made sense to promote himself to Doctor of Divinity and preach a revival in the bargain. The Lord confirmed him in his Call by helping him to unload more copies of the Book in three nights of sweating for Jesus in a torchlit tent than he could in a month on the road. He thrived. Then he converted a matronly lady whose apple cheeks and ample bosom slaked a yearning left over from his moonstruck years. Unfortunately he converted her away from a husband and six children, the eldest age seven, and their idyllic passion was periodically dampened by tears for her abandoned babes. She would weep at the sight of an unfledged robin or a cocker puppy or any single child that was not itself in tears or demanding attention. One by one she had loved her own babies, but all of them together drove her to God and the Reverend Sophman. She had been accompanying him at the organ the night he stepped into the pulpit of a Presbyterian minister in a small Indiana community and was denounced by a visiting parishioner, a native of Vera's home town. A few weeks after the pious faithful had beat them and tarred them and released them barefoot at the edge of town, a cultural bee pollinating America with the notions of Europe gave a free lecture on phrenology that converted Sophman from God to Science. He spent a hasty couple of hours studying multi-syllabic scientific terms to replace his multi-syllabic theological terms, and took to the road as Professor Sophman. His lectures were even more inspiring than his sermons had been, but the infidels of science were as watchful as Christians. The first village idiot he phrenologized un-masked himself to reveal a reputable judge. The next was a bank manager, and after that he spotted them every time—except the night he attributed strong powers of concentration to a gentleman who had not said a complete sentence since childhood when he was kicked in the head by a horse.

Schumberger's performance in the tavern hadn't fooled him for five minutes, but seeing him in the hall outside his hotel room puzzled and frightened him. It was half an hour since his last customer had departed bearing a signed scroll attesting the size and significance of his bumps. Professor Sophman steeled himself for the violence life had taught him to expect. Then he realized Schlumberger was accompanied not by half a dozen rowdies reeking of whiskey and righteousness, but by a small, nervous woman with high cheekbones and a jawbone that knobbed high under each ear. The aggressive tilt of her chin exposed a white long vulnerable neck. Tension made her neck cords vee promi-nently toward her breastbone, forming a hollow a tongue could fill. Then, as Schlumberger began stammering his introduction, Sophman understood exactly how he was to earn his twelve-and-a-half-cent fee. He ushered in the new convert, barely restraining an ejaculation on the mysterious workings of Grace. He sucked his teeth back up and said, "Vera, sharpen another quill."

While Schlumberger bowed his head at every mention of a Latinate term, the professor explained that the lady was meek and pious and loved children and home and had enough Amativeness to make her frisky without the threat of an unladylike lust. During one of the professor's weighty pauses Madame Vera raised her eyes from the paper and glanced at Louise. A sense that they had exchanged a sign, recognized one another as members of a secret society, tickled the follicles of Schlumberger's consciousness. He was far too occupied with other things to puzzle over it.

24 | As Flies to Wanton Boys

AFTER LEAVING the phrenologist's hotel room, Schlumberger and Louise strolled down Milk Street toward Julian Hall, where Rouault was in the kitchen making bullets. He poured molten lead from a deep spoon into a small hole in the mold, then held the mold by the handle while the lead cooled. The liquid-filled hollow reminded him of the dispenser from which the priest shook holy water over the casket in a Mass for the Dead. After a minute he split the halves of the handle and dropped the glowing lead ball into a shallow baking sheet filled with water. As it hit the water, it hissed like something alive.

At five minutes to midnight nothing moved on the street. All the buildings had been placed end to end in two neat rows between the cobbles. The shopwindows that had spilled light and the doors that had spilled light and people onto the cobbles were shuttered and shut. The only voices carried from behind thick wood in a backroom of the tavern, where a chorus of basses and tenors strained to reach an impossible sourness of melancholy. Schlumberger's voice was still competing with crowds.

He had begun drinking after the phrenological exhibition, and continued during the two hours it had taken him to persuade Louise to let Professor Sophman examine her. While he drank, his mind had synchronized with the raucous sounds and whirls of the tavern crowd, and now the stillness and quiet could not drag it back to a normal rhythm. At last Louise wrenched her waist from his hug and refused to be bundled and rushed down an empty street. He promised to mend his pace and she consented to put her arm in his, but no sooner were they walking somberly along than he noticed with secret hilarity that the gaslamps lighting the street were bobbing in time with his stride. Slyly, trying not to aggravate Louise, he broke step or bounced on his toes to see if they could be surprised. They matched him trick for trick.

In the dark intervals between lamps Schlumberger pointed out stars to Louise, who kept her eyes resolutely on the cobbles. The stars hung above the street on a dark velvet ribbon frayed jaggedly by chimney tops and gables. Schlumberger's voice soared to greet them. He made the customary analogy between their constant flame and his love.

A constellation of round black balls lay cooling in the baking pan. Rouault picked up the first and began cutting away the pimple made by the hole through which he had filled the mold. He heard Schlumberger hailing Andromeda in time to scoop them all into a leather pouch and scuttle upstairs to his room. He continued his work by candlelight, shaving each ball with a clasp knife to a lethal perfection of roundness.

Later Schlumberger would remember that just as they stepped inside Louise mentioned that it was hardly cold enough for such a big fire in the kitchen. With barely a glance at the embers he steered her to a place at the table, calculating aloud how long it would take them to save passage money to Europe. America had been a mistake from the start, he explained. Not quite the outpost he had imagined it, perhaps, but still no place for a chess player. Busily talking, he cleared the table of the plates left over from supper, the silverware, the glasses, Rouault's forgotten bullet mold and the deep spoon in which he had heated the lead over the coals.

He rinsed two glasses and reached from a shelf a fresh bottle of brandy. As he worked the cork, the bottle vised on his lap between his legs, Louise slid her eyes away, refusing to let her gaze sanction him, still refusing as he poured two glasses full and pushed one across the table with the back of his forefinger till it nudged her fingertips. He chuckled when she curled her fingers under her palm.

"Aw, one more," he crooned. "Then we'll go to bed, I promise. Rouault isn't expecting you tonight, is he?"

"Do you think you had better?" she asked wearily. "It's past midnight. Tomorrow you are scheduled to play Greco."

Schlumberger waved Greco away along with a fly that had tried to settle on the rim of his glass.

"I know why you're angry," he said. "You bet me Professor Sophman was a diddler and you didn't win your bet."

"Umm. That must be it. He certainly described me down to my toenails, didn't he?"

Not catching her tone, Schlumberger smiled.

"Ah, confession is good for the soul," he said. "Now that you've admitted for once I was right, the honey will flow again."

"After all," Louise said, "any woman would purr with pride to be described that way: lover of God and husband and children and home. In that order. I'd love to love them all, but they're so hard to find. Where do you suppose is my home? I've lived in hotel rooms and boarding houses ever since I was married, and they all look so much alike I can't decide which one to love."

"Your home is with me, in Paris, and we shall be there again within the year, I promise you."

"I'm glad that's settled. I'd hate so to have let Professor Sophman down. Now about my children. Only one, I'm afraid. Died the day I bore him. Buried on a hill south of Arles. Couldn't tell you where. I didn't go to the funeral. Sick in bed. I wept, though, while they were shovelling him under. Wept with gratitude that God had spared me the job of nursing a rapist's brat. That was in the days when I still prayed."

Schlumberger stammered the word, "Rapist?" in a whisper.

"Oh, hadn't I told you? Rouault found it hard to believe, too. If I'd told him it was a bird fucked me, he would have thought I was the Virgin Mary. In fact I think he does. It makes him such a pious lover."

Schlumberger struggled to find something to say that would be soothing, but what finally came out was, "Why are you talking like this?"

"Do I need an excuse? I thought you wanted to know *everything* about me. Or is that just something you say in bed? 'What are you thinking, Louise? *Talk* to me. What are you thinking *now?*' And when I've got nothing to say, no little sweet to pop into his mouth, he sighs and his eyes get juicy."

With dignity Schlumberger said, "That was not kind."

"Oh, did I hurt you? But only an hour ago, when I begged you not to make me get my skull measured, you told me nothing Professor Sophman could say would ever be able to hurt me. And you were right, *he* was right, I've just been telling you how right he was. Especially about what a loving and faithful wife the young lady will make. Except I wanted to ask him, William, who is my husband? I've got Henri's name, but a soldier boy was first to have my cunt, and I'm told that counts for something in these matters. But then he didn't mention his name. And then there's you . . ."

"Stop this," Schlumberger said. He was being steady and authoritative. "I know that hiding behind Rouault's back has caused you . . . anguish. More than I realized till now. Before we leave we'll simply have to tell him, explain it. He will have to understand that in the eyes of heaven, the only husband you will ever have is—"

"Is you of course, William," she said with a sweet smile.

Schlumberger nodded, but when she finished his words for him, he was not quite sure that was what he had intended to say.

"We'll go to bed now," he said. "I don't need to finish this." He indicated his brandy glass. Then, reaching his arms across the table, he placed his hands over Louise's wrists and said, "I'm glad you talked like this, Louise. You've told me something I never knew."

"What's that?" Louise asked. Her voice was that of a schoolmaster who expects precisely the right answer.

"I love even the cruel things you say," Schlumberger continued. A muscle in his cheek was jumping like a chained dog. "Because without them I would never know how you have suffered."

"Umm," said Louise.

"Now we'll go to bed. And make love. And in the morning I will meet Greco. And Louise," he said, gripping her wrists tighter, "I want you to know that tomorrow, when I beat him, I'm doing it for you."

After a moment Louise said, "That is disgusting. Let go of me."

"What?"

She yanked her hands out of his grasp. She went to the counter and began scraping and stacking the plates he had placed there helter-skelter, isolating herself in a small whirlwind of work. She seemed to be moving too quickly for Schlumberger to keep her in focus. At that moment he needed desperately for her to stand perfectly still until his ears stopped ringing. He felt at last that he was about to penetrate to her core, but instead of the cool grotto he had expected to find behind her level gazing eyes, he was on the lip of a fiery cavern. With a scalding splash of lava the walls slipped from one grotesque shape to another. Nothing would stay fixed long enough for him to master his giddiness.

As Flies to Wanton Boys

Rouault tapped the butt of the pistol on the bureau top to make sure all the gunpowder was at the bottom of the barrel. Then he took an oil-stained square of cloth smaller than the base of a chess pawn from his patchbox and held it over the muzzle. He carefully placed on top of it one of the newly made balls. With a cleaning rod he forced them both into the barrel to its bottom. Then he inserted a firing cap behind the trigger and cautiously brought the trigger down against it. After he loaded the other pistol the same way, he tried to finish the last paragraph of his letter. It was so important to get the ending right that the words wouldn't come. It was only midnight. He could take a walk to clear his head and finish it later tonight.

For a few moments Schlumberger panted, opening his mouth like a dying fish. Then he closed his jaw tight and squeezed shut his eyes until he had snatched from the whirl a fierce calm, in which he thought of what he must say, fitting the words carefully and eloquently in place as he did when he was rehearsing in his journal one of the spontaneous quips that had been the foundation for his reputation as a wit in the Café de la Régence. Then he opened his eyes and moaned through clenched teeth, "Won't you let me—are you so—what: proud? Can't I give you anything?"

She turned to him clutching the bread knife with whch she had been scraping pork scraps into a bucket, and held it between them as she spoke. Schlumberger did not know whether the wavering point was a threat or a defense.

"Do what you do for yourself," she said. "Not me. Play chess or drink wine or fuck for you. Don't come trotting up to lay bones at my feet. Don't make me responsible."

Schlumberger picked up his glass and shot the dregs of his brandy into his throat and poured again, pouring not quite brimful because he did not trust his hand to avoid sloshing the liquor melodramatically over the rim. His histrionics with Professor Sophman had taught him what actors learn, that only a whisper can steal a scene from a roar.

"By the time of the match I shall be quite drunk," he announced. "You may tell Maelzel it was your fault."

"No, not mine!" she said. She lunged toward him, the knife branjished unconsciously before her in a gesture so like an attack that Schlumberger barely restrained himself from leaping to his feet. "It's you. You will be responsible, not me." And then, with an incredulous wail, she said, "I don't have that power. I don't want it!" Rouault had heard their voices in the kitchen as he came downstairs, but he didn't stop to listen. In a few hours nothing they could be saying would matter. She became aware of the knife in her hands and frowned at it and laid it carefully on the table. There would be no more hysterics. What came next would be calm. What came next was, "You don't want to be a cripple as well as a hunchback."

Schlumberger was aware, even at the moment, that he barely flinched. His eyes went down and then up too slowly for a blink. That was all. And the word *cripple* had shot a paralysing chill through his legs. He matched her level tone, saying, "You are trying to destroy me."

"Impossible. You never were. It's me I'm thinking of. I want something more from life than to be your crutch."

Then, incredibly, she had turned her back on him, was walking toward the door, and the conversation, unless he did something immediately, was finished. And since he could not leap upon her and smash her to the floor because his useless legs would not carry him across the distance widening each moment between them, he dragged himself to his feet with his arms braced on the table, while his voice, after rasping as though a blow had closed his windpipe, at last produced a strangled bellow: "I. Am. Schlumberger. In chess history. My name—"

Standing in the doorway, she stopped him with a single shake of the head.

"Second rate," she said. "Why do you suppose you got drunk tonight, the night before you play Greco." When no answer came, she shrugged. "When you know you will lose, you drink. Surely I don't have to tell you this most obvious, most transparent thing about you." She held his eyes only a moment longer. "Even a phrenologist might have guessed it."

Sometimes after his orgasm, while he lay cradled between Louise's thighs, Schlumberger would raise himself on his arms and look down at her, at the flushed cheeks and lips, the eyes either downcast showing the delicate tracery of a thin blue vein traversing the horizontal folds, or raised to his own, moist as if she were about to cry, and her hair splayed on the pillow between his hands, which he spaced carefully to avoid pinning a stray strand beneath his palm. Sometimes he would stare at her lying beneath him until his shoulders ached and his arms began to tremble, so that he had to come down upon his elbows again, sliding his lips and tongue along her neck under her ear. Then the spasm would ripple across his shoulders and he would withdraw, leaving a last kiss on her breast or belly. It seemed a long while after she left before he became aware of the ache and tremble in his shoulders, and slowly lowered himself back into his chair.

The fly that had been pestering them at supper that evening woke from someplace and made a small snarl as it danced around the oil lamp on the table. It settled on the hot glass and immediately darted away to resettle at another point. And again dart away from the heat. When Schlumberger saw it next, after it had forayed into the shadows beyond the lamplight's radius, it was on the table examining a fragment of pork fat. Later he found it pacing off the circumference of his brandy glass. He made no move at first. Then his hand went out for the glass, displacing the fly, and he carried it, slowly and with concentration, not spilling a drop, to the slop bucket. He emptied it into the bucket. He recorked the bottle and placed it back on the shelf. With the completion of each of these acts, his sense of buoyancy grew. In his slightest movement he was aware of a calm flow. Somewhere out of sight a fly hummed in a surprising cadence. Each move Schlumberger made reinforced the rightness of his conclusion and his decision, which had occurred to him with a faint sensory shock like the first faraway tones of chorusing voices, their rough melody bodying as the men marched closer into the full glory of "La Marseillaise," and his stride back to the table blended with the brisk heroic rhythm that must so many times have transformed into the most graceful dance the casual acts of Bonaparte. A chorus of huzzahs went up as he turned down the wick of the lamp.

He marched to the stairs in the dark, supremely elated in the knowledge that he understood everything that had happened, understood it perhaps even better than Louise herself did. The logic was conclusive. A woman does not give her body to a man she does not love. Louise loved him. The best proof of it was tonight's cruel scene, by which she had risked losing him. It was impossible to be that cruel to someone without loving him. That had been what first nudged him to search for another meaning in her words. Then, with an anticipatory thrill as the faint music first reached his mind, the realization blossomed. She had risked her own happiness to bring home to him "certain truths," he would be writing a few minutes later in his journal, "that I would never have realized without her.'' There would be leisure for writing tonight, since Louise would not be sleeping with him. Not tonight. But that didn't worry him. He did not even hesitate as he walked past the room she nominally shared with Rouault. He knew she would be there, but he would not discover until much later that she was reading the letter Rouault had been composing for her.

Rouault had left it lying on the bed, intending to finish it later in the evening. There was no need to conceal it, because he was not expecting Louise in his bedroom that night. Puzzling through the convolutions of his script by the light of a flickering candle, she was beginning to understand what Rouault was telling her: that by the time she read the paper in her hands, he would have damned himself to eternal flames by murdering Schlumberger and Maelzel—for love of her.

''La Marseillaise'' dinned magnificently as Schlumberger opened the door to his room. Only a brief journal entry, then he must sleep. In a few hours he would meet Greco. He was on the eve of his Austerlitz. His Jena. And after the battle, when she saw how thoroughly he had obliterated Greco, she would know he had been equal to her desperate gamble with their love. Stepping out of his trousers in the dark he placed his foot square into the chamber pot and sustained a nip on the ankle from its sharp rim that stopped ''La Marseillaise'' in mid-crescendo.

And by morning Louise was gone.

PART III

25 | Profile in Black

STILL GROGGY, Schlumberger swung down from the high coach step into a court paved with dung. In the sunless light steaming balls of fresh dung lay atop old dung flattened to a mealy paste by hooves and wheels and feet. The dung was spongy underfoot as spring ice. He yielded his weight to it without trust and rocked groggily, wondering if this were New York, half struggling to get back inside the dream and not sure he'd left it.

Only a moment ago, before a clumsy passenger stumbled over his legs to the coach door, he and Louise were somehow both inside the automaton box. He was preparing for a game: lighting the lamp, setting out chessmen on the board; while behind him she purred softly in a nest of petticoats. Now, as he blinked around the steaming court, a shadow plunged past his ear. A man in front of him grunted, staggering back, fumbling the bag he had just caught as if it were struggling to escape. On the roof of the coach the driver raised another bag and a voice from the cluster of passengers sang out for it. A desolate echo prowled the court, claiming the bag for someone hiding in the eaves. Schlumberger squinted up at the coachman, who had sprouted a pair of sickle-sharp horns as he threw back his head. When he reached for another bag, the points of his curling hat brim dipped, and Schlumberger turned away.

He stepped this way and that through the knot of passengers, looking for a way out. A plank fence boxed the stable yard. Beyond it on every side rose buildings that made the court narrow and deep as the bottom of a well. Clouds just above the rooftops mortared the sky shut. He couldn't tell where the sun was, couldn't tell whether it was morning or evening, because in the first two days he had been traveling he didn't sleep at all, only strained with each lunge of the horses to close the awful gap that had opened between him and Louise Rouault, and when at last his eyes dropped, it might have been last night or five minutes ago.

He felt he was being stared at. He looked up at a wall, clay colored and peeling, where a pair of windows was set like eyes under beetling eaves. In one a grey oval hovered, upsetting the symmetry like a walleye cocked at an empty corner. The oval was a face, staring at him. He started to recognize Louise peering through the grime. Then the shadow under her nose congealed into a moustache. With the new angle of his next step, it became a yawn. Then the face, which seemed to be regarding Schlumberger with pensive sadness, began to float upward, shrinking as it rose to the edge of the window. A pair of disembodied hands followed it, graceful as gulls flapping lazily away, and the window went black. *But she's here,* Schlumberger thought. *She must be here. She wouldn't have waited another week for the Boston packet, and this is the next nearest port where she can board ship for home— and no matter what she wrote, what she wants is what I want: home.* What she wrote was: I'd rather be dead or on the streets than live like this. She had scrawled it in the blank space on the last, unfinished page of Rouault's letter.

He tried to stretch the kinks out of his back. Just as he was peering about for a door, a yawn overtook him and the court squeezed and wobbled in his tears. Beneath an undulating roof horses knocked their hooves against the stalls and nickered mournfully at horses in the yard, which nickered back and tested the buckling of their traces. By the time Schlumberger's eyes cleared, the sun had melted through the clouds and stained them crimson. He thought of the red felt lining in the automaton box, and how in the lamplight it had glowed like the inside of a cheek. In the dream she had been rustling behind him, testing out more comfortable positions in the cramped box.

He was glad, he remembered, so glad she was with him again, but her movements were jostling chessmen from the board. Groping for them in the shadows he heard a sharp distant whinny as he grasped a black knight; neck muscles squirmed between his forefinger and thumb. No sooner had he pegged it between the king's bishop and rook than it galloped off through the ranked pawns. *It's not her fault,* he thought. *It's because they're so skittish.* He was answering Maelzel, who must have claimed the box would be too small for both him and Louise. But the game was about to start. Turning for a glance, a luck-kiss, he saw that in the floor of the box there had appeared a trapdoor opening into a narrow stairwell. As he feared: *Gone—just as the game is starting.* He lowered his head into the hole and whispered her name. Chill drafts moaned up from below. A harness jingled; or was it a teasing giggle?

A wind sighed urgently, but he could not separate the words.

"Hey, is this yours?"

"What?"

"You want this bag, or can I keep it?"

Schlumberger knew the leather creases of his traveling bag as well as the lines branching his palm. Why was his bag hung from that knotty fist with the wart-knuckled thumb? The face leered expectantly, a slender thread glistening at each mouthcorner.

"That's my bag," said Schlumberger.

The crowd around the coach brayed. Every face copied the leer of the youth handing him his bag. Schlumberger must have circled the yard and started through the gate. As he turned toward the gate once more, the driver was tilting over the edge of the coach roof a coffin-size trunk, and two pairs of long white hands swayed up to grasp it. The warty hand clamped his forearm.

"Hey mister, I fetched yer bag."

The leer had become an anxious, ugly curl. The upturned palm concealed the warts. Schlumberger fed it a York shilling to make it go away.

That was the first of the hands.

SCHLUMBERGER KNEW the only rational thing for him to do was to find the South Street docks and check the passenger lists at all the shipping companies to see if Louise had booked passage for Europe. The narrow street the coach yard faced must slope toward the river. A block downhill the street angled sharply, but beyond the sun-coppered rooftops he saw the gently tilting tips of masts. Yet he had an impulse to trust a hunch, turn up the street toward the sun. Now, for five minutes, while the sun still shone, any alley or doorway was the one from which she might appear. Any face among the crowd streaming past might blossom with recognition. Billows of powdered horsedung stung his eyes. A water carrier bearing her yoke of buckets like crippled wings jostled him into the downhill stream, and he abandoned himself to rationality and the riverfront.

He tried to fall into step with the water carrier. The yoke across her shoulders kept him nearly at arm's length. "Is this the way to South Street?" She didn't turn her head or break stride. A strand of hair dangled across her eye, but her hands never left the ropes that hung the sloshing buckets from each arm of the yoke. As she turned into an alley, she said through clenched teeth, "Just stay on Maiden Lane." A block further a triangular building cleft the street. A signpost reading "Maiden Lane" might indicate either fork of the cleft. Bearing to his right, Schlumberger noticed after a few minutes that he was marching uphill. An alley on his left lowered his horizon enough to reveal, far down the hill between converging walls, the needle tip of a single mast. How, he wondered, had he come to be walking parallel to the river rather than toward it?

While he pondered he was distracted by a vaguely sensed discontinuity in the jingle of harnesses and creaking cartwheels and shuffling feet. An unnatural clarity isolated each sound. What was absent, he at last realized, was the sound of human voices, the chatter and warble that might have woven these scratches on the silence into a continuous melody. Aside from an occasional hawker's cry or the curse of a teamster, this vast crowd moved in silence. No one connected with anyone else. In whatever environment he inhabited, Schlumberger had drawn stature from his isolation; even at the Café de la Régence, where idiosyncrasies clung like barnacles to the older chess fanatics, he was considered an eccentric. It was his secret joy to stand apart. But in this mob there was no society against which to stand—only randomly colliding atoms of flesh.

As he stood shifting his bag from one hand to another, a sow trotted fast out of an alley, four dogs scuttling at its flanks. Three of the dogs were good-sized setter mutts that could almost look over the back of the pig, and one a terrier small enough to squeeze under her belly. The terrier worked its legs twice as hard as the others and panted loudly. All the dogs yapped and snapped at the pig, which ported a trunk thick as a pony keg on pointed trotters that arched like the legs of a woman in high heels. Its ears were pink and tender and the rims of its worried eyes were pink and its trot was brisk but steady as if it had a long way to go to get home. When the pig swerved from the wheel of a cart, a black dog with a patch like dirty snow on its rump leapt at its head. The sow braced its forelegs stiff in the road, whinnied as if it were about to break into song, then swung its head like a bull, yanking the dog off its feet. The dog flipped a somersault and thumped down in the gutter at Schlumberger's feet. The sow, its brow raked by a scarlet kerchief, trotted squealing off amid the high excited yips of the two remaining setters and the runt. At Schlumberger's feet the black dog worried between its paws a red shard thin as parchment.

He threaded his way to the opposite stream of traffic and traced his steps back to the fork. By the time he found South Street, the sun was gone. He turned right toward the Battery and entered a shipping company office in the next block. It was a Liverpool line, he learned. The packet, *Independence,* had sailed with the morning tide. No Le Havre packets could be booked from there. When he asked about ships bound for France, the clerk passed across the counter a tight, officious smile and a much-folded newspaper, *The Journal of Commerce*. Schlumberger stared a moment at a headline about silk imports, then looked back at the clerk, who had already tucked his chin neatly between the stiff points of his shirt collar. His chin rested on his puffed necktie like the beak of a roosting hen. Roused by Schlumberger's stammer, he took the newspaper, folded it to an inside page and passed it back, tapping a forefinger at a column headed "Old Line Shipping." Schlumberger learned there were two Le Havre packet lines. Both ships had sailed that morning. There would not be another for two weeks. He asked directions to the Old Line Havre Packet office, which listed a Washington Street address. "North River," the clerk remarked. Schlumberger produced a tone of pleading interrogation and began to shape the air with his hands. "Other side of town," the clerk volunteered. Schlumberger nodded and smiled as if he were perfectly satisfied. The clerk lowered his eyelids, resettled his chin in his ruff. Schlumberger inquired the location of the second Havre packet's office, which was not given in the advertisement. The clerk inquired whether Schlumberger intended to purchase a berth in the next Liverpool packet. Prodded into inspiration, Schlumberger said there was a chance his friend might have sailed on the Liverpool packet. True, he realized, if she were seriously bent on eluding him—and his mind panicked before an abyss of complexities. What was she not capable of?

He scanned the Liverpool packet's passenger list without finding her name. At the door he turned back and asked to see the book again. He drew from the coattail pocket of his greatcoat an envelope so frayed the corners were worn to holes. He slid it down the names on the list, pausing under one and then another, checking their handwriting against the hand of the envelope's address. Perhaps she would have registered under an assumed name. Feeling the envelope between his fingers again recalled to him the lamp in his cabin swaying with the Atlantic swell as he wrung meanings from each line of the letter inside, recalled how crisp the paper had been the night he broke the seal, sitting at his table in the Café de la Régence a few moments before he abandoned his match with La Bourdonnais. *Please come, mon cher, I am surely lost without you.* What was once a voice had become a document, a puzzling artifact with meanings that must be rethought.

All his actions from the moment three days ago when he learned of her disappearance had been sure as a sleepwalker's. But once he admitted doubt, the possibility that he did not *know* where she would be, his only hope became an infinite cunning. He lingered over the "S" of Mary Ellen Sawyer, which seemed to shape the same voluptuous belly on the downstroke as the "S" in Schlumberger. Miss or Madame Sawyer appeared to be one of the few women traveling alone—another promising clue. He asked what she looked like. The clerk shrugged. He described Louise to the clerk, agonizing over the bluish or grey shade of her eyes until the clerk volunteered that the Sawyer lady had red hair.

On the street gaslight burned yellow holes in the darkness. Teamster wagons swayed along, their vast shadows eclipsing distant lights. The darkness whistled and cursed and creaked. Looming into the lightspill where he stood, one shadow resolved into a wagon piled with barrels. Lashed on top where it would have been dangerous to stack more barrels were bales of cotton or wool. A teamster flicked his whip among the horses, barking and whistling, and the drays, straining to outpace the whip, clopped along in the one direction their blinkers left open. Schlumberger fell into step behind them.

With no clear idea of the address of the second Havre packet's office, he decided to continue down South Street toward the Battery, hoping either to stumble onto it or find a more talkative clerk in another office. He planned now to check the lists of all the London and Liverpool packets as well. If he walked into an office where she had been, he told himself, he would know it. He was fighting to regain his certitude, his faith. The Washington Street office could wait until tomorrow. From uptown he heard a frantic clamor of church bells. Shouts and snarling dogs. A fire. Not even the ruddy glow of flames reflected on a brick wall could tempt him back into those twisting streets tonight. He wanted to keep the water at his elbow.

At a wharf where a sloop was still unloading, a hawker offered the workers his wheelbarrow. Schlumberger felt all his own need flow through the coaxing plea: "Half a shillin' then, mates, only a half a shillin'?" How, Schlumberger wondered, could anybody fill the desire to rent a wheelbarrow with so much woe? Men stamping up and down the gangway ignored the hawker. A shadow leaning at the taffrail cursed him through a speaking trumpet. In the light fanning from the open doors of a warehouse a man stood on a hogshead of sugar. A crowd churned around him. He was preparing to speak. His prophet beard bristled, his eye skimmed the fringes of the crowd. He might have been searching out some homely object or action, an exemplum through which to hurl his mighty bolt of eloquence. He would, in a moment, point a finger at Schlumberger, and his wisdom would crack like thunder: "You seek a woman! You shall find her at . . ." A boy scampered from the warehouse and handed up to the prophet a sheet of paper.

"Naow," the prophet said, and the crowd hushed. "Fifteen bar-relspotash," he sang out. "Twelvechests o' greentea, and twentypipes o' sherry, naow—whatamI-bid, whatamI-bid-bid-bid on the potash." And as Schlumberger passed in the darkness the auctioneer chanted, "Twentytwentytwenty, I got twentydollar, who'll gimme twenty-five, twenty-five! Who'll make it thirty . . ." Far down the street, after the wagon he had been following turned uphill, Schlumberger could still hear him, like a child hypnotized by a nursery rhyme: "WhatamI-bid-bid, whatamI-bid . . ." At last the words blended with the lazy gossip of waves sloshing at a pier, slapping and warbling along the hulls of ships snug in their slips.

Circling around a load of barrels stacked in the street at a ware-house entrance, he passed under a bowsprit held up by a Neptune figurehead. It cradled a trident across its naked breast. Schlumberger glanced up into its nostrils. They seemed wide enough to inhale a squall. *Where is she, old father?* The figure nodded stiffly and smiled beneath its beard of seaweed green, wiser than any sea that broke across its eyes.

In the next block Schlumberger found two more shipping companies and checked their passenger lists and described Louise. He learned there was a shipping company two blocks up the street that might be open another twenty minutes. On the way a breeze slipped up his sleeves and down his collar and his nipples rubbed the inside of his shirt. His shoulders ached from carrying his bag. His stomach ached with hunger. He passed an oyster stall, warm and steaming, and almost decided to let the next office go until tomorrow. *No,* he thought. *I can come back in ten minutes. Besides, this might be the one. Maybe it hasn't even sailed yet. We can cross on the same boat.*

On the corner of Cuyler's Alley a small crowd fanned around the steps outside the shipping agent's office. A beefy man with an eyepatch beamed from the top step and squeezed romantic sighs from an accordion. A fiddler one step down sawed out a brisk reel, throwing cocky, triumphant glances over his shoulder at the accordionist. In the street sailors and longshoremen circled round a dancing whore, clapping with the fiddler. Their hands jumped up and down as the woman jiggled her breasts and kicked her legs. She hiked her skirts to her thick, white-stockinged calves and pumped them up and down and kicked clods of street mud off her heels into the crowd.

Seated beside the accordionist was a man in a wide-brim Quaker hat with the tail feather of a pheasant tucked behind the silver buckle. The man squatted like an insect with all the angles of his knees and elbows acute. As he got to his feet all the angles straightened out and he moved to a spot Schlumberger's path would intersect. Under one arm he clamped a black leather portfolio. Below the hat brim's sliding shadow he opened at Schlumberger a spiky black and white grin and murmured, "Cut you?" The tip of a scissors blade flashed in the coat pocket where his free hand hovered, and Schlumberger bolted past him to the door.

The din from the street was so loud it was only after he had closed the door that he heard the chortle of the doorbell. It bobbed and shivered in a small frenzy of welcome, while the occupants of the room ignored him. A balding clerk was poking coals around the fireplace grate, where it was too late in the day to add another log. Behind a cluttered desk a bearded old man was cleaning his ear with his little finger, scrupulously inspecting what he had mined before flicking it onto the floor. Both went on poking.

Then the old man blinked vaguely up at Schlumberger, extending his tooling finger at an elegant angle, as if he were permitting Schlumberger to sample the scrapings beneath the nail. Without a word to break the stillness, he lobbed a glance to his clerk, who as if by instinct rose from his knees by the grate to meet it. The moment Schlumberger saw their gaze meet, he knew Louise had been here. Her presence was unmistakable as the scent billowing from her petticoats as she peeled them down her hips and rolled him back across the mattress.

But he could not make them say they had ever seen her. He rooted in his memory for some detail of her person they would have to recognize. The clerks answered him in headshakes and grunts. He told them about her eyes and hair, the way her nose thinned away from its broad bridge, its constellation of pale freckles. The clerks corroborated one another with wordless glances that convinced Schlumberger they were lying. At his back there must have been a momentary surge of music and clapping admitted along with the lank figure which deftly raised a hand to throttle the doorbell. But Schlumberger was showing them how high against his cheek the top of her head came, remembering the fine hairs that would cling to his beard and lips, giving them more and more, and feeling each time they shook their heads that he had lost forever each part of her he offered them. The words altered the meaning of his memories, made them public, utilitarian. All the marvelous parts got changed into something that made sense. He stammered to a halt, groping for more.

The balding young man nudged Schlumberger aside and took a seat across from the old man. Hair from below the tonsure line swirled artfully across his barren pate. When Schlumberger saw him slap both palms on the desk and ostentatiously drum his fingertips, he felt the pleasant shock of an exile who hears his native language spoken on the streets of a foreign capital. Long ago, it seemed, he had read such challenges and made them. He was surprised only that he had not noticed it before amid the clutter of ledgers and correspondence on the desk: the chessboard. In a moment he had sized up the tactical balance. It favored the old man, but there was one chance . . . He wrenched his eyes away and told them about her habit of swinging by its drawstrings the beaded reticule she carried when she wore her yellow bonnet. As he listened, the old man scratched out the bowl of a pipe. The bald one contemplated the board, cluttered with traps he did not see. His hand drifted out for a move, wavering, and Schlumberger broke off what he was saying and backstepped two paces, his own hand shooting out. It danced on the end of his arm as if it were doing a mesmeric pass. He spun on his heel toward the door, colliding with the man who had been standing behind him. He started to excuse himself, then recognized the man in the pilgrim hat, who grinned and said, "Cut yer silhouette, sir?"

Catching a gasp, Schlumberger shook his head and started to the door. The man's hand snagged in his coat like a hook.

"Look, mister, this is a chance fer you," he pleaded. "Just look at my folder here, I had Gen'ral Jackson himself sit fer me."

"I am very busy," said Schlumberger. "I do not want—"

The man slipped open the flap of his folder and produced a sheaf of heavy papers. He backed in step with Schlumberger's advance until he was standing against the door. To get out Schlumberger would have to move him.

"Now you tell me if that ain't the spit of ol' Andy Jackson. Ain't it now? Look at that jaw, that's Old Hick'ry's jaw so's you'd know it in yer sleep." The black cutting made a jagged hole in the white paper. The silhouette cutter flipped through his papers so fast the black hole seemed to writhe, bulging here, sucking in there, shooting out tentacles that shrank and reformed, collapsing and bloating like a creature that couldn't decide who to be.

"Wait," said Schlumberger. "Who is that?"

The silhouette cutter flipped his papers slowly in reverse.

"That one," Schlumberger cried. "Who is she?"

"Ah, now," breathed the tall man. "Ain't she a fine lookin' woman. You like the ladies, do ye, sir?"

"When did you see her?"

The silhouette cutter knew he was in no danger of losing Schlumberger's attention now, and he brooded over the figure while he considered.

"I cut out that lady just last night," he said. "She was in a line of people right in this office, buyin' tickets for the packet sailed this mornin'."

"She bought a ticket here?"

"Offered it to her when I was done, but she wouldn't buy it. Told her she was such a handsome lady I'd give it away for a shillin', but it's such a fine piece of work I couldn't take less.''

A petulant buzz diverted Schlumberger's attention to the clerks, whom he discovered craning around his body to peer at the silhouette.

"Sure it is," the young one whined. "That's the one who cried."

"Nossir," glowered the other, stuffing his chin into his beard. "Don't look a thing like her."

Schlumberger tried to lift the portfolio out of the silhouette cutter's hands to give them a closer examination, but the artist wafted it out of reach, smiling apologetically as he said, "Three shillin's. That's my usual price. A man's got to eat."

After a clumsy exchange of paper, Schlumberger's currency for the artist's art, Schlumberger lay the silhouette on the desk between the two men. The balding clerk bent over it eagerly. His hair slipped, opening to view another inch of shiny dome.

"For sure it's her," he said. "The one who was twenty dollars short."

The old man twirled a finger in his beard and pronounced his judgment. "She never had a nose like that one." His poking finger jostled onto the paper a black pawn that rolled on its base till it touched the profile's black chin and gave it a strange tufted beard.

Schlumberger addressed his questions to the balding young clerk, who told him while he fingered his hair back into place that a woman like the one in the silhouette had tried to buy a ticket on the Liverpool packet late the previous evening. She had been twenty dollars short of the $140 fare. Yes, he remembered the silhouette artist had been at work that night, but he couldn't say for sure this was the woman to whom he had tried to sell a profile. He was positive, though, that she was "like a twin" to the woman who had wept when she learned the price of a ticket, and asked them to hold the sailing till the last moment.

"Why did she want you to wait?" Schlumberger asked.

"She said she'd be back when she got the money. But she never came back."

Half to himself Schlumberger murmured, "How could she possibly think to get twenty dollars in a single night?"

"Hah!" barked the bearded clerk, his little finger reaming an itch in the deepest, most succulent pocket of his eardrum. "A woman like that?"

And the two men cackled together, their good fellowship restored. As Schlumberger snatched the silhouette from the desk, he raked his forearm across the chessboard. Striding to the door, he could tell by the old gander's howls that he had spoiled a fine triumph.

26 | The Dancing Flame

BART KIRKY, the silhouette cutter, must have wondered whether the foreigner would pay him or try to kill him if he told what he knew about the woman. He had followed Schlumberger out of the shipping agent's office. Standing on the top step outside the door, he watched Schlumberger watching the whore dance among the sailors. The red skirt flicked at their legs. Strange fellow: he wasn't watching her like a man who liked watching her dugs bounce. More like she was a problem to solve. Twice he drifted away, each time in a different direction. Each time he paused just at the point where the general darkness would swallow his shadow, then turned back, yawing by some inevitable accident back to the circle of light and the clapping crowd.

The bag, Kirky would have noticed the bag. *Must be heavy. Gives him a bit of a stoop. Cut a nice profile of that, but it wouldn't do.* You always had to straighten out the bumps, pretty them up. Only way to sell. Shape a line to the life and they'd turn up the nose every time: That don't look like me. He'd learned early how well they paid for a pretty lie. Trim away the bulb nose, the lump of fat under the chin, and they called you Leonardo. That's what made him a successful artist. Only it got dull, cutting the same face every day.

It may have been, given the luscious attention to detail of the seduction that followed, that Schlumberger fascinated Kirky almost as much as the woman herself did. The question must have prickled like an itch: how was that female with her helpless calculating mews connected to this jumpy hunchback? Runaway wife? Not likely: nobody'd peel off three shillings that quick for a cutout of a woman he'd already had. No doubt of it: he wanted that woman bad. Thick wad in his wallet, too. Not for long, though. Nobody who wanted anything that bad would be able to hang onto money. Kirky smiled. He knew about wanting women: walking the streets with a hot prick under your coat; waiting by mud ruts for the ladies to show an ankle when they hiked across. Mostly you could wheedle cunt when you needed it. A promenade on the green, a big sigh with some and a bumtickle with the wise girls, the ones who'd had it already; then you took a stroll to the bushes. But that was how you got chars—scabs on their knees, red knuckles. Sometimes a man wanted a little silk, a spot of powder and paint, a flower-smell to cover sweat-smell, bum-smell. A few pretty lies. And for lies, he knew, you paid.

When you were young, like Crookback down there, you needed the lies, thought you did. The bigger the lie you needed, the more you paid. First you needed the silk and perfume lie, and paid plenty for it. Then you went for the biggest lie of all, the one young Crookback needed: the lie that only one cunt would do. And for that, Kirky knew—thinking of Janice (. . . or Gerty or Jane . . . *his* Janice, he would probably still call her in the third day of a drunk), who had kept him giddy till he was spent dry and then left a note on the pillow saying when he got another stake look her up—for that lie you paid all you had.

The whole wad? Yes, but careful: if he was reckless enough to spend it all, he was reckless enough to be mean when it was gone. Best not be greedy. Best think first: what does he want to hear—really.

The whore's dance had accelerated into a reel, one sailor after another hooking her waist in a tattooed arm to stamp and prance in the mud. She was panting now, she tried to end it, fall into the arms of one man, who propped her up and passed her to the next. She lurched off again, trying to cover her face with a grin. Kirky saw that Schlumberger had edged closer to the circle. The light from the shipping agent's window compassed his legs. Among the milling sailors' legs, it was easy to keep his legs in sight. They were the only ones not moving to the music. What did he want? Kirky wished he would step deeper into the circle, into the light, far enough to show his face. Once Kirky might have thought Schlumberger momentarily returned his gaze, but if he did, nothing he saw could have warned him. The light was coming from over Kirky's shoulders, and his wide hat brim shadowed his face.

The whore was spun away from one of her partners, and skipped with the torque toward a pair of arms that slyly withdrew their promise to catch her. She back-stepped onto the hem of her skirt and sat down hard; then—settling languidly onto her back, nuzzling her head into the mud as if it were a feather pillow—she cocked her legs up in the one resignation she knew they would allow.

The first brays of laughter snapped Kirky's head back. He felt in his brain a seething, premonitory tingle, like the one he used to get when he still worked at being an artist, and would suddenly see the precise *line*—in a palm wrapping a mug, a muscled calf—that would translate from flesh to canvas. The shadows blending Schlumberger's face with the shadowy street and the pier beyond and the black ocean throbbing behind a row of masts no longer hid anything from Kirky. He filled the dark outline of Schlumberger's face with the look he had seen there when the shipping clerks laughed. That was all the clue he needed to create a world that would pass for real. He already knew, I have reason to believe, one chunk of truth about Louise Rouault, and now he had one good lie, too. He started down the steps after Schlumberger, certain which would do him the most good.

ON THE PLANK FLOOR of the shipping office Schlumberger's heel-hard steps had popped like drumbeats. Each stride rapped, "You lie, you lie," at the chuckling clerks. Once he reached the street he stopped walking as if he knew where to go. He drifted back. Under the light the fiddler still sawed and the whore danced and the men one after another dove at her like wolves bringing down a doe. As he watched her, Schlumberger's mind circled the foul old clerk's jibe. It dizzied him. Or perhaps it was only the circling dance that dizzied him. He squeezed shut his eyes: the shadow dividing her pale back shimmered, purposeful as the stalk of a lily. His hands slipped under her arms and cupped her breasts. They were a palpable weight. The nipples rose, undeniable as the third line of a syllogism. That was real. Its meaning was certain as the salt-taste of the hollow under her ear, firm as the bony cradle of her hips, overwhelming as the last releasing plunge. You couldn't buy that meaning for twenty dollars.

But when he opened his eyes the dizziness came back. The ring of sailors thumped their hands as if they were warming them before the flame-colored skirt, which would not hold a single shape long enough for Schlumberger's eyes to rest. He closed them again, tried to see his hand over Louise's breast, the areola circling her nipple framed between his fingers. But the image, which a moment ago had been tangible proof of his reason for standing in this foreign street, explaining with purest lucidity the burning corns on the little toe of each foot, the gnaw in his belly (he had not eaten since dawn, when the coach changed horses)—now that image was pretending it had never existed. Wheeling red comets filled the darkness behind his eyelids. Once she seemed to be hovering just beyond the swirl—he sensed rather than saw the slope of her cheek, the tendon curving behind her knee—but when he tried to bring her to the center, a movement so elementary, so natural, the red comets meshed into a tight spinning wall of gears. He opened his eyes. The dancers would not stop spinning. The whore spun from one man to another, slipping under one pair of arms, permitting a momentary grasp from another, shrugging away from hands that tried to dart under her bodice. With awe, with horror, Schlumberger realized none of them could fill her—not *all* of them.

He had to walk away. He crossed the street into darkness, took a few steps out onto the wharf. Ten paces down a small greenish coin hovered an inch above the pier: the light across the street, reflecting in the flat disk of a rat's eye. The rat allowed him to approach another three steps, then disappeared over the edge of the pier, straight down, it seemed, into the water. But there was no splash. No sign it had ever existed. Schlumberger began to shiver. Far out in the Atlantic a wind had remembered it was November. On the choppy waves a point of light flashed like a wolf's tooth. It was unthinkable, what the old clerk had said. But she was gone: that was unthinkable. To understand it you had to let yourself think the unthinkable. Starting the moment he had arrived from France—why had she made him wait so long? What had he ever known of her? One night last week as he was dropping off to sleep at her side—drifting out of himself gently as he had a few minutes earlier exploded out of himself—she rolled away from him toward the wall, and he lay motionless until he felt her jerk and catch her breath and shudder, and when he put his fingers to her cheek he felt the tears and said, "What's wrong? What is it?" but she wouldn't tell him, and the next morning she wouldn't tell why there were four welts leaping to her hip from the dark curls of her groin. Why? Why had she gone?

ALL THE ANSWER he had was what he had found in Rouault's

room. The morning after the visit to the phrenologist he had overslept breakfast, trying to sleep through his hangover, and spent a couple of hours in the automaton box rehearsing end games with Maelzel, so he didn't begin to miss her until she wasn't there to make lunch. Rouault hadn't joined them for their usual noon meal either. Maelzel cursed them both and left for a restaurant. Schlumberger remained in the hall alone, trying out combinations against one of Philidor's end games, expecting her any moment, because they had not slept together the night before, and occasionally in the long afternoons she would come to his room to make love.

At three o'clock he found himself listening to the silence throughout the house. Half an hour later he broke through the first layer of silence, and the house began to whisper its complaints: the pigeons nesting in a broken slat of the attic vent; the split beam groaning in the parlor ceiling; and the rats, those two in the cellar that spoiled the butter, gnawing at the panel behind the kitchen cupboard, the splinters filtering down between the walls until the hole the black tip of a nose fills today can tomorrow pass their lean bodies to the grains and sugar.

After another fifteen minutes Schlumberger walked to the market district, hoping to meet her on the street. He came back after a quick tour of shops, expecting to find her waiting. Only the house had waited, the silence. He walked through the silence opening doors: kitchen, parlor, workshop, his own bedroom. Expecting only silence and emptiness, he did not knock before opening the door of Rouault's room. One glance at Rouault told him she was gone. He was sitting on the edge of the bed staring at the floor. His bare feet curled on the floor like tools he didn't know how to use. The weight of his shoulders bore down on his chest, wedging it into the swell of his gut. Between his spread thighs his hands hung limply. He might have been sitting like that for hours. He made no sign of surprise or resentment at Schlumberger's intrusion. He went on staring at his feet a few moments before he looked up, blinking. He didn't seem able to focus the ten feet to the door where Schlumberger stood. In the silence that had grown suddenly more oppressive by his awareness that Rouault sensed it, heard it, too, he said, "Where is she?"

Rouault did not stop blinking.

"Then why, damn you?" Schlumberger said. "If you don't know where either, then tell me why."

KINGKILL

Along with the croak that might have been a laugh, Schlumberger caught a minute tilt of the head. It directed him to a sheaf of papers strewn beside Rouault on the counterpane. He didn't wait for an invitation, and Rouault didn't try to stop him. The top page continued a clause that spread to other clauses and conditions referring to something begun on the previous page which Schlumberger did not bother to read because it was in Rouault's hand. Angled across the blank lower half of the page Louise's large copybook hand spilled out of control. The proper loops and swirls were straining against their center of gravity, breaking every few letters into a chaotic freedom: the downstroke of the first *d* bloated grotesquely; a *t*-cross slashed over the next three words; the final word an impatient slur. The message was like a hoarse voice struggling to shout: "I'd rather be dead or on the streets than live like this."

Schlumberger pulled up the collar of his greatcoat against the sea breeze. "On the streets." Unthinkable. But that she was gone was unthinkable, and her own words confessed the possibility of this new unthinkable fact. Beyond the pilings the ocean churned its salty musk, governed by currents born where no explorer had penetrated. His teeth were clicking. It was like losing a game. You had to rethink every move to discover when you stopped being in control of what happened, when the moves began to mean something other than what you had planned. He remembered the first time he had watched her shrug the chemise off her shoulders, the crescent shadows of her breasts riding her ribs like dark twin smiles against the ivory pale the moonlight gave her body, and he thought, *That, too. Whatever it meant is changed. Nothing has only the meaning it had the moment it happened. Any chess player knows that. His move modifies yours; her move. Any fucking chess player. And you thought when you left Paris you gave up games for good.*

In a few moments it became too cold to stay on the dock, and he rejoined the circle of men around the dancing whore in time to see her prone in the mud with her legs pawing the air like a beetle flipped on its back. When he noticed the silhouette cutter walking toward him, there was nothing he was not ready to believe.

27 | Men of the Sixth

WHAT REMAINED after the fiddler stopped sawing was not really silence. The ring of men had closed like a contracting iris upon the place where the woman went down, but their hoots and bellow jammed the air. And on the top step the accordionist the fiddler had drowned out was still pumping a thin romantic wheeze. His voice was even thinner, a faint hum under the accordion hum, easy to mistake for silence until his squeezing arms faltered or some pressure in his lungs burst and a word or phrase throbbed out: ". . . all my dreams . . . by the blue waters of . . ." But all Schlumberger could hear was a silence like the silence in Julian Hall three days ago, when he knew without yet knowing it that Louise was gone.

A minute ago the silhouette cutter had touched his arm and started writhing his lips. His face wrenched into grins that must have been meant to be reassuring, his hands were smoothing the air, puffing it into strange shapes. When the fiddler lifted his bow from the strings, the words that had been coming at Schlumberger from so far away were at first too near to hear. They were a raspy whine in the silence. Then the whining silence began releasing words like bubbles from a fish's mouth, and Schlumberger was being told perhaps the silhouette cutter could be of some service to him.

It was about the lady. Not wanting to intrude but: a nod to the flame-colored skirt. You like the ladies, sir? *Triangular flashes of flame kept changing shape beyond the scissoring legs of the sailors.* Yes, the lady. Obviously distressed. Delirious talking. *Pinching between brows a fold of flesh:* Two or three places she might have. Yes, quite willing to assist. An inquiry here, a visit to. But first perhaps. *Taking a breath, then gingerly, retractably:* Only a few blocks uptown and huge steaming oysters. *Assured now, the lilt of authority:* To some agreement on terms.

And though the name he said she'd mentioned (Leland? Lemans? Leblanc? Kirky tried them all with a halting air, watching closely Schlumberger's eyes and lips) conveyed no hint or hope, Schlumberger reasoned that he didn't know what name she might choose after discarding the rest of her self, and he let the tall man lead him into the city.

Schlumberger followed haltingly, his feet testing the darkness for jutting cobbles, water-filled holes, clumps of dung. Now and then they entered the nimbus of a gaslamp hovering just over their heads like a phosphorescing sea creature. Schlumberger heard the sinister hiss behind the glass. One pace beyond the lamp his shadow was squeezing from under his heel squat as a dwarf, and four strides later it was a lanky giant being sucked headfirst into the dark. Three stories up, beyond the lampglow, the buildings warped toward each other over the street. The wind in the gables rattled like Schlumberger's fa. er the night he died. Clouds lowered onto the rooftops and dribbled into the standing puddles. The puddles uncoiled sluggishly and slid along in gutters and ruts, points of light winking on their backs and on the seeping walls. Sometimes from a far wall Schlumberger heard a slosh or cough. Once a shapeless bulk lurched against him. It staggered off, snarling.

At a place where the path between ruts narrowed, Kirky nearly edged Schlumberger into the water, and he dropped behind. He couldn't catch up without breaking into an undignified trot. He was exhausted and hungry. His shoulder would begin aching half a minute after he shifted his bag from the other hand. He followed, keeping his eye on Kirky's bobbing shoulders. His Quaker hat had a dent in the crown, Schlumberger noticed, that tilted the tip sideways. It seemed to be pointing down every alley they passed.

They had not penetrated more than a few blocks when Kirky fell silent. Every few minutes he would toss a one word remark over his shoulder, but the rising wind from the ocean made his voice leaf-thin and gusted it away. The narrow canyon of buildings funneled the wind. They raised their greatcoat collars against it and the collars flattened to the backs of their necks as if they were wet silk. The wind worried the coats' loose-flapping skirts. *Maybe he doesn't like to talk against the wind,* thought Schlumberger. But he was uneasy. Kirky seemed to need all his concentration to find his way.

Schlumberger tried to calculate the number of intersections they had crossed; how many turns they had taken. He had a vague idea he might have to find his way back alone. Back to where? No place in the city was home. He didn't even have a room for the night. Back, then, to the shipping agents' office, where he had felt that presence like a perfume, an echo.

None of the mnemonic tricks he used to locate himself on a chessboard worked here. No grid of ranks and files crosshatched into symmetrical squares. Short blocks alternated with long randomly or according to laws he was too tired to decipher. There were no right angles: streets intersected like shards of broken glass. Cross streets exerted a mysterious stress on the trajectory of the main street, first tugging it into an obtuse arch, then cracking it back on itself. Rounding a corner was like tracing the outline of a fang. Kirky would veer to the left, apparently turning off into a strange street. A minute later a trademan's sign would tell Schlumberger they had never left Pearl Street. Or had in some unaccountable way returned to it. Then he realized that for the past five minutes the wind had no longer been at his back, but in his face. Was Kirky leading him in a circle back to the river?

As he was about to challenge Kirky, they heard fire bells clanging on the wind. From the mouth of an alley a hum swelled to a bellowing Hosanna. Kirky flattened himself against the wall as a double line of running men, perhaps fifty in all, spewed whooping and catcalling from the alley, dragging by two thick ropes a firewagon pumper. A man bucking along on its back was cursing into a megaphone whenever he could catch his breath. Behind him came another line of firemen racing ahead of a spooled hose on wheels higher than a man's head.

"Volunteers!" shrieked Kirky. "Sixth Ward crew! Toughest crew in the city!"

The window of a building down the block reflected a throbbing orange glow. Catching sight of it, Kirky punched Schlumberger cheerily on the shoulder and sprinted off. Schlumberger trotted after, tucking his bag under his arm. Some ten yards ahead, Kirky disappeared down a side street just as Schlumberger heard a melodious thud, and a moment later he rounded the corner to see another pumper, rammed broadside by the one that had just flown by, tilt up on the edge of two wheels, balance there a lazy miraculous moment, and collapse onto its side like a shot steer, gushing water from a split plate. The number of firemen seemed to have doubled but the only one who took notice of the accident had his leg caught under the pump handle. The others were busy dancing around each others' swinging fists and kicks or wiggling in red-shirted knots on the cobbles. The foreman, who had apparently leapt from the pumper just before the collision, was scrambling among the grunting red bodies looking for his megaphone.

Schlumberger saw him dart between the legs of a white-eyed horse to retrieve it. Then he jumped back onto the pumper and put it to his lips, screaming, "Get 'em, boys! Show the bastards who handles fires in the Sixth Ward!" He was trying to strike a wide heroic stance, but he had to shake his leg every few seconds to keep off a hand that was clutching at his boot. At last he leaned from one of the polished brass pumping arms and aimed a round kick that missed by inches a bareheaded old man in carpet slippers who wore a pair of spectacles with the glass in one frame smashed to a blind star. The old man gave up trying to get the foreman's attention and pried at a red shirt astraddle the chest of another red shirt lying in the street. The one on top was kneeling on the other's biceps and rhythmically hitting his face, which lolled with the blows, offering each cheek in turn. The old man wandered from one clot of firemen to another and at last climbed the steps of a house where Schlumberger could see flames jumping in a ground-floor window like children wanting to see out. The old man opened the door, stood patiently aside while yellow-black smoke billowed out like hastily departing guests, and as it began to clear, entered the house. He emerged carrying a scroll-back armchair patterned with patriotic eagles, which he placed in the street. Next he brought out an armload of clothing. A few spectators, neighbors apparently, attempted to dissuade him from a third entry. The roof beams had been cracking ominously and the garret window flashed bright orange. The old man shook them off. He came out, staggering and weeping from the smoke, carrying a footstool on which he had placed a humidor lined with pipes and a tinderbox. A fat woman in house robe and nightcap who had been standing at the foot of the porch steps emitting regularly spaced shrieks followed the old man onto the street, beating his shoulders with her fists while he drew the armchair around toward the flaming house. She shied away after he raised a threatening backhand, and he sat in the chair, stuffed a clay pipe and sparked a wick from his tinderbox, his hand trembling slightly as he held it to the bowl and the tears perhaps no longer entirely from the smoke. His pipe firmly drawing, he was well settled in the armchair in the street among the battling firemen—horse dung and mud now quenching the proud flame of their shirts—when a section of roof collapsed, and the sudden splash of sparks raying among raindrops moved the crowd to a unanimous moan of aesthetic delight.

Within another few minutes one team of firemen had driven their rivals from the field and connected a hose to the pumper. Men strung on either side of the water tank were trying to synchronize their seesaw pull-and-release on the pump bars to the megaphoned bellow of the foreman. The hose man was juggling a stream of water toward the flaming hole where the roof had collapsed. The sporadic frenzy of the pumpers shot the water out in bursts that either splattered against the wall five feet below the hole or spent their thrust in the air and sprayed gently over the crowd. Some boys stoned out the garret window to make a more accessible target. The crowd sent up a cheer when it saw water pouring accurately into the flaming window.

From somewhere near Schlumberger a voice of sated resignation said, "It's all over now the roof's gone. The rain will put it out." A minute later Kirky laid a hand on Schlumberger's elbow and said it was like this all the time. Some part of the city was always burning, and if you harked to the bells, you could watch three or four buildings go up in a single night.

He was right: twice again as they walked, Schlumberger heard the clang of church bells calling the faithful to their devotions.

28 | Schlumberger Visits the Oracle

AND LATER in the hotel room, sitting in the stuffed chair drawn up to the window so he could stare down into the rain-grey street where he still kept looking long after he gave up hope of recognizing her among the pedestrians below, he would remember they must have crossed Broadway after they left the fire. As they came out of a side street onto a well-lighted thoroughfare, Kirky grabbed Schlumberger's arm in a grip hard with civic pride and said, "Eighty feet across, and at midday it's worth your life to step off the sidewalk." On the other side they had slipped into a crevasse in the solid wall of buildings and walked in the dark to an alley that connected after a time with the street of colored globes. The windows of all the houses on the street were lit up as if there were a party or a death in the family, but Schlumberger needed to wonder about that only until he noticed over the doorways the gaslit colored globes ornately lettered with names like KATIE-DID and CRAZY JANE and SINBAD SAILOR. Some of the windows were translucently curtained so that shadows could be seen undulating on the rippled surface. At the uncurtained windows women stood or sat in strong light looking out on the street as if they were waiting for someone to come home. Kirky put two fingers in the corners of his mouth and whistled a shrill greeting to a woman in a yellow gown. She called out, "Is that you, love?" but Kirky only gave a laugh like a hungry bark and walked on.

Schlumberger even remembered that the globe over the door where they clopped down five steps and knocked had read STOUT PEG. And he remembered the crowded saloon where the air and cigar smoke had been in and out of so many other lungs it smelled like moldy hay and had to be swallowed down. Kirky had nodded and waved and spoken to half a dozen people before they came to an empty table. Schlumberger sat down and looked under the table for a place to put his bag that wasn't covered with tobacco juice or gobs of well-masticated chew. While Kirky was still craning around and snapping a finger in the air to signal a waitress, Schlumberger said, "Surely she's not here?" and Kirky said, "It's not that simple," and whistled a girl from the bar.

"No Canal Street plan tonight, Bart?" she said, and Kirky told her tonight he would eat sitting down. Without consulting Schlumberger he ordered oysters and whiskey for them both.

Behind the bar Schlumberger saw a gilt-framed painting of an eye-patched, parrot-shouldered pirate with a wooden stump below his scarlet greatcoat. He was about to ask Kirky, since he apparently couldn't yet ask what he truly wanted to know, if the house was named STOUT PEG for the pirate's wooden leg, when the waitress returned with their whiskey and he heard Kirky say, "Is Peg about tonight?"

"Oooo, business tonight," cooed the girl, and Kirky drew her down to whisper something in her ear. *That's when I should have known it,* Schlumberger would think, watching drops of water inch down the hotel windowpane. *Right then, when I saw the way she looked at me before she went off to talk to the woman.* She had rounded her eyes and lips at him the way some people do to show enthusiasm for the ideas of small children, and as Kirky continued whispering she left the look frozen on her face as if she had forgotten about it while her eyes raked Schlumberger up and down till the skin next to every pocket where he carried money itched. Then she broke into a giggle Kirky stopped with a movement Schlumberger couldn't see, that sent her twitching off through the crowd to a corner table where an enormous woman in pink silk was rolling a cigar in her lips. As the waitress bent to her shoulder, the big woman cupped behind her ear a hand wearing a fingerless glove made of some black silky material that fit skintight all the way up her forearm and squeezed out a huge shapeless white bicep. Schlumberger even remembered Kirky saying, "Peg will tell us what's what," though he had not taken his eyes off the woman, who was blowing cigar smoke from her nostrils onto the wobbling ledge of her bosom. The women's corset pushed her breasts up and squeezed them together in a cleft tight as a pair of buttock cheeks. Nodding slowly as the waitress talked, the big woman took the cigar from her lips and held it out as if to examine it, and even through the blue haze of cigar smoke Schlumberger felt a shock like cold water seeping into his boot at the moment when the woman's eyes, without changing direction, refocused on himself. *It's the same look,* he thought. *Only this time with something like pity along with the amusement, the avarice.* And then, *I always thought it would be the men who were weighing and pricing in places like this.*

And he asked again, "Are you finding out if she has been brought here? To this place?"

"Drink first, friend," Kirky said, downing his whiskey and whistling for another. "Then we can talk."

The oysters came with the third round of whiskeys. Kirky taught him to dip the oysters in whiskey and cock back his head to suck them from thumb and forefinger. The texture was slimy at first, and when he tried to chew he would find the meaty kernel slipping onto his tongue or into his cheek like something alive, but he was so hungry he swallowed a few whole and told Kirky he could feel them splash into the whiskey. Kirky laughed and Schlumberger began to like him and feel confident that he was engaged in negotiations that would soon have dozens of sympathetic people ranging the city in search of Louise Rouault.

And that was where his trouble remembering started: he would try to get hold of something Kirky said and it would slip away like the muscled meat of the oyster sliding under its skin.

"It quite often happens," Kirky was saying at one point, "that unattached women"—and he gave a disquisition on what he meant by unattached, which was, he assured Schlumberger, nothing at all disreputable—"unattached women will find their way to Miss Peggy's establishment."

His tone was reassuring and faintly pedantic, as if he were a professor dispelling a sinister superstition attached to what was in reality an odd but innocuous fact of natural history. Schlumberger found himself trying to recall if the lecture was in response to some question of his or if it was a part of some train of thought Kirky had initiated or if he had simply snatched it up as it floated by on one of the floating tables. He had to blink and stare hard at a table to make it stop floating.

"But I thought you *knew,*" Schlumberger interrupted. You said you *knew* where she went after she left the shipping agent's. Are you only guessing, then?''

''I have definite knowledge,'' Kirky said with a vague nod.

Schlumberger couldn't remember how many times during the intricate narrative that followed Kirky's walnut-wristed arm shot up and another brace of glasses appeared on the table. It seemed Louise had burst into tears when she learned the price of the ticket, but Schlumberger couldn't later be certain Kirky had told him that, because he had also heard it from the shipping agent. Kirky had been on hand, it seemed, cutting silhouettes of customers in the quay, and offered his assistance in finding what at first seemed to be an address mentioned by the lady herself, which turned out at a later point of Kirky's explanation to be no fixed address but merely a night's lodging anywhere, which eventually funneled down to Kirky's admission that he had either directed the lady or brought her himself to Stout Peg's.

''Here?'' Schlumberger remembered saying. ''You brought her *here?*''

And Kirky had pushed his palms in Schlumberger's direction as if gently to contain him, and told him soothingly about the lady's obvious distress and the difficulty of finding suitable lodging after a certain hour in the evening and the high repute of Miss Peg's disinterested benevolence in such cases. And Schlumberger had a distinct memory of focusing hard on one idea: *I can't hit him until after I know everything he will tell,* and saying, ''Where is she now, this minute? Is she here, in this building?'' Then Kirky left him and Schlumberger watched him through the smokehaze and floating tables and milling people conferring with the big, cigar-smoking woman, both of them from time to time aiming glances at him. *That look again,* he remembered thinking, but by then he was no longer afraid.

There was a confused argument about money. Schlumberger recalled telling Kirky the price of the supper was an outrage, but Kirky explained there were other expenses involved and Schlumberger at last understood that an introduction to Stout Peg customarily involved the payment of a substantial fee, and Kirky named a large sum of which he said he would be content with a fraction, which he named. ''But she's right over there,'' Schlumberger protested. ''I can just walk over like you did a minute ago.'' And Schlumberger saw Kirky's hand dive for the pocket where his scissors glinted as he said, "Oh no, friend. If you want her to talk to you, you *must* be properly introduced."

Schlumberger didn't remember surrendering the money or his parting from Kirky, whether Kirky had actually accompanied him to Stout Peg's table or simply steered him in that direction before he loped off through the crowd, a head taller than anyone else there and two heads taller in the high-crowned Quaker hat.

There followed another intricate conversation with Stout Peg, whose eyes sliding in their fleshy pockets made him think of oysters, and another surrender of money. Then he was with Stout Peg in a scarlet-draped parlor where half a dozen women sat on chairs and divans and one by one got up and glided past him smiling, and he kept shaking his head, saying, "No, no, that's not her," and describing Louise Rouault in all the detail he could recall, and at last, exasperated, he said, "Don't you understand—I don't *want* a woman." He thought he must finally have made himself clear, because the next thing he remembered was winding interminably up a stairway behind the hollow-clumping feet of a shapeless crone who held the candle in front of her so he had to stumble in her shadow up more flights than he could count and down a hall to a door, which she opened for him and closed after him.

The room was silent. The gaslamp was turned so low it barely illuminated its own globe. The dirty yellow globe hovered above the table like a full moon. A wide circle of shadow skirted the floor around the table. Beyond it Schlumberger made out a stiff-backed sofa, a bed stripped to the sheets, and a window where a female figure stood facing the dark outside. Long moon-colored hair hung in ringlets on shoulders that seemed knobby and frail.

"They said you can tell me where she is," Schlumberger said.

"I can tell you—" began the strange voice, and her head turned not far enough to see him but far enough to rest her chin against one of the knobby shoulders and let him examine the fine straight profile, the nose straight and high-bridged, the chin plumb with the brow; and then the voice, throaty and toneless, giving him only the words to inflect however he might, continued, "—anything you need to hear."

Schlumberger took two steps into the room. Hovering a few inches in front of the lamp globe was an orange rose big as a sunflower. When he forced himself to blink, it retreated to the globe, where the orange color seethed with an angry hiss until he relaxed his gaze and it lifted free again and hovered contentedly in front of the globe. But the hiss in Schlumberger's ears didn't go away.

"I'd like to sit down," he recalled saying, and he must have done so because after that he remembered being on the sofa listening to the woman's toneless voice. She was still at the window but she had turned her back to it and was leaning against the curtain. As she talked she moved her back against the curtain as if she liked the way it felt on her bare shoulders. Her dress was a muddy purple, but the shiny material caught light from the globe and slid it along her breasts and belly as she moved. It was tight enough to leave no doubt of her profession, but high necked with a prim white ruff about the throat that made him think the distance she still kept between them was not coyness but reserve. *Even here,* he thought, hearing the cautious toneless voice, *in a place like this. It's still possible to keep some dignity.*

It was that dignity then, that he addressed himself to, and the soft glow in her eyes that the purple gown made luminous, and at some point as he spoke the eyes seemed to detach themselves as the rose had from the globe and float free of all context, a condensation of pure sympathy. He told the eyes the whole story, going back to Paris the night he saw her climbing out of the machine with her breasts swinging toward him and perhaps further back than that, because there was something about his father dying, and once he even unfastened the traveling bag at his feet and rooted among his shirts and socks for his journal to check the date of her last visit to his Paris apartment, as if he needed documentation to prove she ever existed. He took out the hinged oak box that opened into a portable chessboard, and showed her the black king modeled after Bonaparte. This set went with him everywhere, he said, and with his thumb rubbing the heavy swell of Bonaparte's shoulders, he told her about the strange instant of calm when you know there is nothing to do but watch the wobbling sun till you hit ground, and how before that tumble from a swing his back had grown straight as anyone's. The attempt at thoroughness might have been what garbled his meaning. A long time later, with her beside him now on the sofa, her slender arm arched along the back and her slender, long-nailed fingers sliding under his collar at the back of his neck, she said, "I can be any woman you want."

Which wasn't what he wanted to hear.

That moment, at least, he remembered clearly, as if in the current that had swirled him along ever since he let Kirky lead him up the hill into the dark streets, this snag had given him one close look at the bank before he was again swept away. He looked at the woman, at her thickly painted face. *She must be old,* he thought. Her cheeks and lips were bright as fever under a heavy yellow-orange powder that coated her face well back to the jawbone under her ear. What he could see of her neck wrapped in the high starched muslin was tautly corded. *And not pretty either,* he thought, making out through the powder the deep pores across her nose bridge where the hair had been plucked. Only the shimmering violet eyes seemed capable of a life independent of the mask. The sympathy he had addressed himself to had given way to an impatient flicker, and Schlumberger abruptly realized that what she had just said was not a reply to what he had told her about Louise, not even a comment on it, but an offer prodded by some obscure need flickering behind the painted mask.

Even then he didn't understand Kirky's joke—or Stout Peg's. Yes, it might have been only hers. It seemed possible now: three days later, with the raindrops nudging one another down the windowpane and the gaslights in the street outside his hotel window coming on and three days of walking under his heels, three days of peering into faces on the street, trailing after skirts and rushing to get ahead of them so he could get a look at what was framed by the blinkering bonnets, and turning away from the strange faces not even noticing after a while the startled jumps the women gave at his urgent stare. But at the time it could only have been Kirky, who had known from the moment he led him up that street that if he put him together with Stout Peg that was where it would end. Maybe he had been too tired to understand what the purple-gowned woman was saying, had been saying all along, because he stayed there beside her, his neck cradled in her hand, until the face, the mask, came close to him, the lips parting over his own, and he saw beneath the painted jaw the pinpoint bristles of beard, and the full point of Kirky's joke.

He got his feet under him fast. His lurch raked the wig askew. Its flaxen cascade over the right eye might have been coquettish, but the exposed left ear had a ripe squash outline and a hole sprouting hog bristles.

Schlumberger Visits the Oracle

"You could have just told me you didn't know," Schlumberger said.

Suddenly, as with one of those *trompe l'oeil* drawings in which a shift of perception reveals once for all that the child's hoop is also the left eyesocket of a skull, it was not possible to think of the one in the purple dress as anything but a man. Sprawled on the sofa, he fumbled at his wig. A moment ago, fully inside his mask, both hands would have been fluttering about, flashing the pale underside of the wrists as they patted and stroked it into place. Now he simply spread one palm over the skullcap and twisted it straight. Then he smoothed the hands over the dress, trying to put something pert and birdlike into the defiant look he gave Schlumberger. But his body couldn't believe it any more. His fluttering eyes and puckering chin tried to promise tears, but behind the mask of rouge and powder the man's face confessed itself so abjectly that Schlumberger wanted to apologize.

But when he said, "Didn't you hear anything I said?" it sounded like an accusation. He caught the accusatory tone himself before the man on the sofa could answer it, and tried to complete his first intention. "I mean, don't you . . . can't you see . . . the hair is nothing. I mean, sometime the dress would have to come off, too, wouldn't it? And the kerchiefs or socks or whatever you stuff inside the breasts would—"

"No lectures, please," the man said in a trembling voice much deeper than it had been. "Just go, if that's how you are about it."

Schlumberger didn't know how many times the man had to tell him. It seemed much later when he was standing in the open door, feeling if only he could explain it right, something important would be resolved forever. "Don't you see it yourself?" he was saying.

"We're not going to understand each other."

"How can you think this will—"

But the words Schlumberger needed didn't come, and he was only mouthing air when the man said, "Just get on the other side of my door."

29 | Fireboy

HE KEPT STARING out the hotel window at the street long after the mud-grey drizzle had thickened to black night. He wouldn't have recognized her now. He couldn't tell if that shadow gliding past a rain barrel was woman or man.

But the window connected him with the life of the street. When there was no longer any place he could think of where she might be and he was exhausted with tabulating how many women spied a block away had hair or a dress or a familiar head-down pensive way of walking that counterfeited hers, he returned to the hotel and sat at the window. It was a way of not giving up. A day ago he had seen her driving past in an open carriage, deep in talk with a fat woman who might have been Stout Peg, and he yanked up the window and cried out, "Louise! Wait for me!" And then, "Come back, Louise. I'll never find you." But neither woman looked up and he leaned far out the window to watch the carriage round the corner onto South Street before he drew his head inside and closed the window and controlled his breathing enough to think, *She has never done her hair like that. And it was the wrong color.*

Until it got too dark to see, he had been watching people pass in and out of buildings on the other side of the street. Where he sat he could see a coffee house, Floyd's Cooper Shop, a ship chandler's and Gaylord's Grocer's. Women never visited any store but the grocer's. It was a man's street close to the waterfront. Sailors and longshoremen cruised the sidewalk alone or in restless phalanxes that ricocheted from the chandler's place to the tavern under Schlumberger's window. Men often loitered outside the coffee shop, leaning against the wall. For hours men would lean there in a langourous trance, shifting only the leg they would draw up to prop a foot against the wall behind them. Despite the chill they opened their frock coats and tucked the skirts behind the hands tucked in their pockets so people could see their bright silk waistcoats. All their waistcoats were patterned with flowers or hunting scenes or maritime scenes. On some of them gold chains hung from one pocket to another. Pearl and jewel pins anchored their cravats. They puffed out their bright waistcoats like the chests of competing birds.

At first when the men noticed Schlumberger passing on the street, one or another had offered him tobacco or tilted back his head or the brim of his beaver hat to let him see his face. A few spat tobacco juice near his feet. Others would circle their lips with the tips of their tongues. One grinned as if he had known Schlumberger a long time and was only waiting for him to remember where they had met. After the first day they ignored him.

It was the evening of his third day in the hotel. The steady grey rain that had been sifting through the streets since dawn drove him inside at dusk. He was relieved to find the tinker had gone. Last night an itinerant tinker had been booked into the room with him. "What happened to your face?" he said, and tried for the next hour to penetrate Schlumberger's silence with his grating chatter. The quiet and a bed to himself would be a luxury. He had hung his greatcoat over the brass footrail of the bed. His clothes clung to his skin and smelled like a wet dog. After he had poked up the coals in the grate and sprinkled fresh coal on the flames, he pulled off his boots and hung his wet socks and trousers over the footrail. Then he wrapped himself in the counterpane and drew up to the window the room's one chair, a high, narrow, thinly stuffed wingback. When he rested his head against the back, he felt the wings were about to clamp around his temples.

He noticed the tips of the street poles glowing. When had the lamplighter passed? He tried to estimate how long he had been sitting in the dark. An hour? Two? Long enough to stiffen his calves, which ached when he stood. He drew the bedside table up to the window and lit the oil lamp. Then he sat again in the chair, bathed in light like the women on the street of colored globes. Even with the street lamps lit, he couldn't make out faces below him, but the connection with the street wasn't broken. *When she looks up,* he thought, *she will see me like this. Wrapped in this cloak.* The light inside the room made the window glass an obsidian disk on which his own face floated. Hair was still rain-plastered to his forehead. The shadow of his nose concealed the purple-yellow bruise under his right eye. But the light shone full on the left side of his forehead, where a two-inch gash opened through his hair like a strange red mouth. A ripple in the glass twisted his split lower lip into a leer.

Why couldn't that have been the end of it, he thought, *that closing of the door? That would have been enough.* The man in the purple dress had at last realized that he didn't have to be afraid of anyone who would stand in his doorway for ten minutes evangelizing about some woman who had taught him what love is. "Go fuck her then," he said, and slammed the door, closing Schlumberger into the dark hall. Far down the corridor a candle burned at the stairhead. A draft from below made the flame writhe and dodge. The bracket was so high on the wall the light barely reached the floor. The only other light came from slits under the closed doors. They traced a path to the stairs. Sometimes they seemed to be floating at eye level or tilting upward as if Schlumberger were climbing a ramp. When he got to the stairhead he saw a dead moth mired in the tallow bowl. He groped down the stairs. A candle burned on every second landing. The lightless landings were black tunnels.

He didn't remember how many candles he had passed before he missed it, realized that all he had in his hand was the journal he'd hauled out to check a date, to confirm more for himself than the man-woman he was talking to that he lived in time, owned a past in which Louise Rouault been real—and the bag where he carried the journal was still lying unbuckled at the foot of the sofa in the room he'd just left. For a moment he thought he would simply go on without it. He didn't care about his shirts of shaving tackle. Or even much about the bag itself, though he had lived out of it for six weeks during his Atlantic crossing, and carried it up to Paris four years ago, a present from his father's brother, who along with his mother had put him aboard the coach with his dead father's legacy money to make his fortune in the city. The leather, once shiny as a buffed boot toe, had been scuffed and gouged in the luggage holds of half a dozen stagecoaches since then, and when he opened it the leather wrinkled into lines as familiar as the comic grimace his father used to pull while he puzzled out a difficult combination.

There were only two things in the bag he wouldn't rather replace than go back for: his book of Philidor end games with Schlumberger's own notes so filling the margins that his name might justly have appeared on the title page as co-author; and his Bonaparte chess set. Since the money had evaporated, the chess set was the only remainder of his father's legacy, found in the old man's bureau in the echoing stillness of his room the day after he had ceased forever to inhabit it. Even while he still did inhabit it, lying stone still after that last thrashing convulsion, his eyes closed, jaw tied shut, the crucifix folded into his hands over his breast, the first thing Schlumberger had thought of when he saw the candleflame bounce on his waxy balding crown was the drawer where the old man's treasure lay snug beside his linen.

So he had to go back. His feet thumping up the steps sounded far away, like someone in another part of the building pounding to be let out. On every landing the smell of urine pinched his nostrils. There was no handrail. The backs of his fingers skimming the wall to steady him touched a mossy seepage. He wiped them on his greatcoat. Along the hall he turned down, night sounds filled the dark. Behind the first door a fox barked. Further along: a whirr like battering wings surrounded and stifled a hysterical gobble. Near the end of the passage a heavy sea moaned up the strand and broke and fell back. The door he knocked at was opened by a woman naked to the waist, panting slightly, who asked him with poised, businesslike politeness to wait a few minutes. Behind her on the bed a beefy man with ash-grey skin and epaulettes of hair on his shoulders sat with a pair of trousers over his lap and cursed. The cursing kept on after the door shut Schlumberger into the dark again. He heard it halfway back down the hall.

At the stairwell he leaned against the wall by the candle, trying to decide whether the room he wanted was up or down. Far below him feet thumped and a fiddle skipped along on an endless repetitive reel. A wave of nausea stiffened him to the wall. For a moment he saw himself letting go, floating into the darkness down and down, head over heels in long slow somersaults. He squeezed his eyes shut until the dark stopped spinning. Then he twisted the candle out of its bracket. Hot wax spilled onto his waistcoat and trousers. His hand burned with it, but he held onto the candle till the wax cooled. The wax curling around his fingers hardened, welding the candle to the hand. At the top of the next flight of steps he saw the dead moth in the tallow bowl and knew this was the right floor. The candle in one hand, his journal in the other, he walked down the hall and knocked awkwardly with the hand that held the journal.

"You've got my bag," he said when there was no answer. "You've got to let me have my bag."

The silence on the other side of the door pretended to be the silence of a room that is empty. Schlumberger reasoned with the slab of door. He told it the bag contained his clothes, all he had, and personal items of no value to anyone but himself. He offered it money, explaining how little he had. The silence of the room beyond the door was absolute; he began to doubt. He wandered away a few steps, locating himself in the hall, and then back, convinced that the silence lied. He rattled the doorknob, knocked harder. Kicked.

"Are you afraid, is that it? I won't hurt you. I only want my bag. It's if you don't open that you ought to be afraid. Do you hear?"

He kicked the door hard. The silence beyond it confirmed to him that he was not alone in his fear, that fear could be his weapon. He imagined the shallow breathing, the rigid muscles, the helplessness of the petticoated man. He smiled.

"You can't get away with this, you know. You think if you don't open, I'll have to go away. But I'll be back. And next time I won't have any trouble finding the right door."

He held the journal under his armpit while he groped in his pockets, muttering obscenities and threats that began as a strategy designed to frighten the thief, and rapidly became a rasping chant synchronized to the pumping of his heart. By the time he found in the deep pocket of his coattail the key to his Paris apartment, he was no longer forcing the rage into his voice, and as he used the key to slash a huge X in the doorpanel, he was shouting, "Think you can hide from me? You titless, cuntless shit hunter. Go on, play the woman—see how you like it when I rip off your nuts."

Down the hall doors must have been opening, someone must have scurried downstairs for the bulky, potato-nosed man posted in the bar to run out the ones who thought Stout Peg's whiskey and women were charity gifts. Schlumberger never heard him thumping down the hall. He was on his hands and knees stuffing wads of leaves from the empty back pages of his journal along the doorcrack, saying, "That's all it will take: a minute. You've got that long to open up—or roast in there.''

A slight tilt of his head made an interesting change in the face the hotel window reflected: the ripple which lifted its lips in a gloating leer turned them upside down. They made a gross sad-clown pout. Schlumberger rocked his head back and forth to see how rapidly he could make the face slide from hilarity to pathos. The most hilarious thing he could recollect was that he had imagined his threat to burn down the door was a bluff. He only realized it was not when he saw his hand patiently holding the candle under the crumpled paper until it darkened and a tiny flame skipped along the edge. It burrowed where the edge twisted under the door and puffed out all along it in shoots like ivy climbing a wall.

The first kick hit his wrist and the candle streaked toward the ceiling. The next one tried for his gut and struck his forearm, because the kicked wrist had already clamped to his ribs and his body was curling around it to welcome the bright impossible pain. The candle stubbed out hitting the floor, and someone was smothering the burning papers with a blanket, so the shadows helped him squirm away from the wilder kicks and he kept his journal tight over his groin. After a heel bounced off his forehead he tucked his head to the wall under his shoulder and took many kicks on the hard knob of his hump. The potato-nosed man devoted so much skill to the hump he must have thought, in the shadows, he was kicking Schlumberger's skull. When the chucker-out had satisfied his professional pride, he and someone else dragged Schlumberger sobbing down the hall and balanced him on the edge of the stairs until he toppled. They picked him off the landing and balanced him on the next flight. Teetering on the top step, he was planning how he should pitch onto his back to let his hump take the sharp edges of the steps. *I'll be a turtle,* he thought. *They can't hurt turtles.* It was like his moment of vertigo as he stood by the candle peering down the stairwell. Only Schlumberger wasn't floating.

He came to with his cheek in the cool mud of an alley puddle and something jabbing his ribs: a jutting cobble, he thought, and dragged himself a few inches on his elbows. The pain jabbed again as soon as he lowered his body. He rolled onto his side and put his hand to his waistcoat pocket, where he had put the black Bonaparte from his chess set after showing it to the whore. A few minutes later, when a man found him vomiting over a rainbarrel at the mouth of the alley, he was still repeating the last words he remembered hearing. "The crazy fucker," he croaked. "He tried to burn the place down." His voice mimicked the chucker's bewildered rage.

THE MAN WHO FOUND Schlumberger was a good Samaritan who believed in the rewards of virtue. He wiped blood and grit from Schlumberger's face with a handkerchief dipped in the rainwater Schlumberger had vomited in, dabbing tenderly at the raw places and saying, "Ow, ow," every time Schlumberger grimaced. The he took Schlumberger to a hotel and talked the clerk into admitting him. While Schlumberger, bloody, moaning, cradling his sprained wrist against his cracked ribs, stood by rocking on his heels, the Samaritan explained that he was a gentleman despite his appearance, and had money. To confirm this characterization he looked a little anxiously at Schlumberger, who nodded and began palping around for his wallet while he went on moaning. The clerk said he would accept two nights' payment in advance, and the Samaritan helped Schlumberger find the pocket where he kept his wallet. He lifted it from his fumbling fingers to count out the money and then scrupulously, under the clerk's eye, replaced the wallet in Schlumberger's pocket.

After patiently signing Schlumberger's name in the register, correcting and recorrecting the spelling because Schlumberger took a sudden interest in accuracy and insisted on the *c* between the *S* and the *h,* the Samaritan was about to lead Schlumberger off to his room when he refused to move. The clerk, it seemed, had handed the Samaritan the key with the comment that he had assigned Schlumberger a quiet room facing the rear alley where he could rest undisturbed. Schlumberger insisted on a room facing the street, which the clerk protested he didn't have. "You've got to have one," he explained, smearing blood and mucus into his moustache. "If she's out there, I have to be able to see her." After some mediation by the ever-patient Samaritan, the clerk found Schlumberger a front room where the management had not yet found time to replace a windowpane shot out by a street reveller. It was really only a small hole, he explained, which they could easily cover with paper, but the gentleman occupying the room had insisted on being reassigned because the ball had grazed the tip of his ear.

The Samaritan helped Schlumberger up the steps, explaining that it had been three shillings for the room and twenty shillings for the

Samaritan's time. "That's fair, isn't it?" the Samaritan earnestly demanded. He wouldn't let Schlumberger drop onto the mattress until he moaned that it was fair. "Sure it is," said the Samaritan, pulling off Schlumberger's boots for him. "Lots of folks would have just took the money and left you there. In that alley. Lots of folks."

He woke up the next afternoon. When he began to stir, the mud that caked his hand over the journal lying against his breast cracked like an old scab. That night he was back on the street looking for her. He asked directions to Stout Peg's oyster saloon and stood trembling in an alley across the street, watching everyone who entered and left. At nine that evening Bart Kirky's Quaker hat bobbed up the steps from the cellar entrance. Schlumberger hobbled after him, holding his ribs. "Kirky," he called, but the pain in his ribs kept him from putting much breath behind it. Kirky was loping down the street. Schlumberger sucked a deep, rib-cracking breath and gasped, "Kirky." The silhouette cutter crouched as if he were about to run, but when he saw pain crawling on Schlumberger's face, he swaggered up to within ten feet of him.

"Where is she, Kirky. Please. Tell me."

"Well, well," sneered Kirky, "the fireboy himself. You'd better not let Peg see you out here. She'll sic Yonny on you again."

"You know, don't you, Kirky. You can tell me."

"I can't tell you nothing, fireboy. I'm in bad trouble myself. Peg damn near keel-hauled me. She don't like me bringing in people who try to burn her down. It ain't good manners."

"Just let me see her, Kirky. I've got to talk to her."

"See who, fireboy?" he laughed. He started walking away.

"Kirky, I'll kill you," Schlumberger shrieked.

Kirky turned back and ambled to within a yard of Schlumberger, who was holding his side and keening with each exhale.

"Look at the killer," he said. Then, a slender alloy of pity threading his mockery: "Why don't you give it up."

"Please," Schlumberger whispered. "Take me to her. Got to talk to her. Only a minute."

"You mean your thieving little bitch?" he said. "She's gone. She pawned my watch to buy her goddam ticket. I hope her fucking boat sinks."

And his long scissoring legs bore him off into the crowd much faster than Schlumberger could follow.

HE MUST HAVE NODDED for a moment; when he lifted his head the ripple in the windowpane had shifted from the mouth to the brow of his reflected image. Where its eyes should have been, the creature floating in the darkness had a crease of bulging flesh. It was a certain, blind and bulb-browed. Schlumberger shifted his chair so that his face was in front of the bullet-shattered windowpane, which was covered with newspaper that didn't reflect anything. The wind rattled the paper against the glass like the breathing of a consumptive.

In the past day Schlumberger sometimes doubted whether Kirky had ever seen Louise. He unfolded the silhouette Kirky had made of the woman in the shipping agent's office, and examined each line. It could have been any of a thousand women. Then, wavering in his disbelief, he considered Kirky's last words. They had an authentic sting that made it easy enough to believe Louise Rouault had filched his watch to buy a boat ticket. If it were true, Schlumberger had missed her. Finding Kirky again would bring him no closer to her. She had escaped Kirky as she had escaped Schlumberger and Rouault and whoever else there had been.

And how could he follow her back to Europe? The money for his own packet berth had evaporated. Barely enough remained for another few nights' lodging. Suddenly he sat up straight: even if Louise had money for the crossing, she hadn't gotten it in time. The packet had sailed without her, and there wouldn't be another for nearly two weeks. That meant she must still be in the city. Somewhere. Anywhere. In a hotel. He need only check the hotel registers. As he rose and opened his arms, letting the counterpane drop to the floor like an old skin, it did not occur to him that the elements of this new possibility had always been present, lurking in the wings like a fifth-act messenger until he required it in order to go on hoping. Hope made easy bargains. All it required of him in exchange for what it gave was that he cast aside any doubt that Kirky told the truth about a woman stealing his watch and that the woman whose silhouette he had cut was Louise and that she would choose no other refuge than a hotel in no other city than New York. His clothes were still damp, but he slipped his wrist gingerly down the sleeve of his frock coat and blew out the lamp, buoyantly hopeful.

In the next two hours he checked the registers of five hotels. On the way back to his room, he realized he had not thought to check his own hotel's book. Hope flickered up again. She could be in the same building with him. One floor down. At the next door. He hurried along, his arms pressed against his ribs. Perhaps she had even seen him. He might return to find her waiting in his room, running to embrace him. *No* he thought. *It won't happen.* He remembered those first nights after she left Paris, how on the walk home from the Café de la Régence he would work himself into such a froth imagining her there waiting for him that he leapt the stairs three at a time and threw open the door and spent the rest of the evening pacing off the walls in his empty apartment. He forced himself to walk more slowly. He made up his mind as he scanned the registration book that even if she were in the same hotel, she would use an alias he would never recognize. Not a single female name resembled the hand that had written his name on the envelope he carried. He didn't bother looking at the last few names in the column.

But as he mounted the stairs, it was more than the climb that shortened his breath, and he started down the hall with his heart athump in his throat. Surely the fire in his room must have burnt by now to its coal: why was there such a strong bar of light under his door? Inside the room someone coughed. *It's another peddler,* he thought. Just another stranger booked into the room to destroy his privacy for the night. His key rattled in the lock. As he swung open the door, a stab of feeling—perhaps neither hope nor despair but only exhaustion—brought tears to his eyes, and he stood at the threshold, blinking to contain them. The stranger had not lit the lamp, but the fire in the grate was stoked ruby bright. The chair had been moved from the window to the fireplace, its flared wings blocking his view of the one who sat in it. All he could see through his swimming eyes was a hand on the armrest, a bare calf angled gracefully toward the fire, the glow laying a warm golden ribbon along the shin. That rainy day she came to his apartment for her final chess lesson, the day he first kissed her, Louise had extended her bare ankles to the fire. He approached the chair. A familiar voice crooned, "Willie, boy—I came for the money you stole."

Maelzel's gold-flecked grin gleamed in the firelight.

30 | A Question of Honor

THE SMELL of the room, that unique musk by which an animal takes possession of its burrow, had become Maelzel's. The smell blended expensive sherry and Havana tobacco with an undercurrent of damp wool. Maelzel's greatcoat was flung across the bed, its sleeves spread to claim it. His frock coat slouched over the brass post on the headboard, topped by his beaver hat jauntily raked, as if a sleepy sentinel had covered his eyes for a snooze. On the hassock at the foot of the bed his traveling bag yawned in the abandon of total privacy, a shirt tail lolling over the lip. His boots snuggled before the fire. There was no place for Schlumberger to sit.

On the back of the hand that lay in Maelzel's lap a branching blue vein tracked through a bristly foliage and submerged between the four bald knuckles. As Schlumberger watched, the hand lifted, the forearm pivoted from the elbow out across the chair arm and the palm uncoiled toward Schlumberger, the fingers ready to curl around whatever came their way. "Will you pay me now, Willie, or do we go to the police?"

Schlumberger regarded the palm. The rosy firelight tried to disguise its pallor, but if he touched it, he felt a grainy chalk would fill the whorls of his fingertips.

"There's no question," he said, "of its being a police matter. I fully intend to repay you."

"Then do so."

The hand remained rigidly proffered, like a grotesque variant on the command to kiss the bishop's ring. Schlumberger stared at the muscle bulging below the thumb, and heard his father saying, "You cut this one,'' flopping the slippery trout across the board, and when he cut, imitating the old man's expert slice from anus to gills, the eggs had spilled from the swollen belly onto his fingers.

"You must understand," Schlumberger said. "If I had the money to repay on demand, I would not have borrowed it from you. But I fully intend, once I am agai settled in Paris—"

"Let us speak for a moment, Willie, about the word 'borrow.' " Maelzel crossed his legs, settling himself for a lecture. His trousers were pulled halfway up the calves, which protruded like hairy tusks. "I know you are a gentleman, Willie, and gentlemen do not steal. A fact of nature, is it not? But my room was entered by stealth. It was ransacked, my cashbox discovered beneath a pile of books on the floor, the lock of the cashbox forced, Willie, forced," (the square clipped forefinger wagging under Schlumberger's face was scrupulously manicured) "and a large sum of money removed. To the police this is not going to look very much like 'borrow.' " (How delicately the hand could fondle the grease-smeared rods and wheels of a machine.) "They may even question, Willie, whether you are a gentleman at all."

"In that case," Schlumberger began, and gulped, breathless to hear what words would come to his lips, because this *mechanic* had just called him a thief and in that case you were supposed to force that bubble of air trapped so painfully against the base of your throat to burst with denial in case your honor might in that ". . . case, you may show them the note of honor I left in the cashbox." Of course! and he breathed again, knowing he was not could not be a thief. "You may point out that a thief would have taken *all* your money, and would not have left you a note for precisely the 175 dollars he took. Nor would a thief have offered interest on that sum." Which proved him an honorable man, would prove it irrefutably if he could only say it without that silly tremolo, and he concentrated on eliminating the erratic flutters from his larynx as he said, "And I much doubt that a thief would have signed his name. The only circumstance in which the police could mistake me for a thief is if you have destroyed the note. Have you?"

"Tut, Willie," said Maelzel, accenting his amusement with a circumflex heist of the eyebrows. "I, too, am a gentleman. And it is not possible to beat off the shyster wizards of Ludwig van Beethoven and the Imperial Viceroy of Italy—as I in my time have done—without acquiring a small fund of experience in legal matters. Despite your elegantly worded note of hand, you must concede that, in law, a loan requires the consent of the lender. Which you did not get."

Schlumberger turned away, a gesture which might have had some force if it had carried him to the door, but the chill, the damp and his painful ribs and wrist made it for the moment necessary to endure any indignity rather than return to the streets. He took a few decisive steps, which brought him to the inside corner of the room. In the wallpaper's endlessly repeated filigree he detected a toothless blind lion wearing a symmetrical fringe of whiskers and a crown. Someone had tracked a mosquito to one of the eyeholes, leaving a brown blood splotch in which was glued a single leg small as a hair. He turned to face Maelzel, who was sipping sherry.

"I was in a dreadful hurry," he stammered. "And you were nowhere to be found."

Immediately he recognized the abjectness of this defense, and flushed, and found himself wondering why he was acting as though he considered this discussion of the slightest importance, when all he really cared about was—

"One more point, Willie—your note was 130 dollars short."

"You know that's a lie," he cried, a righteous timbre restored to his voice. "I only took what I needed to get back to Paris and keep from starving on the way."

"Did you really? Then why is it that prior to your loan I had nearly 600 dollars, and I am now reduced to less than 300? Not counting what I had to spend on coach fare following you here."

"I took only 175 dollars. This is a filthy game you are playing."

For a moment Maelzel narrowed his eyes at Schlumberger as if he were aligning a painting with the vertical drop of the corner where he stood. Then he said, "Do you know—I think I believe you," and loosed a shrill cackle. "Hah! What a pair you make, trooping one behind the other into my bedroom after your scrupulously precise *loans*."

"Do you mean . . . did she—"

In order to draw Schlumberger from his corner, Maelzel had only to cast into it the faintest shadow of Louise Rouault. Without willing it, without even thinking it, Schlumberger found himself standing directly before Maelzel, who did not deign to raise his eyes above the third button of Schlumberger's waistcoat as he said, "Of course, William.

The bitch had no more money than you. She was not quite so greedy as you, but then she did not leave behind a promissory note. Perhaps she thought I owed her a dowry.''

"You talk as if she had run away with a—''

Schlumberger had carried the thought this far before he realized he didn't want to complete it. He could only wish it had never occurred to him. An inexorable law dictated that a piece once touched must be moved.

"—run away to get married," he said.

"Married!" Maelzel replied. "You are indeed a gentleman. The refinement of your language is—''

"Don't play with me," he shot back. Behind him the fire crackled and hissed as if it were breaking the bones of a small bird. An erratic draft made it puff and fidget. The shadow of Maelzel's nose darted from one cheek to the other. In the firelight the face seemed to melt and reconstitute itself as if a wind were flipping the pages of a book too rapidly for Schlumberger to read. One moment he read the sly wisdom of a lynx; which melted into a lecherous owl with a mad yellow stare. To make certain of the expression he dropped to his knees before the chair. "If you know something," he said, "tell me. Don't smirk and quibble about words." The threat he tried to put into his voice broke into a raw moan.

"Quibble?" said Maelzel. A delicately sculpted trace of indignation flared his nostrils. "If you choose to call it marriage when a bitch goes into heat and trots off to fuck on the street corner—''

Schlumberger sprang for the throat. Perhaps he had not been kneeling at all, but waiting in a crouch for words he knew he would hear, because his lunge seemed to uncoil a fury he had been straining his whole life to release. In midair, his own bellow rushing with the wind in his ears, he felt his back snap straight, the hump that bent him groundward broken at last, opening his body into a shaft of pure rage hungry to sink in that arrogantly wattled neck. As his hands met Maelzel's throat, even before the fingers could tighten their grip, the bellow rose to a howl. His swollen wrist sustained for an instant the force of his leap, then burst into pain. His wrist and elbow buckled like an unstrung puppet. As his head thudded against Maelzel's breastbone, the chair rocked on its back legs and made a leisurely backward dive. Before it dumped them both on the floor, Schlumberger felt even through his pain

KINGKILL

the unshaved bristles under Maelzel's jaw scraping his cheek. A grunt
broke in his face—a pungent alloy of tobacco, sherry and decayed meat;
a whiff from a lair full of half-gnawed carcasses. The scrape and smell
fused with his pain and all the pain that was to follow the way his
memories of Louise in Paris blended with the *recoule, recoule* of
pigeons on the roofs of the Rue St. Honoré.

On the floor he gargled a cry and tried to thrash and flop toward the
wall. He wasn't thinking of the chucker's kicks—he had simply become
an experienced victim. But with still another yard between him and the
wall that would shield his face and groin, his legs drew up for the final
thrust and refused to uncurl. He put his cheek to the floor and tried not to
breathe, hugging his elbow to his cracked ribs. The slightest movement
would open his side and spill out coils of pain. In his other arm he
cradled the sprained wrist. He let out his breath carefully, sucked it back
a fraction at a time, and let it escape again. The pain ebbed.

Then from some place near the lower wall of his stomach an organ
he had never imagined secreted a strange creature, a live thing that rose
through the meandering caverns of his body, and no matter how hard he
tried to keep it down, it burst from his throat like vomit. Then he
sobbed. At first, choking in his own mucus, he imagined he was
weeping because of the pain. Then he heard himself blubbering, "She's
gone, dead, on the streets, gone, gone."

31 | A Lesson in Natural History

SCHLUMBERGER HAD NOT, I think, immediately recognized that his search for Louise Rouault was finished. In the first minutes of the conversation, he had responded to Maelzel's jabs out of habit, with all his old arrogance and craft, just as if there was something about his honor as a gentleman that was worth defending. Now, while he heard through the sound of his own huge sobs Maelzel rasping and hacking and spitting in the fire, Maelzel setting the armchair back on its legs, Maelzel kicking the broken wineglass into a corner, he realized that long before he discovered Maelzel rather than Louise sitting by the fire, he knew she had been cut out of his life like a gangrenous limb. He had known it the moment the whore on South Street began pedaling her legs in the air. As the sailors whooped and cheered, he had shivered, unable to approach or look away, until the silhouette cutter tapped him on the shoulder and said, "You like the ladies, sir?"

He had known at least since then, and maybe since the night he arrived in Boston, from the moment she had stamped into the parlor at Julian Hall, spraying raindrops from her scarf as she flicked it off her head, and turning, seeing him there with Rouault, she had put that cool, formally polite smile on her lips and nothing at all in her eyes as she said, "Monsieur Schlumberger. How nice of you to come." As if he were a neighbor from three blocks away who had dropped in unexpectedly and perhaps a little inconveniently—not a man who had traveled six weeks across three thousand miles of ocean because she had written a letter saying, "Please come."

[2 2 5]

Sometimes, perhaps often, there are gaps between the moment of an event and the moment the mind begins to experience it. Later, trying to understand it, he remembered how calmly his mother had gone through the familiar motions of preparing a late supper for his three younger sisters after the last guest had departed, how all the regular evening rituals kept their appointments as predictably as the swing of the hall clock pendulum—the washing of dishes, the bedtime bickering of Yvette and Marie, Anne's search for a clean nightgown in the dresser drawer where it had been placed only that morning, and the night prayers in the late summer twilight, followed by Yvette's nightly question, "Does God love everyone, *Maman?*" And his mother's voice, flowing evenly, patient as if it had not made the same reply to the same question each night for a month, since four-year-old Yvette began grappling with the mysteries of theology, saying, "Yes, my sweet." "Then why does he let us be so sad?" And the voice, never faltering from its reassuring steadiness, "God has prepared mansions for us in heaven. On earth we must bear a little sadness." The only departure from that evening's ritual had been that William, the oldest, the only son, had not been sent to bed shortly after the girls. Filled with his new responsibilities, he sat up in the parlor with his mother, trimmed the lamp for her, which he usually did not do, and strained to engage her in grown-up conversation, chatter about the livestock, the disposition of the family textile business. "I'm concerned about . . ." he would begin, and outline with grave pauses and a fretful sucking of his teeth that he had learned somewhere an intricate practicality he thought his mother might be comforted to know he had not forgotten. And she would nod her head, acknowledging or submitting to his need to mention the poor quality goods that were being transported to the Paris retailers, and reply with the same tone of patience and reassurance that she had used with Yvette, "Yes, William, something must be done." And when at last he rose and stretched dramatically and halted halfway to the door as if he had just recollected something trivial enough, and said offhandedly, "By the way, I don't suppose . . . now that everything's over . . . would it be proper for me to just . . . ," her voice had maintained the same flowing calm, as if she had been waiting for the question the past hour, as she said, "Yes, William, you may fetch it."

And how casually, with what weighty tread, trying to create for

A Lesson in Natural History

her—and for himself as well, he was to realize—an auditory illusion that nothing, nothing had changed, did he mount the steps to his father's room, cross to the bureau without a glance at the empty bed, open the third drawer, and without disturbing the fold of the linen draw out of its resting place the hollow, hinged box, barely rattling the heavy-shouldered Napoleons, the low-bodiced Josephines, the befringed marshalls and bayonet-ready pawns. His heart bumping against his throat, his breath coming in heavy, irregular bursts, he wanted to open the box and set them out on the bureau top, inspect them all instantly in the flickering glow of the candle that had lit him up the steps. But a strange impulse made him turn to the bed he had refused to notice when he entered. He left the portable chess set on the bureau and walked with the candle to the side of the bed farthest from the door. There, in the narrow space between the bed and the wall, as if it had concealed itself deliberately from all other eyes for him alone to discover, was his father's meerschaum, flung off the counterpane in the turbulence of his last convulsion. Schlumberger picked it up. It was half-filled. The brittle shag retained the concave impression of the forefinger that had tamped it into the bowl. He placed his own forefinger into the bowl over the concavity. His nostrils caught a faint whiff of the apple slice which kept the bedside humidor moist. The pinch of tobacco in the bowl of the meerschaum could not have left the humidor more than two days ago. It was already quite brittle.

Perhaps it is always this way—that some incidental thing, a pipe of stale tobacco, wedges into the fissures of habit the one irrevocable fact that transforms your life. You open the door of your lodging as you have on all the other nights. You adjust the wick of the lamp as though you had not expected it to be already burning, lit by another hand. You put the teakettle on the stove without mishap, only now and again pawing empty space rather than the sugar spoon. Perhaps you unfold a newspaper, your eyes slide down the tight, narrow columns assuring you that order still prevails. The clock ticks and strikes a little louder than usual, but you will not be bullied into retiring before the usual hour. Only when you at last are sitting on the side of your bed stifling a yawn do you blink away the yawn tears and your eyes rest on a shoe curved to the ball of a particular foot; or a hairbrush, its tenacious bristles snarled with a few dark strands that have somehow, by some inconceivable horror, become keepsakes.

KINGKILL

In the pipe rack on the humidor there was one empty space. Schlumberger inserted the stem of the meerschaum into the hole and went back to the bureau for the chess set. He reminded himself to close the door quietly and remembered just in time that his steps going down the hall should betray no eagerness or elation. His mother would have to find out in her own way that everything had changed.

FOR A LONG TIME before Schlumberger began making any sense of Maelzel's words, he was conscious of a tender purr. Contrapuntal moans made a duet with his sobs. Then he felt strong hands gripping him under the armpits. He let himself be lifted and gently settled in the armchair. He let Maelzel give him a red bandana handkerchief to flush his nose and wipe his eyes and moustache. He let him holler down the stairway for a basin of cold water, and ease him out of his greatcoat and frock coat. He let him peel back the sleeve and adjust the swollen wrist in the water basin on his lap. He let him holler again for a brace of glasses and bring the brimful glass of sherry to Schlumberger's lips as if he were feeding an infant. And he let Maelzel talk.

My God, look at you, Maelzel told him. Not just the wrist, but that lip, that gash on his brow, had they been treated? Where had he got such a beating? And he rattled on, not even waiting for Schlumberger to bother not to answer, telling him he understood everything now, and would not have been so goddam crude if he'd known how Schlumberger felt about the woman, and he knew all about that because he'd been young once and had a few sparks left yet. But he had just assumed that Schlumberger knew what everyone did—that some women had a box so hot it made your prick burn. "Just like an old man pissing," he chuckled, "but you don't need to worry about that for a while, Willie—you wait." And when you meet one like that, you stick it to her all you can in the time you get, he explained, but *God!* don't make the mistake of expecting her to be there tomorrow, too. Why, hadn't Rouault ever told Schlumberger he'd married her while she was pregnant with some soldier's fuck? And hadn't she only waited till her bastard was shoveled into the ground to start fucking the soldier boys again? Ask Rouault, Schlumberger was advised. You just ask him. He couldn't count the times he'd taken her back. She'd start twitching her ass every few weeks, and if he blinked, she was gone, and in a couple days or a week he'd come back from church and there she'd be—a starchy apron over her frock and a hambone boiling on the stove, and a pussy so sore she wouldn't let him drill her for a week.

You couldn't blame her, Maelzel explained judiciously. It was a sickness, and some of them were born that way. You had to learn how to recognize them and not expect more than you could get. It didn't surprise him that Schlumberger had been plugging her, he said, only that he hadn't been more man-of-the-world about it. He confided that "the bitch even tried to rub my fur, but I told her, 'I've had too many of your kind, Dearie.' " Surely Schlumberger couldn't be totally surprised by the turn things had taken. After all, if the bitch threw herself at Schlumberger with her husband under the same roof, one might guess her favors were rather "liberally bestowed," mightn't one? And hadn't Schlumberger noticed that stallion hounding the exhibition since the first night it opened? Big fellow with a spade-shaped beard? He picked his teeth and snoozed through the games, but when Louise was onstage, you could see the smoke puffing from his nostrils. "The bitch would hand me the candle to shine through the gearbox," he said, "and then before she sashayed back to her corner, she'd pass a look out over the house to that damn stud that would make him pop a hole in his britches." Maelzel had guessed then that she was about due for another romp. He hadn't been a bit surprised a few nights ago, just before they left for the phrenologist's show, to see her step out the side door as he was going upstairs to get his collar button. And when he glanced down into the alley from his window, sure enough, there was Spadebeard with his hand inside her bodice, squeezing the melons.

While he talked Maelzel pulled off Schlumberger's soggy boots and frock coat and fetched him a blanket from the bed and refilled his glass from the bottle that stood uncorked on the mantle. He kept on talking as he flicked a dangling shirttail into his traveling bag and swung it to the floor, hooking an ankle around the leg of the hassock to scrape it over to the fireplace beside Schlumberger's chair. Squatting on the hassock with a mock sigh, he placed a negligent hand over Schlumberger's forearm on the arm of the chair, and continued talking, peering up at the regally cloaked Schlumberger with cheery winks and grins.

And Schlumberger listened. Two or three times the blanket that wrapped him rippled while he made little peeps of anguish and squeezed

[229]

out tears that matted his lashes. But he listened: huddled inside the blanket, his toes spread before the fire, he took deep draughts of sherry and let the words pour down his ear and burn him hollow.

When Maelzel saw signs of turbulence, he would pat Schlumberger's forearm and say, "But Willie, this is just man talk, every man knows these things." Once he said, "These are things I learned at my daddy's knee. Didn't your daddy ever sit you down and tell you about women?"

"My father died," Schlumberger told him. They were the first words he had said since he leapt at Maelzel.

He fingered for a dry spot on Maelzel's red bandana handkerchief and filled it. Each nostril emptied like the dying note of a bagpipe. Only false griefs are decorous. He squeezed the handkerchief into a wet ball and looked for a place to put it. Finally he stuffed it between the arm and cushion of the chair. Maelzel watched the operation, nodding approval.

"You can give it back later," he said.

"Thanks," croaked Schlumberger.

Maelzel refilled Schlumberger's glass, advising him to "Drink it down" as if it were a purgative, then propped a foot on the fender and an elbow on the mantle and swirled the contents of his own glass, raising his eyes every few moments to Schlumberger, who would then direct his own eyes at the dying fire. Maelzel appeared to be waiting for some comment on his man-talk speech. He hummed through his nose a brisk skittish tune. Later Schlumberger would recognize it as an air from the climax to Beethoven's Battle Symphony, the one Maelzel claimed Beethoven had stolen from him. He never tired of explaining the intricacies of Beethoven's slanderous lawsuit, always ending the story with its moral: "Never trust a genius, Willie—he's a man of no principle." And then, because Schlumberger's genius as a chess player was commonly conceded between them, he would always break into a cackle that exposed the gold of his eyetooth to show every rule has its exceptions.

He hummed and swirled his sherry and waited. At last Schlumberger said, "I've come so far. What will I do now?"

Maelzel knocked back the last of his sherry and clapped the empty glass on the mantle. "Dooo?" he crowed. "What will you *do?*" He squatted again on the hassock and laid his palm over Schlumberger's, which lay on the chair arm. Schlumberger felt a tingle of panic at the sudden intimacy of Maelzel's flesh covering his own, but the grip was tight as an owl's talon. The skin on the back of Maelzel's hand was tough, translucent parchment. The blue vein that humped across the bones seemed to throb as if it might burst through the skin.

"You'll do what you've always done, Willie," he said, spreading a fierce grin.

Schlumberger stared at him.

"It's very simple," Maelzel told him. His grip tightened painfully. "You'll play chess."

Schlumberger repeated the word as if he were trying to master the sounds of a foreign language.

"Listen, Willie," Maelzel explained. "That wooden dummy with his head wrapped in a towel is the most ingenious diddle trick that's ever been devised. But it's only as good as the man in the box. With William Schlumberger as the Turk's brain, we can make—"

"But I don't—I never," Schlumberger seemed to be amazed at the discovery, "I never wanted to play chess inside that box."

"Willie, there's something you haven't understood yet. You were in that box two weeks, and you turned the Turk into a national celebrity. If you don't believe me, count the newspaper articles. I'll bet back in '18 they didn't give as much space to Andy Jackson's Seminole war as they did to the Turk's last game. And chess? There's a new chess club in Boston, another in Philadelphia. Have you seen the chess books hawked in the stalls? Another month and chess is going to be more popular than Indian killing. You did that, Willie, you and the Turk, and you can't just walk away from it."

"It's the machine Americans are interested in, not chess. I want to play chess in Paris."

Maelzel released Schlumberger's hand and stood up.

"You're forgetting, Willie," he said. "You owe me."

"I'll send you the money from Paris."

"Not good enough, Willie. Have you got, this minute, enough left of what you took from me to buy steerage fare?"

"No."

"Where will you get it?"

Schlumberger mumbled about giving lessons.

"Shall I tell you how you can get that money, Willie? And lots more? Let me bring you up to date. You remember Greco."

KINGKILL

"Somebody who wanted a game, wasn't it?" Schlumberger guessed.

"Wanted a game?" Maelzel said. "He came all the way from New York for a game with a thousand dollars in his pocket. You were supposed to take it away from him the day you disappeared."

A couple of weeks ago Maelzel had sat down to supper babbling about a newspaper article while Schlumberger was thinking of the scratches on Louise Rouault's belly. Now he explained it again. He got out his wallet and unfolded a page from the *New York American* that said a New York chess club claimed its players were better than Boston players, because they had beaten the Turk three times. "That was when the bitch was in the box," Maelzel said. Schlumberger reminded him that the Turk had lost in Boston, too, with him in the box. "But they don't know that in New York," Maelzel said, "and when they do, they won't believe it." And while he was trying to explain why what really happened was unimportant, Schlumberger lost interest. You could track the welts into the pubic hair, but there was no way of knowing what he suspected—that she had slashed from deep inside, as if she were trying to rip out her sex.

"When the Boston players made an arrogant reply," Maelzel said, "the dispute, *mon cher* William, moved into what my ex-colleague Ludwig would call *presto! presto!* tempo." A member of the New York club who signed himself "Greco" offered to wager one thousand dollars that he could beat the Turk, and dared the Boston gang to back its own boast with more than words. He had arrived in Boston the night Schlumberger left, and went home disgusted when Maelzel canceled the game. They could patch things up and reschedule the match, Maelzel was certain of that, but it would have to be in New York. "Do you have any notion, Willie, what your cut of a pair of thousand dollar matches could be?"

Schlumberger shrugged and said, "I'm not interested in money."

"Goddamn it, Willie," Maelzel howled, "you *owe* me money!" He leveled his voice to a murderously patient snarl. "You're interested in your honor, aren't you? You took, by your own account, 175 dollars of my money. I won't call it stealing. But I want it back and you don't have it—and when I offer you a chance to get it, you goddamn well don't have any *right* to say you're not interested in money."

Schlumberger sighed, trying to seem resigned, or at least petulant.

But the sherry was puffing up his brain to a horrible gaiety, and it felt so good to be bullied, he almost let himself break into a grin.

"Only till I've paid you what I owe," he said.

"Of course," nodded Maelzel, beaming.

With rare shrewdness Schlumberger added, "And made passage money back to Paris."

"Of course."

As Maelzel skipped ponderously about the room plucking up his cravat and collar studs and shaving tackle and fitting them into his traveling bag, he explained that he needed only one day in Boston to raise the thousand dollars to back Greco's bet. They could be here in New York again by the seventh of the month with a challenge that would force Greco into a match. "By the way," he asked, "Where is your bag?" It had been stolen, Schlumberger told him. "No matter," Maelzel said. "We'll get you another with the Greco money. Meanwhile you can share mine." His hand on the buckle, drawing the belt tight, Maelzel offered Schlumberger a patient smile.

"What is it, Willie?"

"I was only thinking," Schlumberger stammered, "that if we plan to return—that is, wouldn't it save money if I just stayed on here and—"

Maelzel let the belt go slack. He put an arm around Schlumberger and gave his hump an affectionate rub.

"I need you with me, Willie," he said softly. "If those boys are going to put up a thousand dollars, they're going to have to see proof that you are the *best*."

While he finished buckling his bag, he told Schlumberger the thousand-dollar match with Greco was only a beginning. He claimed America was mad for machines and the Turk was going to make them both rich enough to wipe their asses with dollar bills. Schlumberger and the Turk together were an unbeatable combination.

"Maybe you don't know it yet, Willie," he said, sweeping open the door with a courtly bow, "but you *are* the Turk."

Schlumberger didn't bother to remind him it was only until he earned passage money.

PART IV

32 | The Lost World

IN THE YEARS that followed, the story of how Schlumberger's stupidity enabled the bastard Greco to welsh out of a thousand-dollar bet was one of Maelzel's favorite dinner-table rants. Schlumberger, who was usually absorbed in contemplating his next move, listened through it patiently every time, even waiting for a break in the narrative to interject his own comments. Then, when Maelzel had stopped talking just long enough to sink his teeth into a turkey gizzard or lubricate his throat with a gulp of Médoc, he would say, "Move your pawn," or "Defend your queen, for god's sake," or "*Échec.*" And Maelzel would abruptly frown, wipe the grease from his fingers into the napkin on his lap—a concession to Schlumberger's outraged fastidiousness about the turkey fat and fingerprints that for a time were accreting on the chesspieces—and move his pawn or whatever the piece was Schlumberger had called to his attention. Then he would seize the bottle by the neck and shake the last drop into his tumbler, bellowing out, "Rouault, bring another bottle of the Médoc up from the cellar," and continue the anecdote, usually beginning with, "And then the bastard . . ." Schlumberger heard the story so often that eventually, without being aware quite how he acquired it, he had pieced together a fairly coherent account of the whole affair.

Over the years he in this way accumulated a good deal of information about Maelzel—information dropped like crumbs on the table at their evening meal, and during the ritual chess contests that accompanied it, which Schlumberger ritually won though he matched Maelzel glass for glass of whatever they might be drinking. Spurred by connections that occurred to him as he related the day's list of grievances, Maelzel would plunge with scarce a pause for preamble into an incident in his association with Beethoven, the lawsuit brought by the bastard Winkel to defraud him of his right to the metronome, the price the viceroy of Italy paid to peer into the empty cavities of the automaton. Though Maelzel's reminiscences seemed to obey no principle of organization save the associative whims of his fancy, many of them were linked by an inverse chronology. He would suspend a given tale indefinitely, choking into it digressions within digressions that thrust its true beginning ever deeper into the past. Later in Havana, when the fire dream had seared Schlumberger's brain clean as bone, he sifted all these rambling anecdotes for the anagogic proof of the crimes that demanded Maelzel's death.

Concerning the Greco match, it took Schlumberger a long time to understand why Maelzel had greeted his good news with howls of rage and frustration. As a border-dwelling Alsatian, Schlumberger was a passable linguist in German as well as his native French. But the molten eruption of Maelzel's wrath welded the most colorful obscene idioms of each language into a catalogue of bodily smearings and stuffings and lickings and possible and impossible hyperbolic copulations with both humans and an improbable menagerie. Though he had heard it before in snatches, this confused Schlumberger. The eclectic mix of French and German confused him, particularly when it entered into combination with Yankee whorehouse slang—an idiom it would take him yet a while to master. The necessity to make a mental picture of some new anatomical grotesque while he was still dealing in a far too literal-minded way with a previous suggestion concerning a teaspoon and a rat's asshole confused him. And even if Schlumberger had possessed a more nimble poetic fancy, Maelzel's howls could not have mystified him more if they had been the jabbers of a baboon in a silk waistcoat, because from Schlumberger's point of view the confrontation with Greco had been a splendid success. Maelzel had explained it all to him while he was howling, but it was difficult for him to follow the argument as he was being beaten about the shoulders and poked in the midriff with a walking stick that Maelzel used with the dexterity of a fencer. When Maelzel had calmed down enough to run through it again, during one of their evening meals with the tumblers and dishes and silver and the ever-present wine bottle flanked around the chessboard like captured pieces, Schlumberger's attention was often diverted at crucial moments from the intricacy of Maelzel's explanation to the sporadic intricacy of his board game. But at last he got it all, understood the long series of calculations that had been abruptly foiled the night an unexpected rap on the door made him put down a life of Napoleon which he had been furiously and indignantly annotating, and admit to his hotel room what proved to be the most satisfying antagonist of his chess career. Maelzel's rage began to be intelligible to Schlumberger once he realized, probably about the fifth time he heard it, that the great chess rivalry between New York and Boston, which had drawn headlines in the presses of both cities for a month, was entirely the creation of Johann Nepomuk Maelzel. The creation, a work of art in itself, was also an example of one of his cardinal maxims.

The secret of business success—presented in some versions of the story as the secret of life itself—was, according to Maelzel, the ability to turn a stupidity to advantage. In Maelzel's English lexicon, which was serviceably precise in dealings with shopkeepers and laced in society with a rich patina of old-world French and German that nicely covered its deficiencies, the word *stupidity* occurred with the frequency of a leitmotif, and applied to two broad catagories of experience. Accompanied by a harsh bark of laughter, it described his amazement at one or another of the bizarre customs of the natives in whatever nation was currently hosting him. In America these included chewing tobacco (though after a few years he acquired the taste himself), the Yankee drawl, and the classic revival in American architecture: he could not come within fifty yards of a building fronted by a two-story row of Ionic columns without muttering something about the god-damnedest stupidity he ever saw—a habit that made Schlumberger think of his mother crossing herself each time she passed a church. When the word was used with a contemptuous writhe of the lips and a spray of fine hot saliva erupting from the *p*, it usually referred to one of Schlumberger's blunders.

Maelzel was constantly on the spy for ways to transmute stupidities of both categories. Those that fell into the blunder category, being unpredictable, once-only occurrences, were more rarely subject to his alchemization, therefore more highly prized when they were.

That was why the Greco scheme was particularly sweet to his palate. The sweet taste of the handsome financial stake was doubly sweetened by the opportunity to turn profit from a blunder, and Maelzel was a man whose day was crossed with gloom if he could not dump into his morning tea three spoonfuls of sugar. Schlumberger had seen him dip a forefinger into the drained cup and bring the glutinous undissolved residue to his mouth with the glazed rapture of a sucking babe.

The stupidity Maelzel transformed into the Greco scheme had been authored not by Schlumberger but by Louise Rouault. Both the offending act itself and the way Maelzel appropriated it illustrate Maelzel's extraordinary passion for publicity. "Let them say any fucking thing," he would confide, his fork breaking the crust of a meat pie, "so long as they have to admit you're like nothing else on earth." His favorite pastime in the short winter days of slush and mud and drizzle was scissoring newspaper articles, even advertisements, any scrap of paper with his name on it (and how he fumed when it was misspelled!). He pasted them into a huge scrapbook that Schlumberger liked to call his journal. "Your diary," he would chide. "The repository for all the little intimate details of your life." Maelzel would frown over the tops of the half-spectacles he wore during such work and abstractedly smooth his fingers across the seven thick black letters of his name. Once when Maelzel had been gone most of the day Schlumberger rummaged through the trunk in his closet and found, among the greasy machine parts wrapped in designs for extravagant unworkable inventions, three more books like the one he had seen so often on Maelzel's lap. Their covers bulged wide, obese with clippings, dating back to 1804, the first performance of the CELEBRATED PANHARMONICON ORCHESTRA.

To Maelzel, newspapers were bread, thick-spread with the black butter of his name. After the automaton's first performance in a new town, he ceremoniously read the press reports of the event at table. He read them with the edifying piety of a patriarch intoning scripture. He read the most exclamatory laudation with a flat-voiced somberness that made each compliment no more than his due, and at peak moments, his lips pursed, eyes half-closed, he would incline his head like someone sustaining a barrage of applause. The only time his solemnity cracked was when he read attempts to explain the automaton's secret. Speculations about legless chess geniuses, midgets, peepholes in the Turk's chest to expose the board to a hidden operator—all sent him into nervous whoops of laughter.

The Turk's press celebrity and the rhythmic recurrence of Maelzel's name in each account were only partly the result of a spontaneous combustion of enthusiasm. On tour, not fifteen minutes after the coach had rattled into a town, Rouault would be unpacking crates from the special trailer wagon he had built to attach to coach axles (there would have been no room for the baggage of other passengers if all the automaton boxes and the mechanical trumpet player and rope dancers rode on the coach itself); Schlumberger would be washing the grit from his mouth with whiskey, pulling off his boots, dropping inert as a grain sack into the hotel bed to groan and nurse his aches to sleep; but Maelzel, his hair brushed, sideburns drawn out to feline points, would be poking the studs into a fresh shirt, snarling at the servant brushing the shoulders of his frock coat, snapping at another to brighten the shine on his boots even as he pulled them on, and holding out a stiff leg for the lad to button the strap under his instep. Then he would set out for the establishment where he invariably flourished his first calling card—the local newspaper office.

Behind the closed doors of the editor's inner sanctum—to which he never failed to penetrate within moments of arrival—amid the cigar smoke, over the midday brandy broken out in his honor, Maelzel assumed like a clever actor whatever face he judged would spread itself across the greatest number of column inches. Schlumberger never was certain which Maelzel he would discover in the next day's paper. Sometimes the front page would announce the visit, for a limited engagement, of the inventor of the panharmonicon and the automaton chess player. But the polymorphous gentleman he had supped with the previous evening might just as often be the royal mechanic of the Austrian court; or the confidant of Beethoven, inventor of the metronome and a professional musician himself (Maelzel always accompanied the automaton trumpeter's shrill cacophony with a thumping rumble on the piano); and sometimes, in the more intellectual journals, Schlumberger would read of a scientist engaged in researches which would have profound reverberations in the areas of mathematical calculation . . . or transportation . . . or agriculture. Maelzel displayed a serene assurance of the importance to the world of whatever he was engaged at the moment in promoting—his lofty projections for the future of what he was calling the Age of Mechanics raised the tone of any publication. The chess automaton was remarkable not simply in itself, he pointed out, but in its *application,* a word he wafted on its way in a suggestive fog of cigar smoke that roiled with grandiose possibilities.

Schlumberger noticed a peculiar formal tone in Maelzel's style of speech. Often there was scarcely any difference between his preperformance oration introducing the automaton and his table talk or casual remarks. He frequently spoke of himself in the third person, curling the corners of his mouth as paper curls just before it bursts into flame, and saying, ''Mr. Maelzel will just take that bishop you've so carelessly exposed.'' Or, delicately patting his lips to screen the widening maw of a yawn, ''Tomorrow Mr. Maelzel will call on the director of the city's largest manufacturing establishment.'' Eventually, with a faint shock, Schlumberger recognized that Maelzel talked just like a newspaper account of the doings of Johann Nepomuk Maelzel.

When he did use a personal pronoun, it was frequently *we.* He would tell a new acquaintance about the journey from Philadelphia to Baltimore or Cincinnati in a way that made Schlumberger question the reality of his own experience. Instead of the three of them, Maelzel, Schlumberger, and Rouault, jolting along in a springless coach, smacking ruts with a force that tumbled them into one another's laps, Maelzel would conjure a royal progress, himself gliding at the head of a retinue of courtiers. ''Thence we were conveyed to an inn fifteen miles south of the metropolis,'' he would explain. Schlumberger once heard him say, ''We retired early that night, troubled with a toothache.'' After that he knew Maelzel's *we* did not include himself and Rouault at all. It was the *We* of regal solitude.

Though Maelzel talked almost constantly and always about himself, Schlumberger knew scarcely more of him than he might read in the newspaper. Only three decades after Maelzel's death did Schlumberger discover the elementary fact that the man who had been his constant companion for twelve years had a brother two years his junior. He found that information in a biographical dictionary that identified Leonard Maelzel curiously—as the inventor of the panharmonicon. The article contained a number of other factual discrepancies. But by the time Schlumberger read the *Nouvelle Biographie Générale* article, he was no longer surprised to find in published information on Maelzel's life strange blurrings of outline, as if the subject were being viewed through the pocked, wavy pane of a stained-glass window. A few years earlier he had read the essay by George Allen on the automaton's history in America, and he knew that Maelzel was still getting the story told exactly as he had dictated it to dozens of eager newspaper editors.

In the years since Maelzel's death, Schlumberger had not played a single game of chess. He had renounced chess as a godstruck sinner renounces gin. But even a man who lived alone, balancing his mind precariously between Ovid and Epictetus and detouring two blocks around the headquarters of the Chess Club, could not avoid news of the exploits of the American chess genius, Paul Morphy. The *New York Gazette,* which Schlumberger scanned each night over dinner in a Broadway restaurant, was slow to discover the prodigy. In August 1857, three paragraphs tucked low on an inside page had announced the coming chess congress. Schlumberger veered his eyes away from the word. Living since his mother's death on the capital from a small inheritance had taught him discipline. He would not even have learned the news if a casual acquaintance had not drawled, "Imagine what's announced in tonight's paper. Rather exciting news for chess players, I'd say. D'you know the game?" "Not me," replied Schlumberger; as he spoke he calculated how to shift his dinner hour to avoid the man's company.

A few weeks later the press announced the coronation of the Chess Champion of the Western World. Schlumberger did not read far enough to learn the fellow's name. In the days that followed the journalists haltingly discovered that the incidental details of the new champion's life could be puffed into the simulacrum of epic. At the outset the minstrels missed a beat. Heroes have to appear heroic. The new standard-bearer of American promise was a lad barely out of his teens. He had a tinny soprano voice and silky sideburns that wouldn't grow past his earlobe. Then an inspired biographer transformed the embarrassing facts by saying that if Morphy was no Davey Crockett, he was yet a David. The *Gazette* pounced on the Biblical analogy, and the other epic makers quickly found the proper rhythm. The ground resounded with the thud of felled Goliaths. The David's physical eccentricities which early stories had muted, now swelled the boast. Was he five feet four inches in height? Call him barely five feet, wearing lady's gloves and shoes made for a child. The tale had it that one opponent who couldn't beat Morphy on the board threatened to stuff him in his pocket. Soon there were choruses for all the traditional episodes in the hero's legend, even the childhood marvel casting its shadow into the future. Crockett killed his bear. Morphy, at the age when the Nazarene stunned the Temple elders, met and humbled the Hungarian master, Lowenthal.

By now even Schlumberger knew his name, knew the New Orleans Chess Club had raised $5,000 to pit its champion against the masters of Europe. Each headline bit like a drop of acid into the granite of Schlumberger's resolve. There were so many. When the papers reported the fall of Harrwitz, he struggled, yielded and read. The Anderssen match he followed with controlled interest. The fruitless pleas for a match with Staunton, the terrified champion whose every excuse for postponement was reported with scornful rage, excited Schlumberger past all pretence of detachment. Sometimes he thought how Maelzel would have purred over the headlines. Or perhaps not: people change. Passion becomes petulance: a stiff-fingered reach for the softest chair, the accurately timed egg. If he had lived, you might pass him unaware in the street. But how thoroughly had Schlumberger himself changed? In his sixth decade of life his hands trembled with envy and vicarious triumph as he followed the account of Morphy defeating eight *professeurs d'échecs* in blindfold play at his old home, the Café de la Régence.

In 1859 he purchased *The Book of the First American Chess Congress* to read about Morphy. He carried it to his favorite restaurant with furtive excitement, the same anticipation of self-discovery he had felt at the age of eleven, when he filched from his father's bookshelf and bore to a loft in the carriage house a volume of Rabelais. Both books contained forbidden knowledge. He placed the book in the center of the table. Between himself and the book he placed a plate of steaming roast beef with boiled potato and green beans. He ate with disciplined pace for a few moments, then dug through the rest of the obstruction. He had a second slice of bread to mop the gravy, ordered another glass of wine, and drew the book toward him. It opened not to the Morphy article, but to one called "The History of the Automaton Chess Player in America." He closed it immediately. He drank his wine, paid his bill, and was nearly to the door before a breathless waiter hurried up with the book he had forgotten. At home he threw it on a table and forgot it again. Newspapers accumulated over and around it. When the night breeze whirred and fluttered their pages, he weighted them with a guttered candle in a heavy metal holder. Then one night he came home drunk and swept the whole pile onto the floor. He picked the book out of the nest of papers and cursed it for five minutes, recognizing in his own voice as he cursed his horrible fidelity to the nuance and rhythm of all the old stock phrases and many of the rage-sparked unique ones. They hissed and bubbled to the surface as if he had heard them last only the day before. When he could no longer pretend he didn't recognize whose voice had been coming through him as if he were a medium, he sat on the floor by his bed, the book in his lap, and wept. Then he read it. That same night he rooted on closet shelves and in the back corners of bureau drawers till he found his chess journal. He opened to the first blank page, well into the second half of the volume, and began to write. He neatly copied into the journal three sentences from the essay he had just read. ''Some kind of negotiation or scheme appears, at any rate, to have been occupying the mind of Maelzel, for on the third of March he advertises, that he suspends his exhibition here in order to make arrangements in New York for an exhibition there. To New York he went, undoubtedly, but—from some unknown cause—he did not exhibit there during this year. His short visit, it is likely, had some other object in view.'' Under the last line he made a dash and carefully wrote the name of the author, George Allen, and ''Page 457.'' Then he dipped his quill again, but let the ink dry on its tip. An hour passed. When he wrote again, the hand sprawled recklessly, as if a new intention had superseded the original one. ''If he decided,'' Schlumberger wrote, ''to blow his nose and fart on the same day, the old bastard would have written up an advertisement for the papers. But that time, at least, I thought I knew what 'object' he had in view. Until I saw him at the door with his travel bag in his hand and that look on his face that seemed to be sadness and pity and relief, I didn't realize I'd had enough cunt for a while. But him coming all that way *again* (and all the other times, too, that came after) was a testimony, or I thought so. And he didn't just say, 'You've got to come home, Willie.' He said, 'I need you.' And I started looking for my boots. But I should have known—with him it was just another kind of advertisement, a way of getting his diddle. Words were only words.

The important thing to him was never the 'object in view.' That was only a screen for whatever he wanted or what he was afraid of. What had frightened him into coming all that way was . . .''

That night Schlumberger got no further. He had been drunk when he came home, drank more while he read, and drank as he wrote. But that was the first of the Maelzel entries that were to swell the journal to its final pages. What he had not the courage or coherence to say that night, what he began to discover only in the months and years of writing ahead, was that Maelzel's mania for publicity bred in him two great terrors.

The first was that the automaton might be exposed. During travel the automaton was dismantled into five separate boxes, no two of which would have yielded clues sufficient for a deduction of its secret. When Maelzel settled more or less permanently in Philadelphia in 1827, the store room of the automaton was double-locked and its windows barred. Even with these precautions Maelzel insisted that the house never be left untenanted. Perhaps this is one reason why he tolerated the continued presence of Rouault. His services as mechanic, handyman, cashier, and operator of the "Mechanical Rope Dancers—the Fabulous Funambulists" were readily dispensible, but Rouault, no matter what the holiday or how lengthy his previous incarceration, was always willing to stay behind. How he occupied himself alone in the big old house on Chestnut Street neither Schlumberger nor Maelzel troubled to determine. There was another reason, of course, for keeping Rouault. He knew the secret. Anyone who knew the secret was dangerous to Maelzel. What had mystified Schlumberger for a long time was why, since Louise was gone, Rouault wanted to stay with the troupe. But it would take twelve years and the steaming heat of a Havana night before the last disguise had been peeled from Rouault's core of hatred and love.

Schlumberger was no further trusted than Rouault. Maelzel kept him away from society as much as possible, particularly the society of chess players. He sometimes felt uncomfortable if they were seen together on the street by a person he judged "capable of calculating twice two." When the secrecy fit was on him strongest, he would even insist that Schlumberger take separate lodgings. It was this, not any particular austerity of taste, which explains what had been observed—that Schlumberger frequently occupied more humble quarters than his employer. Whenever he asked permission to take a walk or attend a theatre, Schlumberger could sense in the glowering calculation behind Maelzel's eyes a powerful desire that his every moment of life outside the automaton box might be erased from the earth.

It was at these times, when Schlumberger was testing the limits of his bondage, that Maelzel would talk wistfully about making a chess automaton that was a genuine machine. "Not as impossible as you think, Willie," he would say. "It's merely a question of devising a chessboard on which the opponent's move can trigger the move of the automaton. Just remember that."

Schlumberger never took such jibes seriously. He knew their purpose was to fret him. Yet he was never certain that Maelzel was entirely bluffing: the desire behind the threat was real. He had listened to Maelzel's claim that his invention of the metronome had made a science of music. *"Allegro, andante, adagio, presto,* bullshit!" Maelzel would explain. "What do they mean, when no two men have the same heartbeat. One conductor's *presto* rocks you to sleep, another shakes the fillings out of your teeth. But with my metronome: ah! You have a precise mathematical gauge. Each time you hear a symphony, it will be played the same way." Schlumberger also heard Maelzel say hundreds of times that the music of his panharmonicon orchestra surpassed any human performances he had ever heard. "It's only reasonable, Willie," he said. "A mechanical trumpeter doesn't get drunk, fight with his wife, or worry about his debts. The sound that comes out is disembodied, absolutely pure!" One of the grim pleasures Schlumberger got from the newspaper eulogies that surfaced in the wake of Maelzel's death was a line in the *United States Gazette* which read, "He has gone, we hope, where the music of his Harmonicons will be exceeded."

If Maelzel's fear of exposure made him impose drastic limits on Schlumberger's life outside the automaton box, it also inspired many compensating privileges. Schlumberger's craving for chocolate and pastries was indulged without quibbles. Little wrapped packages of sweetmeats appeared on his dresser or by his place at table as if he were the object of a particularly solicitous courtship. Only his queer nervous metabolism prevented him from fattening to the point where he would be incapable of climbing inside the automaton box. The wine cellar was stocked with choice vintages. Maelzel's only restriction: that Schlumberger not drink more than one bottle with dinner on the night of a performance.

The principal concession made to Schlumberger's need for society was, of course, the long dinners over the chessboard. If Maelzel enforced upon his employee a monastic retirement from the world, he would attempt to embody the lost world in his own person. The whole range of intellectual stimulation, companionship, and affection the world might have offered, Maelzel condensed into the ever-twirling, multifaceted bauble of Maelzel's wit, Maelzel's ideas, Maelzel's skill as chess antagonist, Maelzel's moods and rebukes and flatteries. When Schlumberger had a cold or a hangover from one of his periodic attempts at self-annihilation in alcohol, Maelzel cooed and fluffed his pillows. When Schlumberger ranted and wept over a lost game, Maelzel, after his own tantrum had subsided, thought up wise stoic consolations. When Schlumberger was disobedient, sneaking away to a chess club for an anonymous evening's play, Maelzel punished: rage, sarcasm, the threat to retire the automaton. All these supplied the similitude of a richly varied life of the soul. Surely they would have proved insufficient to any but a man for whom the carved grotesques that people a chessboard had personalities complex and capricious as any he had ever discovered in the human heart. Maelzel had no great love for chess, but he had the shrewd versatility of an aging mistress inventing fresh ways to tease her lover. The chess players among his society friends taught him new combinations, and he spent just enough time studying end-game theory to keep his restless partner from losing interest. Often a game begun at breakfast would be left on the table all day, the pawns brought out with the poached eggs and stacks of ham, the struggle for center control joined over and around the light lunch of cold cuts and wine, hotly contested through the varied courses of the evening meal, leaving the end-game stalk to finish along with the last bottle of claret and the last cigar before bed. At morning, noon, and night Rouault would clear the plates and silver with the same methodical concentration with which Schlumberger cleared the board of Maelzel's pieces. And clear them he did, though he typically accepted a rook-pawn or knight-pawn handicap to keep the contest in jeopardy.

But Maelzel was not a woman.

The Lost World

The eunuch slumber of Schlumberger's first twenty-five years gave way after he met Louise Rouault to periodic spasms of sensuality. After his daily foray into the elite society of the city, Maelzel would occasionally return to their Chestnut Street quarters to find that the rook-queen gambit he had left Schlumberger mulling over as he stirred a third cup of coffee had been swept from the board. Chesspieces would lay fanned across the floor like grapeshot. He would find a dark explosion staining the wall, dripping rum from its lower rays to the baseboard, where concave shards of glass mingled with pawns and knights. If the stain was still damp, Maelzel hurried to the chess club. Then he tried the taverns on Chestnut Street. Or, if there was a place in whatever town they were staying that the local clergy advertised from the Sunday pulpit with threats of hellfire, he would climb the stairs of the alley entrance and sneer at whatever snickers he got when he told them he was looking for a horse-faced drunk with a lump on his back, and no, he didn't mean in his pants, though he would probably have one there, too. If the stain was already dry and Rouault told him Schlumberger had asked to borrow money, Maelzel wouldn't even bother to search locally. He would hang out the sign that told people the evening's performance of Maelzel's fabulous automaton chess player had been canceled so that repairs could be made on its delicate mechanism. Then he would buy a ticket on the first Concord coach for New York City. There he would go to the streets where the colored balls hung over the pavement, lettered with names like RED RIBBON SAL or PROUD PAMMY. He would make his tour leisurely, perhaps lingering a while if he happened upon an establishment that could satisfy his own rather special tastes.

Eventually he ran Schlumberger to ground in the room of whatever woman had adopted him—and he always seemed to find someone breasty and hollow cheeked who would curtail her customary business to transform the lumpy mattress where she plied her trade into a throne in which Schlumberger reclined on a heap of pillows drinking and interminably talking. Sometimes when he saw Maelzel in the doorway, Schlumberger would weep gratefully and start stuffing his shirts and socks into his bag. Sometimes he would yank a candle bracket from the wall and throw it at Maelzel's head. Sometimes he would just drool and leer up at Maelzel and offer him a glass of rum without remembering his name. Once Maelzel, in a fit of exasperation that Schlumberger could not content himself with a whorehouse closer to home, mockingly accused him of continuing in his New York expeditions the search for Louise Rouault. "What an absurd idea," Schlumberger replied. "Haven't you told me yourself that one cunt is like every other once you're inside it?" But he never explained why it was to New York that he had to go. The girl would always curse Maelzel after he had finally got Schlumberger sobered and dressed, and sometimes Schlumberger, too, but for him there would always be a last sniffly embrace and usually a present: money, a box of chocolates, once a garter that Schlumberger catapulted into a mudpuddle just as he boarded the stage. Maelzel gave way to a rather envious curiosity and asked, "How do you make them act that way?" After a dumbfounded pause, Schlumberger shrugged, "I don't make them. I let them."

Maelzel accepted these disappearances philosophically, as you would accept the periodic absences of a favorite cat which was a good mouser. They were the price of Schlumberger's fidelity, and of his silence. Maelzel's terror of exposure made him tolerant. Once in a while he would mention in a fretting way a former operator of the automaton, a man named Mouret, with whom he had apparently parted on bad terms. The name always came to Maelzel's lips reluctantly, after much teeth clicking and sideburn tugging. A peculiar inner tension, one that nothing in his repertoire of blasphemies and obscenities could ventilate, was released only by this name. But whatever demon the forbidden syllables exorcised, they always seemed to call up another of equal potency. No sooner had the name passed his lips than Schlumberger began to sense that Maelzel was placing his words like the footfalls of a man who hears the ice creaking beneath each step. Despite all his caution, once the name had been summoned it barged and clanked through his subsequent conversation like a sinister poltergeist. Observing his obvious torment each time the name slipped past the locks Maelzel repeatedly reset against it, Schlumberger realized he was in an agony not to suggest anything to Schlumberger that he hadn't figured out for himself. On rare occasions Maelzel tried to master his superstition by facing it, and he spoke his fear almost candidly, almost conceding to Schlumberger that minimal degree of shrewdness to grasp that what Maelzel feared from Mouret was a power also held by Schlumberger. Once after a closely fought match played out to Schlumberger's inevitable victory at 3 A.M., a drunk and weary Maelzel had slurred Mouret's name into *morte,* so that Schlumberger experienced a slight *frisson* as he heard Maelzel soothing himself to sleep with a muttered, "We're safe as a bank—Morte doesn't even know we're in America."

Schlumberger never mentioned Mouret first. He waited with infinite patience for the name to poke its moist trembling nose into the conversation. When that happened, as it inevitably did, he flexed his claws. How good a chess player was Mouret, he would drawl, as good as the *professeurs* in the Café de la Régence claimed? With a chuckle like the rattle of dice in a glass Maelzel would reply, "Not in the same class with you, Willie." Then Schlumberger would affect the curiosity of a lover jealous of his partner's past *affaires de coeur:* what had they quarreled about? Why did they part? And he would suck a string of cartilage from the gap in his back molars while Maelzel fell into a shaky rasp. "He was a drunk. Undependable. Like you." Leaving the moral unspoken. And if Schlumberger persisted, as he did with ritual doggedness, Maelzel would rise, the legs of his chair snarling, flicking his napkin from his throat, and intone, "Never mind why he left. I dismissed him. I can dismiss you. Forget Mouret. Why are you always pestering me with Mouret? Never mention the name again."

And Schlumberger, with a merciless shrug, would reply, "Hang out the repair sign for tomorrow's performance. I'm due for a holiday from that fucking box." He knew he would never see that look of anguished pleading again if Maelzel suspected it filled him with such tenderness.

Once at a crowded inn on the Boston Post Road Schlumberger shared a bed with Maelzel. What woke him, he thought, was the erratic squeak of an unoiled socket in the Turk's elbow. He shook himself awake in a small panic. If he had dozed off how could the Turk be making a move? But it was Maelzel who was squeaking, whimpering in his dream like a dog stretched by the fire, producing abortive yips and twitches that were all that would translate of the dream's fine, arm-flailing diatribe. At first, his mind still tracking the maze of his own dream, Schlumberger merely knuckled him in the back and said, "Wake up, you can't fight them all."

With perfect clarity Maelzel moaned, "Betrayed."

Schlumberger, rubbing the heel of his hand in his eyes, recognized his opportunity. Softly, close to Maelzel's ear, he whispered, "Who? Who have you betrayed?"

Maelzel shook his head impatiently and said, "Lies." Then he breathed from a sigh to a snore.

Schlumberger shook his shoulder. "What lies? Who?" he whispered.

In the moonlight Maelzel's face writhed as he struggled against the words. Schlumberger pulled them out like a dream gardener, shaking clammy loam from their roots. "Three columns . . . ," he heard, and asked, "What—on a porch? Greek columns?"

When he had found the right question, the proper magical formula, the dreamer said, very distinctly, in quotation marks, " 'Hoax Exposed.' " Then he choked a sob, rage or grief, and volunteered a lengthy explanation. Schlumberger grasped only an occasional word or phrase from the tangle. When this monologue crumbled into a snore, Schlumberger prodded him again, and dislodged the single word, uttered with deep reproach, "Leonard." Curiously, it was this word in a biographical dictionary, the name of Maelzel's unmentioned brother, which years later recalled the entire scene to Schlumberger's mind. At the time there had been no leisure to reflect on the word's significance. A sudden timbre filling the dreamer's voice—as if, after calling from the end of a long passage, he were suddenly standing quite close by—warned him that the seance was over. Schlumberger turned on his side and began to breathe deeply just as Maelzel raised himself on his elbow and poked him. "Close your mouth," Maelzel ordered. "Your damn snoring woke me up."

At breakfast the next morning Schlumberger said, "Last night you had a nightmare."

"Not at all," replied Maelzel briskly. "I was sitting in the dining room of the National Hotel on Broadway. Across the table the Turk was sipping coffee. He said, 'This should interest you,' and handed me a newspaper. I recall it quite clearly, as I do all my dreams."

Thus Schlumberger learned that the first of Maelzel's great terrors was betrayal: a nightmare headline proclaiming the secret corruption wedged in the immaculate polished teeth of his machine like a piece of rotting meat—giving off the sour putrescence of human flesh. The second of Maelzel's great terrors, deducible without the divinatory arts of dream probing, was that the automaton would lose its reputation as an infallible chess master. This made between his terrors a fraternal link. Both were a denial that human hands had defiled the purity of his machine. Both expressed themselves as a fear of public exposure—the sinister obverse of his craving for newspaper immortality.

After that first disastrous week he spent in the automaton box, Schlumberger lost a game only on rare occasions. He would be drunk and fall asleep waiting for his anonymous opponent to move. Or he would be embattled with Maelzel, and lost to remind him how valuable he was when he was winning. Once or twice he may even have been outplayed. That was why, when he learned that in the automaton's New York debut Louise Rouault had lost two games, he could hear exactly how Maelzel must have greeted her as she climbed out of the box—the purpled face, the breathless shriek ludicrously muted so it couldn't be overheard by customers still lingering outside the building, saying, "Stupid! Stupid! Do you think anyone will want to see an automaton that *loses* games? If it can't win, nobody will believe it's a machine! Stupid, stupid, *stupid.*" And then, after a typical procession of obscenities, his final damning judgment: "You are guilty of the most colossal . . . *stupidity.*" Schlumberger sometimes wondered if there were not another thought straining for expression in that pause preceding the word of ultimate contempt; wondered if the real word, unspeakable even to those lips which passed so glibly the most excrement-dripping obscenities, were not *betrayal.* Unspeakable because the idea of betrayal was too searingly close to what he really thought, what he most feared, and the bare utterance of the word would have constituted an incitement to the act.

The potential betrayers were whoever had learned the secret. All the former directors; Schlumberger never learned exactly how many there had been. Chiefly Mouret. But also, in Maelzel's moments of wholesale mistrust, Louise Rouault. "It would be just like the bitch," he would warn. "No woman born can keep her mouth around a secret longer than it takes to melt a sugar cube. What a fool I was even to teach her the difference between a pawn and a queen." Whatever fear he had of Schlumberger and Rouault showed itself obliquely. It was an occasional stammer in the midst of his most sarcastic denunciations, a shying back from the unforgivable insult, an unexpected delicate regard for his victim's rawest wound. With Schlumberger he never mentioned the chess prowess of La Bourdonnais except to belittle it. With Rouault he attacked God but not Louise Rouault. And whenever rage had mastered prudence, small gifts would appear. Not money, which was almost freedom. But an embroidered waistcoat. An expensive sherry. And when money was scarce, praise—always a cheap but valued commodity. For Rouault, who wanted nothing Maelzel could ever give, he left coyly on his workbench religious tracts, acquired perhaps from street hawkers, perhaps sought out in church vestibules. He never troubled to notice what Schlumberger had quietly observed, that Rouault did not even read The New Testament anymore, that he ripped each tract, unread, once across the center and used it to start the stove fire. Sometimes even in those days Schlumberger wondered how Maelzel would have treated Rouault and himself if they had been somehow divested of that reserve of power—the ability to betray.

Under his breath, then, Maelzel might have been muttering *betrayal* when Louise Rouault marred the Turk's American debut, but all he said aloud, no matter how contemptuously, was *stupidity*. And it was to transmute this stupidity to an essence of pure profit that Maelzel exercised such elaborate craftsmanship in stoking the Greco scheme. Perhaps he was especially eager to sear away all memory of Louise's blunder because he recognized that it would not have been nearly so colossal if he himself had not abandoned the caution that habitually governed him in anything that threatened the Turk's reputation. But the American press had a weakness for spilling frothy rivers of newsprint in praise of anything novel and mechanical, and Maelzel, the country's newest citizen and possessing a machine that stirred the imaginations of editorialists, had an irresistible weakness for gratifying it.

There is evidence that he tried to resist. The *Ship News* journalist who interviewed Maelzel on the South Street docks on February 3rd 1826, the day he landed in America, introduced him to the New World as "Mr. Maelzel, Professor of Music and Mechanics, inventor of the Panharmonicon, The Musical Time-Keeper &c." What reserves of modesty must Maelzel have summoned to refrain from proclaiming himself the impresario of the marvelous chess-playing automaton, fresh from a generation of triumphs in the capitals of Europe. But Maelzel had a weighty reason for his modesty. He was afraid that if he exhibited the automaton or so much as acknowledged it was in his possession, he would be jailed and the Turk impounded as stolen property.

Maelzel's legal title to the automation was fogged by ambiguities

The Lost World

Schlumberger was a long time penetrating. From the fact that the phrase "Maelzel's Chess Automaton" frequently appeared in the advertisements for the Turk's performance, most people, particularly in America where the automaton's true history was not so well known, assumed that Maelzel was not only its proprietor but its inventor as well. Maelzel himself was too busy a man to scruple over trifling distinctions between possession and conception. He let people think what they would. If he had not actually invented the chess automaton, he might well have. He was, after all, or claimed to be, the inventor of the metronome, an array of mechanical dolls and panoramas, and his masterpiece, the panharmonicon—"A far more complicated piece of machinery, Willie, than the Turk."

In fact, the automaton had been invented in 1770, two years before Maelzel was born. It was designed by Baron Wolfgang von Kempelen, Aulic Councilor on Mechanics to the Royal Chamber of the Viennese court. He had been commissioned to construct a toy for the amusement of the Empress Maria Theresa. Because people did not yet depend for their bread on machines, the principles of mechanics could still inspire delight and mystery. The chess machine became the subject of scientific speculation throughout Europe. Von Kempelen found himself a famous magician. At his studio in Pressburg his researches into the mechanism of human speech and the science of hydraulics were constantly interrupted by visitors requesting a demonstration of the Turk's powers. Eventually he spread the tale that the Turk had been damaged in a move and he was too busy with more important work to repair it. But some men are doomed to be celebrated for their trifles. In 1783 the Emperor Joseph II commanded Von Kempelen to resurrect the Turk. It was received with such admiration that the emperor calculated that the fame of his court would be magnified by pressing the Turk and its creator into service as roving ambassadors. He arranged a two-year tour of the capitals of Europe. Von Kempelen consoled himself with the prospect that this would give him an opportunity to bring the world's attention to his improvements in the design of water pumps and fire engines, and his "speaking machine"—a talking doll with a vocabulary of enough polite clichés to make smooth conversation in the most refined ballrooms; which is to say, about thirty words and phrases. Unfortunately, the crowds which attended Von Kempelen's performances had an unswervable taste for chicanery. They tapped their toes and muttered behind their fans during the talking doll's *repartée* and the serious lecture on speech mechanism that accompanied it, and showered enthusiastic bravoes upon the mysterious Turk. "And no wonder in that," Maelzel would explain. "Who would care a rap for a 'speaking machine'? What could you ever *do* with it?"

Maelzel's opinion, delivered between moves during his chess dinners with Schlumberger, was that Von Kempelen was a gifted man who lacked the ultimate vision of true genius. The Turk was ingenious enough, to be sure, but Von Kempelen hadn't recognized its potential. "When he died, Willie, I was just putting together my first panharmonicon. My father had an organ-building factory I used for a workshop, working over that damn thing every night till I got headaches that would *blind* me. And just as I began organizing my first exhibition of the thing, I read that old Von K.'s estate was selling the Turk, and I thought, 'God-damn, with that chess automaton and my Panharmonicon, I'd have such a colossal show.' "

So Maelzel's title to the automaton was solid enough when he purchased it in 1804, though Schlumberger never learned how he could afford the 15,000 franc purchase price on the wages of a Viennese piano teacher. And for the next six years the "colossal show" made his fortune. The trouble began, according to Maelzel, with that damned popinjay bastard of Bonparte's. In 1810 Maelzel found himself in Milan exhibiting in the court of Prince Eugène de Beauharnais, the stepson of Napoleon, whom the Emperor had installed as Viceroy of Italy. "The minute I saw him come mincing into the hall," Maelzel would say, "I knew he would make trouble. Didn't even have his old man's guts—had some court fop proxy for him in the chess match. At least when Bonaparte met the Turk—that was in 1809, Willie, right after the battle for Wagram—he stepped up and played the game himself, even if he did cheat. But not de Beauharnais. He just sat there stuffing his nose with snuff and sneezing and whispering bad advice in his proxy's ear. And when it was over up he comes with his drippy nose and watery eyes, and he slips an arm around my shoulder and I knew exactly what he was going to say: Couldn't I, as a courtesy to royalty, mind, reveal the principle of the marvelous automaton's fucking operation? You have to understand, Willie, that it's not prudent to hoodwink royalty, and I knew how much trouble I was in. In those days it wasn't just a question of sticking a key in the Turk's back before a performance and winding up the clockwork in order to give the audience the idea of a machine. I was using a little casket Von K. had made, that he kept in the big cabinet, and when I hauled it out, I would give a long spiel about the mysterious power it contained to guide the Turk's arm and how it couldn't be revealed to the public, and *this* was what that *arshloch* wanted to get his hands on!''

Maelzel had said that surely His Majesty would understand that only the automaton's owner could be privy to the intricate details of its operation. But the Viceroy of Italy was a man accustomed to having his curiosity gratified. Taking the most direct route to his end, and one which seldom failed of effect, he asked Maelzel to name his price—''Not just for the secret, Willie; he wanted to buy the whole thing! What could I do?'' Thinking of his livelihood, Maelzel refused until his refusals became ungracious. At last he named what he thought was an outrageous and prohibitive price—30,000 francs—which the Viceroy promptly paid. After Maelzel's tantalizing eloquence about mystery power sources chaining the secrets of the universe, his apology for the empty casket was met with dumb frigidity by the entire court, and when he went on to explain the real secret of the automaton's operation, exposing all the functionless machinery, Eugène de Beauharnais began to realize that what he had just bought was not the secret of the universe, but a 30,000-franc conjuring trick. He felt Maelzel's price had been outrageous.

''Willie, I swear to God,'' Maelzel would say, and even years later his complexion would pale and his jowls tremble as he recalled it, ''if the entire court hadn't been standing around, if they hadn't all seen me begging that little snuff-drunk pimp not to buy my machine—I would have been clapped in irons and thrown into the darkest hole in the kingdom of Italy.''

As it was, when the workings of the bogus automaton had been thoroughly exposed, there was a rather terrible silence in which the only sound was the periodic sniffing of the Viceroy's nose, and then the viceroy turned to his treasurer and said, ''Write Herr Maelzel a draft in the amount of 30,000 francs.'' Such a superb demonstration of magnanimity and of the fact that their sovereign could toss away the price of a lucrative ambassadorship without spoiling his digestion drew frenzied applause from his courtiers. Maelzel breathed his relief and took his money. The Turk went into a storeroom, and Maelzel went to Vienna and made an ear trumpet for Ludwig van Beethoven.

"Why should I feel sorry for you?" Schlumberger would ask. "You had 30,000 francs in your pocket, and if you move that rook where you're planning to, the game is over."

"I tell you, I was a pauper," Maelzel would insist. "That money was gone, don't ask me how, within eight months. I had to go back to giving lessons. *There,* smart boy, I had better plans for my rook than you thought, hah? Then one day I walked into a tavern, ordered a bock, and struck up a march on the piano. After a few minutes this gent comes up and raps on the lid. 'I don't know who you are,' he says, 'but I can hear you just well enough to know you are a dreadful musician.' I knew who he was well enough, and I saw the chance I'd waited three years for, so right off I said, 'Since my playing is so offensive, you probably wouldn't thank me for a little advice I could make that would give you an ear like a fox.' "

"Check," said Schlumberger.

"Because immediately, Willie, I thought of my panharmonicon. If I could once get Ludwig van Beethoven to write a piece of music for the Maelzel panharmonicon, I could tell all my darling little piano pupils to take their fingers off the keyboard and stick them back up their asses. So: a deal. An ear trumpet for a Beethoven composition. I even gave him his subject: Wellington's victory at Vitoria, and I said, 'Start with "La Marseillaise," the cocky little corporal strutting around the battlefield. Then come in far away, far, with "God Save the King," and *build* it, make us see the cavalry thundering over the plain, and have them battle it out until "God Save the King," is roaring, plowing them under.' God, the idea alone was worth—what do you mean, check?"

"I told you not to move the rook there. If you had—"

"You impudent little shitsmear, you haven't even been listening to me, have you? Why don't you forget chess long enough to learn something about life for a change? What I'm telling you is that I practically *wrote* the most popular piece of music Beethoven ever did. When he finished the panharmonicon piece I said, 'Ludwig, this is splendid, but I'll get a bigger audience if you score the thing for orchestra. You need money to go to London, so do I. We appeal to patriotism, arrange a charity concert; print posters: "For the benefit of

Austrian and Bavarian soldiers disabled at the battle of Hanau.'' And you and I ladle off enough cream to finance our travels.' Hah! by the time I was finished, we had enough to go around the world. Shall I tell you, Willie, how much we made in *two performances* of that concert? Four thousand six gulden!''

"Do you want another game? It's early yet.''

"Oh, go ahead, set them up. Are you listening to me?''

"Of course. If you made so much money, why did he try to sue you?''

"Because we made *too* much money, Willie, and suddenly the welching bastard remembered that he had made me a present of the music for the panharmonicon. When I tried to use the piece myself, he claimed I stole it.''

"But it wasn't even a present, was it? Didn't you say you made him an ear trumpet in exchange for—''

"I made him *four* ear trumpets, and the liar said none of them worked. I kept telling him, 'You can't expect it to work if you hold it a foot away from your ear. You have to put the damn end of it right inside your ear.' 'No, no, I can't do that,' he says. 'It makes my eardrum itch.' Can you imagine, Willie—he has to fill every piece of music he writes with those damn cannons because that's the only noise that sinks through the cotton in his skull, and when I give him a chance to *hear* again, he says to me, 'My eardrums itch.' ''

"So who won the lawsuit?''

"Never mind that, it's your move. If you're going to play chess, keep your mind on the game.''

In fact the lawsuit was never contested, because Maelzel abruptly left Vienna. For more than a year he toured Germany with his panharmonicon and automaton trumpeter, which reproduced a piercing repertoire of French and Austrian cavalry signals. During this time Maelzel completed the array of mechanical entertainments that he later brought to America. He devised or acquired a panorama called *The Conflagration of Moscow,* in which, to the accompaniment of a staccato frenzy of mechanical trumpets, drums, triangles, and cymbals, a red flame inched across a skyline of onion-domed minarets while Cossacks and soldiers of the Grande Armée painted on paper rollers pursued one another in and out of alleys and avenues. The effect was strikingly realistic, especially when the candles that were passed behind the translucent scarlet paper to simulate sudden explosions of flame were held too close and set fire in earnest to the towers. The show was completed by the Funambulists, a pair of loose-jointed puppets with round eyes and identical fatuous smiles. When their hands were clamped round a slack rope strung across the stage, Maelzel would play a waltz on the piano, and the clever lad and his lassie would appear to dance and tumble on the rope, more or less in time with the music. The rope on which the puppets danced was threaded through sturdy pulleys out of sight on either end of the stage. By tugging on the ends Rouault, standing behind a curtain, could alternately tauten and loose the rope, making the puppets twirl and flip in their well-oiled joints. This operation wound up an interior mechanism, which at intervals caused the pair to roll their eyes and raise their eyebrows, while their painted lower lips dropped on hinged jaws and a bellows contraption in their chests emitted a tortuous barking squeaking chorus recognized by all as male-female laughter.

"At this point," Maelzel would say, describing the premier performance of the merry pair, "the applause became deafening. Even bloody Ludwig could have heard it."

In America, the Funambulists climaxed the show, puncturing the tension of the chess duel. Intellectual titillation was fine, Maelzel said, but he judged the audiences would be more ready to return if they were sent out into the street with a brisk massage of color, motion, and sound. Schlumberger invariably remained closed inside the automaton box for the duration of their performance, feeling stifled, bored, trying to occupy his mind by devising novel ways to stretch the cramp out of his legs. Perhaps this is why he seldom lost an opportunity to attack the Funambulists.

"It's not deafening."

"What? How would you know, were you there? You can't hear anything inside that box."

"Polite, perhaps. Never deafening."

"Just keep that shit-eating grin on your face," Maelzel would say, lurching from his chair. A moment later he would return, puffing from the quick climb up and down the stairs to his bedroom, bearing one or the other of the scrapbooks. With a reckless, unsteady hand, he would clear aside bottles and plates, snarling at Schlumberger's caution to keep from jostling the chessboard, then leaf through the pages with

The Lost World

hasty reverence till he found the item he wanted. " 'Still another in Mr. Maelzel's ingenious repertoire of automata,' " he would intone, " 'are the Funambulists, contrived with an uncanny mobility of limbs and physiognomy, which closed the evening's festivities to the spirited applause of all.' "

"Spirited is not deafening."

"God damn you, it was deafening!"

Then Schlumberger would shrug and say perhaps American audiences were less sensitive to culture, and Maelzel would be so annoyed he would forget he had a plan to immobilize Schlumberger's queen. Sometimes, particularly when Maelzel began hinting that the chess automaton was a dispensable adjunct to their livelihood, Schlumberger could not resist asking why, if the Funambulists, the panharmonicon, the *Conflagration of Moscow* and all his other automata had been such an unqualified success, their tour had been so brief. Could it be that, with the Turk repining in one of Eugène de Beauharnais' dungeons, the remaining automata were not sufficiently compelling to an audience? Nonsense, Maelzel replied. They could live comfortably with the panharmonicon alone, as Schlumberger damn well knew. Why then, Schlumberger wondered, was the Turk always given the most prominent billing in the posters? Then Maelzel would explain that he had cut short the tour of 1815 not because it was a failure but because he had an opportunity to make a fortune with a new invention. The year 1816 found him in Paris, where he had elicited sufficient financial backing to rent a storefront next door to a perfumer in one of the shops in the basement of the Palais Royal. Over the door he erected a large sign, lettered in gilt-edged scarlet against a purple background, proclaiming J. MAELZEL & CO., THE MAELZEL METRONOME. Here he employed three assistants knocking together his totemic tick-tocking pyramids. He arranged demonstrations in music schools and presented Maelzel Metronomes, affectionately inscribed, to noted symphony conductors. He devoted much attention to the phrasing of posters and advertisements. After a few trials with "Maelzel's Musical Time-Keeper," he settled on "The Maelzel Metronome—A Maelzel on Every Piano." At about this time he began receiving the first in a series of outraged communications from Amsterdam, where a swindler named Winkel was claiming to have constructed a device remarkably similar to Maelzel's.

Whether Maelzel was countering some vaguely sensed threat to his security emanating from the Winkel letters or simply yielding to his inveterate restlessness, he journeyed the next year to Munich, where he had a brief audience with Eugène de Beauharnais. The life of a commander in the field in the years when Bonaparte's empire first bloated like a blood-fed mushroom and then shrank and blackened on the stalk, had toughened him. The courtly flourishes had been drawn from his speech like pus from a wound, leaving him curt and shrewd and bitter. The winter retreat from Moscow, during which he was left to hold together the tatters of the Grande Armée while his stepfather fled to Paris, had frosted the fringes of his sculpted curls. In the debacle following Waterloo he had shed both his pastry-fed chubbiness and the Italian throne. When his stepfather went into exile, de Beauharnais went to Munich, where he came under the protection of his father-in-law, king of Bavaria. Here, as the newly created duke of Leuchtenberg, he lived more modestly than in the days of the Empire.

Maelzel inquired after His Excellency's health. Since Borodino, not the best. Maelzel commented philosophically on the misfortunes of war and public life. De Beauharnais flicked his forefinger impatiently. Maelzel stalked closer to his purpose. If His Excellency would not consider it impertinent, could Maelzel inquire whether he had managed to salvage from the Italian court any of his personal treasures? Yes, and the Von Kempelen automaton among them. Ah! Maelzel exclaimed, then perhaps Maelzel was in a position to perform a small service for His Excellency. Since the automaton had been, if he was not mistaken, in storage during practically all of the seven years de Beauharnais had possessed it, perhaps he would be pleased to dispose of it. Maelzel was organizing another tour of automata, and since he had a nostalgic fondness for the old Turk, and found himself with a handsome capital—2,000 francs to be precise—not grand by His Excellency's standards, but surely a fair and not unwelcome sum in these difficult times . . .

"Take it if you want it," said de Beauharnais, "but the price is 30,000 francs."

Maelzel so far forgot himself as to say 30,000 francs was an exorbitant price.

"I quite agree," replied de Beauharnais.

One question Maelzel consistently evaded, no matter how often

The Lost World

Schlumberger asked, was why he didn't simply make a duplicate of the automaton, and let the Turk continue to gather dust in de Beauharnais' closets. He billed himself a master mechanic, after all, and claimed to be a former official mechanician to the Austrian court—the same office, in fact, that Von Kempelen had held. He expressed himself always eager to roll back his shirt cuffs and dip his fingers in a greasy tangle of bolts and sprockets. On the other hand, Schlumberger reflected, when the panharmonicon had been jarred out of synchronization during a bumpy stage journey, he often directed Rouault to finish the more extensive repairs. His own time, he claimed, was more valuably spent as publicist for the troupe, composing poster advertisements and shaking the hands of editors.

As for the automaton, constructing a copy might involve months of delay. Maelzel may indeed have been nostalgic, or more probably superstitious about the Turk, which seemed to hypnotize audiences with a visage that suggested not lifeless immobility, but passion rigidly controlled, a rage to dominate harnessed by a supreme concentration of intellect. Though it never varied from its small repertoire of movements—an occasional lazy sweep of the head to suggest a mind contemplating the board, the graceful inclination which accompanied its final *"Échec,"* and, most powerfully suggestive, the sharp click of its raising eyelids signifying that an error had been made on the board, the sudden piercing grey gaze of its glass eyes, blind and all-knowing—these sufficed to convince audiences that, like certain busts of the mad Viennese sculptor Messerschmidt, if the Turk didn't come alive it was only because he didn't choose to. Perhaps it was this quality that Maelzel feared himself unable to duplicate.

Also, it is quite probable that he accepted the duke's price because he knew he didn't intend to pay it. De Beauharnais had enjoyed his little revenge, but Maelzel was not wrong in his calculation that he needed money. Maelzel argued that the sum set by De Beauharnais was absurdly beyond his present means, and could be raised only by exhibiting the automaton. Accordingly, De Beauharnais agreed, while insisting on the full 30,000 francs as purchase price, to accept Maelzel's 2000 francs on account and receive the balance in quarterly installments. On the battlefield, too, he had proven stubbornly faithful to principle, but not a brilliant tactician.

A world exhausted by war welcomed the bloodless conflicts of the

[2 6 3]

chessboard enthusiastically. In Paris, then in London for three years, the Turk was one of the most talked of personalities in Europe. Particularly in London, where, with the brilliant Mouret directing its moves, the Turk offered pawn and move to all challengers and conceded, according to Maelzel's frequent boast to Schlumberger, only six games in three hundred. The Turk's immense popularity must have enabled Maelzel to fulfill his contract with de Beauharnais several times over, if that had been his serious intention. Thus Maelzel's only excuse for falling in arrears—the poor response to his tour through Holland in 1821–22—rings hollow. After the success of the four previous years, what could have remained of the debt if he had not already fallen into the habit of paying de Beauharnais late and short? He would have been encouraged in his delinquency by the knowledge that for such a simple toy, 30,000 francs was after all an outrageous price.

During 1822 the tone of de Beauharnais' letters of complaint shifted from sluggish to vexed, then settled into a climbing scale of threats. Maelzel responded by keeping the Turk on tour as much as possible. Papers bearing the Leuchtenberg seal that from time to time caught up with him found their way unopened into his waste basket.

At about this time the Amsterdam inventor, Winkel, instituted legal proceedings against Maelzel, claiming that the Maelzel Metronome being marketed in Paris was in fact the Winkel Metronome. He asserted that Maelzel had copied every particular of his design except the calibrating scale, which had been needlessly complexified. In fact, the main advantage the Maelzel Metronome had over its rival was that Maelzel had known how to make people want it. Somehow, whether in a business agreement or as a byproduct of an unrecorded reconciliation, he advertised his metronome with an endorsement by Ludwig van Beethoven. His posters, taking full advantage of the happy alliteration which welded the name of the device to his own name, brought it to the attention of every musician in Europe. And his factory made it available in quantity.

In the de Beauharnais affair an unexpected deliverance seemed to be presaged in 1824. At the age of forty-three, exhausted by a lifetime of court intrigues and military campaigns, Eugène de Beauharnais died. Within weeks, however, Maelzel discovered that the Leuchtenberg heirs were more clamorous for payment than their departed relation. He received notice that he was being sued both for the return of the Turk and all proceeds from its exhibit. There were rude hints of criminal charges for fraud.

Schlumberger would remember Maelzel, gnawing pensively at the scant meat on a turkey gizzard, muttering, ''That damned tin soldier . . . must have told them, in his *death rattle* to get me. Willie, my boy, remember one thing,'' he would say—and, remembering the move he had been contemplating, he would drop the meat onto his plate and reach for the piece.

''Ah-ah,'' Schlumberger would caution, and the hand would stop directly over the piece.

''What's wrong with that move?'' Maelzel would squeal. ''I'm going to take your goddamn knight.''

''Your fingers.''

And Maelzel would obediently wipe his greasy fingers on the tablecloth, take Schlumberger's knight and continue with, ''Willie— one thing: diddle anybody you like, but never, not if he threatens to burn you at the stake, never give in to the temptation to let him know he's been diddled. He'll never forgive you for it, and he'll make your life miserable even after he's dead.''

As with all prophetic statements, it would be a long time before these words yielded to Schlumberger their full significance. At the moment all he could do was advance his queen into the space newly occupied by the piece which had just taken his knight, putting his queen on a lethal diagonal with Maelzel's king.

''*Échec et mat,*'' said Schlumberger, smiling complacently.

During his altercation with Beethoven, Maelzel had devised a simple, effective strategy for slicing through legal verbiage— exodus. With his valuable automata and the ''Battle of Vittoria'' score, or as many of the instrumental parts as he could filch, he had boarded a coach under an assumed name and disappeared from Vienna. He left his Viennese attorney locked in battle with the attorney representing Beethoven's affairs, busily stewing a rich compost of words. The attorney was to realize only months later that his Augean labors, too, would go unpaid. Then, as the winter of 1825 drew close, the Winkel lawsuit loomed. The Leuchtenberg heirs maneuvered with implacable, passionless thoroughness. On December twentieth, again under an assumed name, he embarked on the packet ship *Howard*. In the hold lay the Turk's several amputated parts, distributed in five separate crates labeled with innocuous incognito. He was bound for America, a *tabula rasa* awaiting the seven magic letters of his name.

Prudence demanded, however, that the slate remain unmarked, at least until he could be certain that his enemies in Europe had been lured onto a false scent by a discreetly planted rumor that he was in rapidly failing health and had taken refuge somewhere in Hungary. By carefully husbanding his funds he calculated that he could support the troupe, including himself and the Rouaults, in idleness and secrecy for three months. A packet from Europe docked in New York every two weeks. That would allow the Leuchtenberg-Winkel bloodhounds six opportunities to prove whether they could track him. If they had not done so in that time, he might safely conclude that the trail was cold. Then he could discard his alias and launch his campaign to put Maelzel's Fabulous Chess Automaton on the lips of every American.

But he had not anticipated the hunger of the American press to make him famous. Before such coltish eagerness half his prudence succumbed before he had been on the soil of the New World five minutes. Coming down the gangplank he was accosted by a frisky young man, who asked if he had the pleasure of addressing Professor Gebir. It had been six weeks since Maelzel had signed the ship's register as I. Gebir, professor of polypharmacy and author of *Summa Perfectionis*. His response, therefore, was a curt, "Certainly not," followed by a stammer that was tilting toward an acknowledgement that he was indeed Professor Gebir, when at the last moment, sniffing ink on the fellow's fingers, he instead asked the gentleman's reason for inquiring. When he learned that the fellow dancing along to keep in step with him was a representative of the *Ship News,* a sudden access of candor demanded that he confess himself. Probably only the raised eyebrows of the Rouaults, who stood by during his interview, prevented him from proclaiming the Turk as well.

Whatever remaining hope Maelzel had of resisting temptation he abandoned within the next forty-eight hours. On his second evening in New York he left the Rouaults in their quarters in the National Hotel, 112 Broadway, announcing his intention to explore the metropolis. An hour later he had found his way to Blin's Chess Rooms on Warren Street, headquarters of the New York Chess Club. "I hadn't planned to say a word, Willie," he once explained to Schlumberger. "I only wanted to size up the competition." Among the first persons to whom he was introduced, however, was William Coleman, one of the strongest players in the city. Mr. Coleman was the editor of the *Evening Post*. Within a short time the editorial page of the *Evening Post* was describing to its readers a remarkable invention.

In the weeks that followed, articles relating to the automaton continued to explode with the regularity of grapeshot in a systematically planned artillery barrage. Each day Maelzel would meet at Blin's with the likes of Coleman, Ezra Weeks, Antonio Rapallo, and Judge Fisk, a brilliant old curmudgeon who clung to the Johnsonian periwigs and breeches of the previous century. Maelzel filled the expansive bonhomie that followed a closely fought contest with fascinating, mysterious talk. Over the brimming claret glasses, while some men softened up a plug of tobacco and others, Maelzel among them, puffed long currents of cigar smoke, he spoke of the coming uses of androids and hinted about the mysterious power source that had been harnessed to govern the automaton. A day or two later the *Evening Post* would be treating its readers to speculations on the future utopia to be created with android slaves, or to countless speculations on the nature of the mysterious principles operating the yet unseen automaton. Only Judge Fisk, who was generally acknowledged as the most powerful American chess player until the appearance of Paul Morphy, seemed to demur, and he was met with an embarrassed silence when he had the poor taste to suggest that Maelzel was talking gibberish.

At a certain point Maelzel realized that the *Evening Post*'s readers had been tantalized to the point of being cloyed. Without some release, frustrated desire would spill over into irritation, and stagnate. And after all, Maelzel reasoned, the secret was out. His presence in America and the existence of the automaton could hardly be more public. An actual performance by the Turk could only augment its celebrity, and bring money as well. Four packets from Le Havre had already docked in the East River since his arrival, and they had not unleashed upon him threats of impoundment or prison. After a hasty business conference with the manager, the lobby of the National Hotel was outfitted as a theatre. Curtains were strung from pillars, chairs assembled, a slack-rope strung for the Funambulists. An announcement of the Turk's debut, along with the "Automaton Trumpeter and the Incredible Funambulist Rope Dancers," was published in the April 11 issue of the *Evening Post*. Two nights later, the "Turbaned Turk" raised its head, swept its sightless gaze over the lobby with serpentine smoothness, and nodded regally to signify that it was ready to receive its first American challenger. Inside the cabinet was Louise Rouault.

She was not a strong player. Maelzel accepted necessary risks, but tried to minimize them. Prior to the performance he explained that the automaton had been damaged in passage, and that extensive repairs were still being made. For the present, therefore, the Turk could play only composed end games, and the machinery would not function properly unless the Turk retained the privilege of making the first move. These end games could be selected from a little book bound in green morocco, which Maelzel passed around the room. It contained about fifty end games. What Maelzel did not tell the audience was that the book had been compiled by a London chess master named William Lewis, one of the automaton's former directors. They were constructed in such a way that Maelzel could offer challengers either side, black or white, and win every time. Most challengers sized up the board and chose the side with the most powerful and numerous pieces. With the Turk moving first, that side was sure to lose, usually within about five moves. Occasionally an acute or suspicious challenger would deliberately choose what looked like the weak side. Then the Turk's first move privilege would be used to spoil the sure-win solution, and the contest would be fought, more uncertainly perhaps, but with all the piece values that had made the challenger suspicious now weighting the contest for the Turk.

During the Atlantic crossing and for three hours a day since the troupe had been in New York, Louise had been catechised on the contents of what they called the green book. She had memorized all the endings. The problem was that inferior players did not always make the best, most logical move, the one she had memorized. Then the game was in jeopardy. On that first night, playing both sides of Philip Stamma's forty-first ending, she won both games. The audience was relatively small compared with those to come, but most enthusiastic. At the close of the exhibition the Turk was wheeled off "amid great and deserved plaudits." These were the words of the enthusiastic Coleman. Soon crowds were being turned away for both the afternoon and evening performances. The hotel manager, who was collecting a percentage, strutted the lobby beaming and bowing, almost as officious as Maelzel himself. The next week the Turk lost two games.

The Lost World

Maelzel called that a monumental stupidity. He did not, however, replace Louise Rouault as the automaton's director. The story George Allen relates, that he flattered Coleman with the secret and engaged his son to direct the automaton and later solicited the additional assistance of two other friends from Blin's, is totally incredible. With the Turk's secret Maelzel was never promiscuous. And he would most especially not have confessed it to Coleman. A journalist was the last person to whom he would have confided a truth that made him so vulnerable.

What he did was to close the automaton for immediate, emergency repairs. The repairs consisted of two fourteen-hour sessions with Louise. He worked out as many possible variants as he could imagine on the fifty end-game solutions and made her memorize them. Then the exhibit reopened, and the Turk played two performances a day for another month, winning often by a hairsbreadth in games that twisted the original problems into bizarre shapes, but winning consistently. He had no intention of making the June first performance the last for more than three months.

"At least the bastard waited until after the game," Maelzel told Schlumberger. "I was at the lobby door shaking hands as I always do, and suddenly I've got this envelope in my hand. I look up and here's a wiry little fellow grinning at me like this, with his tongue laying on his lower lip. 'What's this?' I say. 'A court summons, Monsieur Maelzel. I am the legal agent of the late prince, Eugène de Beauharnais.' Fuck!"

The next day at noon, customers for the first performance found posted at the lobby entrance Maelzel's Performance Canceled sign. For the following month, in courtrooms and out, Maelzel fought with every resource of language in his arsenal to keep possession of the Turk, while the Turk itself, with an expression on its face of calm, meditative patience, sat in a wedge of shadow under the hotel's grand staircase, staring at the blank squares of the chessboard before it. On July 3 Maelzel paid the Leuchtenberg agent $800 and was given a piece of paper granting him clear title to the Von Kempelen automaton. By the fifth he and the Rouaults had crated the automata and were on a coach for Boston.

Maelzel was both furious and chastised. He was in a fury that he had been chastised. He considered the $800 settlement an outrage, though in later years he would boast that his skill in negotiation had forced upon the Leuchtenberg's a considerable compromise with their first demand. He seemed to be cursing each particular rut in the road, which meant that as they traveled the Rouaults were treated to an almost constant monologue of mumbles and barks. But his chastisement had also wrought in him a resurgence of virtue. He resolved with the fervor of a penitent once more to embrace prudence. The automaton must be kept from public display until he found a knowledgeable chess player to be its brain. A few nights before they left New York, at a time when the final mocking outline of the Leuchtenberg settlement was looming through a fog of rhetoric, his fury had given way to a moody ruminativeness. He ate listlessly, rearranging peas and potatoes on the plate as if they could be made to yield a message. His mind was groping among the tangle of threads by which he made his world dance. He grasped the one he wanted, gave a tug.

"Louise," he said, and Schlumberger could imagine his eyetooth flickering its gold plug at the corner of his grin, "when is the last time you wrote that damned Alsatian?"

Maelzel would have known Louise had been corresponding with Schlumberger. Each packet that sailed since the second week of May had carried a thick envelope in which the record of her impressions of America and her homesickness provided the occasion for a sinuous dance of hint and flattery. In the light of subsequent events Schlumberger considered it probable that her correspondence had been encouraged if not actually suggested by Maelzel. As for the letter of June 29, it was a melody constantly changing tempo until he at last became convinced that it was composed at Maelzel's direct instigation. What he could never resolve was the nature of that instigation. At one time, sick with love, he would imagine Maelzel raging, bullying, threatening, and a terrified Louise penning a tearful and nearly truthful plea. Later, when it became necessary to anesthetize himself against the possibility that Louise had ever felt the slightest affection for him, he convinced himself that the letter had been drafted by them both. He saw them clearly as the first memory of childhood, cozily side by side at the table, her hair drawn so tightly down from its center part that the candle flame bounced off the surface of a black mirror, Maelzel rolling brandy in his cheeks and offering suggestions: "Tell him you dream of his cock." Merry giggles; a blot on the manuscript. Through hiccups of laughter: "Be sensible; he'd never believe that." "Dearie, any man would, and get stiff just thinking it."

The Lost World

Thus Schlumberger, stretched on the rack, writhing, sketching in the details of a likely, unknowable world. Thinking how Maelzel must have arrived in Boston confident that the trap was succulently baited. All he had to do was last twelve weeks: six for the letter to find its way to Schlumberger, about thirty seconds for him to decide what to do with it, and six weeks more for him to cross the Atlantic. And if Maelzel had been allowed—as Schlumberger became convinced he must have been—to see Schlumberger's replies to Louise, those ever more arch and ardent confessions of bondage that he regularly floated with the Atlantic tide, he would have known that the bait was right and that if he could cultivate prudence until the end of September, virtue's reward would be gold. But Maelzel couldn't wait.

In America opportunities hounded Maelzel, hurled themselves at him in the street like unpaid creditors. Walking down Milk Street in Boston he saw the For Rent sign in front of Julian Hall and peeled off a deposit from his freshly changed roll of American currency without even knowing he was setting up his theatre next door to the boarding house of Mrs. Lydia Vose, who kept a parlor where the best chess players in the city met. Stopping there for dinner, how could he avoid seeing the strewn copies of the New England *Galaxy* and *Columbian Centinel,* folded to the pages that gave detailed reports of the Turk's New York exhibition? When he found that without any attempt on his part to fuel controversy, the merits and workings of the Turk were the subject of simmering debate, how could he refrain from admitting that he himself was the celebrated Maelzel and the automaton they spoke of was sitting, still in its travel crates, at the next door?

Schlumberger didn't have to guess or deduce or invent what happened next, because Maelzel told it himself. He talked automatically while his hands kept up a frantic swing from plate to mouth, stuffing it with turkey or oysters or whatever they were eating that night as if for all his garrulity a hysterical demon inhabiting his body were trying to plug up the word hole, jam it closed, drive them back. It was the first episode of the Greco story. Telling it, Maelzel would do Abe Fuller bulging his eyes and choking on his greens until he could sputter, "Yu-gak-*you* are Mr. Maelzel?" He would take all the other parts, too: Doc Greene, Tom Eckley, Bob Paine and the rest, but chiefly he would act the central role, Maelzel, as Maelzel, ever so calmly, urbanely, expertly drawing them in, so that within five minutes the abstract argument about whether a machine could play chess had become a question of whether they could beat it, and more—whether they could beat what Maelzel was strongly hinting the New York Chess Club couldn't beat. Because that was where the rivalry was born, though the newspapers wouldn't pick it up for a few weeks yet.

By the time he said goodnight that evening, the coaxing had already turned into a clamor to see the Turk in action. But Maelzel remembered prudence and told them his repairs to the delicate mechanism would doubtless take until the end of September. Later, when he began running low on money, he hinted that perhaps the Turk would be ready for end games a little earlier. He kept his vow of prudence until September 13. He gambled that if he could stay firm in his resolve to decline full games, Louise Rouault knew the green book of end games well enough to keep the Bostonians at bay until Schlumberger arrived. The gamble failed. Within two weeks Louise had lost three games.

That, Maelzel shrieked, was the most colossal display of stupidity he had ever seen. And Schlumberger could hear how, even in his rage, he would hesitate at the word *stupidity,* summoning in the last instant, with the aid of a convulsion that made his cheeks shudder like a luffing sail, the control to keep from calling it the betrayal he truly thought it, but was afraid to utter; so that the word exploded with more intensity than the word itself could hold but also a faint lack of resonance. For a week Maelzel ground Louise's stupidity in the crucible of his rage, following her from room to room with curses, filling the air with their sulfurous odor, as if the sheer corrosive power of them were a fuming *aqua regia* that could dissolve the facts, dissolve history itself. By the time Schlumberger arrived, his cursing had given way to another, more subtle form of verbal attack. He strode the streets humming as if he had at last discovered the universal solvent. He had devised a way to make the civic pride of the Bostonians and New Yorkers ease the sting of the Turk's humiliation.

And when he explained the plan to Schlumberger, told how he had stood for five minutes in front of a mirror before he left the house—until he could set his face like clay hardening in the sun in that mask of duty and outrage and Tell-the-truth-though-you're-damned-for-it that he knew he would need to make the plan carry—Schlumberger, no matter how many times he heard it, would begin chuckling, snorting the way he would over a poisoned pawn play, when the poor arse-worm who thinks he is picking a little sweetmeat from the dish gets that eggsmell look on his face and realizes you've pinned his queen. And when Maelzel told about being ushered into the inner sanctum of the *Centinel* editor, doing for Schlumberger his first view of Mortimer Salt perched behind his desk like a rabbit in the vegetable garden who hears someone coming and can't decide whether to drop the lettuce and run or try for one more leaf, Schlumberger would whinny and gag and pound the table even if it upset the board, ruined a combination he had spent an hour developing and couldn't restore—not because he didn't recollect the placement of every piece but because Maelzel didn't, and wouldn't believe or claimed not to trust Schlumberger's reconstruction.

Schlumberger never met Salt, but he knew all about him from Maelzel. Though not a chess player, Salt had made space in his paper for the Turk's exploits because he knew the future was going to be shaped by machines and stirring interest in Progress was his journalistic and patriotic duty. He did it because his readers would argue, vigorously and at length in his editorial columns, about whether the Turk was a real automaton and how it worked. He did it because the *Galaxy* did it. And Maelzel told of freezing that flair-nostrilled nobility on his face while he explained to Salt that he had come to him as one gentleman to another with a serious ethical problem, and showed Schlumberger how Salt, sitting behind the scrolled oak desk in his private frosted-glass cubicle in the *Centinel* offices, had stiffened his back like a bunny when he hears a twig snap. Maelzel said he had told Salt the last thing in the world he wanted was to advertise the fact that occasionally, when its sensitive tuning had been damaged by travel, the automaton *could* lose a game, and he did Salt saying, "Uh-huh, uh-huh," which was how Salt filled every pause in the conversation, and showed how Salt pumped his jaw against a small plug of tobacco in quick jerky chews that bulged a muscle in Maelzel's cheek and made him look exactly like a worried hungry rabbit. And Maelzel told how he said to Salt that a man, a *gentle*man had a duty to put aside personal inconvenience if he had genuine respect for truth, and did Salt saying, "Uh-huh, uh-huh, any decent gentleman." Maelzel said he confessed that he knew one of Salt's writers was in the audience last night, and he would not dream of asking Salt to suppress the report of the automaton's defeat. "Uh-huh, couldn't do that," Maelzel would say, quoting Salt, and chew faster and squeeze his elbows to his sides with his forearms cocked in front of him and the hands dangling from the wrists like bunny paws. And then Maelzel would lean forward over the table toward Schlumberger and put in his voice a tone of solemn intimacy and show how he had told Salt, ''But I thought this might be a proper time, perhaps the most fitting time, to correct a vile untruth. A lie.'' Then, doing Salt, he would perch stiff-backed on the edge of his chair, stop chewing and tilt his bifocals onto his forehead and give a rabbity twitch to his nose.

''The fact is, I told him,'' Maelzel would say, his brow drawn and creased as it had been when he was actually talking to Salt, ''the reports of the automaton's games have been, putting it generously, misrepresented in the New York press. Defeat? In New York? I tell you, sir, there's not a single chess player in that city who is decent competition for the Turk.'' And then he would sit back again, showing how Salt's jaw became rigid as his back, and say ''Huh?'' and settle his glasses in place with another rabbity nose twitch and give Schlumberger the startled blinking look Salt had given him.

''Truth will out, Mr. Salt, I told him,'' he said, leaning forward again as he had over Salt's desk, ''I have to say it. The automaton chess machine never suffered a defeat in this country until—'' and he held the sentence suspended while he filled the pause with several Saltish uh-huh's gabbled rapidly, ''—until last night—at the hands of—a Bostonian.'' And here Maelzel, who had done the whole thing straight-faced while Schlumberger roared and sobbed with laughter, broke down as well and whooped, ''By the nuts, Willie! I had his nuts in the palm of my hand and when I gave a little squeeze I could make him dance a jig on the ceiling.'' And Schlumberger's own whoops slowly dropped into contented sighs as he wiped his eyes and poured another glass of sherry for himself and Maelzel, thinking how the world was full of gullible people like Salt who deserved what they got.

That was how Maelzel transformed the Turk's humiliation into a crusade for truth. The next day's *Centinel* claimed the honor of the first American victory over the automaton for a Bostonian—''reports from the Commercial Emporium to the contrary notwithstanding.'' The New York *American* replied with acid dignity to ''slurs upon both its veracity and the honor of the metropolitan populace.'' Its earlier reports were unequivocally reaffirmed: it was in New York and nowhere else that the automaton had been first defeated. What was more, it had been defeated

The Lost World

there not once but twice. That same night Louise lost two more games, and the *Centinel*'s next issue said that even if the *American*'s boast were true, (and the editors had authoritative information to the contrary) the automaton had now been defeated by Bostonians three times.

Until this point Maelzel had been able to orchestrate the debate with the despotism of a symphony conductor. He wafted his baton, and the *Centinel* stroked the buoyant chords of the first movement, cocky, aggressive, the bows bouncing along the strings; a frolic. With a dip of his powerful wand, the *American* trumpeted, all brass and bustle, bass tuba, trombone, kettledrum. *Zing-tiddle-dum,* replied the strings: *No, you shan't, I'll dance my dance.* And the *Centinel* readers' column swelled a woodwind chorus of mail. It was a verbal "Battle of Vittoria," with the *Centinel* and the *American* dueling like the English and French to what Maelzel hoped would be a similarly profitable cacophonic finale. It was the only tune Maelzel knew, but it had a rousing beat, and he knew well enough how to disguise it so that you might hear it again and again without recognizing it.

Now, with the commencement of the lyric movement, Maelzel found his autonomy challenged by a revolt among his musicians. After the lumbering blat of *American* brass had been outrun by Boston's three quick victories over the Turk, reported in the *Centinel* with breathless flourish, there followed a pause. An entire issue of the *American* passed without mention of the Turk. The editorial in the next issue commenced temperately, a solo voice fragile as an oboe suggesting that end games were not chess, full games were chess. The threat was muted, hardly perceptible to any but Maelzel's delicate ear. The second paragraph, insidious as piccolos, swelled the movement: The Boston end game victories could well be flukes. There were New York chessmen the Turk in full games could never defeat. When would full games grace the automaton's board? A letter in the same issue broached an angry scherzo quite unplanned by Maelzel. With authoritative scholarship the author asserted that end games were problems with certain solutions. Known in advance, they erased from the game the surprises of chance. If one knew solutions the other did not, they were no true test of a chess player's worth. Had anyone analysed end games played by the Turk? Were they true contests with multiple possible endings? The letter was signed "Greco," an alias that recalled a seventeenth-century chess bandit who played for high stakes and had once in a few months won 5,000 crowns, enough in that time to secure a man's comfort for five years.

Breathlessly Maelzel flailed his baton. Ridiculous theory, riposted the *Centinel*. New Yorkers were churls in defeat. And Boston, proud Boston would prove its mettle in full games as well as it had in end games whenever the chance was forthcoming. In the final movement the *Centinel* and the *American* joined in a strident terrifying climax. Supported by the full blast of percussion and brass, the woodwinds shrieked and the strings sizzled a single clamorous question: When would the Turk play full games?

Maelzel, his baton pitifully wilted, awaited Schlumberger.

"So, everything depended on me," Schlumberger said, because that was the way Maelzel had explained it. He never asked how Maelzel knew he would come. That was one of the things they agreed without talking about it not to talk about.

Schlumberger had won the last game of the evening half an hour ago. The board lay as they had left it, Maelzel's king trapped between Schlumberger's knight and bishop. The oil lamp flickered. Black smoke rose from the chimney. Maelzel reached across the table and twisted the knob just enough to allow the flame another quarter inch of wick. It would burn lean but steady for fifteen or twenty minutes, then begin another paroxysm. Schlumberger had watched him play with it like that all evening. He refused to let himself wonder why it disturbed him. When Maelzel leaned over the lamp, the black of his pupils seemed to split open and spill two slits of golden light.

A saucer at Maelzel's right hand cupped four cigar butts strewn among their ashes. In the heat of the game Maelzel had stubbed the burnt ends so hard the leaf wrappers bent and split, making pedestals. Three of the four butts stood on their pedestals in a grey, flaking loam. The saucer looked like a forest of burnt-out stumps. The soggy ends were wetly frayed. They still retained in the pulpy brown leaf wrap the print of Maelzel's teeth.

The lamp smoke rose through the heavy silver waves of cigar smoke like strands of black hair coiling in an underwater current. Cigar smoke filled the room, pouring listlessly. The windows had been opened to admit a night breeze, but none stirred. The window admitted mosquitoes impervious to the smoke. They whined and resettled boldly

The Lost World

exactly where they had been slapped away. The rasp of cicadas in the oaks outside the window rose and died like steady snoring. It must have been August, though the same conversation probably took place half a dozen times in as many years.

They were in the old Fifth Street building in Philadelphia where they made their headquarters off and on from 1827 until the end. The room might once have been a parlor, but they had dragged in a table so they could take meals there in the overstuffed easy chairs where they could sit for hours rather than in the hard stiff-backed chairs in the large bare dining room. The scars and debris of use crusted the room. Maroon splashes stained two walls. The rug around the spittoon was matted and sticky. A stray cat Schlumberger had admitted one rainy night carried table scraps to odd corners of the room, where they grew a bilious mold. They distracted the flies from the table food, Schlumberger contended. Just the same, Rouault would sweep it all out every week or two. On the fireplace mantle stood a dozen books haphazardly stacked, three metronomes, a windup drummer boy in a French uniform, a clay pipe with a bowl so charred your little finger could plug it, and a stuffed owl. Its eyes followed you to every corner in the room. The walls were hung with hunting prints and old posters from cities in Europe and the United States where the automaton had played. All bore Maelzel's name in red letters edged in gold. Three frock coats were draped on chairbacks; three pair of boots were scattered on the floor. One pair stood guard by the spittoon. Another lay on their sides under the table. A third was set with the toes pointing parallel and the heels against the armchair where Rouault lay sleeping. Rouault sprawled with his right leg over the arm of the chair and his left hand palm up on the floor. His head lay tilted back in the crook of the chair's other arm. His mouth was open as if his tongue were awaiting a host.

"It's an interesting problem in tactics," Schlumberger said, wrapping his tongue carefully around the words. He was ponderously drunk. "You had to give them full games. I can see that. And the bitch couldn't do it." (Schlumberger, too, had learned to avoid her name.) "It was up to me. But—"(He swallowed a hiccup with a refined yawn) "but why did you close the show for two weeks? I could have learned the Turk in two or three days." Then, as if the estimate must be precise as a metronome calibration, he reconsidered and said, "Surely, two or three."

[2 7 7]

Maelzel held the sherry bottle to the light. Less than half-full. He poured first for himself, then for Schlumberger. Three bottles like it, empty, sat among the chesspieces and uncleared dinner dishes and the corpses of insects that the flame had sucked in through the window and danced with until they died. The table between them was stacked and cluttered. Schlumberger's side had only a plate with the fork and knife lying among the fat scraps he always cut away from his beef, a goblet full of wine, and most of the chesspieces. The chessmen stood in clusters like prisoners of war plotting an escape.

Everything else on the table belonged to Maelzel. The two empty sherry bottles and the partly full one. The forest of cigar stumps. His own goblet and plate, along with a deep dish for soup and Schlumberger's soup dish, which he had passed to Maelzel because he didn't like the taste of potato soup. A dessert plate scraped clean of cherry cobbler. Several bones and a gnawed turkey gizzard that he had snacked on at about 11 P.M. while he was absorbed in beating off Schlumberger's encroaching end game, and had not bothered to find a place for on his plate. Serving dishes, too, gravitated toward Maelzel's end of the table, so that he seemed to have collected the bowl of sour-cream biscuits, the remaining wedge of a sweet-potato pie, the plate on which a gob of butter had melted into a rancid yellow pool. Everything on the table seemed to have been sorted and gathered close to the one who needed it most. They were like a pair of misers who had agreed not to covet the same treasures.

Maelzel, also drunk, was being judiciously prudent in his answers: "You might have learned it in two days, Willie. But I didn't know you then. I didn't know whether you could or not." He didn't remind Schlumberger of his nearly total mechanical ineptitude or of his habit of falling asleep in the box. He also didn't mention that Louise Rouault had announced that she would have nothing to do with the chess player once he arrived, and he would have had to plan on at least two weeks to get that problem under control.

"But you promised them full games by the middle of October. You must have trusted me that much." Schlumberger coarsened his voice like a scab of ice to cover the plea beneath.

"Willie, I did know what kind of chess player you were. It was only a question of teaching you how to operate the pantograph."

Two flies had mired in the pool of rancid butter and died there, an irresistible lethargy of oily golden syrup weighting their wings. A third, unawed by their fate, perched on the rim stirring the pool with its forelegs, making up its mind.

Maelzel explained how on the thirteenth of October, when he knew Schlumberger could operate the Turk, he had gone back on the offensive in the newspaper campaign. It wasn't just a question of announcing that on the sixteenth the automaton would play Bostonians in full games. The art of it was to suggest that Bostonians were the first challengers truly *fit* to meet the Turk in full games. It was all a question of carefully turned phrases like "with all due respect to the manly efforts of the cavaliers of the Commercial Emporium, we nonetheless feel . . ."

"And that was the bait you thought would get you Greco?"

"But it didn't. Not yet."

"And what did you think that first week, when I lost two games?"

"Best thing that could have happened. *That's* what got him. The *Centinel* brayed so loud about Boston chess players, those dumb buggers in New York must have thought they had lye up their holes. If Greco or somebody down there didn't say, 'We'll play that goddam machine for big money,' they never would have been able to get a stiff cock again."

Schlumberger didn't, for once, join Maelzel's cackle.

"I meant," he said, "what were you thinking of *me*. I'd lost two games. Weren't you afraid he was going to beat me?"

Silver cigar smoke hovered in the wiry silver bristles of Maelzel's side whiskers and crown. The smoke seemed a silvery secretion of his concentration. Carefully, more carefully than Schlumberger noticed at the time, he said, "I trusted your chess game, Willie."

"You didn't always. Remember the night you put back one of my moves? Occasionally a gear slips, you said. The automaton has erred."

"And you moved the piece again."

"I had to do it three times before you let it stand. I was damned if I was going to let you spoil that game. I had a bishop sacrifice that would make the bastard's queen fall into my lap on the fifth move. You should have left me alone. You should have trusted me."

More than once on nights when the oil had burnt low in the lamp and Schlumberger had passed and repassed his glass for a refill, Maelzel had seen these abrupt breakdowns in his mellowness. It was like changing the setting of a metronome from a lazy largo to a presto. A cord in his neck stood out and began to throb. His eyes blinked rapidly. His voice quivered as if he were a rag doll clutched and shaken in the jaws of a fierce hysterical terrier. Maelzel knew the evening was careening toward violence. While he deliberated how to respond, he took from his pocket a jumble of gold coins that he liked to play with. He set them on the table behind his gold-rimmed bifocals. Often while he was thinking out a move he would stack them into a tower, as he did now. Then he would cup his hand over them, pick them up by the bottom coin, and release them one by one, letting them chink onto the table top with diminishing resonance. They would chink together rapidly or slowly as his calculations came swift or sluggish.

Chink, went a coin, and Maelzel said, "Willie . . ." (Chink.) ". . . you'd already . . ." (Chink.) ". . . lost . . ." (Chink.) ". . . two games that week." (Chinka, chink.) "How was I to know?"

"By looking at the board."

Maelzel made his face as unreflecting as he supposed the Turk's was. At these times Schlumberger parsed the slightest gesture. Maelzel might be required to justify the twitch of an eyebrow, a fractional lift at the corner of his mouth. An exhale long enough to be called a sigh or forceful enough for a snort would call down a lengthy, violent rebuttal. He watched Schlumberger with what he hoped was inoffensive blandness. He had once seen Schlumberger in a crowded restaurant absentmindedly bring to his lips a raw oyster. He didn't seem to have any consciousness of what had gone into his mouth until the slippery meat was too far back on his palate to recall. The change came first to his eyes, which bulged as if a pair of fingers inside his skull were trying to push them out the sockets. A fraction later, like a spreading ripple, his mouth and throat contorted with nausea. He got it down, but it leached all the color from his cheeks. A single contraction of his brow squeezed out pimple-sized beads of sweat. "I hate oysters," he said, trembling. "Hate them." And he left the table. Now, as if to overcome a similar nausea, Schlumberger gulped hard. The metronomic artery in his neck, which had been throbbing boldly, detumesced, almost dissolved into the smooth flesh of his neck. A fresh tempo, a longer swing of the pendulum succeeded.

"But you were right, weren't you," Schlumberger said. "I proved it: you couldn't trust me. After all that planning. Weeks, months of it.

Just when you had him. Had Greco willing to bet a thousand dollars. I picked that moment to disappear." Almost inaudibly, he added, "Following that fucking bitch."

Maelzel could take a breath. Risk a comment.

"You didn't know," he said. How long did Schlumberger have to maneuver before he extracted this benediction? And how often, unable to believe it, did he force its repetition? Perhaps he never learned to trust that as the years passed Maelzel's rage over the Greco stupidity had dissipated, exorcized at last by the endless repetitive obscenities through which he vented it. Perhaps he always suspected that the sense of betrayal burned hot as ever, damped by an expedient lie: the kind of lie that made a life under the same roof possible. For Schlumberger, no subsequent revision could cancel the violent sincerity of that first eruption. From the first contemptuously expectorated "Stupidity!" and the dysenteric flow that word unblocked, the hatred was so powerful Schlumberger could never fully or for long believe, no matter how many times he was assured of it, that he had been forgiven.

Because in the Greco scheme all Maelzel's genius for transforming reality through rhetoric was charged tight and lethal as the mouth of a cannon. But in those last weeks it was as if a mad artilleryman were packing the charge, pouring down the barrel more gunpowder than could ever be needed just to sail the ball far enough and accurately to the target, packing down the waiting mouth so much in the way of physical exhaustion and suspended hopes and interminable calculations that the slightest spark could only erupt in a suicidal explosion of the weapon itself.

The night Maelzel found him in the waterfront hotel where he had burrowed himself, Schlumberger had just spent two days roaming the streets with a sprained wrist, a pair of cracked ribs, and a face more scab than skin. Maelzel had just completed a three-day coach trip from Boston over roads made of felled tree trunks dragged onto the highway, haphazardly trimmed, unplaned, and leveled with mud that had washed away in the first storm. Within two hours of their tussle on the bedroom floor Maelzel started back over the same road, Schlumberger in tow. Rattling into Boston twelve hours into the third day of the return journey, which had begun at four-thirty that morning after a four-hour nap in a wayside inn, they deployed sleepless and unfed. Schlumberger helped Rouault to dismantle and crate the automatons and see to their loading on a specially hired coach, while Maelzel, pausing only for a shave and a vigorous brushing to get the road grit off his shoulders, spent the next eight hours hunting down all the chess players he knew to put them on notice that Boston's prowess and veracity and manhood had been insulted by an upstart New York tyro who called himself Greco.

And he couldn't just spit the story out onto the table and expect it would do its own work. The story wasn't that good. It had a false-bottom drawer that was hard to disguise, a space filled only with words. No matter how important it was to crank the last sprocket of tension into the rivalry between the two cities, every art had to be simultaneously employed to conduct all that passion through the automaton. Maelzel's eloquence had to be a precise vector spinning the gears of the Greco scheme fast enough to blur the fact that the Turk was only an incidental focus of the dispute. Telling the story more than a dozen times to men all over the city, he had to balance force against force, each time with the vividness he brought to the first time, whirling each tooth through its socket in the same artful acceleration from outrage to ferocity, so that before he got out the last word, his audience would be rolling with such velocity they would seize it away from him and continue under their own momentum. He wouldn't have to ask for what he wanted, it wouldn't even have to be his suggestion, because they would already be diving into their desk drawers for the checkbook or counting off bills, pushing the money at him with a fervor that combined bloodlust with patriotism as they said, ''You take this now—no, don't refuse, I'll not have it—you take it back to New York with your automaton and tell them when a Boston man wins a chess game, it's not by luck, by God.'' And when he had raised a thousand dollars that way in a few minutes less than eight hours, it was midnight, and still with no sleep he had climbed aboard another Concord coach along with Schlumberger and Rouault, and spent his third set of three days in two weeks rattling over the hard-rutted, jolt-studded ribs of the Boston Post Road.

And after they arrived, moments after their bags smacked the floor of a rooming-house hallway, off he went again, a perpetual motion machine, this time to the editorial offices of the *American* with the story that the chess community of Boston was puffing the accidental wins they had scored while the automaton's mechanism was out of tune by claiming—with the arrogance of a $1,000 wager—that their fluke couldn't be duplicated by New York's own Greco.

The Lost World

Then he went back to the rooming house to wait for Greco's response. The story appeared in print on November 7, the very next day. Maelzel read it aloud to Schlumberger and Rouault and explained what it meant and how Greco wouldn't be able to resist it. Taking their indifferent silence for skepticism, he repeated the whole explanation, until Schlumberger cleared his throat and said, "Oh yes, of course," in a thin facsimile of enthusiasm.

When that same evening the landlady announced a messenger at the door, Maelzel cried, "Now, you doubting Thomases, see if I'm not right!" He bounded back up the stairs waving a letter like a captured flag. "He accepts the $1,000 wager and suggests a match on the eleventh, only four days away." He tossed the letter on the chess table in front of Schlumberger and groomed himself to go out, creating a small whirl of hum and preen that Schlumberger remembered because it was the first time he saw Maelzel's cut-glass scent bottle. Beaming at his mirror face, Maelzel moistened his fingertips and stroked them along neck and jowls, then sprinkled his handkerchief and took a deep sniff as he clattered down the stairs to arrange with the manager of the National Hotel on Broadway to convert his lobby once again into a theatre. Schlumberger and Rouault settled to wait in a room redolent of cherry blossoms.

The two men, who loved or had loved the same woman, had scarce a word for each other. Rouault sat at the table opposite Schlumberger, drinking the last of his coffee. His cup and saucer occupied a corner of the table where Schlumberger's chessboard sprawled. As he brought the cup to his lips, his eye followed his hand. The act required total attention, like a fine adjustment in the panharmonicon. When he had replaced the cup on the table, he put his hand over his knee and stared at the knuckles. Now that the silver crucifix Schlumberger used to see on a chain around his neck had disappeared, Rouault lived alone inside the tight boundary of his gaze, which did not stray past the tips of his fingers. When the cup was drained, he left the room with lowered eyes. His room was at the end of the hall from the one Schlumberger and Maelzel shared. He stayed there most of the time alone. Occasionally he would wander down the hall and sit on a bed while Schlumberger outmaneuvered a grimacing Maelzel on the chessboard. He said nothing unless he was directly addressed. Though his eyes seemed to be on the board, he would sometimes rise during an end game and shuffle out the door and down the hall to his own room. Probably nothing less than this total insularity could have stifled Schlumberger, who confided to his journal that he felt Rouault "a brother in grief." He wanted to lock his arms around Rouault's neck and sob with him over Louise.

That night and for much of the next few days Schlumberger was alone in the room, but he had little temptation to stray outside. The streets he had roamed searching for Louise still branched in his dreams, shooting out alleys that led him to doors he didn't want to enter. He preferred his room, despite boredom. He could plant himself in a chair and know the wall behind him would not creep closer, the floor not drop away. There were comfortably permanent promontories and planes in the faces he met there. He left the rooming house only for meals, and was always glad to recognize it when they rounded the last corner— porchless, boxy, squeezed between a warehouse and a millinery shop on Maiden Lane. The upper story was top-heavy. A pair of gables hung over the street, casting afternoon shadows on the cobbles and up the wall of the tobacconist's opposite.

When the three men returned from the hotel restaurant on Water Street, they would have to knock and wait and knock again to be admitted. The door was kept locked and latched. When she eventually heard them, the landlady would rattle her locks and crack a slit in the door wide enough for her eye to inspect the perils of the rude waterfront street. Then she would back into the hallway, keeping the door between herself and the street like a shield, leaving the men a twelve-inch crevice in which to file past her, thick-backed Schlumberger usually nudging an extra inch. She relocked the door quickly. He never heard what she was mumbling as he passed, but his impression was that she felt anyone who rented one of her rooms ought to stay there and not gallivant about all day. She always seemed to have come from a long way to answer the door, but she refused to trust her roomers with a key. She was a squat woman with a large busy bosom.

She kept three cats which she complained about and shooed off the steps and broomed down the hall. They were a mother and two well-grown kittens with identical markings. The twins tumbled in a ball down the steps and fell often into the hall spittoon. As soon as a door was opened they darted into the room to play tag on chairs and counter-panes. Schlumberger discovered he needed to catch only one of them, because if he did and tossed it into the hall the other would follow, streaking between his legs. They made the dim stairway dangerous. They had a habit of sleeping together against the side of a stair, each head pillowed on the haunch of the other. When Schlumberger complained, Mrs. Moore said she couldn't stand them underfoot either, but nobody would take them both, and anybody could see it would be an awful cruelty to separate them. Schlumberger, less from real concern than to relieve the tension and boredom of waiting, said it would be an awful cruelty to let somebody break a leg falling down her stairs, and the startled look that darted across her eyes gave him the satisfaction of knowing he had made her aware of a danger she would not have discovered without him. Her face was buttressed with a broad overhung brow and a jutting jaw that made a trough where her small eyes and nose and mouth huddled. She considered a moment, lowering her head so that her brow cast all her features but the tip of her chin into shadow, then stumped away down the hall.

By the third day Maelzel refused to play another game of chess. He shrugged into his greatcoat, deftly plucked from a corner his gold-handled stick, and said he was going "out" with an inflection Schlumberger later learned to recognize as a euphemism. He was really saying that he was off to a whorehouse and if anyone wanted to accompany him he only had to grab his hat and his pecker. The past week Schlumberger had spent nearly every moment under the eye of Maelzel or Rouault or both. Jammed shoulder to shoulder between them on the three-day coach trip, sleeping two in a bed at the post road inns, drinking, playing chess, he nestled in a cozy, convivial lethargy. It gave him the balming sense that he was no more than what they saw. Now, however, he wanted to be alone a while to discover what it felt like being nearly two weeks severed from Louise Rouault.

Once the door slammed him into the empty silence, he felt at first simply numb. He eased off his boots and lay back on the bed, closing his eyes. Then, tenderly, like a tongue exploring the gum around an abscess, he applied a tentative pressure to certain memories—her rare laughter, a guttural juggling of more syllables than she could ever catch; the sharp tumescence of her nipples when he kissed them. He sprang from the bed, his skull throbbing. A few minutes later he was in the hall, knocking at Rouault's door. "Do you want to play chess?" He decided a noise that might have been a groan or a cough meant no. Back in the empty room, he felt an ominous straining and testing of knots, as if some creature inside him had sensed the vacuum and were swelling to fill it.

His eye ranged the room, frantic for distraction. He glanced at the chessboard abandoned in midgame, saw how he would checkmate Maelzel in three moves, and paced to the window. Heavy, wet snowflakes were plunging past it and melting the street to mud. Dancing along through the puddles, a girl in a flame-colored skirt flopped on her back and smiled up at him. He moaned and spun away, noticing on the far wall a framed print, perhaps a salvaged calendar decoration, that his eye had barely grazed before. It showed two fishermen on the bank of a stream, both expensively dressed in high boots and wide-brim hats with pheasant feathers in the bands, whose ambitious casts had hooked the wrong prey. One man's line was strung through a tree branch and hooked in the seat of the other's green trousers. While the man in green trousers cocked over his shoulder a frown of comic dismay, his own line led off the tip of his pole and traced through the clutching branches an uneven pentagonal web. Its last strand dropped to the hook snagging his companion's earlobe. The companion had one foot up in a painful hop that had spilled from the fancy catch basket hanging on his shoulder a single small sunfish. A dog was sniffing it without much interest. On the other bank a barefoot boy in patched pants hanging by one suspender was yanking from the water a huge, tail-whipping trout like a dozen others that lay in a row under an oak behind him. The boy had a wide freckle-cheeked grin. His toes in the water created an intricate swirl that smoothed into a profile of Louise Rouault sleeping with the flowing currents of her hair spread on the pillow. Further downstream her swollen breast filled a quiet eddy.

He hadn't lived long enough with Maelzel yet to know that by preference he entered a room with a pounce, never knocking till he had tested the lock. He was surprised, then, opening to the four quick raps, to discover in the doorway not Maelzel but a short, fat man with a tall, thin man leaning behind him on the other side of the hall like a sunset shadow.

"We're here to see Mr. Maelzel," said the short man, walking past Schlumberger into the room. His long companion unglued his back from the wall and followed, his head bobbing at each step like a pump handle. Before Schlumberger could stop them, the twin grey cats glided between his ankles and disappeared under the bed.

"Mr. Maelzel is out. I can't tell when he'll return."

"In that case," said the short man with a satisfied nod, "he may be returning any moment. We'll wait."

He swept off his hat and settled with a genteel plop into the armchair drawn up to the table at Maelzel's side of the chessboard. The tall man peered around, blinked rapidly at the chessboard, and walked directly to the comic print Schlumberger had been studying. He put his nose within two inches of it and stood absolutely still for a few seconds, then made a sound like several rapid hiccups and turned around to share the joke. He got the short man's attention by hiccuping a few more times, then said, "Little kid catch alla fish." He had spectacles with thick circular lenses that made his eyes loom from his face. When the short man snapped, "Willie!" the tall man's eyes blinked hugely, and he bobbed away from the print as if he had been caught looking at something artistic.

The short man set the hat Schlumberger hadn't offered to take on its crown on the floor, and glanced inside it before smiling up at Schlumberger as if the round hole where his head had been made a witty point. His face was shaved to a red tenderness, and his head was hairless except for a little belt of mousedown on his neck. He had pouchy cheeks and a hairless pouchy brow ridge that looked as if it would pucker his eyes tight as a sleeping baby's if he once relaxed the piercing blue candor of his stare.

"I'm Barnaby Sunderson," he said without rising or extending his hand. "This is Willard Wilson. Sit down, Willie."

Wilson cocked back his head to focus the room, leaving his lower jaw asleep on his Adam's apple. Watching his nose twitch the spectacles back into position, Schlumberger could not for a moment tell whether Wilson hoped to discover a chair by sight or sniff. He made a complete circle of the room, staggering on the sloping floor, came upon the cane-back chair next to Sunderson's with a startled grunt, and lighted there quickly to make up for lost time. Sunderson crooned approval and wafted Schlumberger to the remaining chair.

With Sunderson and Wilson on one side of the table and himself alone on the other, Schlumberger felt off balance. The slope of the floor, which placed him slightly above his visitors, made him feel that he and the chessmen on the table were about to slide into their laps. After sitting down, Wilson had glanced covertly at Sunderson, then removed his hat and placed it on the floor next to his right ankle. He crossed his leg when he noticed Sunderson's crossed, and uncrossed it to cross the other to match Sunderson's when he saw he had got the wrong one on top. That and his slack lower lip edged with a pasty coat of mucus made Schlumberger decide Wilson was an idiot. While Sunderson made pleasant, vaguely probing comments about Mr. Maelzel's famous automaton, Schlumberger watched Wilson's head bobbing around the room. Once it bobbed around to the fisherman print and started hiccuping until Sunderson, without interrupting his question whether it were true that the Turk had once given pawn-move odds to all challengers, knocked Wilson's crossed leg to the floor with a sharp kick. "Ouch," Wilson complained, and started bobbing again almost immediately. Thereafter, whenever his head strayed toward the picture, it jerked back with a quick round-eyed glance at Sunderson before straying off again. Soon the lids were lowering, slowly extinguishing the huge eyes.

"Sorry," Schlumberger said. "I don't know about the Turk's European career. I don't take much interest."

He had just decided that whatever business these two had with Maelzel could not be important enough to make him suffer their presence another five minutes when Wilson's head stopped bobbing. The huge eyes—with moist pearls of mucus like the stuff on his mouth at their inner corners—were fixed on the chessboard.

Schlumberger looked at the board, where his bishop and knight kept Maelzel's queen pinned. He was about to slap the idiot's hand away. It had shot out over the board, hovered there, hanging from a wrist with a bone the size of a pigeon egg, the fingers twitching. The fingers were broad and flat and caked by a skin disease that reddened the knuckles and made them scale. The nails were nearly buried in blunt puffy pillows of flesh. Schlumberger didn't want those hands touching his chessmen, but he wasn't in time to prevent it. The fingers closed nimbly over one of Maelzel's bishops, skimmed it through a hole Schlumberger had never imagined his last move left unguarded. There was a gentle click as the bishop changed places with the knight that had been pinning Maelzel's queen. The hand deftly deposited the captured knight on the sidelines and retreated to the edge of the board. The fleshy fingers did a nasty little victory dance. The newly positioned bishop would in another two unpreventable moves be on an uncluttered line with Schlumberger's queen, which could defend itself only by a pawn move that would open a gap in his king's line of defense. The big lids behind the spectacles again began to narrow, but not sleepily.

Schlumberger turned to Sunderson.

"Does he play chess?"

And Sunderson, with a sweet, oddly familiar smile, said, "Want to find out?"

SCHLUMBERGER could hardly wait till they were out of the room to skip over to the bed, his high gleeful whine swelling into whoops as he tore back the counterpane and sent a pillow soaring off the end of his boot. The glass water pitcher it thumped onto was still tottering at the edge of the washstand when Maelzel opened the door. He didn't notice its musical smash.

"Did they come out of here?" he rasped.

Schlumberger whooped at him and dived for the bed. With his hands planted in the small of his back, he rocked onto his hump and neck and spun his legs in the air like a circus tumbler balancing a red ball, letting out more whoops and whinnies.

"Those two on the stairs—answer me, damn you!" shouted Maelzel. "Were they in here? What did they want?"

"Hah! They left a damn sight sorrier than they came! Yip-yip!"

Schlumberger's flailing legs made him hard to grab as a fish. Maelzel poked his gold-handled stick at the wheeling legs, but a lucky kick flicked it clattering across the floor. He lunged for the lapels of Schlumberger's waistcoat. One of the spinning knees clubbed him behind the ear and he fell to his knees beside the bed, which seemed to be emitting shrill feline protests. He stabbed the heel of his hand viciously at one of the forearms propping Schlumberger's body; Schlumberger collapsed on the mattress still whooping, but the whoops abruptly became a moan.

"Ooooh, careful! Ouch, God, what am I doing? Those bones are still brittle." Since the day after he was beaten, he had worn against his ribs a tightly wrapped cummerbund improvised from a pillowcase.

Maelzel, still kneeling, his hands leaning on his thighs, said, "Now tell me," with simmering patience.

Schlumberger rolled onto his stomach and propped himself up so his eyes were level with Maelzel's and let his hands fall open with a triumphant giggle as if the whole story were there in the lines of his palm.

"Was he still crying?" Schlumberger asked. "You passed him on the stairs, did you see those eyes? Those bottle-glass specs made his eyes like full moons, and when they got all bright and teary—"

"You beat him then, didn't you? Didn't you?"

"God, it wasn't that easy," Schlumberger said hotly. "I haven't seen anybody like that since Paris. Not since La Bourdonnais. At first I thought he was an idiot. You saw that fly-trap mouth?"

"How bad, then, damn you—how bad was it?"

"Awful. He scared me: that first game it was all I could do to draw. And when he won the second I was really scared. Then I started to win—"

"How many?"

"And I thought—he's got to break. He can't go on losing like this, one game after another and he's like the Turk, some machine that can't be hurt. All he does is drool spit on his big lip and blink those moon eyes at the—"

"God damn you, how many games?"

Schlumberger would have accounted for that first loss with a fairly elaborate excuse, but he never got to it. Maelzel bellowed and sprang. Schlumberger's yelp as he was dragged to the floor mingled a frisky pup's delight with the pain from his cracked ribs, and when Maelzel's cane began whirling and jabbing, glancing off his shoulders with a sting that convinced him the rage was real, he still found it so remarkable that a four-game win could spark such fury that he could barely dodge and duck for laughter. Hugging his ribs and moaning through his whooping, he scrambled back onto the bed and bounded off the other side with Maelzel right behind him, stepping the mattress like a deck in high seas and shrieking "Stupid, stupid, stupid!" At last, flailing the cane in the wake of Schlumberger's cackling caper round the chess table, Maelzel made an ambitious lunge that brought his foot down on the spine of one of the twin cats streaking for the door. The cat got clear, but carried the foot along well past the point where Maelzel could get his weight under it again. He skidded down on his rump. In the hall, board-stiff, bosom aquake, stood the landlady. Under their sheltering ledge her small eyes peered as if some horror from the street had slipped past her locks.

The Lost World

"So I FAILED YOU again," Schlumberger said. "You should have warned me." He surveyed the littered table between them—the flies in the butter, the dregs of the wine, the meal, the game—as if they represented the wreck of his life.

"Willie . . . ," Maelzel was trying to be gentle, so his muted tone heightened the sarcasm, "common sense should have told you—nobody bets a thousand dollars when he knows he can't win."

"You talk as if I knew it was Greco. How was I supposed to know?" The dangerous edge had slipped back into his voice. "Was I supposed to *guess* they knew the Turk wasn't a machine—"

"They probably didn't know for sure," Maelzel interposed.

"—and then guess they would be waiting for you to leave so they could trick me into a game and see how good I was?"

"You're too trusting, Willie. You've got to learn what the world is really like."

"Yes, trusting. And how is it that my trust didn't ruin everything? If they knew I was the Turk, why didn't they tell the world?"

"And confess they had been afraid to risk money on the game? After all, Willie, what they did was less than gentlemanly. They weren't going to brag about it. Besides—" he was warming as always to a discussion of the calculations that filled his pocket, "knowing is nothing. The world is full of people who *know* a machine can't play chess. That's no help at all in figuring out how the Turk manages to do it. Until someone can answer that, they'll have to go on believing what they know is impossible. And that's easy—easy as God on a cross. Easier, because any time they want to hand me twelve and a half cents, they can *see* the miracle."

But Schlumberger was only interested in trust. His voice quavered as he said, "It wasn't my fault, Johann. I want to know you believe that."

"Of course, William. I believe it."

"It was . . . that bitch. Little fuck machine." Schlumberger had adopted many of Maelzel's pet phrases. His vocabulary was malleable as hot wax. "She had me so . . . ." He trailed into quivering silence.

"Willie, let's go to bed."

Maelzel got to his feet carefully, as if he had noticed a scorpion among the turkey bones. Schlumberger lurching to meet him jarred the table. A few chessmen spilled to the floor. He clutched Maelzel's shoulders.

"But Johann . . . Johann . . . she was so . . . she would slide her hands up her body and . . ." (he dropped to a whisper) "cup them under . . ."

His sob choked the rest. Trying to tell it was hopeless then. Of what he had lost, the body was only the halo, and the halo all he could recall.

"Come to bed, Willie. If you like, you can bed down in my room tonight."

Schlumberger shed about two circles of drunkenness as he replied that his own room was only a short walk down the street and he preferred an uncrowded bed.

"Of course." Maelzel smiled without rancor. "That's why you're a bachelor."

It was an old game they played, almost as venerable as their nightly chess bout.

Maelzel lit a candle from the lamp and turned out the flame. Arm in arm, with Maelzel lighting the way, they walked through the hall to the street door. Maelzel murmured something about not stumbling on the cobbles and closed the door, turning back alone into the hallway, passing on his way to the stairs the entrance to the parlor where they had been sitting. After his unsteady steps had climbed out of hearing to his sleeping quarters, someone stirred in the dark parlor. A slow slap of feet crossed the floor. The glass chimney of the lamp ticked on its metal base. Sparks jumped from a flint. A smouldering flame, barely alive, floated toward the wick, and the lamp once more glowed. Rouault surveyed the same table Schlumberger had surveyed a few moments before, with what might have been a similar expression, then scooped from the floor a black bishop and queen. He placed the bishop on its rank, the queen next to it, then finished setting up the board for tomorrow's game and began scraping the dinner plates. Soon he had a big stack of bones and gristle, dried grease and loose flaps of skin.

33 | Peeping Toms and Inventors

FOR A TIME Schlumberger's history becomes the public history of the automaton. In later years when he was reviewing the events of this time in his journal, he recognized—with a rather chilling naïveté—that attacks on the automaton coincided with periods of decline in his own fortunes. "And the attacks are always directed through the press," he exclaims. Not strictly true, though there was a curious maidenly quality about the Turk that made absolutely damning to his reputation any suggestion that there was a man inside him. The licentious pleasure the press took in such suggestions, insinuations, and eventually the published account of a pair of callow spies always drew Maelzel snorting to the defense of virtue like an outraged papa.

In his researches Schlumberger may have been infected by a strain of Maelzel's publicity mania. When it struck he spent the better part of an afternoon rummaging through trunks and drawers for the scrapbooks where Maelzel had embalmed every shred of paper mentioning the automaton and himself. After Maelzel's death Schlumberger had stolen the scrapbooks to make sure they would be destroyed. As year followed year they lay on his closet shelf, mantled with a dust that marked them sacrosanct. At last he accepted that he had become their custodian. He lifted them down and wiped away the dust to see what he had salvaged. A name in one of the cuttings from the year 1827 sent him on the first of those expeditions that were to lend documentary ballast to a certain shimmering spectre that hovered in his dreams during the second half of the century.

The endless revolving of coach wheels and paddle wheels during his travels with Maelzel had confirmed him in his reclusive habits, and he would return from these forays into his past breathless with relief. Settled once more in the bedroom-study he shared with a wall-eyed cat, he would hastily sharpen a quill and leaf to the first blank page of the journal.

"Reginald Pike still lives in Baltimore," he wrote, wincing as the cat on his lap delicately, deliberately needled his thigh. "Not now, Hodge," he said and stroked its neck and filled its bowl and dipped his quill again to write, "He keeps a yellowed copy of the same cutting from the *Federal Gazette* that helped me trace him. Even when I forgot myself and seconded his recollections of that May heat wave, he didn't recognize me. Not surprising, really: he saw me only for a few moments, and of course it was not me he saw, but that damned chess boy. And in those days I had hardly any hump."

Reginald Pike remembered the heat because he and Varney had peeled off their winter underwear only two days before, but Varney hadn't yet got his spring dunking. Standing shoulder to shoulder with him on the rim of a rain barrel, both sweating even though the sun had gone down an hour ago, Rags could tell his own stink from Varney's and didn't like Varney's. But it was the only way to see. They kept their eyes level with the window sill, ready to duck if someone spied them. They were too far away to make out positions on the board, but they weren't interested in chess. What interested them was the Turk, and they had a good profile view of it.

As Pike spoke, Schlumberger experienced a strange disorientation, a sense that while he had no memory of the spectacle Pike was describing, he was invisibly present at its heart. He had no memory of the crowds hawking and craning; nor of the challenger fidgeting with self-conscious arrogance at a table set inside the velvet rope that kept spectators back from the Turk's sanctuary. He never saw the ladies fluttering their fans between moves, the men fanning themselves with their hats and sliding their forefingers around their collars. He never heard the solemn mutters of explication that followed each move, nor saw the man Pike called Old Greywhiskers who paced between the challenger and the automaton, duplicating for each the move made on the other board. As Pike's eyes kindled to his subject, Schlumberger thought of the airless box where he would shake himself awake at the approach of Maelzel's heavy-heeled stride.

"Sometimes Old Greywhiskers would plant himself to watch the game right in front of the Turk, and Varney'd whisper to me, 'Old fart, he's gone to sleep on his feet, old baldy fart, should we go down to the next window?' and I'd say, 'No, he might move and we might miss it.' The night it happened was the third night in a row we spent standing on that rain barrel.''

"Why?"

The old man, his thighs spread to his hearth fire, waved the question away. Who could remember why a boy does anything. But Schlumberger didn't even have to repeat the question. Still waving, as if a bluebottle kept trying to settle on his porridge bowl, Pike was already biting his moustache, hem-hemming, struggling to explain what it had been like to be Rags, and telling how after that first night, walking home up the beech-shadowed street, Rags had straightened his back the way the Turk held his. He showed how Rags had tried to set his jawline at an exact horizontal. He showed Rags bringing his arm up from his side with indolent steadiness and lowering it over the darkness with the fingers narrowing to a cone the way the Turk's did when it fastened on a piece.

"It was because it was so smooth," he explained, "so certain, not like a machine at all, like something human might be if it had never made a mistake." And Schlumberger understood how much fifteen-year-old Rags would have given to be able to surrender the lurch, the surprise of his own body for the Turk's grace and chilling precision.

"But it did lose occasionally," Schlumberger said. "It wasn't invincible."

"Oh, I know, later they said it did." And Schlumberger caught that tone of half-sleepy reverence. "But you wouldn't understand how . . . you'll never believe how . . . disappointed I was, how mortally saddened when I saw that man climb out of the box."

Standing on the barrel rim waiting for the next move, he and Varney had been arguing, he explained, about whether it was really a machine.

And Varney had just said it was all a trick, there had to be a man in there somewhere, when a voice below them said, Would you like to know where?

And Schlumberger wrote, "How long had you been watching them? Did you see them the first night, and take two days to figure out

[2 9 5]

how to use them? Or did you just step into the alley one night for a smoke before the Funambulist routine, and know what to do the minute you spotted them? They jerked around so quick the barrel began to tilt, and you clamped both hands onto the rim. Pike remembers how the hairs on your forearm tickled his ankle. He wanted to jump and run before you grabbed his ankle and pulled him down, but Varney was playing tough, asking who you were, and Rags couldn't run till Varney did.

" 'Who I am doesn't matter,' you said, and Rags never got a good look at you.

"Pike didn't recognize the engraving I showed him, the one of your wedding day I stole because it had her in it. All he could remember was thick shoulders, thick arms clamping the barrel, holding it steady, your hands ready to grab his ankles in midair if he tried to jump. You were so close beneath, you had to look straight up, Pike says, your face seemed to grow out of your shoulders, like mine does. The light from the window was dim, and whenever it hit your face, you stepped into Varney's shadow.

"And later, when you opened the shutters, the light was behind you, so he never did really see you, but he remembers you saying, 'Who I am doesn't matter,' which was not the last lie you told, and he remembers you saying, 'What matters is that you boys have a chance to be famous.'

"Did you know I thought you were being kind? Because I *was* melting inside there, and cursing Maelzel because even on a night that hot he had to wait till the last applause died and the last customer pawed his hand at the door before he told you to wheel the Turk behind the backdrop, and while you were pushing I heard above the grind of the wheels when you said, 'It's stifling tonight. Let me raise that window and open the shutters.' And Maelzel said, 'Idiot. Somebody in the alley might see.' And you were patient as always, saying, 'The window sill is six feet off the ground, Johann, there's nothing out there but the back wall of a stable.' You didn't mention the toolshed leaning against it, or the boys waiting on the roof. And Maelzel said, 'All right, open it up. I'd better uncork our boy here before he faints.'

"What else did you never tell?"

It took a long time to convince Varney's pap, Reginald Pike said, because they didn't tell about the man in the alley. Varney's pap kept asking why they would drag a barrel over to the toolshed and climb up on the roof to look at a shuttered window. How did they know that was the window in the room where the automaton was kept? How did they know someone would open the shutters? If they had just left out the part about the shutters not being opened yet when they first got up onto the roof, they would have been all right. It was a hunch, they said, and Varney's pap said, "Yeah?" The man in the alley had told them if they mentioned him nobody would believe them. He made them promise not to. Then he said he would not like to find out they were not honorable boys and told them about a drawer in his room where he kept two pistols to do God's work. They didn't tell Varney's pap any of that. It took more than an hour before Varney's pap would believe they had seen a sweating man with a lump on his back climb out of the automaton box and take a long swig from a water bottle.

"Then he said, 'You scrub up your faces, you boys. This story is worth a week's wages.' He was mortally disappointed when the editor at the *Federal Gazette* would only offer them five silver dollars for the story. I was afraid he was going to get mad and leave until Varney tugged on his arm and said, 'Please, pap—I got a chance to be famous.' And we were famous, too, even if the story told more about Varney and his pap than about me, because it had been Varney's pap who went along to the editor's office."

Reginald Pike laughed as he said he never did forgive Varney for not saying "we" even if he never said anything about it, and a few weeks after it was over, he and Varney quarreled about something else and after that never saw much of each other. He'd heard about five years ago that Varney'd died.

But Rags's name was in print, too, he said, and that was when he got up to fetch the newspaper cutting before Schlumberger could tell him he had a copy of it in his own wallet. He kept it pressed in the pages of the family Bible, which he got from a kitchen drawer.

"All my children seen this," he said, "and pretty soon my oldest grandson will be old enough to know what it means." And he passed Schlumberger the yellowed brittle cutting reverently on the palm of his hand. When Pike asked, "You got grandchildren?" Schlumberger pretended he was busy reading. The headline was "The Chess Player Discovered." The dateline was Friday, June 1, 1827, the last day for fourteen months that the automaton performed in public.

And with Pike leaning across his shoulder while he read, his quavering forefinger underscoring one phrase and another, appending to each lengthy footnotes that exhaled into Schlumberger's nostrils the beer and sausage breath of Pike's past, Schlumberger understood that even more than Pike's own memory what verified his act was the yellowed paper, because the printed story was the only thing about what happened that didn't change, that lasted after the men up and down Walnut Street had stopped calling Rags over to slap him on the back and say he was an enterprising sprat who would go far, and after his father, who usually didn't pay attention to anything but his cards, saw the announcement in the next day's *Gazette* that Mr. Maelzel had closed his show for the summer, and took Rags down to the tavern and heisted him up to the mahogany bar like a prize hog to dangle his legs and look at the cut on his toe while he told his cronies how old Slocum had puffed his kid up for the press but it had really been Rags who got the idea to climb up to that stable roof, telling it so well with all those men grinning through their chews and offering to set him up with a man's drink the day he turned sixteen and Rags's pap saying, You can just give me that drink and I'll deed it on to the boy when he's of age, that Rags could almost believe that's how it had happened until Tuesday's paper came out.

The story in Tuesday's paper didn't say the boys had lied. It said nobody could verify what the boys had said they saw. It said one of the boys had wanted money for the story. With elaborate tact it laid before its readers the incontestable fact that the automaton had been baffling the crowned heads of Europe for more than forty years, and upon reflection it seemed the hypothesis that a mystery this simple had not been discovered years ago was more than surprising. Patriotic feeling aside, did not the crowned heads of Europe possess resource and acumen the equal of that of a pair of curious youths? And would the inventor of the panharmonicon and the celebrated automaton trumpet player taint the authenticity of his accomplishments by allying them with a hoax that mocked the very Genius of Mechanics?

People on the street stopped calling Rags over to talk. The smiles they turned on him as he passed suggested he was a rascal who had tried to put something over, but now a sense of proportion had been restored. When this happened Rags and Varney got together and decided what they had tasted and were losing was more real than a drawer they had never seen that had God's pistols in it, and they began telling about the man in the alley who had told them what window to look through. They said the man in the alley was the same one who later opened the shutters in the room just before the tall man with the crooked back climbed out of the automaton. If people didn't believe them, they could go ask that man. People pounced on the shift in the story, and told the boys they had almost been taken in once, and just because somebody was a fool didn't make him a damn fool.

Then the mail coach brought in a Washington, D.C. paper, the *National Intelligencer,* that printed an editorial claiming the whole story had doubtless been fabricated by Maelzel to keep his exhibit in the news, and the *Gazette* should not have permitted its columns to be used for advertising. Rags and Varney talked it over and decided the man who told them where to put the barrel and what window to look through must have been in the pay of Maelzel, and they had been the victim of an advertising stunt. The next day the *Gazette* conceded that it may have been taken in, and when people on the street talked to Rags's pap, they said the automaton chess player was a marvel of the age, and somebody ought to take those two boys in hand and teach them to respect the truth. That night Rags's pap told him he had been shamed in front of all the best people in town, and that was getting off easy because Varney got a strapping from his pap, and on the street they both got kidded or lectured at by everybody they saw so bad that after a while they decided it was easiest to just say they'd learned a good lesson that people weren't fools or damn fools either. When he'd told it that way a few times, it was as if the man he'd seen climbed back inside the box and disappeared and each time he told it again he drove another nail into the box lid, so that ten years later when that writer Poe pried it up, he saw the man climb out again with something like astonishment. In the first week after people started talking about the story, the only one he reminded that he'd told it first was his wife, and only later, when it looked like the lid was off for good, did he start reminding his friends, too.

It was a good lesson, Varney's pap said, and Rags had learned it well.

WHAT SCHLUMBERGER learned gave him a strong notion of what to look for in Maelzel's scrapbooks, or so he thought, but when he came across the cuttings that sent him out of his study again to hunt down the

Walker brothers, it was from nothing more tangible than one of those hunches that used to help him sense the right combination on a chessboard—an obscure sense of symmetry. Rags and Varney jostling for a perch on a shedroof were a pair of clowning rooks. Here, he thought, might be another. But he knew that when you paid for information, you were likely to get the story your informant thought he had been paid for. He was careful not to suggest his suspicions to Hiram Walker, even though he realized within moments after they met that the precaution of a false name had been unnecessary—the little man with snuff-stained teeth did not remember him, did not associate him with Maelzel and the automaton.

He had traced Walker to a Canal Street hotel for men only. The clerk led him to a door that opened onto a long, low-ceilinged hall. On both sides bunkbeds honeycombed the walls. At the other end of the aisle between the beds a window turned the morning light the color of a tarnished spoon. "You want number thirty-eight," the clerk said, and told him to leave the candle at the desk on his way out. Schlumberger shuffled down the aisle checking the numbers on the footrails of the bunks. Boots and bundles lay in the slots between bunks. His light caught a gaptooth hole, a knot of driftwood gnarled like a foot. In his wake snores faltered, a restive lowing rose and sighed away. Straw ticking rustled sluggishly and churned up a smell of sour flesh and piss and whiskeybreath. In number thirty-eight, a lower, Schlumberger peeled a blanket back from a head tightened around its sleep like a fist. He set the candle on a pony keg and rocked a shoulder, whispering, "Walker," until the mouth closed. Slowly the eyelids unclenched. "Are you Walker?" The eyelids blinked. "Are you *this* Walker?" Schlumberger held in front of the eyes a cutting from a Saratoga newspaper. It was from the summer of 1827. It described an American chess automaton that rivaled the one displayed by Maelzel. American genius had not long been baffled by the mechanical marvel, it said. It used the word American eleven times. The American chess player had been constructed by two American brothers named Walker. The man in the bed danced his eyes over the paper, then shifted them to Schlumberger. "Get out of here," he whispered. "I don't care what you want."

But Walker wanted gin and to get it he gave Schlumberger what he wanted. They went to a tavern. Over the first glass Walker asked questions. Schlumberger told him he had been directed to the Canal Street flops by Walker's son. "The last one he sent down here wanted money," Walker said. "He didn't get any more than you will." Schlumberger told him he didn't want money, he was an investigator. "What for?" Walker asked. "Maelzel's dead. Long dead." "Someone else isn't," Schlumberger said. Walker took a drink and said, "Then you know about the murder." Schlumberger waited.

After a successful tour through upstate New York Hiram and Orville opened in a hall on Reade Street at Broadway. It was May, 1827. When the papers said how good the automaton was, Maelzel showed up one night and offered them $1,000 for it. "I wanted to take it," Walker said. "But Orville, he was planning to get rich."

Six months earlier they had offered to make Maelzel a duplicate automaton for $500. "He laughed us out. We gave him another chance after it was built and he told us to kiss ass. He wouldn't even come see how good it worked. So we thought since we had the damn thing, we might as well hire us a chess player and use it ourselves. By the time he got around to offering us double what we ever thought we'd get for it, we were making near a hundred dollars a week. Orville said, 'We give you two chances, now you can cram them bills up what we didn't kiss.' "

After New York they played Saratoga, Ballston, Philadelphia, other places Schlumberger knew better than Walker himself because Maelzel hadn't even passed over the stories that didn't mention his name or the Turk. In a little town in upstate New York, Hiram and Orville started quarreling and Hiram said he was tired of traveling and let Orville buy him out. "He never wanted a partner. He just needed somebody to build it for him. I was a 'prentice joiner then, and I let him talk me into giving up my job. I took $500 for my share, plus half the profits up till then. I was going to come back to Manhattan and set up as a cabinetmaker. I liked woodworking." He looked quickly at his hand curled around the gin glass. "Haw: I made it back, but the money didn't." A few weeks later Orville was traveling the post road to Baltimore. He and the chess player braked the wagon at a tree felled across the road. "The chess player got away, but they shot Orville right out of the wagon and put five more balls in him while he lay in the road."

"Maybe it was robbers," Schlumberger said. "Highwaymen."

Walker snorted. He grabbed his lower lip between thumb and forefinger and sprinkled snuff against his gums.

"Then why'd they turn that wood dummy I made into kindlin' wood?"

Schlumberger was quiet for a minute. He hadn't thought Maelzel could ever surprise him again.

"It would have been an accident," he said. "He never would have told them to do it that way. He would have said, 'Here's the money. Take care of it, I don't care how. Just make sure it never bothers me again.' And they would have thought that's what he meant. Do you see?"

"What do you care?" Hiram said. "Orville don't care none."

Schlumberger didn't know why he cared, but he did, it seemed: there were still things about Maelzel that he wanted not to believe. He cared enough to risk dropping his mask as impartial investigator. "You don't understand," he said. "He wasn't that kind of person. He would squeeze you dry, but not . . . In Austria he was the queen's mechanician, he was . . . a gentleman. I knew him."

Walker sucked snuff.

"Gentleman?" he said. "Ain't that somebody who can eat ham without bloodin' a pig?"

Schlumberger reminded himself that he had got more than he came for, but still not what he wanted. He fed Walker more gin and asked him how he had built a working automaton chess player.

"It started out just talk," Walker said. "Like us, sitting over a drink. Orville come into the tavern one night, and he'd just been to Maelzel's show. First thing he says to me is, 'That thing's a gold mine, Hiram. If we could make one like it, half that gold would be ourn.' 'That's where you're dead wrong,' I told him. You couldn't build one like it, the thing was a secret invention and had been a secret forty years and that was why people paid to see it, because they couldn't figure it out. And Orville said, 'But if we could,' and I said, 'We can't. If we could it wouldn't be no gold mine.' I told him the thing that made it a gold mine was that it was the only one in the world. If somebody could make another one, pretty soon there'd be a dozen and nobody would give spit to see it, so where's your gold mine? And of course that's where Orville got that look and said, 'Hiram, you just give me a gold mine idea.' 'Two in one night,' I said. 'That's a record.' And he said,

'Don't you see it? We don't even need to buy the lumber. We don't even need to learn how to play chess. All we got to do is worry that old heinie into thinking we could if we'd a mind.' That was Orville. He'd rather bluff than bet a straight flush.''

So the first time Orville went to see Maelzel, it had been pure bluff. Orville hadn't even got Hiram to knock together a box and prop a block of carved mahogany on top of a scarecrow. Which was probably why Maelzel, who knew bluff like the smell of his own socks, had sent them packing. Hiram waited for Orville in the Liberty Tavern on Amsterdam Avenue. Orville came in looking just like Hiram knew he would, mean and beaten. "The bastard laughed at me," he said. Hiram nodded. "Like I said," he said. He noticed the man who followed Orville as soon as he came in, because before he went up to the bar he had stood in the door looking around the room till he saw Orville. Hiram hadn't been surprised five minutes later when the man came over to their table.

"He didn't even tip his hat," Walker said. "He just sat right down and said, 'I'll tell you how to build one.' "

Schlumberger had begun trembling.

"What did he look like?" he said.

34 | Schlumberger in Eclipse

BACK ONCE MORE in his study Schlumberger spread across his desk the Walker automaton cuttings and the Rags and Varney cuttings and considered, while Hodge stepped gingerly among them switching a grey tail in his face, how these paperscraps had clogged the smoothly whirring gears of his life. The attack had come in the guise of an attack on Maelzel, but its effect on himself had been no less devastating. He began to understand it as a pinning movement, with a flamboyant attack developing along one flank to worry Maelzel's defenses while along the other its lethal component was subtly maneuvering for a leap. Once Maelzel realized he had been hasty in dismissing their bluff the Walker brothers became the obvious menace. By the time of their New York opening he was sufficently concerned to write his friend Coleman of the *Evening Post* for a first-hand critique. Schlumberger dimly recollected the cruelly honed enthusiasm of Coleman's reply. Though its end game lacked refinement, Coleman said, the Walker automaton moved its arms and shook its head with a lifelike fluidity that made the Turk's gestures appear lurchingly mechanical. Far more infuriating to Maelzel was the news that the crowds turning out for it were swept on a wave of patriotic enthusiasm. He cursed the glee Coleman made no effort to suppress for the Walkers' ''Yankee pluck.'' Then, just as he was arranging a New York trip and calculating how much it would take to buy off the Walkers, a movement on the ignored flank sprang the trap, and the Baltimore *Gazette* spilled across its pages the lurid peepings of Varney and Rags.

In his panic the first thing Maelzel did was to close the exhibit for the ever-recurring "mechanical repairs" and spend the entire day and into the evening hysterically impressing upon Schlumberger that he was the first chess player in the automaton's forty-year history stupid enough to allow himself to be seen. In the days that followed, Schlumberger saw little of Maelzel, but when the boys' story was discredited, he had little doubt that it was due at least in part to Maelzel's happy faculty for ingratiating himself with members of the press. The troupe continued through the next four months to live on savings—an index of the depth to which Maelzel had been shaken. During their sparse dinners he frequently pointed out that the food Schlumberger was eating amply discharged any biblical obligation Maelzel had to the virtue of Charity.

When his Mechanical Marvels Exhibit at last reopened in October, it featured a splendid version of Maelzel's musical diorama, *The Conflagration of Moscow*. The buildings burned more brightly than ever, the lines of Cossack cavalry rolled through the alleys in relentlessly extended ribbons. Cresting the wave of ink that heralded this fresh marvel was the phrase "Newly Arrived From Paris!" It stood boldly in each poster like an imprimatur of cultural authenticity. At the bottom of the page was the information that the Automaton Chess Player would be "exhibited only to private parties, on application to Mr. Maelzel."

During the first weeks of the automaton's eclipse Schlumberger demanded passage money to Paris. Not, apparently, with any great show of determination, for within a short time he was meekly developing other skills. He learned to operate the Funambulists. He became Rouault's assistant, oiling the intricate wheels of the panharmonicon and the *Moscow*. He lived on the daily chess game rationed him by Maelzel and on the promise that the Turk would be reinstated in the exhibit as soon as Maelzel judged the suspicions of its authenticity had been forgotten. "They forget everything, Willie, you just wait. How long did it take them to forget how many thousands of Frenchmen Bonaparte turned into worm food? A hundred days!—and the soldiers sent out to shoot him down were embracing him with tears in their eyes. You wait." But when the show opened in Philadelphia in January of 1828, it was again the *Moscow* that headed the posters, and Schlumberger was behind a curtain making the Funambulists spin and jerk on their rope while Maelzel pounded out a piano waltz. It wasn't until June 4, exactly a year after the Baltimore exposure, that Maelzel felt safe giving an occasional public performance of the automaton. By that time Schlumberger was floating along cozily in his new routine, buoyed on half a dozen bottles of claret a day. He played his daily game with Maelzel and drank and talked about someday returning to Paris to challenge La Bourdonnais. "Go ahead," Maelzel would answer. "We don't need the Turk to draw a crowd." He was correct. Audiences did not tire of his dancing, trumpeting dolls and panoramic spectacles for another six years.

What was it, Schlumberger wondered, that kept him and Maelzel together during those years? He pondered Maelzel. What he knew of his mind he had learned in their chess games. Little vision, he recalled, but a tenacious cling to what advantage he could spot, and a tendency to wring it dry. As he did with the Turk. Though the Turk had lost its value as his primary moneygetter, it had by no means been retired. He contrived to make its seclusion exclusive, and levied a high fee for the occasional "private parties" at which it performed. Could he have had, in addition, a certain irrational fascination with the Turk itself? Doubtful—but he did have an irrational confidence that the public fascination for it could never be more than temporarily dimmed. And as long as the Turk retained its value in his mind, so did Schlumberger, the best director to be had.

Maelzel's chess was also cautious, sometimes to a crippling fault. A Schlumberger at loose ends was a potential betrayer. Safest to keep him under control, where his temptation to commit one of those "stupidities" Maelzel feared could be constantly monitored.

But if these things were true, why did Maelzel seem so blithely to dismiss Schlumberger's threats to return to Paris? "Go ahead," he would say, and draw from the air the names of half a dozen men he claimed could take Schlumberger's place. And when Schlumberger's answering jeers became particularly arrogant, Maelzel would say that as soon as he had an evening free, he was going to develop a genuine mechanical Turk that would make Schlumberger superfluous. The mechanical problem, he explained, was elementary: a simple question of devising a cylinder that would trigger a move in response to the move of a live opponent.

Every time the subject came up Schlumberger would affect a contemptuous parody of Maelzel's own logic. "That's a purely defensive player you're describing," he would say. And Maelzel: "I'd make it so certain moves would cause the Turk to initiate an attack." And Schlumberger: "One that could be modified and remodified in response to successive moves?" And Maelzel: "Yes, damn you, that's possible, too." And Schlumberger, ending it, the statement beyond which he would retreat into snorts and chortles: "You make a Turk that knows Philidor by heart and has a few surprises not even he thought up, and beating it might work me into a healthy sweat." And Maelzel would slip into a maddening mechanical jargon that never failed to reduce Schlumberger's confidence to a furious splutter: "Impossible! Do you think I don't know it's impossible? Why do you go on like this?"

Pondering this same question years later, Schlumberger returned again for his insight to chess. On the few occasions when Maelzel had maneuvered a crucial advantage, his face became suffused with an uncontainable glee that popped his eyes, purpled the veins in his cheeks and nose. Once when Schlumberger was wine-fuddled Maelzel had captured his queen. While Schlumberger played out the difficult game remaining, he watched with terror and disgust as a thread of saliva dribbled from Maelzel's lower lip onto his empty king's-rook square. And Schlumberger eventually decided that one further reason why Maelzel needed him was in order that he might constantly be able to remind him how little he was needed.

And what might it be that Schlumberger required, if not the knowledge, despite all Maelzel's taunts and threats, that he was needed? Nothing. The cat's belly whine became an interrogative prod. No more than this? Perhaps a little more. The taunts, for instance, were easy enough to absorb, when each evening Schlumberger had the regenerative pleasure of making his tormentor behave like a cretin at the chessboard. There were other strands in the net, perhaps less quantifiable. There was the comfort of feeling that his reputation and accomplishments had been artificially stunted by the Turk. No limit threatens a potential never tested. There was convenience—the balanced compromises characteristic of a practical marriage, one of those marriages in which one partner, in exchange for a not too gougingly luxurious level of creature comfort, consents not to the other's infidelities but merely to a certain casualness in accounting for time that makes infidelity possible. Infidelity? Call it such. Valued for what he valued most in himself, Schlumberger, like a tepid wife, did not inquire into certain other areas of Maelzel's need in which he had come to be aware he was a disappointment.

In Philadelphia a hall on Fifth Street near Chestnut Street became the semipermanent headquarters of the exhibition. Maelzel ingratiated himself among the local businessmen, chiefly John F. Ohl who would one day finance his last voyage, while Schlumberger settled himself like a retired colonel in a rooming house next to the hall. His room faced an alley. He kept it spare as a hermit's cave. He entertained himself by devising elaborate ironic compliments for the landlady's monotonous menus.

For a while he frequented the backrooms of a Swiss clockmaker with a passion for cheese and chess. While Maelzel pursued his fancy in tavern and drawing room, his employee would be hunched over a chessboard washing down with white wine delectable wedges of Gruyère. When the shop bell tinkled Gustav would rise with a sigh and shuffle to the front room. It was a henhouse: a hundred gossiping clocks, each asserting the truth of its private hour. The wine and cheese were better than the chess, but Gustav spiced their games with a waspish hum about the financial and sexual intrigue of the town's notable citizens. He had known them all since childhood, it seemed, and required but the slenderest clues to deduce their present peccadilloes: Two gentlemen in conversation outside a bank meant the ruin of a third; a swain stepping down from a certain lady's carriage set horns on the brow of a congressman. Schlumberger enjoyed creeping into the pockets and under the skirts of all the people Maelzel never let him meet. After Maelzel found him out and cursed him for risking the Turk's reputation with a talky old man, he drifted a while, sulking and drinking more.

Then he discovered at the corner of Second and Dock streets a hotel restaurant that kept a room for chess players. It was nothing like the Café de la Régence. He was known there as Schmidt. Maelzel found him there, too.

After that he spent more time in his room, which was papered with lilies of the valley attended by hummingbirds. Each needle-pointed bill hovered at the same angle above the faded blossom. It grew more difficult for him to leave the room on Maelzel's periodic expeditions to Boston and Baltimore, New York and Saratoga.

Schlumberger in Eclipse

By 1834 *Moscow* had burned twice a day in the same way too many times for the world to care, and the automaton again became the principle attraction of Maelzel's handbills. The prospect of once more regularly playing brilliant games as the Turk's hidden director at first pleased Schlumberger. Soon he began to complain of backaches and the heat in the box. He said that nobody in American was a fit match for his genius, and he was tired of wasting his best gambits on dolts. Sometimes he even allowed himself to suspect it might be chess itself that bored him.

35 | The Hoaxer Hoaxed

BY THE SUMMER of 1836 anybody who read a newspaper from Massachusetts to Virginia knew as fact that a man with a stooped back hid inside the automaton. In the previous autumn Maelzel had found it necessary to borrow money from his friend Ohl to pay rent on his exhibit hall. After a decade in America the gilt on his marvels had begun to tarnish. The Turk, once more headlining the show, drew to each performance a faithful coterie of chess amateurs, but Maelzel had always been keenly aware that it was not chess that paid the bills, but the Turk himself, his mystery, his machinelike infallibility. He determined to cast his nets beyond the well-worn circuit of the Eastern seaboard and seek fresh audiences in the South. The Christmas season, therefore, found the enigmatic Turk in Richmond, Virginia, under the eye of a man fond of repeating Sir Thomas Browne's opinion, "What song the Syrens sang, or what name Achilles assumed when he hid himself among women, although puzzling questions, are not beyond *all* conjecture."

One evening—it must have been shortly after they arrived, because after they had been in a new town long enough to make acquaintances Maelzel seldom associated publicly with Schlumberger—they were drinking together in a tavern after the performance. A man with protruding grey eyes and a broad forehead approached them and congratulated Schlumberger on an excellent "demonstration of method." Standing over them he clicked his heels together as he said it and gave a curt, respectful nod. He kept his back and shoulders squared in a way that Schlumberger could not help admiring, and wore a military cloak frayed at the edges. On its sleeve was an off-grey patch. Schlumberger thought at first the man was a soldier, but the dark curls arched around his brow with a flamboyance too studied for what he knew of the military. His soldierly air was like Napoleon's, Schlumberger decided, with something in it luxuriantly female. Perhaps it was only the lilt of his southern accent, the edge of coyness in his assumption that Schlumberger would know what he meant by "demonstration of method." Schlumberger didn't and raised his eyebrows to say so.

"I refer of course to your chess game this evening," said the man. He slurred through the formality of inviting himself to join them. As he drew his chair to the table, Schlumberger caught a whiff of his breath that explained the brightness in his eyes. All accomplishments of the analytic faculty, the man explained, were the result of a scrupulous application of *method,* chess being no exception. The man himself had made a few trifling experiments with method—had employed it, in fact, to deduce the automaton's secret, and felt quite confident that he was addressing the author of the automaton's games. He addressed most of these remarks to Schlumberger, with an occasional glance toward Maelzel, a courteous way of not totally excluding him from the conversation. Maelzel, in a broody humor, complaining about poor revenues and insufficient publicity, had taken a few moments to marshal his outrage. But as the abashed Schlumberger was about to take the congratulatory hand extended across the table, Maelzel's modulated bellow interposed.

The gentleman, Maelzel said with a sarcastic leer, was obviously unaware of the automaton's venerable history. Did he think that Maelzel, the court mechanician of the Austrian kingdom, would have the audacity to perpetrate a fraud upon the crowned heads of Europe? Upon the Emperor Napoleon himself who had met the Turk at Wagram and bowed to his mechanical prowess even in the flush of his own victory on the larger battlefield? The man in the military cloak listened to Maelzel with a smile that stretched his moustache, but didn't narrow his large round eyes. He listened through a long record of the Turk's triumphs and then said that he was not at all the provincial Southerner Maelzel seemed to imply, and not unacquainted with the automaton's history. He had studied the articles relating to it in both *The Edinburgh Encyclopedia* and Sir David Brewster's stimulating *Letters on Natural Magic*. In addition, he would be happy to sketch the elementary steps by which the analytic mind could demonstrate that no machine could duplicate the action of the human brain in chess.

"Nonsense," Maelzel replied. "Look at the Babbage calculating machine. It computes astronomical tables, navigation tables to the farthest decimal, and never makes an error. The automaton merely applies a similar principle to chess, and—"

"I beg your pardon," drawled the stranger. "There is a vast chasm between a calculating process which moves from step to step *inevitably*, like Mr. Babbage's calculator, and one which is subject to whims of temperament and judgment. Surely you are aware that no single move in a game of chess follows of necessity from a preceding one. The rules of chess are not like those of algebra, where a prescribed order of steps leads to an unvarying solution. A chess game might more aptly be compared to the composition of a sonnet, in which rules serve merely as a conduit for the expression of a temperament unique as—"

"I don't care to hear your fucking theories," Maelzel said.

One corner of the man's thin smile pushed up into his cheek. The flesh bunched along his nostril like a flexing bicep. He stood up.

"Nonetheless, you shall hear them—by and by," he said. "I suggest you keep an eye on the columns of the *Southern Literary Messenger,* which I have the honor to edit."

After the man left, Maelzel was uneasy. It may have been the first time in his life he had antagonized a journalist. At the next performance he spotted the journalist in the audience. His luminous grey eyes were a vortex drawing toward their deep cores every detail of Maelzel's routine. His only relief from their stare came when they dropped momentarily to the journalist's knee, where a sheaf of paper was rapidly filling with notes. The next day Maelzel brushed his whiskers and paid a beaming visit to the *Messenger* offices. He learned that an assistant editor named Poe was indeed preparing an article on the automaton. Poe refused to see him. But that night he was again in the audience with his note pad. Maelzel had been planning to outflank the harsh northern winter by quartering in Richmond until spring. He closed the exhibit on January 13 and scuttled back to the troupe's Philadelphia headquarters like a shivering bear that had just remembered to hibernate.

His flight was not quick enough, however, to stay Poe's avenging pen. In April of 1836 the *Messenger* published a list of seventeen "observations" upon which Poe based his assertion that a concealed human being operated the automaton, along with a detailed, wrong explanation of how the deceit was practiced. Charge number sixteen in Poe's indictment states that a man named Schlumberger with a pronounced stoop in his shoulders traveled with Mr. Maelzel and was never in sight during performances. When Schlumberger had fallen ill, the automaton performances were canceled.

That summer, waving the paper in Schlumberger's face, Maelzel shrieked, ''And you weren't even sick either—only puking drunk! See how your stupidity serves us?''

Wherever the Turk had played, Poe's article was reprinted and discussed. The Norfolk *Herald* said, ''The essay on the Automaton cannot be answered, and we have heard the Editor challenges a reply from Maelzel himself.'' Maelzel's reply, scribbled in the margin of his faithfully preserved scrapbook clipping, was ''SHITEATER!''

There was nothing else to say. It didn't matter that many of Poe's explanations were absurdly wrong: that he claimed the wheels and cogs of the machinery cabinet were multiplied by mirrors—which did not exist; that the director observed the board from a position in the Turk's hollowed chest where Poe had spied a gauze-covered hole—which did not exist; that the director moved pieces by operating a lever—which did not exist—in the Turk's armpit. It all sounded so true that the one way Maelzel could have discredited it was by permitting an inspection that would have substituted for Poe's crude conjectures the true elegance of old Von Kempelen's inventive mind.

Maelzel couldn't risk that, any more than he dared reveal that Poe had plagiarized his wrong explanations of the automaton from Brewster's *Letters on Natural Magic*. Directing people to Brewster would ultimately lead them to the source Brewster had plagiarized. That was a book called *An Attempt to Analyse the Automaton Chess Player,* published in 1821, by a brilliant young mechanic named Willis. It is written in dense technical language that Brewster misunderstands and distorts into what nearly amounts to a fresh creation. Locked inside Willis's syntactic labyrinth is an accurate account of the pantograph and the magnetized chessboard that were the Turk's mechanical heart.

Poe's challenge was unanswerable not because it was true but because for the first time in the automaton's history it was believed. It had, as Poe himself was to say of his detective tales, *an air of method.* It was the first blossom of his reputation as an infallible analytic mind. All through the clamor it roused, while the jeers of the one-time believers grew more vicious in proportion to the fervor of their once belief, Maelzel howled as if his hand were being held on a hot stove. Because he couldn't tell anyone else that Poe was a fraud and a pompous fool and a plagiarist shiteater, he told Schlumberger, again and again. His talk about building a chess automaton that would be a real machine swelled to such intensity Schlumberger began to worry that Maelzel might forget he needed magnets and false-bottom drawers to make people believe the impossible.

Poe needed only words. He once floated a balloon across the Atlantic and brought it down on Sullivan's Island off Charleston, South Carolina. The New York *Sun*—which paid him for the story—was "the sole paper in possession of the news" until the adamant denials of the next two post riders from Charleston finally convinced people it never happened. He proved the immortality of the soul by hypnotizing a man on his deathbed. Six months after his death the spirit spoke in the throat of a corpse, and the "facts" in the case of M. Valdemar were laid to final rest only when Poe raised his high whinnied admission of fraud. And his words explained the Turk's operation as convincingly as the empty cabinets and intricate gears Maelzel exposed at each performance.

Thus did the master literary hoaxer of the age meet and best the great Cham of Mechanics.

36 | Questions of Trust

IN 1834 HAD OCCURRED the ultimate stupidity, the betrayal Maelzel had always dreaded. Penniless, drunk, ill from the alcohol that made him a pauper, Jacques François Mouret—fellow alumnus with Schlumberger of the Café de la Régence, director of the automaton from 1819 to 1825, who had given pawn-move odds to all comers and yielded but six games in 300—sold to the *Magazin Pittoresque* for thirty francs a 10,000-word reminiscence of his partnership with Maelzel, including a detailed explanation of the workings of the so-called automaton. By spring of that year Mouret had drunk the money, and the article, like a windborne seed, had begun to sprout in the pages of newspapers and other periodicals. Once it took root in the chess magazine *Palamède,* translation to foreign soil was assured. It crossed the Atlantic in 1837 and settled in the fertile loam of the *National Gazette*. Across the front page of the copy Schlumberger found in the pages of Maelzel's scrapbook had been savagely penned the words, "Like all the others."

For a short time after Poe's article appeared, audiences had swelled. They came, however, not with reverent awe to behold the mysteries of science. They came with eyes knowingly aglint, with lips uplifted to bare the needle points of their eyeteeth. Maelzel conducted his introductory spiels amid audible titters. No matter: he glowered the more, drew out to greater length the Turk's European pedigree and the list of its victories in capitals far more illustrious, before audiences vastly more sophisticated than the one before which he now stood.

While the smirks grew he pressed doggedly on, like a scold locked in the town-square stocks, fiercely impenitent.

The crowds soon thinned. Mystery is an eternal source of refreshment, but spectacle quickly palls. Each night Maelzel wheeled the Turk, its countenance aloof and noble as ever, before a sparse audience scattered like chessmen in a tacky end game. These faithful ones came, it seemed, for a game of chess. The fresh publicity of Mouret's disclosures completed Poe's work, but brought no new audiences. Everybody who wanted to see the Turk had seen it.

Not even a new score for the Panharmonicon could bring them back. The jaded mob looked at the posters describing its brass and mahogany exterior and said it probably concealed a forty-man orchestra. The Turk disgraced Maelzel's other ingenious mechanisms as well. The rope dancers lay side by side on the workbench, their red lips stretched in a smile of fortitude while their glass eyes slowly filled with dust. And the trumpeter, his uniform and cheeks newly painted, his lung capacity newly expanded, could blow no call to wake the credulous.

One night in the autumn Schlumberger slipped away after a performance. Not even the promise of a chess game could keep him with Maelzel when the weekly gross fell below the hall rent. He was tired of tirades about Mouret's treachery. He was tired of vows to invent a machine that would expose the bastard Poe's fraud. He stayed away until he thought Maelzel would be in bed. On the way home he saw a light burning in the workroom. *Still ranting,* he thought, and passed with no intention to stop. Next to the hall doors was a huge poster describing the mechanical marvels within. An EXHIBIT CANCELED ribbon slashed the poster downward. Another crossed it going up. The top ends of the ribbons were curling down. A misty rain was creeping into the glue. *Maybe he will say we're bound for Paris,* Schlumberger thought. He waited for that thought to excite him. Instead his mind filled with hummingbirds, and he thought, *I will have to leave my room.*

He found Maelzel pacing among the exhibits. The Funambulists had been hurled from the workbench to a corner, where they lay with legs entangled. Under the grime on his face the boy puppet smirked. The girl's jaw hung in a voluptuous gasp. The Turk, wheeled to the center of the room, was bareheaded, its skull glazed with a moss of grey flaking paste. But the lowered eyes still focused inward, its concentration imperturbable. As Maelzel paced, the long strip of crimson material that had been the Turk's turban floated from his left hand. When he saw Schlumberger, he turned on him as if he had left the room only moments ago.

"We'll beat the bastards yet!" he cried out. "Here's the fact, Willie: Mouret's lies have only been published in towns where we've played. So—it's a big country. Boston, New York, that's not the world. Do you see?"

His flourish had wound the crimson banner round his arm.

"Oil spots," he growled, shaking the banner in Schlumberger's face. "All over the Turk's turban. Sloppy, disgusting, no wonder the people stay away. When Rouault gets in, he and I will have a little talk. He's responsible for this." Then he said "Stupid" with a little shudder of revulsion. It shook his jowls like a sneeze.

Rouault had been back for less than two weeks. After Louise had been gone a year, he began dropping out of sight, sometimes for weeks, occasionally a month or two. His most recent absence had coincided with the onset of heavy press attacks on the automaton's authenticity. He had been away more than seven months and Schlumberger thought they had seen the last of him. Then one afternoon Schlumberger had stopped by the exhibit hall looking for Maelzel. He wanted a showdown: for a month Maelzel had paid his salary in promises. That had happened before, but the previous evening Schlumberger, walking the streets, had glimpsed Maelzel entering a plush hotel tavern with a pair of cronies. *He's still got money somewhere*, Schlumberger thought, and when he came to the hall he was planning to demand it, and if Maelzel wasn't in he would ransack his sleeping quarters (Maelzel always slept under the same roof as his automatons for fear of burglars). Instead of Maelzel or money Schlumberger found Rouault. He was in a corner of the workroom, asleep on his old mattress under the shadow of the panharmonicon.

Schlumberger saw a moist slit between Rouault's eyelids and asked, "He know you're back?"

"Not yet."

"You might as well clear off again. We don't do enough business to support even two of us any more."

Rouault's tongue patrolled the scum on his teeth, bulging his cheek.

"Where is it you go, anyhow?"

Rouault sat up and leaned heavily against the wall of the panharmonicon. Inside the cabinet a cymbal gave a muted shiver, and its vibration traveled along a tightly coiled spring.

"You go whoring like me?" Schlumberger pressed. "Aren't you getting too old for that?"

Rouault rubbed a palm across his thinning hair, as if in reply. He never talked with anyone except to make strange warnings that were never understood until later. While Schlumberger and Maelzel were drumming their heels on their trunks, waiting restless and bored for a coach, Rouault would amble up and say, "Three, four hours yet," and not even stand to hear Maelzel's outraged cry that it would be along in five minutes and Rouault damn well better be ready to board. Only half a day later would they learn that Rouault had talked with a post rider who had passed the coach on the road trying to fit a new axle. Schlumberger disregarded on principle all Rouault's warnings and advice, and always regretted it. He spoke to Rouault seldom because there was much he wanted to ask and he was afraid his curiosity would betray him.

"How come there's no food?" Rouault asked.

"I told you—there's no money." Then, thinking of why he had come searching for Maelzel, Schlumberger added, "At least that's what he says. We're finished. You'd better clear off for good. He'll tell you the same."

As always, Maelzel took him back. He railed about the stupidities of his employees and contrived to blame Rouault for a host of reversals, but the next day the pegs above the workroom mattress were again hung with Rouault's cap and jacket. *He's still afraid of him,* Schlumberger thought. *After Poe and Mouret, what can there be left to betray?*

Now, as Maelzel, crisp and aimless as a toy soldier, paced the workroom, Schlumberger learned the answer. Maelzel believed the automaton could still make their fortune.

"Ah, Willie, they'll wind up with shit in their craws yet."

Schlumberger had heard the tone so often he automatically gave spectral reality to the amorphous "they." *They* were the ubiquitous company who spent their lives thwarting Maelzel.

"In '26 they thought they'd driven me out of Europe," he said. "Ha: Was Bonaparte driven out of Europe when he sailed for Egypt?"

Questions of Trust

"A poor analogy," Schlumberger observed. "Bonaparte left an army to rot in Egypt."

Maelzel checked his pacing to croon "Willie, I love you for your pedantry," then strode on, rounding the stalwart trumpeter with a comradely clap to its shoulder, rapping his knuckles on the Turk's bare skull, explaining that all they need do to net fresh audiences was to cast further from the Eastern seaboard.

He dismissed Schlumberger's rhetorical groan.

"No more jolting coaches," he promised. "This time we travel smooth as Moses on the Nile."

"Large on Egypt tonight, aren't we," Schlumberger said. "Don't joke: I've had my fill of washing in a packet berth. It makes me vomit till I vomit air. I'll tell you now—if there's any traveling, it's to be by coach. At least every sixteen hours I can plant my legs on solid earth."

Maelzel told Schlumberger that steam had revolutionized travel while he had been sleeping off a drunk. Somehow he suggested that he had known all about steam as a power source and would have put together a steam locomotive and a paddle wheel steamboat long ago if he hadn't been kept so busy wet-nursing Schlumberger. Steam would soon do every sort of labor quicker and cheaper than men could. Coaches would be out of business. Railroad tracks would belt the world. Already they could travel by rail clear to Pittsburgh, and then board a steamboat that would run the Ohio down to the Mississippi and run the Mississippi clear to the Gulf of Mexico. It was the most luxurious mode of transportation known to man, and Schlumberger was the last man to hear the news. That jab put Maelzel in such a good humor that he ignored Schlumberger's obscene comment on it and told him they would stop off at every good-sized town on the river and give the frontier boys a show.

"We'll suck the lint from their pockets," he said. "We'll—" and he broke into the leering chuckle that signaled his best *bons mots*. It sounded like a stack of coins funneled through his fingers with a chinka-chink-chink on a tabletop. Chuckling that way, he leaned across the table at Schlumberger and said, "Ever see a deerskinner lay open a hide, Willie? We're going to slit this country from neck to nuts."

His good humor lasted till they reached Pittsburgh. They played four days and wheeled the crated automatons from the rented hall at three in the morning. They shivered on the pier in a dawn fog waiting for the first downriver boat to bear them beyond reach of their creditors.

Next stop was Cincinnati, where they rented the ballroom of an inn with a promise to pay at the end of the week. Just before his piano warmup Maelzel bent to the airslit in the lid of the Turk's box, and Schlumberger heard him mutter that the room was bare as a baby's gums. Schlumberger was for crating up after the first show, but Maelzel said it was a Thursday, bad night, and they would stay through the weekend at least and still be able to get the crates smuggled out to the pier Saturday night if they hadn't made enough to pay the hall rent.

Friday night as an unexpected crowd filled the hall he gloated. He didn't care that it was filling with rowdies who perched on the backs of chairs and passed a jug along the rows. He didn't notice as he rumbled into his piano fanfare that the hush was cracked by ravenous chortles. They let him get through his introductory spiel, the opening of the doors and drawers, the lifting of the Turk's drapery. They offered a swaggering blackleg for the first game, and as the man came to the challenger's table, Maelzel saw the audience was full of teeth.

"So what, I thought," he said later. "We're not in Boston. It's their money I want, not their manners."

The challenger tried to answer Schlumberger's gambit by advancing a pawn on the diagonal. Just at the moment Maelzel realized the challenger had never before seen a chessboard, someone in the hall yelled "Fire!"

Other voices chorused: "Fire!" and the mob set up a mock-panic holler.

When the thumping inside the Turk's cabinet began spilling chessmen from the board, the holler changed to a howl like hounds baying a fox. Maelzel dived for the board and kept his weight over it as he wheeled the Turk off. They made their exit in a barrage of spoiled fruit that had been stolen from pigs rooting in the street. Once a door was between them and the mob, Maelzel let Schlumberger finish thumping loose the lid. As he stood up in the box Schlumberger had a glimpse of Maelzel's purpled grimace, the piece of tomato clinging to his shirt like a glob of crimson sputum. Then the back of Maelzel's hand whacked his ear and slashed across his face. A heavy emerald ring made blood stream from his lip. H stood quite still. The hoots and stomping on the other side of the door came to him through a roar like tumbling water in his left eardrum.

His stinging cheek filled his eyes with tears, and he blinked them away, while dimly, far beyond the cataract surging inside his head, a voice was shrieking, "Stupid asshole! Don't you trust me? Answer me—can't you hear?"

Next morning at breakfast Maelzel gave him a salve for his cut lip and said things would be better down the Ohio. The peasants there hadn't even invented the wheel. They would flock to the Turk. It would be like the Second Fucking Coming. They tried again in a town called Rising Sun. Poe's fame had preceded them. After Lousiville they boarded the *Delta Belle,* and Maelzel said they would run straight down to New Orleans without another stop and Schlumberger said, "About time," and got drunk.

PART V

37 | Aboard the *Delta Belle*

ON CLEAR NIGHTS running a deep channel the captain would shout "Fire up!" and Schlumberger, lying in the narrow berth of the cabin he shared with Rouault, would hear the clatter of firemen heaving wood into the furnace. A few minutes later, the safety valve on the boiler hissing, the boat would shudder from stern to bow like a man in fever, and the rhythmic slap of the paddle wheels would quicken to a stutter as the pistons thumped a groan from every joist and the bottle on Schlumberger's table rattled to the edge and toppled off. Cursing the waste, wide awake now in the airless room separated only by a wall from the boilers, he would mutter to Rouault that the heat was worse than inside the automaton box, and grope for another bottle to keep him company on deck. He would pass the open door of the boiler room where the firemen, their shoulders and backs streaming like molten gold, were still at work, pitching cordwood into the gaping mouth. No matter how they gorged, it only roared for more.

He would go up to the hurricane deck and stand far out toward the bow to see the twin stacks glowing cherry bright, as if they were translucent. From their mouths sparks flared a solid column two yards up. Dispersing, the sparks wafted in feathery swirls and arced like shot birds. The heavier debris, some almost clinker size, fell with a raindrop pitter on the dry roof of the pilothouse and the cotton bales stacked on the texas deck.

After a heavy shower Schlumberger would peer anxiously up at the dark pilothouse. He expected some action: the bales covered with tarpaulin, water sloshed on the decks. At the least, buckets filled and

[3 2 5]

readied. Sometimes he would stare half an hour at the dark window without a shadow changing shape behind it. *Abandoned,* he would decide. *We are adrift. The first snag will rip out our belly.* Then his eye would catch a brief flare behind the window, as if a spark had burned through the roof and dropped inside. He would watch the mocking throb of the pilot's pipe. *He must,* Schlumberger argued, *be able to see the sparks fly past his window. He must know steamers burn to water level quick as tinder.*

In the first week they were on the river, before they had reached the falls where the Ohio opened into the broad glare sheet of the Mississippi, Schlumberger had shared a few pulls from his bottle with an old keelboat man whose trade was being eroded by steamboats. He didn't have anything good to say about them. They were built cheap, he claimed, because the owners knew they would last only four or five years. Six at the outside. Schlumberger said he was surprised that structures so huge and complex should have such a short life. The boatman ticked off with enthusiastic malice how they blundered to their ends blithely as seasons of mayflies. Sunken logs gutted them like fish bellies, he said, and sometimes they ran aground in storms. But most got done in by speed-fool pilots. A pilot trying to set a new record from Cairo to St. Louis would tie down the safety valve on the boiler to get more steam. Sometimes the boiler took it, and sometimes it burst apart. Sometimes bad insulation in the furnace room or the stack shafts started fires that could sweep a boat in minutes. The ones that didn't burn or explode got shook to pieces by their own pistons. Keelboats might not be so fast, he said, but the cargo got to port, and nobody got killed. Did Schlumberger know about the *Old Hickory?* Boiler explosion, he said, gloating. His voice dropping reverently, as if disaster was a holy mystery, he said, "Near two hunderd souls kilt."

Schlumberger tried to make him be reasonable. No one would deny there were accidents, he said, but river pilots would not risk their own lives wantonly. "You're wrong there," the old man said, his voice becoming strident. "They're men who want to die, every one." When he hauled out a Bible and began chanting about the death by water and the death by fire, all Schlumberger could do was try to laugh, which got the old man started on how bad it would be for those that were with child in the time that was coming. The conversation ended when Schlumberger demanded to know why the old man wasn't traveling by keelboat if steamboats were deathtraps. Was he one of those who wanted to die, like the pilots? The old man stopped ranting as if he had been slapped. "My sister lives clear down Cairo," he said, his cheeks shaking. "Can't afford to spend a month on the river." The Bible had disappeared like the head of a turtle under the mud-crusty folds of his buckskin. He stumped away.

Looking up at the sparks whirling past the window of the pilothouse Schlumberger felt his smug victory evaporate. Why would the pilot not raise the alarm? Behind that dark window was there really anyone at the helm? Schlumberger could only tell the room was not empty when the man sucked on his pipe. By its momentary glow he thought he could detect a mouth hooked up at the corners in wicked glee. His first night on deck he forced himself to make that mouth a mask of leering confidence, and trust it. But the next day he had climbed to the texas deck and inspected the black pockmarks where the clinkers had burned out. That convinced him they had survived the night run only by chance. He resolved to alert the captain that his pilot was drunk or mad. That evening after supper he loitered by the texas deck ladder to intercept the captain as he made his nightly visit to the bridge. He heard a guffaw and the captain rounded the corner, clapping on the shoulder a grinning man with a cob pipe clamped in his teeth who had obviously just made a clever jest. They climbed the ladder chortling and entered the pilothouse together. That night, and in the nights that followed, when the heat and the throbbing pistons drove Schlumberger up to the deck, he would alternately stare transfixed at the fiery stacks and the madman at the helm; or, taking a long pull from the bottle he brought up with him, he would resolutely face the wide alley of the channel, surrendering to the monotonous throb of the engines and the current tugging him southward.

Sometimes he spent the whole night leaning on his elbows over the rail of the hurricane deck, a gargoyle figurehead, his nervous hands exhorting the river and waving away its objections, his lips susurrating the words of conversations long dead. He was the victim of a spectral visitation. It had taken him three years to decide that he would never see Louise Rouault again. Missing her, he finally admitted, bored him as much as Maelzel's constant chatter of machines. All that remained of her now, eleven years after her disappearance, was the rheumatic back and bad digestion that he had grown to accept as reason enough for whatever pain he no longer let himself account for by her absence. The ghost that joined him one night on the hurricane deck, therefore, had at first only a feeble hold. It had nothing so gross as a visible manifestation. It was merely that when he talked to himself she was somehow present—at his side on the deck or in the dark channel beyond the bow—and she heard. For a while he engaged her as he would his own memory, reviewing their past conversations, quarreling with her, stopping to demand an elaboration of statements he had once too quickly understood. Soon he no longer had to strain to imagine that her responses were not simply the words he had assigned her, but born of an intellect other than his own, speaking through his lips, perhaps, but capable of surprising him, resisting him.

Not long after that, she no longer needed his voice. One night in his berth he came wide awake and lurched onto an elbow shouting, "Yes! I'm here!" In an instant he realized it had not been his own voice that woke him, but hers calling into his dream. It had come from the other side of the cabin wall. Quite impossible. The cabin to his right was occupied by an elderly lady with a bass voice and her infant grandson. To his left was Maelzel. On the other side of the inside wall was the boiler room with its roaring furnace. Across the corridor from his door was the river. Yet he got out of bed, careful not to wake the snoring Rouault, and walked the decks for the next hour, not quite admitting to himself that he was searching for her. When he finally settled at his usual place on the hurricane deck, he said, "You were here, weren't you." Her reply, wafting from the point of purest darkness in the channel ahead, was in the same full voice he had heard from the dream, and from that moment her impalpable presence was augmented by a voice that was not the water, not the furnace, not the thumping of pistons and paddles.

Even so, he could banish her with a gesture, and more than once had found it necessary to prove that he could. Draining a bottle he would fling it far out into the channel where she hovered, and listen for its faint splash above the constant churn of the paddle wheels and the slurring of water creased by the bow. He would concentrate on spotting it in the inky channel among the glinting reflections of the stack fires, and keep it in sight while it slid alongside and bobbed into the darkness astern.

Aboard the Delta Belle

And she would be gone—until he looked again out into the channel and whispered "Are you there?"

She would stay till sunrise. As the moon waned, mist rose from the swamps. It rolled in currents like the river's ghost. Then a red disc, crisp as the rim of a gong, made the wall of mangroves on the port bank flat and deeply black and sharply etched. Its slow elevation cloyed the mist, burning it back into the stagnant swamp wells. The last tendril sizzled away. A reverberant chime that might have been the rasp of mangrove branches made him blink awake. The gong suspended above the trees shimmered as if it had been struck, and lobbed into the sky, erupting, a diamond now, pulsing unbearable brilliance. He closed his eyes against it. The blood in his eyelids teemed as if it were coming to a boil. "Where are you?" he would say, and then, wincing at the loudness of his voice, avoiding the eyes of an early-stirring passenger nearby, he would turn away, his shadow shriveled underfoot like a drying rain puddle, and shuffle down to his cabin. The rest of the morning and into the afternoon he would sleep.

He called it sleep, but after three bottles of Médoc the line between sleep and stupor blurred. Sometimes as he made his way with hazy deliberation down to the cabin deck, he would pass Maelzel or Rouault on their way to breakfast. He seldom exchanged words with either of them. They never bothered him when he was staying in bed. On days when he wasn't working he had a habit of answering their attempts to shake him awake by mumbling into his pillow, "I'm staying in bed today." That meant he was drinking. On board the *Delta Belle* he was always in bed, even though he spent most of his nights on deck. He planned to stay that way until they docked in New Orleans.

At first Schlumberger thought Maelzel was more optimistic about New Orleans than he had any right to be. Either that or he had lived high too long to know how to practice economy. He booked cabin passage for the three of them for the entire run from Louisville to New Orleans. When Schlumberger saw him counting off $120, he whistled low and asked, right at the ticket counter, for his back salary. "Don't be an idiot," Maelzel said. "This stash is for emergencies. You want to sleep with wild Indians? They'll rob the fillings out of your teeth." Later Schlumberger figured out that the real reason Maelzel needed cabin space was because deck passengers couldn't get the same gambling credit in the grand salon, and that was where Maelzel planned to make

[3 2 9]

his killing. He might have misjudged the gullibility of the Midwestern river towns, but he still knew the difference between extravagance and investment.

What Maelzel had called the wild Indians were the deck passengers, who planted themselves like barnacles all over the forward area of the main deck and slept on blankets and skins for a hundred dollars a head. During his sleepless prowlings Schlumberger often wandered among them. On the *Delta Belle* there were usually about 150 deck passengers. At each town where they docked the number dropped or swelled. When there were less than 100 he could walk from the paddle boxes to the bow without threading sprawled legs. As the population neared 200 the deck festered, seething. Fights erupted like boils. Schlumberger stayed clear of the fights, but watched them with fascination. Groups formed and dissolved at each landing. Schlumberger stayed on the fringes of the groups, spun from one to the next, member of none. Kentucky riverboat men and lumberjacks clustered to drink whiskey and dance to a jewsharp. Knife sharpeners, cobblers, and other itinerant craftsmen huddled together, guarding their tools. Where they talked hands were always busy pounding or stitching or whetting. A company of soldiers cursed loud as the lumberjacks and was made to sleep in two long rows as if they were in a barracks. There were itinerant peddlars that sold snake oil rheumatic cures and preachers that sold God. Sometimes the preachers also carried cases of snake oil to minister to the corporeal as well as the spiritual needs of their flocks. They had, they claimed, a more potent remedy than the secular peddlars, because the natural medicinal properties of their ancient Indian recipes were augmented by a Christian blessing. At Memphis sixteen slaves bound for New Orleans to be sold were boarded. They were herded amidships and quartered next to the cacophonic dash of the paddle boxes. Their group was the tightest on board because they were chained ankle to ankle. Only one of them was allowed to roam—a mulatto girl with a wide, rouged mouth and eyes that her *café au lait* cheeks made a brilliant blue. Once a pair of lady cabin passengers, who toured the deck murmuring to each other behind paper fans that fluttered whenever someone looked back at them, inquired about the mulatto's condition. Schlumberger overheard the mulatto tell their escort with saucy pride that she was worth eleven hundred fifty-five dollars and her master kept her for his own use, not to sell. "My name Daisy," she said, as if that afterthought authenticated what she said.

Schlumberger liked to drift alongside the groups where people were gossiping about the river. One night he heard about the earthquake of 1811 that made the river run backwards and sucked whole islands underwater. Another night he heard the history—with details and emendations by half a dozen passengers interrupting the principal teller—of a river bandit named Wiley Harpe, who had killed his own son for bawling in his crib. He was finally shot by a man named Stiggal whose wife and children he had massacred. Stiggal cut off Harpe's head and jammed it onto a sapling stake, and that's how the town that grew up nearby got to be called Harpe's Head. The head itself was a roadside landmark for some years and was a caution to lawbreakers. Before it finally disappeared it got to be pretty well cured, an old man said, with cheeks rough as a cat's tongue. Many men had theories about the disappearance. The one most agreed on was that a certain old lady in the area—some didn't hesitate to call her a witch—stole it for a medicine that needed powdered skull. The man who told that story wore a pistol at his belt and seemed to know all about river lore. He said river pirates made it a practice to disembowel their victims so the corpses wouldn't float. Once he gave a sharp whistle and the mulatto girl brought him a leather case full of cigars. He was the owner of the sixteen slaves.

Outside the door to Schlumberger's cabin was a plush salon lined with the doors of other cabins and filled with round tables. Only men were allowed in the salon except at mealtimes, when the ladies could foray into the men's sanctuary, coughing at the cigar smoke, and take their places for a meal that usually lasted no longer than fifteen minutes. After the ladies had been courteously but firmly escorted back to their section of the deck, a sitting room crowded with sofas and chairs where there was nothing to do but knit or gossip, the men again broke out the whiskey and cleared the tables for gaming.

On his third night aboard the *Delta Belle,* Schlumberger woke from his afternoon nap at about sunset and stretched his legs on a divan against the salon wall, sipping Médoc from the bottle as he watched Maelzel play cards. Maelzel's table was directly below a huge chandelier set with three tiers of gas globes and hung with crystal pendants that reflected the soft white light. The thumping pistons made them tinkle like tree branches coated with ice. Vibrations shivered the whole salon. An etching, tilted out from the wall beyond the table, was mounted behind glass that caught the light. Reflections on the glass obscured the image now, but earlier, on one of his promenades, Schlumberger had paused to contemplate it. A woman garbed in flowing white stood in a forest glade walled in by shadowy trees. She had a proud upraised chin and downcast eyes. It was clear to Schlumberger that she had been awaiting a rendezvous with someone who didn't intend to come.

Schlumberger said he felt like he was in the belly of a whale with indigestion. The only one close enough to hear him was a white-coated Negro stationed against the wall near Schlumberger's divan. Periodically he circulated among the tables, lighting cigars and pouring champagne with effortless sweeps of his forearm. Between his promenades he stood very straight, though once in a while Schlumberger saw his shoulder blades rest against the wall. The Negro's profile gave no indication he had heard Schlumberger's witty remark. It was high in the forehead and heavy in the nose and jaw, with sullen downturned lips. When he stepped forward to answer a call for champagne, Schlumberger saw his face reflected clearly in the glass that covered the etching beyond Maelzel's shoulder. The lips had cracked and spilled out a double row of white teeth. He passed Schlumberger on his way for the champagne, and Schlumberger told him to bring him a bottle, too. If Maelzel could drink it, he could too, and Maelzel could damn well pay.

A few minutes later the Negro presented Schlumberger with the champagne bottle, flourished along with a sparkling glass on a silver tray. Schlumberger recognized the same grin he had seen in the glass when the Negro had used it on Maelzel and the other card players. The grin showed its great pleasure that Schlumberger was going to drink a bottle of champagne. It complimented Schlumberger on having made the wisest possible choice, the one the Negro himself would have made if circumstances permitted. Its subtle complicity in Schlumberger's pleasure prompted him to tip the Negro another two pennies. The grin broadened momentarily, the dark head dipped and went away. A moment later the Negro had again taken up his station beside Schlumberger's divan, his profile somber and grey.

"Are you a slave?" Schlumberger asked.

The grey face twitched and turned, blinking as if it had been momentarily asleep. The grin was a half step behind the worried blinking eyes.

"Can I fetch you somethin' more, boss?"

"I don't want anything. I was only curious. Are you a slave?"

The grin slipped and came reluctantly back. The Negro seemed to have decided he was about to be teased, and was going to make the best of it.

"Why no, boss," he said. His voice was caramel thick, but lower than it had been, and tremulous. "All us steamboat niggers is freedmen."

Just then somebody at one of the gambling tables snapped his fingers and called, "Boy," and the Negro snatched up his tray and hurried off.

38 | Pairings

SCHLUMBERGER SIPPED his champagne and watched the chandelier above Maelzel's table bouncing nimbly on its chain. The four immobile men studied their cards oblivious to the shimmer and tinkle of its pendants. If the chandelier were to drop from the ceiling, the gas globes bursting into fireballs among the jacks and queens, their concentration, Schlumberger judged, would remain unbroken—Maelzel with his back to the wall, sucking his gold eyetooth; flanking him, a pair of book-end cherubs, pudgy youths with smooth cheeks and red lips and identical dips in their soft yellow hair; and, with his back to Schlumberger so he could make out his features only by the reflecting surface of the glass-framed etching tilted toward the table, a man with small, puffy eyes and raised eyebrows that gave him the bewildered look of a shopkeeper stuck with a full inventory of last year's fashions. He was chewing tobacco with moist lip smacks and winning everybody's money. While Schlumberger was wondering whether the tilt of the etching gave the shopkeeper a view of Maelzel's cards, the man spat neatly across his left shoulder at the cuspidor, and the tableau in which they had been judging the hopes and perils of the fresh deal unfroze. One of the book ends asked the shopkeeper for a card, and Maelzel turned to the other youth, continuing an enthusiastic discourse on steamboat mechanics with frequent explanatory references to his panharmonicon and other inventions.

"As an inventor," he was saying, "I am much like a musician—Beethoven, say. The only difference being that where Beethoven orchestrates sound, I orchestrate motion. A well-functioning machine,

Pairings

such as this steamboat, is a symphony of motions. Power pumps the pistons, and everything rolls.''

While Maelzel talked, the shopkeeper fiddled his cards and the other book end, the one Maelzel wasn't addressing, fiddled the wispy droop of his moustache. The shopkeeper had interrupted more than once to tell Maelzel to bet. Now he again reminded Maelzel which cards were wild, his politeness vibrating at a pitch close to the brittle tremor of the chandelier glass. Despite these distractions Maelzel rattled on, his cadences locking the attention of the youth he favored as if they pulsed to the inexorable gulf-bound will of the steamer's pistons. Now and again the youth would escape into an eddy to play a card, but he never had the sense to improve his hand or fold. After the momentary dreamy swirl of the game, he yielded once more to Maelzel's eloquence, his forefinger absently straying to his cheek to palp a tender carbuncle the color of a strawberry.

"Ever see a man too tired to fuck?"

Maelzel raised his eyebrows back at the raised eyebrows. He might have said nothing less appropriate than, "I'll see that bet and raise you five." He went on: "The analogy is, I think, appropriate. I speak of the substitution of metal machines for flesh machines. It's the nineteenth century's contribution to the cause of Liberty, just as important as our Declaration of Independence. The Revolution freed man's spirit from the British tyranny. The machine frees man's body from the odious tyranny of work. Work—the curse of the man too tired to fuck.''

"You gonna see that bid, mister?" the shopkeeper commented.

"All day he swings a hammer," Maelzel answered, flipping two chips at the pot. "Heists bales, whatever. At night—too spent to spend. A good machine is a way to diddle nature's juice so you can spend your own whatever way you crave.''

His ingratiating leer embraced the whole table before settling upon the youth, to whom he said, "What you've got in your cock,''— pitching another pair of chips—"is fire: steam. Firing up a machine works just like cocktickle: boiler pressure builds and builds, till those two big pistons start to pump, and the paddle wheels churn.''

Schlumberger knew Maelzel sometimes chattered to annoy and confuse him during a chess game, but if this was his intention now, he should have been hypnotizing the shopkeeper, who was taking nearly every pot. For all his apparent preoccupation, Maelzel was betting

KINGKILL

cautiously and folding early, leaving the youths to feed the pots the shopkeeper claimed with an affectionate two-armed embrace. But Maelzel's prudence didn't placate Schlumberger. He was grimly calculating Maelzel's losses, and planned to demand a sum equal to their total as payment on his back salary. *You can pay me at least as much as you give that damn steamboat blackleg,* he planned to say. The higher the losses rose, the more outraged he got.

"All machines are wheels, you know that?" Maelzel was saying. "Paddle wheels, clock wheels, printing press rollers. One wheel rolls the next. A gear is a wheel with teeth."

Maelzel showed how gears worked. He fisted his hands and locked the knuckles of one in the other's grooves. Scowling, he rolled the knuckles in the grooves as if he were grinding something between them. From where he sat, Schlumberger could see the tension in Maelzel's braced fists. The knuckles whitened, the forearms trembled. Or perhaps it was only the piston tremor, which at that instant racked the salon like fever chills.

"Learn how gears work," Maelzel advised, "and you can make fire and steam do anything. The secret is in linkage. One gear links to another, three times as big. It's got to go around three times whenever the other turns once. That triples the energy I get from my fire and steam. Keep your bolts tight. Fix the linkages so they can only make a single motion—the one you choose. Power in Nature is random, messy. The energy wastes away, or kills you by accident—earthquake, volcano, stampede. You've got to master it, the way you break a horse. Rods and gears, they're your harness and spurs. Rein tight—and don't be afraid to blood your spurs."

As Maelzel spoke he leaned toward the youth with the strawberry carbuncle, his elbow so close the youth discreetly edged his chips away to prevent the neat tower from spilling. Maelzel's voice had lowered as his intensity drew him closer, so that Schlumberger would hardly have made out the words if he hadn't heard most of them before.

"Once you know the secret, the rest is simple. You learn how to stoke a fire right, how to get steam under pressure, and be sure to leave a safety valve on the boiler: better waste a little steam than get scalded or blown to pieces. Any schoolboy knows that—a private grease job now and then keeps a host of fine ladies pure. You know what I mean?"

The two youths broke into nervous whinnies and the shopkeeper

[3 3 6]

snorted through his nose. Maelzel laughed too, nudging the youth with his elbow. "You know what I mean?"

The youth's tentative chuckle said he had no idea what intention meshed with Maelzel's labored metaphors. Schlumberger didn't laugh. He had heard it all before, till he was no longer shocked nor amused. Over the years Maelzel's standard arsenal of obscenities had developed the mazelike filigree of an illuminated manuscript. As the pious monks discovered lily and fish and crucifix in the simple twists and angles of the alphabet, Maelzel made each object he encountered yield its secret affinity with pubic hair, penis, ass-hole, semen, menstrual blood. Never to his face, but once in his journal and once to Rouault, whom he thought it would goad, Schlumberger said Maelzel's obscenities were like the words of Consecration in the Mass. Rouault said, "What?" giving Schlumberger a chance to elaborate. "Transubstantiation," he said, and when Rouault's brows strained toward each other to squeeze out the meaning, he explained, "The Word made randy flesh," and preened himself on his wit. For a while Schlumberger had relished Maelzel's obscene metaphors. There was something terrifying about the relentless regularity of pounding pistons and the power of exploding boilers to fling legs and arms at the sky. Thinking of them as cocks and cunts writhing toward the sweet explosion of orgasm made their grease and metal human. Only much later did it occur to him that Maelzel's intention might have been quite the opposite.

Even at the time, Schlumberger's amusement soon palled. Since Poe and Mouret had made a gold calf of the Turk, Maelzel practiced his perverse transubstantiations with smiling fervor. That smile, that urbane tone in which nothing could not be said, kept threatening to slip its gears and whirl off into sobs and shrieks. It made for unpleasant waiting.

At a break in the game the other players stretched their legs on deck while Maelzel retired to his cabin to relieve himself. Schlumberger followed without knocking and found Maelzel bracing one hand against the wall, the hot stream gargling hollowly into the porcelain pot. Schlumberger closed the door behind them and demanded his money.

"You've just given that sharper half my back wages, you lying bastard," he said. "Before I let you through this door again, I want all you owe me. What's left over you can gamble or wipe your fat ass with, but I want what's mine."

Over his shoulder Maelzel said, "Your game is chess, Willie, and it doesn't pay the bills any more. I'm about to let that so-called sharper donate the rent on our next hall."

Schlumberger braced his back against the closed door. "You don't leave here till I get my money."

"Be a good boy, Willie, or I'll kick your nuts."

"Think you can? I don't have two cracked ribs and a sprained wrist this time."

"But you're drunk," Maelzel said. "You're always drunk." He turned and gave his penis a languid flick in Schlumberger's direction before tucking it delicately inside his fly. A single drop specked the tip of Schlumberger's boot.

"You need spectacles," he said. "You just mistook my leg for a tree."

Maelzel cackled and Schlumberger laughed in spite of himself. His laugh was like the scrape of an eggshell down a windowpane. He glanced again at the urine spot on his boot toe, a fat teardrop with a tail pointing back along the line of its trajectory. He tried to hang onto the fury and contempt it roused in him, but it was easier to laugh. It probably wouldn't even stain.

"Give me ten dollars," he said. "Ten dollars, and I'll tell you a secret."

"Oh, secrets! How very sinister."

But Schlumberger saw he was already reaching for the tail pocket of his frock coat.

"That sharper is cheating you," Schlumberger said. "Why do you think he asks for whiskey when you're buying the table champagne? He's drinking colored water. I talked to a deck passenger who told me how they work."

"Ha! That's supposed to be worth ten dollars? How much do you think I'm drinking? Count how often I fill up those two boys, and how much I dribble into my own glass."

"Dribble?" Schlumberger reminded Maelzel that he had just spent two minutes standing over the chamber pot, producing a vigorous stream that could scarcely be called a dribble. "And here's something else," he added. "That sharp sees every card in your hand. The glass in that picture behind you is a mirror. Stop breathing on the boy next to you and play close to your vest."

Pairings

For a moment, noting the dilatory twitch of Maelzel's nostrils, Schlumberger thought he had told him something he didn't know. In their chess games Schlumberger had come to watch for that twitch. It signaled that Maelzel had spotted an advantage. But he said only, "No, Willie, that's too crude, even for America. It didn't even fool you, did it? The real mirror is that flat silver cufflink on his left sleeve. Every card he deals passes over that wrist." He smirked at Schlumberger's astonishment and drew from his wallet a fan of bills. "You still haven't earned this," he said, tucking them into Schlumberger's waistcoat pocket. "It's a gift."

Then, with an absent-minded wave, like someone parting a gauze curtain, he nudged Schlumberger away from the door. "Now stand aside, boy," he said, "and watch me squeeze that tin horn."

Schlumberger's first impulse was to spend the rest of the evening on the hurricane deck proving that he didn't have to do what Maelzel had suggested. But, he told himself, he wanted to see the sharper beat Maelzel. And if Maelzel was really going to outsmart the sharper, he decided he had to see that, too. Why was Maelzel always telling him to do what he had to do anyway? He wandered toward the ladies' quarters in the stern, but turned back before he got there and ambled slowly among the other card players, thinking he might pretend another game had proved so exciting he forgot to watch Maelzel's. He stationed himself near a table halfway down the salon from Maelzel. A man with a gold chain across his waistcoat asked him if he wanted to draw up a chair. Schlumberger, cradling his champagne bottle, said he didn't play cards, and the man told him to move along. He got back to the divan opposite Maelzel's table just as the game was resuming.

Within fifteen minutes Schlumberger thought Maelzel had lost his nerve. He had expected a dramatic win when it was Maelzel's turn to deal. Instead, a small pot went to the shopkeeper and an even smaller one to the carbuncular youth.

Then, after a clumsy shuffle, Maelzel yawned as he lobbed the cards around the table, and said the edge was wearing off the game and he would like to retire after another few hands.

First time I've seen him lose his nerve, Schlumberger thought. *He's old.*

The two youths protested that they would like an opportunity to recoup their losses. The shopkeeper shrugged and said a good compromise would be to hike the ante. Why not open with nothing less than, say, fifty dollars, and bet high. That way the game would have more bite for Mr. Maelzel, and the two youths would have a chance to improve their fortunes rapidly.

Watching Maelzel hesitate, chew at his lip and hem as if the thought of high stakes made him timid, Schlumberger thought, *Christ in heaven, it's as if he wrote out what they were supposed to say on a scrap of paper and told them to read it on cue.* The fizzing of the champagne had transferred itself from his glass to the inside of his head. Little bubbles were exploding all over his brain. They roared like the applause that came to him through the walls of the Turk's box at the end of a game.

Maelzel stopped chattering and played serious poker. The youths bet nervously from their dwindling stock of chips. The shopkeeper was sitting stiffly and passing his hand over his hair as if he were gentling a skittish horse. He saw each bet with a show of guarded optimism. Maelzel played his cards from the plateau at the third button of his waistcoat, his back squared, Schlumberger noted, against the reflecting glass behind him. *He pays me more mind than he admits,* he thought. *Was his face always so puffy, or is it simply the way he shoves his chin against his collar to see the cards?* Under Maelzel's eyes pouches of loose flesh folded soot-grey over the purple veins of his cheeks, and under each cheek the dewlaps bagged like full blisters. *All wrinkles,* Schlumberger thought, especially around the eyes hooded over the cards. Turtle eyes, ancient and wary and evil. Maelzel was raising every bet five dollars, and each time he did the roar inside Schlumberger's head swelled, roaring cheers now cresting the applause. Once on a shopping trip to Paris, his father had said, "Watch that window," and hoisted Schlumberger to his shoulders above the throng, and when the Emperor appeared on the balcony, silk clad and jaunty, fresh from Austerlitz, the cheers filled the square, so loud Schlumberger would have thought he had gone dumb but for the strain in his chest and throat, while his eyes searched the ancient wrinkles for some assuring sign of mortality and his ululating brain pulsed the word *Die, die, die.*

The shopkeeper folded leaving eighty dollars in the pot. Maelzel bullied the other two into sending another twenty dollars after that before the one with the wispy moustache had the sense to call him.

Pairings

Raking in his pot, Maelzel unhooded his eyes to pass Schlumberger a single glance.

Schlumberger lied a smile and hoped Maelzel would be too flushed to remember to get out before it was the shopkeeper's turn to deal. But he didn't need to wait. On the next hand, with over twelve hundred dollars in the pot and nearly half of it Maelzel's, he confidently called with three jacks and a pair of kings, and seemed more puzzled than surprised when the carbuncular youth exposed an ace of hearts and laid down card by card a royal flush.

The sunset hues of Maelzel's nose and cheeks deepened and drained. His mouth hung open, his cheeks luffing.

"But . . . that's impossible," he stammered.

The youth said, "Why?" and everyone awaited an answer.

The other book end, the one with the wispy moustache, tongued a drooping corner of it into his mouth. The shopkeeper meditatively clipped the end of a cigar.

Maelzel's upper lip curled back as if he were showing how dangerous his teeth were, and then kept on baring teeth until the snarl had flattened into a smile. Through the smile he said, "A . . . such a . . . surprisingly good hand . . . so seldom occurs." Then he clapped the youth on the shoulder and sang out a jovial obscenity. Since the youth had so depleted his stake, Maelzel said, perhaps he would stand him a drink at the bar.

"Sure, old man," the youth said. When he stood, showing the profile not disfigured by the pimple, he looked ten years older. He had a more good-natured version of Maelzel's snarl—a wide, high-chinned smile that put his teeth on display like family heirlooms. As he walked off with Maelzel, he clamped in the teeth a cigar he had lifted out of the shopkeeper's case, still open on the table.

Sitting rigidly on the divan, Schlumberger watched them wedge into the crowd around the bar. He picked his champagne bottle off the floor and held it at eye level to estimate how many unpoured glasses remained. He gave it a waggle—no bubbles—and carefully edged it under a leg of the divan. *It doesn't matter where he goes for what he can't get from me,* he thought, *he still needs a chess player.* But Schlumberger had checkmated Maelzel a thousand times without seeing him pale like that. He never before had truly understood that Maelzel didn't give a damn for chess. *The sprat better keep his hand over his pocket,* he thought, *or in ten minutes it will be empty again.* He wanted very much to believe it could happen.

Schlumberger went to his cabin and fell into a heavy champagne sleep. When he woke only a few card games were still in progress. Maelzel was nowhere in sight. He spent the dregs of the evening among the deck passengers. The blue-eyed mulatto danced to a jewsharp. When everyone settled to sleep, he went to his post on the bow of the hurricane deck. He watched the flying sparks, the empty pilothouse and the dark channel ahead, waiting for the ghost of Louise Rouault to join him. But she only appeared in the midst of a profound thoughtlessness, and tonight he could not empty his mind. At last he decided to try sleep again, and if that didn't work, another bottle of Médoc.

Passing through the salon on his way to his cabin, he heard the moans and sighs of sleepers behind the cabin doors. His approach and passing orchestrated their deep rhythms. From the crack under one door slithered faint whispers. Schlumberger paused a moment, but the words were drowned by a rattling snore. Someone was working at his sleep like a miner far beneath the earth. He walked on, the few candles that would burn all night in the salon dipping and swaying to the lurch of his step. As he poked his key at the lock, he heard a door open. *Perhaps the whisperers,* he thought, looking back the way he had come. Someone stood in the salon outside an open door, dimly silhouetted in the gloom between candles. A whispered litany—curses. Schlumberger slipped inside his door and closed it, all but a crack for his eye. Down the hall a voice said quite clearly, "Plug your own ass, old man," and the door closed.

Among the sleepers' ebb and flow—a cough. The bulky shadow twisted, staggered, growing bulges that flowed into other shadows, the backs of chairs, the drape of a table cloth. The shadow shuffled toward him, dragging a third leg. The limp third leg took a surprisingly high step and became the sleeve of a frock coat swung over a shoulder. Schlumberger closed his door before the shadow got to Maelzel's cabin. Some things he would rather not know for certain. But Maelzel's cabin was next to his own, and a moment later a key was searching for its lock. The constant thump of pistons muffled other noises, so that Schlumberger with his cheek pressed to the thin membrane of wall between them felt rather than heard boots thudding to the floor, the gurgle of whiskey in the glass, and another cough—harsh, dry, repeated as if it

Pairings

were trying hard to locate enough moisture to become a sob. As it approached Schlumberger the shadow had continued to curse and mutter, and the words he heard before he eased his door closed were: "Pair. Pair of them. Fucking pair."

Schlumberger thought he was talking about his poker hand until the *Delta Belle* docked in Natchez and he watched the shopkeeper bob down the gangplank arm in arm with the carbuncular youth.

Like you said, he thought. *One wheel turns another.*

39 | What Will Die Dies

ON THE UPPER RIVER, with the paddle boxes drumming a stately march as the disciplined banks passed in review, the ghostly presence Schlumberger courted each night could be coaxed closer. Her habitat, ever receding at the pace of the boat's advance, was the mist that rose from the channel. But sometimes, murmuring and crooning into the dark waters, he would sense her just beyond his elbow, still out of sight yet so close behind him his ear tingled with her whisper, and against his cheek he felt her breeze-blown hair.

After the night of Maelzel's gambling loss, however, Schlumberger's ghost withdrew. As a boy walking home after confession, he would feel God racing in his veins, pounding under his breast, and exult at the sacred mystery—his body itself the tabernacle, temple of the Holy Spirit. Talking half aloud as he cantered along the path, he would heap flatteries upon the One who dwelt within. Later—in a few days or a day, a few hours or an hour—when his corrupting lust had once more defiled the temple, its inhabitant fled, his remorse would seize him with the sense that he was utterly alone inside his body, alone with the unappeasable hunger to which he gave himself, loathing the giving. Now, leaning over the hurricane deck with a drained bottle in his hands, he felt once more abandoned to his body, his despicable humpbacked husk.

He sensed her near presence, but when he tried to speak to her, he was only talking to himself. He felt a fool and stopped and, as soon as he did, heard a faint call, some swamp loon he would say if he wanted to deny the truth, and knew she had fled his side and was slipping ahead of him through the channel mist. But what his sin was or how to confess it and make himself again a fit temple, he did not know.

Below Natchez the channel had become intricate and devious. She was out there, beyond the next turn, retreating under his steady moonlit advance, and the turns were many. The river, grown sick with flowing, kept circling back upon itself. Remembering his room in Philadelphia where he had left his books and the carpet slippers he had forgotten to pack, Schlumberger thought, *The river wants to curl into a lake.* And because his ghost would no longer let him talk to her, he went on murmuring nonsense, saying to himself, *Around the next bend all this will stop—we'll drift into a little lake, placid, cozied under a green coating of duckweed, an island in the middle, and on the bank she'll be waiting.* But always, no matter how full the arc the channel made, how close to complete its embrace seemed to come, before it was joined, some revulsion against the stasis the river yearned for made it veer away, recoil, writhe sluggishly further down, dreaming its valley nest around a lower, ever lower bend.

Suspending between his propped arms the weight of his back, he sipped Médoc and remembered another river journey, when he had stood straight and eager in the bows to spy the smoke of Le Havre, the needle masts in the harbor, and the packet that would bear him across the sea to the arms of Louise Rouault. The banks of the Seine had opened to embrace the heaving Atlantic. But what embrace could clip an ocean or a woman? The woman was gone. He was eleven years older on a different river, and each hour the walls of swampy forest inched not wider to receive the sea but closer, closing around him. Overhead, branches of cypress and oak entwined, roped in thick nets of Spanish moss that swung from the bent boughs, trailing strands in the current that wrinkled away downstream. Recently he had read of the maps of Mercator, whose plotting of ocean currents forced him to deduce the existence in the Southern latitudes of a gigantic whirlpool that sucked the seas into the earth's hollow core and spat them back. In that gentle, constant, beginning-to-quicken current he found it easy to imagine himself on a remote lip of that funnel.

Stop this, he had to tell himself. *You are not bound for the world's end. You are less than a day from New Orleans, a town like a hundred others where you have played your game and gone just as the hotel*

[3 4 5]

bed was beginning to yield a hollow for your swollen damned back.
   Why, then, should he so strongly sense a pending destination? And what of this river ghost? Conjured solely, he insisted, by the accidental similarity between the name of the state of Louisiana through which the river wound, and that of a woman he had seen more than a decade ago for too short a time to claim he had loved, and never begun to love if loving meant knowing.
   Yet she was near. He breathed the steamy richness of the swamp like perfume in a room she had just departed, leaving behind a glove, a purse, a landscape strewn with intimate messages. At night along the banks of sugar plantations heaps of cane husks smoldered, burning from the core outward, winking ruby eyes through the smoke. One morning as he rolled out of bed, the light he struck to dress by made her groan awake and look up through a dark wave of hair at his candle. Yes, she was near, and against all sense and hope he could not prevent himself from yearning, imagining that if he saw her beckon from the swamp he would pursue without a thought—and that frightened him.
   Deep in the swamp forests he sometimes made out a different fire, a phosphorescent pulse that silvered the branches and vines and the fanned spikes of palmettos. It was, he knew, the vigil lamp for a corpse, some beaver or turkey buzzard, possibly even a man, fallen into the final swoon, surrendered to the heatless passion of the swamp. And in the mornings, when the sun was nowhere and everywhere in the moist, clinging air, he would hear from what seemed deep in the swamp a wailing, and think of a woman lost in grief, the sway of her body tossing gray coils of Spanish moss. Then the steamboat would round a bend where the cypress wall dropped like a curtain to reveal a cultivated plain on which, wheeling into view, the charred glistening backs of darkies bent toward the earth. The steamer's wake smacking the banks beat an irregular time to the moan and wail of work songs. Giddy with heat, Schlumberger would pluck his shirt from his sides and stomach as if his flesh were hung with leeches, and marvel that they could work under the sun's eye. *God, they must die of it,* he thought. *It's hotter than inside the Turk.* Often the moist air bore a fetor that seeped into his clothing, into his skin. As the boat, rounding a bend, shaved the bank, he would see fish that had been trapped in pools when the high water fell. They flopped in the drying mud till they died. Then flies ate them, starting

with the eyes, opening a pit to tunnel below the brittle, prism-glinting scales.

It's not her that's coming nearer, he told himself. *It's only death. Only this stinking fertile cycle of decay and growth. Maggots born in rotting bowels, hosted in slime, crawling to sunlight through the eyehole of a fish.* Yet when the pilot left the main channel to run a chute cut by a flash flood, Schlumberger could not suppress a wild gaiety of anticipation. It was like threading the streets of Boston for the first time, knowing she was there, knowing at each corner he might come upon her walking toward him, see her miss stride, disbelieving, then fling open her arms and break into a run. Their actual meeting in Julian Hall, the rain-dripping stranger who had so glancingly acknowledged his presence, was less real to his mind than the hundred meetings he had imagined. And now, as the steamboat nosed into this greenly arching lane of cypress, as the rank swamp pinched his nostrils and he found himself breathless, palpitant, he thought, *It might never have happened. I could step off this boat and meet her on the landing and follow her again all the way to that New York whorehouse where they kicked me down the stairs. There's nothing it taught me that I wouldn't give up for the chance to endure it all again.*

In the bayou the current poured like a wound that won't close. It was still cleaving fresh earth. Bushes dipped toward the stream and gave it their shriveled leaves, while beneath the undercut bank their roots had been sucked clean as chicken bones. As Schlumberger watched, a clod gave way and the brown water snatched a shrub and pulled it under. It surfaced downstream with the washed roots groping for something to cling to. The swirl dizzied Schlumberger until he made himself watch the bank. Giant cypress trunks had been drawn like sinewy taffy from the ooze, and hardened and crusted with moss. Their roots humped away in all directions, making knobby islands in the water. Ahead, a branch bowed across the stream. Under it hovered a dancing shadow, looming, and with a veer of the boat he was in it, a cloud of insects that took him for their sun. He raced to the door and slammed himself inside. A pair of ladies talking on a sofa watched him slapping at himself as if he were putting down small rebellions all over his body.

When he came back onto the open deck, the boat was shearing a close bank. He leaned his back against the bow rail to see the Spanish moss tangling the stack wires. The wires thrummed and the great stacks shook. Strands caught in the deckled rims were ignited by the boiler fires leaping up the twin stacks. The burning ropes combed through the deckles until the branch they clung to sprang away with an angry rustle, and they fell coiling onto the deck. From one a serpent detached itself as if it had been generated by the flames. It lifted its head, peering first at the parlor door and then, the flat head wheeling a level arc, at Schlumberger, who stood with his hands clamped to the bow rail and his eyes held by the intricately calculating tongue. Then it poured across the deck toward him and dropped over the side within a yard of his left boot. He could not move until its tail slapped the water. A wake like an arrowhead whipped toward the bank and shot into a cavern of mangrove roots.

He glanced around to see if anyone had witnessed his panic and decided to go to his cabin. He preferred to see death from the safety of the main channel, where it was only a silvery throb of phosphor, not this enveloping venomous jungle. On his first step toward the door the pilot cried out. Bells clanged. The huge boat stammered to a halt, the paddle swish and piston thud diminishing to an easy slur and murmur of water, almost a silence, that quickly filled with caws and screeches.

Blocking the channel was a derelict steamboat: gutted by a sunken log, perhaps, and rammed up the bank to prevent sinking. The stern was underwater halfway up the sloping hurricane deck, and a blanket of duckweed was tucked around it. The paddle box housing had split like a melon rind, exposing the ribs beneath. On a window ledge a sunning lizard watched them come as if he hadn't expected visitors and didn't mean to put himself out for them.

The *Delta Belle* dropped anchor a few yards from the derelict. The captain had scrambled up the ladder to join the pilot on the texas deck. They filled the air with oaths and speculations. They goddamned the luck. They wondered how that tarnation heap had got there and why nobody at Natchez had mentioned it when they told about the chute. They looked for a name on the goddamn thing and guessed how many hours it would cost them and how long it had been there. *Long enough,* thought Schlumberger, *to become part of the forest.* Where the wreck touched land it had been invaded. Vines covered the hurricane deck and trailed a thick curtain from the rail. On the pilothouse moss was replacing the paint. What showed of the decks was weather-warped, the wood splitting ledges wide enough to cool a fat copperhead. Spanish moss draped the tilting stack. For the first time Schlumberger noticed how the deckled rim of a stack resembled the head of a chess king. From each rivet in the metal cylinder spread rust stains that a circling vine was doing its best to hide. The lowering sun, breaking through a bare patch in the wall of foliage, hit the stack with a red deeper than rust, made it red as a stack full of fire, as if the fire in it were unkillable.

But it was dead enough, and the speculation in the *Delta Belle*'s pilothouse settled down to talk about the best way to remove the carcass. The captain and the pilot strode back and forth across the texas deck scheming. The pilot was for running a cable through the hurricane-deck supports and pulling the hulk into the channel to sink. The captain argued that the channel wasn't deep enough. If they tried to walk over the sunken boat, they were likely to get stove in by the stack or the roof of the pilothouse. Pull down the stack, the pilot said. Rip off the pilothouse, too. A few men with hammers and crowbars could flatten that deck in ten minutes. The captain wouldn't hear of it. It would be more work, but less risk, just to chop away enough of the stern so they could squeeze past. That might take all night, the pilot said. He was disgusted. He had a bet that he could beat the time of a pilot on the *Jonathon Trace*.

By the time a work crew rowed through the duckweed and boarded the derelict, the sun was gone. After a few minutes one of them rowed back for lanterns. Schlumberger went to his stateroom to lie on his bunk and drink. Rouault was in the upper bunk running his fingers over the ceiling planks.

"We're stuck," Schlumberger told him. "A derelict's blocking the channel."

Rouault raised his eyebrows as if that was no surprise and gave his attention back to the ceiling. Any wood that came his way he fondled like a carpenter.

Schlumberger drifted off to sleep and woke to shouting. He heard a pistol shot. He went up on deck. Rouault, sublimely incurious, stayed below picking at splinters. Schlumberger found about a hundred and fifty passengers milling on the forward decks. The pilot and captain and a few other crewmen on the texas deck were peering restlessly into the forest and the sky. The pilot was reloading a pistol. The men on the deck of the derelict were also looking at the sky and making quick turns like cats trying to surprise their tails. There were two lanterns on the deck at their feet and each time a man said, "Thar she is," and took a step, a long shadow whipped over the water and up the forest wall. Lamplight flattened the foliage arching over the channel into a single shifting texture, a living membrane trying to close over them. Where the branches couldn't stretch across the channel, the sky was moonless and starless black.

Schlumberger grabbed the arm of a passenger and said, "What are they looking for? What's happened?" Before he got an answer, a crack like a luffing sail flapped a hot gust at his face. A white streak dipped past him toward the pilothouse of the derelict, and shrieked as it veered away from the shouts and the light. Its heavy wings churned the darkness. The shrieks were hard to place as an echo. One of the work crew had scrambled up to the derelict's texas deck. He was at the door of the abandoned pilothouse, calling, "Here it is, Cap'n. Goddam nest of 'em right in the pilot house. Goddam egrets!"

"It's divin' agin," someone shouted. Above him Schlumberger heard the pilot's pistol slam. The egret bucked as if it had hit an invisible wall and tumbled into the water. All the men cheered the pilot's marksmanship. From the water by the far bank came a thrashing and a slap-slapping splash. At the port rail Schlumberger made out beyond the lantern glow a ghostly white writhing. It sent gentle ripples arcing into the light. There was another shriek, a croak, and sporadic slapping. Schlumberger ran up the stairs to the texas deck.

"Finish it," he cried. "She's still alive. Kill her."

The pilot was putting his pistol into a black case. He and the captain laughed. "She'll be done soon," one of them said.

Schlumberger ran to the rail and peered into the darkness. One broad wing shot up and beat feebly against the black water and was swallowed. As it swooped past him, the tip of the wing nearly brushing his cheek, he had caught a glimpse of a round liquid eye, an eye mad with rage or grief.

IN NEW ORLEANS, Maelzel couldn't find anybody who would rent him a hall in the Vieux Carré on credit. After two days of scouting he negotiated a boarded-up meeting hall on the corner of Camp and Poydras streets, a few blocks farther away from the thickest flow of the city's bodies than he had ever before needed to go. That was all right, he growled. Where they pitched their tent didn't matter. The cheapest and most valuable piece of artillery in a businessman's arsenal, he said, was still words. He could draw a crowd to a plague ward, and claimed he once did, but that was another story he never finished. Schlumberger believed him.

Within two days after they opened, Maelzel had dined with the editor of the city's newspaper, and the Turk's marvels filled half the next day's front page. That night in his box Schlumberger could hear the murmurous gargle of the crowd filling the hall, swelling up to the velvet rope that was Maelzel's levee to shore back the seeping flood of curiosity, keeping the Turk dry and distant and once more potent with mystery. Maelzel had cut a chute, drained off the main channel of bodies into a healthy, rising, cash-at-the-door lake. After a week they moved to a better hotel.

When he wasn't playing chess or drinking, Schlumberger drifted with the crowds in the Vieux Carré. The French street signs made him think of Paris. He would loiter by a market fish stall to hear French spoken. After eleven years of flat Yankee accents his mother tongue was an undulant seduction. In bed Louise had purred certain words no Yankee whore could translate. Now their echoes snagged his memory and drew him down side streets and alleys that would empty into neat private courts where strangers would abruptly stop talking and keep their eyes leveled at him till he bowed and backed out.

One afternoon he took a walk under a sun that seemed to make the white walls of buildings steam. On one side of the street or the other, depending on the caprice of its turns, the buildings let down a slender ribbon of shadow. He walked in it as much as possible. The shadow was the only direction his walk had. It led him to a sun-drenched square where a crowd gathered around a wooden platform. From a distance Schlumberger thought he had come upon some kind of theatrical entertainment. Toward the back of the platform, where it abutted the plaster wall of a building, a line of people stood in the shadow of an overhanging eave. Closer to the crowd that closed around the platform's three open sides were two more figures. One seemed to be circling the other as it addressed the crowd. As soon as Schlumberger left the shady wall to approach, the sun struck his brow like an ax blade.

On the platform stood a Negro woman, bare to the waist. Behind her were other blacks, women and men, more men than women, joined at the ankles by a chain with links thick as fingers. They stood or leaned against the wall or squatted with their forearms dangling over their knees watching the white man walk around the woman who had been dragged down to the customers. While he took bids he raised and wagged her forearm to show the firm bicep or nudged a riding crop under her chin to tilt her face toward the sun. Schlumberger pressed to the front of the crowd, close enough to see a bead of sweat break from her collarbone and runnel down her breast, curving with its curve into the crescent shadow where it lay against her ribs. The auctioneer lazily maneuvered his drawl around a thick plug of tobacco, his words a honey and whiskey gentlemanly slur. He palped a breast like a careful buyer in a vegetable market, then released it with a spank that set up a lewd jiggle. As the bidding rose the woman seemed to be staring at some point of clear sky beyond the tiled roofs of the square. Was it that untouchable concentration that made Schlumberger feel he had seen her before, or only the glistening breasts? No: it was not these hard black cherries he recalled, but a rosy aureole where the bud would nest until he teased it erect.

When she was handed down to a jewel-fingered man in the crowd, Schlumberger saw her brief backward look, listless, beyond all feeling but an idle perplexity, at a wail that rose from the line of chained blacks. What Schlumberger had thought was sky became a tight blue lid clamped over the square as the wailing swelled, pressing at each wall for a way out, rebounding from one to the next, and when Schlumberger thought the sound would press him flat to the ground a white man stepped over to a black in the line and swung a length of pipe that thocked against his skull. Schlumberger knew who had screamed when he saw who dropped. A word separated itself from the wailing's ululant echo, a name, and looking after the slave being led away he recognized the blue-eyed mulatto from the steamboat who had boasted her master wouldn't sell her.

Suddenly, as if there were nowhere else his eyes could bear to rest, he looked straight into the sun and said "Daisy" and all the echoes in the square flew down his throat.

THEY PLAYED six weeks in New Orleans. When they closed it was not because the audiences had dried up, but because Maelzel's southern raid was proving so successful he wanted to turn it into a full-scale invasion. That meant breaking out the full arsenal of Maelzel marvels that were packed in dusty crates in a corner of John Ohl's warehouse in Philadelphia. They had traveled light to New Orleans. Along with the Turk they carried only what Schlumberger called the dolls—the Funambulist puppet dancers and the automaton trumpeter. Now Maelzel wanted audiences to see his own inventions: the panharmonicon orchestra and a new version of the *Conflagration of Moscow* diorama (he had sold the old one to meet rent on the Adelphi Hall in Philadelphia). The new one would have twice as many buildings, dozens more Cossacks, and French grenades bursting every minute with a splash of lava in the clouds. He even had a plan for a new trumpeter who would be able to hold a note longer than any human musician.

"We'll show them the real genius of mechanics," he said. Restored to himself by the crowds and their money, he told Schlumberger the public was a flock of sheep. "If people had any notion what it takes to put together a panharmonicon, nobody would look twice at that damned fake Turk." The Turk was the bastard child who supported the family. Maelzel never forgave it for having been invented by Wolfgang von Kempelen. "You wait, Willie," he would say. "One day I'll make a real one—a real machine."

His enthusiasm was making him giddy, Schlumberger decided.

Schlumberger didn't want to move South permanently. He hated the heat, and the mosquitoes frenzied him. "You make one, then," he told Maelzel. "Build a machine to play chess so I can stay home. I don't care a rap."

"Nonsense, Willie," Maelzel said. "You know I need you. And you won't be stuck here in New Orleans. We'll play here a few months and then keep right on traveling."

"Where?" Schlumberger asked. "New Orleans is the end. There's nothing beyond it but the Gulf of Mexico."

"Wrong, Willie. Out past the water is Cuba. Havana—thousands of people in Havana. And beyond that, who knows? There's no end."

"Beyond that is alligators and swamp. Savage Indians. Indians don't play chess. They hunt with poison arrows."

Rouault came, too.

40 | Mosquito

WITH A WALL at each elbow it should have been easy to kill a mosquito. Usually once Maelzel clamped the lid down, darkness for a few minutes dissolved the walls. The box became a starless void he could fill with dreams. Until the game began, he drifted, dreaming the mirrored walls of the Café de la Régence. There he had also drifted—from the game on the board to the game in the walls, where he could see Schlumberger meditating a move, Schlumberger taking a knight, Schlumberger saying *Échec*—and beyond him, more games, more Schlumbergers, receding until he could no longer distinguish their features. He didn't need to see them in order to know that what he did in the room went on in the walls forever. Here in the box, the Turk's real skull, the walls of its brain, only the void went on—and not forever. If he stretched his legs, his heels jammed his spine against a wall. The hump on his back had grown a callus where it rubbed the wall. Even the darkness was not total. After those first few minutes his eyes could make out the airslits hidden by the lid's overlap, faintly tracing the confines of his cell, diluting his cozy void as the first robin-heralded lesser darkness dilutes night.

And that night in Havana when Maelzel clamped him into the customary dark, it was not the void that rushed upon him, but a whine like the high nasal *Kyrie* of the parish priest in Mulhouse, the one who had said Mass at his father's funeral, the one to whom Schlumberger at age eleven had confessed with terror and self-loathing his first mortal sin, kneeling in the narrow box watching the grey lips on the other side of the grille for a purse of disgust. The mosquito whined close to his ear.

Mosquito

When he slapped, the whine thinned to a pinprick. He wanted out, he wanted to rap on the lid for Maelzel to open up so he could shoo it away or kill it. But the wheels were rumbling along the floor, Rouault was wheeling the box from the storeroom to the hall where the first customers might already be chatting. They were running late that night, rushed because even after six months in Havana, Schlumberger had stayed so close to his hotel room that he still didn't know the city and had lost himself on a rare after-dinner walk among the narrow streets. He had found his way back only minutes before.

As he was legging over the box rim, Maelzel hooked the armholes of Schlumberger's waistcoat in two meaty fists, and pulled him up to his face. With the earnest concentration of a winetaster he took a long evaluative sniff and said, "Are you sober, you bastard? Can you play? Because if you can't—" and not detecting more alcohol on his breath than the dregs of their dinner wine, he stuffed him down like a pile of rags that has to fit into a bulging carpetbag.

It was too late to shoo it out, but, he thought, *I'll have plenty of time before the game to kill it,* and gave his cheek a slap that made his ear roar. For a while it was quiet in the dark, and he thought he'd got it. He even dozed through the first of Maelzel's muffled spiel. He woke with a start when the opening of the first cabinet door brought Maelzel's exclamations suddenly close to his ear. As he listened for his cue, he found himself gnawing at the first joint of his middle finger. He took it away from his mouth burning. He flexed it to make the skin across the knuckle tighten and ache, and risked a thin moan, the sensual hosanna of the connoisseur. It was the hand he would have to use all evening to work the pantograph that moved the Turk's arm and closed his fingers on the pieces.

On cue, he folded back the partition and slid his trunk into the narrow third of the cabinet and reclosed the partition. With the door of the gearbox open, this was as close as he came to the audience. While Maelzel opened the double doors of the compartment where only moments before he had been curled, Schlumberger held himself rigidly still, arms at his sides, so the audience could not see even a shadow's shadow move behind the intricate interlocking curtain of gears. Then he heard the whine again. The bogus machinery admitted pinpoints of light. Maybe the mosquito would get lost in the maze and thread its way to the other side. Something tickled his eyelid. He gave a fierce wink, and it resettled on the wing of his nostril. *Wait till I can light that lamp,* he thought. When the demonstration was over and the cabinet doors reclosed, he folded back the partition, lighted the lamp, screwed the handle into the pantograph rod, set up the small chessboard on which he duplicated the moves made over his head, and took the lamp out of its bracket. Somewhere, glutted with his blood, it would be resting heavy and content. He tracked the lamp along all the walls and ceiling. Then he heard Maelzel insert the key in the Turk's back and wind the gears, his signal to make the Turk's first move. He rebracketed the lamp and opened, queen's pawn to queen's pawn-four.

Once during the game he saw it on the ceiling among the hanging metal flaps that made magnetic connections with chesspieces on the board above. He couldn't slap quickly for fear of upsetting the board. When he cautiously raised the back of his hand, it purred lazily away. In all it bit him three times that night: another knuckle bite, this time on the forefinger, and in the short hairs under his left eyebrow. After the game, when Maelzel lifted the lid, Schlumberger watched it float out of the box and make for the window, where it dissolved into the shadow of a curtain. He claimed to Maelzel that it was the mosquito that made him lose that night, and tried to claim it to himself as well, but the fact was that someone in Havana played better chess than Schlumberger had met with since he left Paris.

"Who was the lucky one?" he asked.

"A boy, just a boy," said Maelzel. Then as if he were conjuring a rage he had grown tired of feeling, "You hear that, drunkard—you were whipped by a boy!"

His smile was edged like the blade of a scythe.

YEARS LATER the edge of that smile was still sharp. Walking home late, the street narrow and dark, Schlumberger would flatten against the wall at a sudden clatter, a horseman galloping drunk. In the whirling breeze, whiskeybreath and horseflesh choking the narrow street, hoof sparks struck from the cobbles, there the smile would be forming, invisible still, hovering behind the gaslight spilled from an upper window. He would try to see only dark, the silhouette of the horseman's flying cloak, the sparks like bright needles, and as a spark winked out, there in the space traced by its arc would be Maelzel's grin sharp enough to chip ice.

•

Mosquito

Why should his memory of a moment like many another be so clear? He couldn't get rid of it. There were things he couldn't get rid of and things he couldn't get back. The sound of her voice, gone. In the dark he would whisper, *Willie, William,* but it was gone. Her eyes were going; sometimes blue, they faded to grey, and he knew that once he had been able to hold in his mind for minutes their precise shade and flecking.

Another thing he had tried to get back was the game that followed. Not the next evening's game, a quick dull victory, but the game he played the night after that. He tried to get it into his journal. He wanted every move, the whole sequence so he could replay it. He still had many games that way. He could pick up his first game with La Bourdonnais at any move, and try a new variation. But all he could get back of the Havana game was the tightness in his chest. The feeling of being crowded off the board. Within five minutes, it seemed, enemy pieces jammed the center. Ten minutes later his queen was pinned. To free her he needed a bishop, his king's only guard. Without the bishop he had only one chance: queen's knight. *Queen's knight to*—he recalled; that was the one combination of the game he could remember with perfect clarity, and he remembered reaching his hand for the queen's knight, how his hand, yellow in the lamplight, began to tremble as it hovered over the board. Because the queen's knight was gone. Lost in the first minutes of play. Keeping his head back tightened his windpipe; his breath sluiced like wind in a tunnel. In most games he waited for the *toc* with his eyes on his own board or on the lamp flame, looking up to the ceiling only when one of the metal flaps ticked down, the magnetic contact broken, showing that a piece on the board had been lifted. But that night he kept his head back the whole game, the base of his skull rolling back and forth over the crown of his hump like a mill wheel, his eyes ranging the squares. And when a flap clicked up against the ceiling, it was always in a place that nudged him tighter. The eight-by-eight square was a cage, and it came to him that the only way to win now was to break out, move his pinned queen to a square outside the board, shoot his rook up the new, unblocked flank. And he thought what he could do with a new row of squares on his flank until a sudden clatter startled him—the sound of the key Maelzel wound in the Turk's back to "restart the machinery," which was designed to cover Schlumberger's occasional coughing fit or to wake him when he passed out in the box between moves. And he blinked and looked at the board: still eight by eight, still his move. And he had no plan, no possible combination, and the queen's knight was lost.

In the last minute before it was over, he felt he would have to brace against his hump and kick the wall out. Or stand. He saw himself pushing up the ceiling, bearing it up on his shoulders and hump right before the audience—standing, straightening his back, spilling pieces over the floor, shrugging the weight of the board from his back. He would laugh like a schoolboy caught at hide-and-seek. Surprise, he would shout at Maelzel, and take a bow. Show how little it mattered.

Then it was check and mate, and the Turk was being wheeled off, and whatever it mattered to the audience didn't matter to him. Only later, when he realized that was the last time the walls of the box ever held him and the last game of chess he was ever to play, did it seem to matter, and when he tried to get it back all he could remember was the tightness.

He was braced for Maelzel's fury, but it was Rouault who lifted the lid. Schlumberger grabbed the sides of the box and pulled himself to his feet. His body dutifully unfolded up to his crooked back, a last joint no grease could limber. He climbed out of the box and paced around the storeroom, thinking what he would say to Maelzel. Rouault had scooped the chessmen into a cigar box, which he was sliding into the cabinet drawer.

"It's that coffin I have to play in," he recalled saying to Rouault's broad stooping back. "That arm is sticking again. That's your job, Rouault. How can I play chess against a real chess player, when I've got to think about all that damn machinery?"

Rouault got an oilcan from a shelf. He put it on a table and scraped the table close to the Turk's back and scraped sparks from a flint to light an oil lamp that was on the table. He positioned the lamp to baste the Turk's back in a yellow glow deep as rancid butter. Then he stooped behind the Turk and grasped the fur-trimmed edge of his coat. He had the touch of a discreet manservant who invests what he touches with quality. As always the Turk's eyes were lowered. His lips looked ready to part. Perhaps simply for a sigh. Rouault draped the coattails over the Turk's head and opened the door in his back. The turban made the Turk's cloaked head bulbous. The bulbous head peered from the elegant, fur-bordered cowl of a sensual monk. Schlumberger could see only the mahogany tip of the Turk's chin. The shadows disturbed him. He had an uncomfortable sensation that under the shadowing cloak the Turk had opened his eyes. He circled behind it to where Rouault was working oil into a joint in the rod that ran up the Turk's back. His arm was inside the Turk's back up to the elbow.

"If I could see his face," Schlumberger said, "I'd know when he's worried."

Rouault's back shrugged. "Nobody sees your face," he said. "All he sees is the Turk's face." Inside the Turk's trunk the oilcan pumped like an erratic tin heart.

"It was the same one, wasn't it?" Schlumberger said.

"Yes."

"I could tell. By the fifth move, I knew him." He paced over to the wall where the automaton trumpeter stood with his trumpet arm bent at the elbow, offering the horn to whoever might shake his hand. The painted cheeks were puffed, the bright lips always pursed, so that he looked like a cherub about to belch. "A boy, he told me."

"Nineteen, maybe twenty," Rouault muttered.

"How can a kid know so much?"

Rouault's arm appeared, placing the oilcan on the table, then disappeared inside the Turk.

"At that age," he said, "you were pretty good, too."

The Turk's left arm extended and floated back and forth over the empty board as if a blind man were searching for the pieces.

Schlumberger laid his cheek against the trumpeter's wood epaulet. He felt more tired than he had since the day he knew there was no place, Paris-bound ship or whorehouse, where he was going to find Louise Rouault.

"For God's sake," he said, "why didn't he stop it?"

"He tried," Rouault said, standing up. He reached both arms over the Turk's shoulders and lifted the coat gently so as not to disturb the turban, and draped it around the wooden trunk. The lamp beside him threw upon his jowl and cheek a waxy yellow crescent. "There was a crowd," he said. "All the ones who missed it night before last. He was their champion. When Maelzel saw how it was, he let it happen."

Schlumberger paced to the door and opened it a crack to peer into the empty hall.

"What's keeping him?" he asked.

Rouault arched his eyebrows as if he expected Schlumberger to have known the answer himself. Then he turned away, replacing the oilcan on its shelf, and said, "When I went out to wheel in the Turk, he was at the door, talking with the boy."

Schlumberger's teeth ground back a cry. He jabbed a short kick at the trumpeter's shins. The trumpeter rocked onto its heels and then nodded obsequiously forward, offering its trumpet with diminishing gusto.

"He's buying him off," Schlumberger moaned. "He thinks he has to buy him off. Christ, doesn't he know he doesn't have to do that?" He came up to the table, where Rouault, bending over the lamp, his cheeks puffed, lips pursed to blow it out, was the trumpeter's momentary twin. "I can beat him, Rouault. He knows that. Just let me out of this fucking coffin, let me play him face to face."

A wall bracket near the door held a single flickering candle. When Rouault huffed out the lamp, it left just enough light for them to see the shadows scamper like night-prowling mice.

THAT EVENING in all the saloons along the Paseo de Paulo, Schlumberger hunted for Maelzel. He wanted to find him with the boy chess player so he could force the boy into a face-to-face game and beat him before Maelzel's eyes. Then he wanted to tell Maelzel they had to leave this city where the rain that fell every day rotted their clothing and never cooled the air. They had to leave because of the heat and because the bay they could see from their hotel windows was clogged with garbage and shit that made a stink you couldn't close out, and everybody knew the yellow fever was carried on the putrid air and you couldn't breathe it without inhaling a mosquito. They could go home, he wanted to tell Maelzel, home to Paris where nobody had seen the Turk for twelve years. They could make a fortune and live in a civilized climate among people who knew who they were and respected them.

Havana had never lost for Schlumberger the uncanny menace of a carnival mask full of horns and teeth. They had timed their arrival to coincide with the carnival crowds that would be rioting through the streets right up to the moment the priest laid his ash-smudged thumb on their brows and said, "Thou art dust . . ."

Standing at the bow rail with Maelzel and Rouault before the

Mosquito

gangplank was lowered, Schlumberger had heard a silvery piping and a clanka-clank like hollow bones knocking together. Weaving down the street among the crowds of shoppers and sailors and whores came a human chain that bristled with masks. To Schlumberger their music was like a leper's warning bell. On the pier Maelzel whistled at a man with a barrow to wheel their bags to the nearest hotel, and they merged with the crowd. Shuffling along to the sinuous pipes, splashing wine on Schlumberger's sleeve and trouser leg, the revelers lurched among them, and each papier-mâché gargoyle leered at his hump. Every other person was a harlequin or a mock princess tilting a bottle to her lips. On the curb people shrieked a warning at him in a strange tongue. The barrow man, who had a few words of English, cackled at the shrieks and told him it was only pimps selling their girls. He was a wiry man, thin as a fasting anchorite. All the fat in him had drained into a goiter that jigged with his stride like a breast.

A skeleton with bad teeth stepped in front of Schlumberger and put a hand on his chest. Its face was powdered white with flour. Soft coal blacked over the nose and gouged dark crevices for the eyes and slashed a hollow under the cheekbones. It wore a black skullcap and black tight-fitting clothes striped in white to outline its bones. The stripes made a riblike cage across its chest. The skeleton said something to Schlumberger in Spanish and held out to him a huge scarlet chesspiece, a bishop. When Schlumberger tried to back away, the skeleton gripped his arm and grinned. It had a sparse crop of teeth set in liver-colored gums. At the roots the teeth were a livid green. With the tongue and gums, they made a colorful hole in the bone-white face. The skeleton tried to thrust the red bishop into Schlumberger's hands. A whiff of putrescence blew from secret pockets in the diseased mouth, and Schlumberger threw up his arm to fend it off.

His gesture caused a loud moan of disappointment in the crowd. He was surrounded by moaning papier-mâché demons. The shoulders of the demons all looked puny, powerless to shake off whatever vice had bloated the huge echoing heads. Sometimes inside the eyeholes and mouth holes Schlumberger could glimpse another, more human face trapped behind the demon's fanged grimace.

A third time the skeleton held out the red bishop, attempting to place it on Schlumberger's head.

"I don't want it," Schlumberger croaked. "What is it? What do you want from me?" He heard the goiter-necked barrow man's cackle and turned to him. "What does he want from me?"

"You be pope, he says," the barrow man explained. "You lead parade."

The skeleton and the demons brayed eagerly and drew closer. A brick-red gargoyle with horns on its temples tried to throw over Schlumberger's shoulders a silky yellow cloak. Another tried to hand him a crooked staff. The skeleton again held out the bishop—not a chesspiece, he saw now, but the tip of one: a bishop's mitre set with cut-glass emeralds.

"A great honor," the barrow man urged. "They feed you, give you free whiskey."

"No, no, I don't want it," Schlumberger said. "Why have they chosen me?"

The barrow man said something in Spanish to the skeleton, who stepped up to Schlumberger giggling and briskly slapped his hump.

That was why, after five months in Havana, Schlumberger knew barely enough Spanish to order meals and preferred to stay close to his room in the hotel. Hunting Maelzel in the night cafés and whorehouse parlors, he found only gargoyles jabbering what he took to be curses or japes.

On his way back to the hotel he was crossing a street when he heard, faintly, a familiar intonation. Stirred by some current circulating through the dark street, it lifted, droned like a mosquito passing his ear, and dropped back, lost in the chatter spilling from an open café door. He started toward the sound tentatively, afraid to stray beyond the streets he knew. It was not Maelzel's voice—he recognized that immediately—but a voice he had once suffered with similar impatience. He came to a long wall of open windows that ventilated the sound, and entered by a side door. The red tongue of the sanctuary lamp barely outlined the main altar, but from the shadowy vault above the choir loft, a chain suspended a lavish candelabra over about a dozen people, the light it cast glowing a golden brown upon the curve of the organ pipes. Schlumberger stayed in the side aisle in the shadow of a pillar.

At a nod from the conductor the organist pressed his hands to the keyboard with the full weight of his shoulders, summoning a mighty tone which poured into the conductor's body and hurled his arms above his head. His hands seemed to burst from his sleeves and the fingers stiffened, sustaining the organ's note. At last they gave a minute twitch that allowed another note to fall on top of the first, and another and yet more, dropping like infinite rows of dominoes, and then a sudden lilting of the hands released from the choir tiered before him the words, *Credo in unum Deum*. . . . His arms made a rolling sea swell that conjured *Patrem omnipoténtem*. His left hand traced the curve of Louise Rouault's breast, and as Schlumberger began walking toward the center aisle, the organ pipes made the floor beneath him tremble with *factórem coeli et terrae*. On the last long note of *invisibílium,* the conductor's forefinger narrowed toward his thumb at the tip of her nipple, and when finger touched thumb sound ceased. In the hush he began anew, shaping from the living air the *unum Dóminum* while the shadows of his arms and swaying torso rolled in the nave below, leaping halfway up the center aisle and across the pew rails on either side, enveloping Schlumberger where he stood.

At *sub Póntio Piláto passus, et sepúltus est,* a sharp voice interrupted and said something in Spanish. Schlumberger was amazed to hear the conductor speak without his hands, without music. The organ sounded a pitch note, the phrase was repeated, interrupted by another scold from the conductor. It occurred to Schlumberger that Maelzel would claim he could design a machine to do it exactly on pitch every time. After the third interruption the director must have noticed that his choir was looking past him. He glanced over his shoulder, then turned to confront the source of distraction, clamping both hands over the rail of the loft to fire down a sharp Spanish staccato. Schlumberger was out the door before they began again, and barely heard the *resurréxit tértia die* as he hurried up the street to the hotel.

By 11 P.M. he was pounding on Maelzel's door. When there was no answer, he walked down the hall to Rouault's room. The hall was dim enough for him to see there was no light along the bottom edge of Rouault's door, but he knocked anyway. Rouault's voice said, "Come in," immediately.

"Why are you sitting in the dark?"

Rouault was in a wicker chair beside the window, his bare feet propped on the bed, his arms hanging from the chair arms.

"My eyes need a rest," he said. His voice was a breath above a whisper, as if he had been a long time talking only for himself and didn't

[3 6 3]

KINGKILL

care now if Schlumberger wanted to overhear. "Close the door."
In the dark the smell of stale sweat thickened as Schlumberger
approached the bed and sat on something hard. Rising, he groped along
a smooth cylinder till his hand discovered the hammer and butt of a
dueling pistol. He sat again, holding it.
"A pistol?" Schlumberger said. "What are you doing with a
pistol?"
"I was cleaning them."
When he laid it back on the mattress, the barrel clicked against the
barrel of its mate. Near it he made out the flat case they came from.
"I never knew you had pistols."
"I've had them a long time."
The night was hot. The faintest of breezes crossed the window sill,
smuggling in the usual harbor stench.
"If you leave that window open, the mosquitoes will have a
feast."
Rouault glanced over his shoulder as if the window were a third
person who had silently entered the room. Gaslight three stories below
made his profile palely luminous. As he turned back toward Schlumberger, the line of his nose and jaw disappeared inside the gaslit
contour.
"It's too hot to worry about mosquitoes," he said. He was still
again, but the wicker, resettling against his weight, continued ticking
for a while. The darkness separated itself into shapes of black and
grey—bedpost, chamber pot, bureau; the sparse furnishings of a man
who made his home in his head rather than a room. No tools, books,
pipes, miniatures of loved ones. But two pistols. In the open case
shadows filled the hollows where the pistols would lie. The pillow
beyond it kept the impression of a head in a shadowy pool. Schlumberger probed the darkness for a place to begin.
"I've been looking for him," he said. "He's not in the bars.
Where would he go?"
"It's a big city."
"I want to tell him we're leaving. Going back to Paris. I thought
we might both tell him. He'd have to listen to us both."
Schlumberger waited for a reply. The wicker gave a small tick.
"Will you say it, too?" he asked. "You want to leave, too, don't
you?"

"There's nothing to stay for anymore," said Rouault.

"Good. We'll tell him together. He can't ignore us both, can he?"

"He's done it before."

"How could he? He'd have to replace us. Who could he get? That boy, after twelve years? For two lucky wins, you think he'd risk—"

"Before you," Rouault said flatly, "there was Louise. She replaced Mouret. Mouret replaced someone else."

His level tone was dispassionate and precise, as if he were tracing a biblical genealogy. Schlumberger had the chill feeling that Rouault could have traced the Turk's history of sin and misery back to Adam.

"You think he could do it, then?"

"The only one who never gets replaced," said Rouault, "is the Turk."

The harbor stench mingled with Rouault's sweat. A heavy nausea flexed the coils of Schlumberger's bowel.

"You know, Henri," he said, "we could have been friends. Better friends, I mean."

"We have a lot in common."

Even with the stench, Schlumberger was glad for the open window, the slightest breeze. "Did you ever hear from her?" he said, and was astonished at the sudden thudding of his heart.

From the dark bulk in the wicker chair there came a rush of breath sharply clipped, something like a hiccup caught before it jams the throat, and swallowed down. But the voice was still flat and steady as it said, "Now and again. A few lines," and then added, after a brief convulsion of wicker, "But not any more."

Schlumberger didn't know how far he dared go.

"Do you know where she is?"

Too far, he sensed it immediately. Rouault withdrew his feet from the bed and stood up. He went to his bedside table. When Schlumberger saw the quick shudders of his broad back and heard a dry chipping, it took him a moment to call back the grief-spent sob he had conjured and recognize that Rouault was merely scratching sparks from a flint. The wall beyond him declared itself a pallid yellow; and while the tinder flared, Rouault reached a candle from the wall bracket behind his chair. He snuffed the tinder and replaced the candle and sat beneath it.

"No need to keep you in the dark any longer," he said. "My eyes are quite rested."

Schlumberger's question hung in the still air between them like a small bird under a vacuum jar. At last Rouault breathed it to life.

"A year ago she was in New Orleans."

"When we were there? Oh, God," Schlumberger said. It was as if he had known it, sensed her, heard her calling him down a thousand miles of river, and then grazed her shoulder in the street without recognizing her. He said it must be the sudden brightness of the candle flame that made his eyes blink, and felt embarrassed because he suspected it was actually tears. The light came from above and beyond Rouault, who didn't seem aware that it was proper to look away from someone overcome by emotion.

"Did you see her?" Schlumberger asked.

"Yes," Rouault said. The wicker chair crackled like a bonfire. "But I wasn't the one she came for."

"She wanted . . . she came for me?"

Rouault's head nodded.

"Then why . . . ?"

"Maelzel sent her away."

Schlumberger waited till his breathing steadied, then said, "Henri, I know how you feel. But you've got to tell me. Tell it all."

"Do you? Do you know how I feel?"

"Please, Rouault. I've got a right to know."

"Do you? Then I'll tell you." He pulled his shirt away from his body and flapped the damp cloth, fanning his torso, but when he let it go, it clung to the bulge of his gut like a plaster. "She was sick. There was some man in it. Some railroad builder in Chicago. He'd thrown her out. Maelzel offered her money. She wouldn't take it. Wanted you."

"Where was I? Why didn't she wait for me?"

"Oh, you were gone. Out roaming the city, drinking, whoring, whatever you do when you're gone. You never made it back that night. It was one of the nights we had to cancel. Put out the Mechanical Difficulties sign."

"And she didn't wait?"

"Maelzel didn't want her to," Rouault said, and paused to pinch from his lip a piece of dead skin. "He offered her all the money he had—"Another pause, while Rouault inspected what he was rolling between thumb and forefinger."—but this time it wasn't enough."

"This time?"

Mosquito

"Hadn't you guessed? Do you think Maelzel would ever have stopped chasing her if she had actually managed to steal his precious hoard?"

"Are you telling me she left Boston with money Maelzel *gave* her?"

Rouault flicked the shred of skin to the floor and ran his tongue along the lower lip with the care of a cabinet builder testing the texture of his planing. "She'd never have gotten far without it," he said.

"But why would Maelzel—?"

"So long as she was around, he judged you would never settle down and play chess."

Schlumberger thought he had few illusions about Maelzel, but with nearly a third of his life shifting its center of gravity like poorly stowed cargo, he wanted to believe Rouault a liar.

"But she left a note," he said. "There was a scrap of paper, something about going on the streets." Which he could have quoted verbatim.

"The note was part of what she had to do to get the money."

"Twelve years . . ." Schlumberger said. His mind was drifting into an eddy of the current; he had to think hard to pull it back toward the channel. Then he said, "But I don't understand—if she wouldn't take his money this time, why wouldn't she wait for me?"

Rouault flapped his shirt. Sweat rolled down his neck into the hairs matted on his chest.

"Maelzel convinced her you wouldn't want her," he said.

"Convinced her? How?"

"He said you were fucking him now."

Schlumberger stood up and immediately forgot why. He thought he might have wanted to put his head out the window for a night breeze. Slapping absently at a mosquito, he felt the nausea that had been nesting in the coils of his intestines come sluggishly awake. It poured through the caverns of his body looking for a way out. As he opened his mouth to say something to Rouault, who was staring up at him with eyes that mimicked the pendulum sway of his body, it made a sliding rush for his throat and choked him. He heard himself gagging. When Rouault's face went by again, he noticed in the way it looked at him a vexing composure, which he decided to violate. He grabbed the damp front of Rouault's shirt, intending to yank him to his feet. His sharp tug toppled him into Rouault's lap, his lips grazing Rouault's ear as if he had bent over to whisper a secret. Rouault expelled a grunt and a shove that propelled Schlumberger backward with just time to imagine the single graceful half step that would get his feet under the colossal weight of his hump before it slammed into the bedframe. Then he was slumped on the floor, the green counterpane he had clutched to break his fall draping his shoulder.

Rouault was still seated, blinking, surprised by his own violence. He said, "Don't touch me," the way he might explain something simple and important to a child.

On the crown of his hump there was only a numb tingle, but in all the places his flesh had pressed against Rouault, Schlumberger felt as if his skin had been scraped away in brittle scales.

"Where is she now?" he said. "For God's sake, tell me."

"Where you can't touch her. Where none of us can."

Then Rouault told about the letters from Chicago. Two of them, one from Louise, asking Rouault's forgiveness. The other a brief note from the man, explaining the circumstances: his profound regret to inform; following so close upon his marriage; a certain imbalance exacerbated perhaps by; the body hoisted onto the pier, the heavy petticoats streaming; and in the next day's post, the final recriminating note, with an enclosure to be passed on to Rouault.

"You never told me," whispered Schlumberger.

"It came with yesterday's mail."

"Show it to me."

Rouault pulled himself out of the wicker chair. He looked down at Schlumberger on the floor as if he couldn't recall how he got there. Then he walked slowly to the bureau and put his hand on the knob of a drawer. Schlumberger could see the moment when his mind changed. There as no shift of posture, but the heavy back, made for burdens, which Schlumberger had seen a thousand times patiently bend to the weight of a crate, became a wall. Rouault turned and put it against the bureau. "I've got rights, too," he said. "What she gave me is mine."

Schlumberger knew when not to argue. He got to his feet. The rawness of his flesh had spread to his whole body and he needed to vomit and the yellow walls of Rouault's room were so bright he could not stop blinking tears from his eyes. As he walked to the door, Rouault

Mosquito

blew out the candle. When Schlumberger turned in the hallway to look back, Rouault was again in the wicker chair by the open window in the dark.

"I'm going to kill him," Schlumberger said, and there was not a sound from the wicker chair to distort the toneless whisper that answered, "Yes. I know."

AFTER HE LEFT ROUAULT, Schlumberger went to the lobby of the hotel and asked the desk clerk for the key to Maelzel's room. He told the clerk that his business partner was negotiating an important purchase and required certain documents. As he handed Schlumberger the key, the clerk commented that Mr. Schlumberger's eyes appeared a bit red and asked if he were catching a cold.

Schlumberger let himself into Maelzel's room and sat down to wait in the dark in a chair positioned behind the door. He found himself fingering a fresh mosquito bite on the tightly stretched flesh just behind his left ear. The room was stifling, and he wondered whether Maelzel would notice if he opened the window. Then he didn't care anymore, because his sweat chilled and made him shiver. He thought of Rouault's pistols and went down the hall to get them. Just outside the door he got dizzy and had to lean against the wall. He had heard of people who were going to be hanged having to be carried to the scaffold, but he didn't know it could be like that when you were the executioner. He was afraid that once Rouault realized he meant to use the pistols, he would not want to let him have them, and wondered if he could stop being dizzy and hot long enough to wrestle them away.

But Rouault was gone. When all Schlumberger got for his knocking and calling was silence, he felt an eerie panic and had to remind himself where he was. Then he tried the handle. The door swung open. Before he crossed the threshold, something about the squeak of the hinge told Schlumberger the room was not just empty but abandoned. He went in. Rouault's drawers were open and empty and his boots were gone; the Bible he kept unread on the trunk by his bed was lying in a corner of the floor and the tinder box that had been there with it was gone. The only things of Rouault's left in sight were the two pistols in their case. The case was lying open on the bed, facing the door.

Schlumberger closed the case and put it under his arm and ran tiptoe down the hall to Maelzel's room, because he had heard footsteps on the stairs. After the footsteps continued up to the next floor, he went back down the hall, breathing harshly, and stuck his hand inside the open drawer of the bureau where Rouault had stood when he told Schlumberger he couldn't see the letter from Louise. He had done it only to be certain, and was puzzled when his fingers closed around a thick envelope.

Back in Maelzel's room he risked lighting a candle. He didn't trust his fumbling with the pistol hammers in the dark. Finding a round lead ball in each barrel didn't surprise him more than anything else he had discovered in the past hour. He was concentrating on one thing at a time, and his hands were trembling so that he had to put both thumbs over the hammer to lower the pin back into place. Then, since everything was going so well, he felt confident he would hear Maelzel's footsteps in time to snuff the candle, and opened the envelope.

The manuscript inside had yellowed since he last held it. Once he recognized it was Rouault's hand, he skimmed to the last page, where he found the words he had read before: "I'd rather be dead or on the streets than go on like this."

It gripped him in a convulsion like vomiting. Harsh racking detonations doubled him over in the chair. He groped to snuff the candle, spilling tallow in his lap, and buried his face in his sleeve to muffle the sound from Maelzel. Each time he thought it was over, it would grip him again and he would go on sobbing in the dark, a pistol in each hand, holding his breath, choking back sobs whenever footsteps passed the door. It must have been close to 2 A.M., and if Maelzel were sleeping at home, he seldom stayed out past that hour. That thought, at last, quieted him. A familiar tipsy shuffle on the threadbare carpet turned out to be an echo of the rasping flint from which he had sparked the candle. Mixed with the occasional clopping of a horse in the street, he heard other echoes: the click of the hammer when he pulled it back; the crackle of a wicker chair; a voice saying over and over, *Take this damn furnace but don't make me take this to America tomorrow but don't make me love this damn furnace.* Sometimes he was afraid he wouldn't be ready when Maelzel opened the door, because he couldn't distinguish the street noises and the sound of his own breathing from the echoes.

One of the pistols slipping to the floor woke him. He was trembling. He pulled back the covers of Maelzel's bed and stuck Rouault's

Mosquito

manuscript into one of his boots before he climbed into the bed. The pistols he tucked under the covers next to his thigh. Then he closed his eyes and felt lapping at the fringes of his sleep the first purifying flames of the fire dream.

41 | Kingkill

WITH A STORM LOOMING, no rites but a nervous *God'a mercy*. No coffin, but a burlap shroud so wide stitched that as the weight slides down the flank of the *Otis,* a spike head peels it half away, and the last sight of those gathered at the gangway in Maelzel's leathery bald crown like a disk at the heart of a blossoming splash swiftly slipping astern.

What follows happens in darkness: the slow explosion of sand as the four-pound shot fastened to the ankles buries itself in the shelf off Charleston; the body, buoyed on the gases of dissolution, twisting in the current, the arms feebly waving away fish that come to nibble the tender meat of eyelids, lips and fingertips. Later the purged carcass settles, stretching along the sand, face to the sun that glimmers palely far above, and a current hollows the rib cage and the arch beneath the upturned jaw till the bones are polished to a pearly lustre, purified at last of flesh.

At night Schlumberger follows him down. On these nocturnal descents, made with tireless fidelity, he witnesses each transformation: Does coral crust the skull? Its pink and orange blisters lodge beneath the cheek. Does the sand sifting through the ribs cover them? On his next visit fish will be threading in and out, and over the years he will find what remains of Maelzel covered and uncovered and recovered like a restless sleeper tossing his blanket.

None of this matters to the biographer. Once the final date is noted and the brackets closed, all that remains of his task is a quick rummage through the battered trunks. A tidy inventory—twelve gold doubloons; a gold medal presented by the king of Prussia to the great mechanician;

and a little green book filled with sure-win end games. Then a hasty eulogy, ending on this curious note: "Whatever there may have been in his private morals, that might have detracted from this favorable impression" (fondness for children, charitable donations, "amiable and obliging disposition"), "was forced upon the attention of nobody, and was never inquired into; and I do not consider it any part of my office, as historian of the Automaton, to draw from their dread abode the personal frailties of Maelzel."

George Allen's essay on the automaton's American career disposes of Maelzel's death in a bare three pages. Schlumberger read them with incredulity, trying to recognize the man they spoke of. Could it all be reduced to this? To Captain Nobre welcoming him aboard the *Otis* with raised eyebrows at the "remarkable change . . . in his appearance"? The pocket chess set, and a last game with Nobre? The petulant snarl when Nobre asked his advice in the end game? The sick man excusing himself, retiring to his berth, instructing the steward to place within reach the case of claret, his only nourishment as he lingered through the final six days before his corpse was discovered "early on Saturday morning, the 21st of July"?

And then, *finis*. A four-pound shot fastened to the ankles. As if a four-pound shot could ballast twelve years in a man's life. As if death was ever an ending. The sleep of the historian and the curious whom his fables mollify is peaceful. Only Schlumberger must plumb and plumb again the chill waters off Charleston, tracking a sunbeam through amber to depths of emerald till it finds a spot on the locked teeth that throws back a golden spark.

In the late afternoon of July 12, 1838, Johann Nepomuk Maelzel was leaning against a forecastle rail watching a gang of stevedores. The sky had the texture of rumpled sheets. The stevedores were lowering the last of the five crates containing the dismantled limbs and innards of the chess automaton into the main hatch of the brig *Otis*. In the steamy sunless heat most of the crew had brought their work on deck and stripped off their shirts. Four men behind Maelzel on the forecastle were caulking the longboat. Their main business seemed to be an interminable lazy argument that Maelzel was too preoccupied to follow. Another gang sprawled on the main deck mending sail, working with the gossipy abstraction of a quilting bee. A few lucky ones, off duty, dangled their bare feet from the afterhouse roof, whittling and spitting tobacco juice into the harbor at the white bellies of fish. The unlucky had work that kept them below. Maelzel might have noticed from time to time that someone stepped to the foot of the aft companion ladder for a trace of breeze. All Maelzel could see of the fellow was a pair of hands twisting a potato and the peel coiling away from the blade of his knife.

Maelzel had learned the *Otis* was in port just a week earlier, four days after he abandoned Schlumberger to the death agonies of yellow fever in the Hotel de Habaña. The discovery was a fortuitous accident. Descending the outside steps of a waterfront rooming house some blocks from his old address, he had been hailed from the street by Joseph L. Nobre, the captain of the *Otis*. Nobre was an acquaintance from Philadelphia. After expressing some surprise at Maelzel's startled response—the sound of his name sent him abruptly scuttling back up the stairway, where Nobre's earnest cries checked him only at the landing, his hand on the doorknob—the captain explained that his employer, John F. Ohl, had charged him to deliver to Maelzel certain business correspondence. In Philadelphia, Maelzel had frequently stored his automata in a warehouse owned by Ohl, and it had been Ohl who loaned him the money to finance his Havana expedition. Captain Nobre apologised for not delivering the correspondence earlier. At the hotel where Ohl had instructed him to call, he was told that Mr. Maelzel had departed leaving no forwarding address. Nobre tactfully omitted the manager's complaint that Maelzel had left his account unsettled.

Maelzel, who had regained his composure, interrupted the captain's apology. He said the Havana tour had met with disaster. His most valued assistant, Schlumberger, had died of yellow fever, and his other helper had deserted. For a time, Maelzel explained, he had hoped to replace Schlumberger, but the promising young man he approached had declined the offer. Even if he could find a chess player—here Maelzel stammered, realizing he might have revealed more than he intended, and made sure Captain Nobre understood that while rumors of a concealed operator for the Turk were damnable lies, only a superior chess player could make the delicate adjustments that the Turk's mechanism constantly required. Despite the slanders of Mouret and Poe, Maelzel guarded the Turk's reputation as if it were an unmarried daughter. Even with a new assistant, he said, there was no point in continuing the tour. They had drawn good crowds till Ash Wednesday, but Lent had been disastrous, and after Easter the crowds seemed to have lost their taste for the miraculous. A stupid lot, these Cubans, Maelzel said, uncultured, uninterested in scientific progress or the art of chess. He continued in this manner, his voice rising to a nervously quavering pitch as he became more insistent, while Captain Nobre must have begun privately wondering whether Maelzel were confusing him with Ohl himself, with whom Maelzel's financial relationship made these justifications more appropriate. The upshot was that Maelzel told Captain Nobre that he would be requiring hold space for his automata and a first class stateroom for himself on the *Otis'* return voyage to Philadelphia.

Seeing they had business to discuss, the captain suggested they repair to a nearby café. He would later recollect that as they were seating themselves, Maelzel expressed a sudden preference for a chair close to a potted palm with leaves that shadowed the table. Though he talked volubly, concentrating on what he said was difficult. Maelzel's eyes kept darting to the entrance to scan each new arrival. At first Nobre had thought Maelzel was looking out for a friend. He was no fool, however, and when he noted the stammers and glances and the quick medicinal determination with which Maelzel drank, he realized that the shading palm under which he was seated was a good place not only for observation, but for concealment.

Maelzel expressed great disappointment that the *Otis* could not put to sea the very next day. Captain Nobre had to be embarrassingly emphatic in resisting his persuasions, explaining that proper stowage of the *Otis'* return cargo would prevent them from sailing until at least the fourteenth, and perhaps later if his search for additional crewmen to replace a pair of deserters were protracted. A problem, deserters. Scoundrels, for the most part, or romantic lads in love with the sea who soon got a bellyful of hanging in the yards.

When Maelzel first suggested that he would like to board the *Otis* immediately, Nobre objected, saying that with all his other duties it would be impossible to outfit a stateroom properly in so short a time. For the moment Maelzel dropped the subject, but after two or three glasses of whiskey he said that he had reason to believe he had enemies in Havana—in the alley outside his apartment he had noticed a prowler; he was certain he was followed in the street; and he had received definite indications that there was a plot afoot. All this was conveyed in hints and whispers, as if speaking out directly would give what he said a more potent reality. Nobre could not be certain whether Maelzel feared a personal attack or—as he explained it the next minute—an attempt to steal the chess automaton and learn the secret of its operation.

In any case Nobre relented his earlier decision, and that very night Maelzel moved his effects aboard the *Otis* and took up residence in the last of the temporary homes he was to occupy in a lifetime of travel. Maelzel not only slept aboard ship, he left it only to see to the proper crating of his automata. In fact, he seldom left his stateroom, despite the relative confinement of even the most spacious shipboard accommodations, and when he did take a stroll around the deck, it was usually, Captain Nobre observed, after dark.

Nobre privately concluded that Maelzel's anxiety might be traced to the unpaid hotel bill, and who could guess what other debts unsettled. He had never known Maelzel as an intemperate businessman, but in the boredom of the tropics, even the most virtuous men sometimes gave way to the artificial stimulations of the gaming tables. All these speculations he discussed at a dinner conversation with his first officer on the day Maelzel died, while one of the new crewmen shuffled around the table, clearing plates and refilling wine glasses.

Just as the crew stowing the automaton crates was hefting the cover back onto the hatch, Captain Nobre joined Maelzel on the forecastle deck. He had good news. That morning he had signed on two crewmen to replace the deserters, and the *Otis* would be able to embark for Philadelphia on the fourteenth as scheduled. Though Nobre did not mention it, one of the new hands had been rather hastily chosen—a gangly fellow with no previous experience before the mast, hollow-eyed and pale as if he had been recently ill, and with a knob on his back that pushed his arms into a simian dangle. Nobre took him on because he wanted to accommodate Maelzel, whose nervous prodding had become an irritation. Besides that, the fellow, who called himself Bishop, was eager—ready to tackle any job on board, even the most menial. Nobre put him to work as galley help, washing dishes and peeling potatoes.

As the *Otis* was clearing the harbor on the morning of the fourteenth, Maelzel appeared on deck in a state of unnatural jubilation. While the crew were hauling lines and dancing up the rigging, he hooked his thumbs in the armholes of his waistcoat and strode about briskly. Each time a sail unfurled and caught the wind he gave a nod as if that were exactly the way he had planned it. The captain was giving an order to his helmsman when Maelzel grabbed his bicep with an air of great urgency and walked him a few paces away. "Up there," he said with a satisfied grin. A sailor was edging along a rope that hung in loops beneath the foresail yard. "Much more nimble than that," Maelzel informed the captain. He had the tone of a man discriminating among wines from the same vineyard. "Easiest thing in the world to build one. And more graceful, too." Captain Nobre at last was made to understand that Maelzel was comparing the crewman on the yard with one of his inventions, a mechanical rope dancer called a Funambulist.

No sooner had Nobre excused himself than Maelzel was again at his side. He produced from his greatcoat pocket a small inlaid marine chessboard and proposed that Captain Nobre join him in a game. The captain, impatiently noting that the ship was still in sight of Moro Castle, said he had no great skill in the game and there was yet some business with the ship he must see to.

"Nonsense," Maelzel loudly declared, "chess is a child's game. I can make you a master with half an hour's instruction."

Maelzel swung about, bumping into a cabin boy, and promptly ordered him to fetch up a deal table and a pair of chairs. The boy hesitated, eyeing the captain, who—apparently unwilling to offend an important friend of his employer—gave the nod. The table was placed toward the lee side of the afterhouse. Just as they were about to be seated, Maelzel crumpled his face in a broad wink and disappeared down the companionway. Even from the galley port an observer might have seen Captain Nobre's cheeks and ears flush purple. After a longish minute Maelzel reappeared. For all to see he held up a bottle of claret and two glasses, as if he had conjured them from an empty hat. He had no hat and the bottle was already a third empty.

Maelzel won the first game handily. By the second, however, he had, with scarcely any assistance from Captain Nobre, drained the claret, and their skills were leveled. The captain barely paused to calculate his moves. Maelzel explained the significance of each, gaily crowed each time he took a piece and winced whenever his own fell. The game became a rapid, boring exchange until the pieces dwindled to three pawns on each side. Here Maelzel uttered a cry like a predatory bird and explained to Captain Nobre and the other passengers, about half a dozen, who had gathered to witness the great entrepreneur's spectacle, that the play had accidentally resurrected a problem similar to one of the automaton's favorite end-game demonstrations. Here he blithely plucked one of his opponent's pawns and dropped it into a new position.

"There!" he cried. "Let us see if you can solve it as the Turk did." Leaning over the table to make his words sound confidential, he whispered huskily, "It all depends on which pawn you move *first*!" then beamed up at the tightly gathered spectators and left Nobre to ponder his advice while he skipped off below to fetch another bottle of claret.

When he returned a few minutes later, the captain and the other passengers did not immediately notice a change in his mood. Perhaps later they might remark that he had uncorked and poured the bottle in silence, with only a muttered, "Woopsy," when he poured an ounce of liquor onto the table half an inch to the left of Nobre's glass. At the moment they laid his silence to respect for Captain Nobre, who was wrestling with end-game strategy.

Ruminatively, addressing himself rather than anyone else, the captain said, "This pawn is closest to your king, but if I push him along with no bodyguard, you'll swallow him at the third move. Should I try this one instead?"

Maelzel replied with a snarl that made the spectators take an involuntary step back from the table.

"You must play your own game," he said. "I cannot tell you what to move."

Nobre made no reply, only advanced a pawn, and after three more quick exchanges he said "Checkmate" and excused himself.

At dinner that evening Maelzel was among the passengers at the captain's table. He sat with his back to the galley entrance, stirring his soup as if he were prepared to dislike what he found in it. A Havana merchant was boasting in a solemn tenor about how many tons of sugar or tobacco he was importing to the States per month or per year. He announced that the future growth of the United States would depend on its tobacco crop and paused to let someone ask how this could be, so that he could have the pleasure of explaining. This was one of the challenges Maelzel customarily accepted *en passant,* and twisted till the subject became mechanics, which would shortly become his own inventions and himself. But he continued his silence. Another passenger filled the pause with a growl about the long interval between courses. Then the cook, a large man constantly sucking his lips, bumped open the galley door with a hip and brought in a stacked steaming tray. After a hasty glance he skittered to a sideboard and put the tray down with a jolt that spilled the gravy boat. The entire table heard his whispered curse. Then, stirring small sweat-smelling whirls in the still air, he circled the table, bobbing in and out over the shoulders of diners to collect soup plates. When he had a stack of them—Maelzel's, still full, had to be carried separately—he left them in daringly high piles on the sideboard and began slapping in their places plates of roast beef.

Captain Nobre had been nodding and depositing appropriately inflected grunts in the intervals of another passenger's monologue. Now he looked up and said, "What are you doing in here? Where's that new galley man?"

"He's ill, sir," replied the cook, careful to modulate the contempt in his voice so that the captain would know it was not directed at himself. The full force of his grievance came through, however, in his next remark: "I'm cooking and serving too, until he's better."

The captain made a vexed reference to landlubbers and instructed the cook to slow down and pass the plates like a gentleman. He added that the cook could inform the new man, Bishop was he called? that he might either find his sea legs by morning or swim back to Havana.

A few minutes later Maelzel, too, said he was feeling under the weather, and retired to his cabin. Shortly thereafter, the man called Bishop appeared with the coffee pot and a brief apology to the captain, and served the rest of the dinner without apparent difficulty.

An hour later Maelzel was still sitting on the edge of his bunk, staring at the small carved object he had discovered earlier that day. During his chess game with the captain, when he had come below for a fresh bottle of claret from the case he had brought aboard with him, he noticed that one of his waistcoats was lying on the mattress. He was annoyed that he had somehow failed to hang it properly over the back of his chair—one could never tell when one would be entertaining guests in his stateroom—and as he was picking it up something fell from its folds and clattered to the floor at his feet. He picked up a black ivory chess king carved in the likeness of Napoleon Bonaparte. The long military overcoat shaped the figure's back to a buzzardlike stoop. He had seen it for the first time more than twelve years ago, when a little windup drummer boy he had set in motion on Schlumberger's chessboard sent it sprawling.

He had seen it often since then, during a thousand tipsy chess dinners with its owner, who habitually installed it on the table to overlook their games like a brooding talisman. But Maelzel hadn't brought it aboard the *Otis*. He had left it in a muggy, yellow-walled room in the Hotel de Habaña with a man who had the stink of death sweat on him.

How had it got in his stateroom? In his haste to be gone from that reeking room, could he have packed it by mistake? He tried to imagine himself tossing clothing into a trunk, scooping a bundle from the edge of the bed where Schlumberger lay sleeping, dreaming, stirring now and again with a faint whimper. But there had been no bundle on the bed. Even if, somehow, the chesspiece *had* been packed among his things, he would have discovered it when he unpacked at the rooming house where Captain Nobre chanced upon him the next week. Or when he repacked his things to move aboard the *Otis*. Then how had it got in his stateroom?

He preferred, I believe, to repeat the question rather than consider the possible answers. Otherwise why would he spend such a long time sitting on the edge of his bed twisting the little black Bonaparte in his palm? When the possibilities are so limited, it is only a problem we do not wish to solve that has no solution. But each time Maelzel's mind sent out a tentative probe in the direction of the one solution, he winced and caught his breath. More than once he hugged his arms over his chest and bent double, his forehead nearly to his knees, and if—in the galley next to his stateroom—someone had pushed through a knothole at the back of a pantry, an eye sighting past the candle on Maelzel's bedside table might have seen a bright thread of spittle stretch from his lower lip to be absorbed, unnoticed by Maelzel in his pain, into the knee of his trousers. Maelzel in his pain. Yes. The little windup drummer boy winding down. The spring slackens, the gears slow, miss their bite and catch a few last times with a jolt that numbs the entire chest and leaves him drooling.

I think Maelzel's terror was not simply at the possibility that Schlumberger might be somehow alive and stalking him. That possibility had been tugging at his sanity for the past ten days—at least since the night he had been walking down the dark hallway toward his room and sensed rather than seen a stooping figure leap from his door and disappear around the corner. By the time he got to the corner, the door to the outside stairway was clicking shut. He did not, for some reason, throw it open and try to glimpse the intruder's flight. Perhaps he should have, or would have but for the chest pains, which might have begun even then to tell him that any excitement, any exertion would clog that delicate gear ticking in his chest. That might have been when the chest pains began. It would account for the sudden grunt and clutch he gave the next evening just before he turned on his heel and hurried off down the alley after catching sight of a shadow hovering behind a rain barrel.

Given these hints and premonitions, the possibility of Schlumberger alive—Schlumberger sitting across a chess table in a dark room with some sinuously crafted new end-game strategy, barely suppressing his glee as Maelzel tentatively dropped his queen into the baited square—that possibility had for a time already been worrying at him like a playful pup with its fangs sunk in a rag. It was enough, surely, to frighten him. But fear was something with which Maelzel ordinarily had no patience. In his best days he would have hefted his heavy oak walking stick and loosed a snarl that would send any alley-lurking cur yelping off at a brisk trot. Maelzel was disturbed, not by an ordinary fear, but by that peculiar terror against which the soul instinctively knows there is no defense. He sensed, I am convinced, that it was Schlumberger stalking him; but he did not quite believe Schlumberger had not died. Not that he feared a ghost—emphatically not. He had only scorn for the vulgar graveyard haunts of romance. The Age of Reason had cast him in its uncrackable mold. He was the supreme rationalist, God was a clockmaker, and clocks had no souls. This Schlumberger, then—and he was by now convinced that, against all probability, Schlumberger had survived: with the Bonaparte chesspiece tight in his fist, it was the only supposition reason would permit—this Schlumberger had not survived quite.

This shadow lurker, who spoke not and could not be confronted, defied all rational expectations. To have spent twelve years dancing a man on a string, and find him suddenly unpredictable, beyond rational control, could admit of only one rational explanation, and it shot Maelzel with terror. It must have seemed a Lazarus stalking him, one who had descended into fever and survived the death of his mind. The worst dread of the rationalist is insanity. It bows to no physical law, and

its power is uncanny. Against the malevolent insanity of a Schlumberger who had uncannily survived and was uncannily aboard the *Otis,*
Maelzel for the first time sensed himself helpless.

It is this, I believe, that prevented him from simply raising a holler,
demanding that Captain Nobre search from forecastle to steerage for a
hunchback stowaway. This new Schlumberger, potent with madness,
could elude any search, would fade into walls and float his mocking
laugh on the wind. And a fruitless search would make Maelzel a fool.
To speak at all would make him a fool. *I saw his corpse,* he had told
Captain Nobre with a sigh. *He was buried on such-and-such a day.*
And was he now to say, *I was mistaken?* The rationalist is not such a
fool. No. Maelzel was old and exhausted, ill and in debt, returning with
a cargo of mechanical toys to a land that had tired of them, and he knew
he must face this insane Schlumberger alone.

Maelzel never felt entirely comfortable in a room that seated less
than a hundred people. His cabin on the *Otis,* heavy with bilge-rank
air, left him strolling space little more than the length of a coffin. At
about midnight he climbed the steerage companion for a breath of air.
There was no moon, not a single star on the night of Maelzel's last sight
of the sky. At the taffrail leaned the deck watch, two old men murmuring over the bowls of their pipes. As he passed, one said, ". . . eat you
alive if you let it . . . ," and the other solemnly nodded. Noticing
Maelzel they fell silent and drew a glow into the bowls of their pipes as
if part of their job were to suck the last currents of light from the
universe. Maelzel continued on toward the forecastle. He heard a clink
above his head. Hanging in the shrouds was a dark lantern, one of the
running lights the ship customarily burned at night in heavily trafficked
waters. He reached up his hand. His fingertips touched a bowl still
warm. It had probably blown out in the breeze. He would mention it to
the watch on his next turn past the taffrail. The gaffsail caught a breeze
and struggled to hold it.

The breeze stiffened, and with the gaffsail swollen, the boom
straining at its point, the *Otis* rolled into a leeward yaw that quickened
the murmurous susurrations of waves along its hull. Maelzel lurched
into the windlass and steadied himself against it, cursing softly. The
foremast groaned back at him, the shrouds set up a faint thrumming, and
he tightened his grip on the windlass chain, clinging to the back of a

great undulating leviathan, capricious as any creature with a will. It was not at all like the predictable thumpa-thump of the *Delta Belle*'s pistons.

The breeze slackened. He walked on. As he was rounding the corner of the forward hatch, he saw a shadow slide behind a water barrel. Walking lightly, Maelzel turned back the way he had come and circled the hatch. Edging along the port rail as far from the hatch as he could get, he came abreast of the corner, his oak stick half raised at the innocent rain barrel, while a fleeting movement at the starboard corner of the forecastle house was followed by a ratlike skittering. Maelzel ran to the starboard rail and looked forward, stepping gingerly past the entrance of the forecastle companion. From its shadow a cloud of darkness detached itself, and before he could turn to meet it a whirling rush collided with his flank, lifting his feet from the deck. For a breathless moment his head and shoulders hung beyond the bulwark rail, suspended over the water by a force thrusting from under his armpits; then he was released, gasping, groaning, mewing, clutching a shroud line to keep himself on his feet. When the pain ebbed enough to let him look, the deck was empty.

Then he heard a strange hysterical *wek-wek,* like a mouse with an owl's talon in its scruff. He raised his eyes. Aloft, high in the shrouds, a figure was leaning toward him. He took a step back. I think he said "Willie" at it, but the only answer he got was a repetition of the *wek-wek* giggle, and when he heard it, he began backing along the deck toward the steerage companion. He never again left his berth in the forecastle.

The steward who called Maelzel for breakfast the next morning reported to the captain that he was behaving curiously. The steward had called and knocked repeatedly without a response. At length there was a feeble croak, and the door was unlatched. Hesitant, wondering whether this was an invitation to enter, he heard a heavy thud. He swung the door open and found Maelzel on the floor beside his berth, conscious but unable to rise. He was trying feebly to raise himself on one arm. The other was pinned under the weight of his body, and he made no effort to use it. The steward helped him to bed, then asked if he would like his breakfast brought to his berth. Maelzel declined with a hand gesture, but as the steward began to leave, motioned for him to approach the bed. When he was within reach, Maelzel—again using the left hand—took hold of the collar of his coat and drew him down toward his face. He tried to speak. What came out was a slurred croak, as if he were in the last stages of intoxication. The right side of Maelzel's mouth was pinched up in an odd stiff smirk. By a combination of gestures and half-articulated words, the steward was finally given to understand that Maelzel wished him to take up the case of claret standing in a corner of his room, and place it near his bedside. The steward protested that the case of bottles would make it cumbersome for Maelzel to get out of bed. Maelzel's response, he decided, was that it "dunmadr," and he did what had been requested.

The steward suggested that Maelzel may have suffered a paralytic stroke. The captain replied that it would not be possible to get medical treatment until they made port, and in any case it was far more likely, judging from the symptoms the steward described, that Maelzel was simply in the midst of an alcoholic debauch. He added a few remarks reflecting the conventional pieties of the temperance societies, then instructed the steward to check on Maelzel's condition at mealtimes, but otherwise let his madness run its course.

In the next few days the captain made occasional inquiries about his passenger, but it was clear that he had formed a distaste for Maelzel that left him with no desire to check on his condition personally. The only other person on board who expressed an interest in Maelzel was the galley assistant, Bishop, who regularly joked with the steward about the special duties he had taken on as innkeeper and chinwiper. The steward had told Bishop that the only request Maelzel made of him was to draw the corks from fresh bottles of claret, but that once, during a rolling sea, he had assisted him in changing his shirt after a sudden pitch had spilled liquor down the front. The steward said Maelzel apparently never left his berth, where a rolled-up greatcoat on top of his pillow propped him at sufficient elevation so that he could bring the bottle to his lips with his left hand. Though he was consuming an average of two bottles of claret a day and refusing all other nourishment, he began after the second day to speak a bit more clearly. The cabin smelled strongly of urine.

When the steward entered his stateroom on Thursday morning, Maelzel, addressing him as Leonard, told the steward he had no right to something if he didn't know how to use it. Bishop found this conversation sufficiently amusing to inquire about it in detail. The steward, whose name was Simpson, enjoyed his talents as a mimic. With his head angled against a raised right shoulder, rolling his eyes and slurring his words, he showed how Maelzel, addressing him in a querulous whine as Leonard, explained that he had no right to create a pandemonium, that he was creating a pandemonium he had no right to, that he had no right to it if he didn't know how to make money with it and what did it matter locking in a few gears if he was the one who knew how to make it fight him in every law court in Europe, even if he was his brother. Bishop inquired whether it might not have been a panharmonicon that Leonard-Simpson had been accused of creating. Certainly not, Simpson said, and what anyway was a panharmonicon. Bishop said that it was a mechanical orchestra, and explained that last month he had been in the audience at one of Maelzel's Havana exhibitions.

At the noon meal on Friday, Maelzel recognized Simpson and asked him graciously to draw the cork on another bottle of claret. He remarked that there were only six left in the case and wondered if that would be enough. Simpson ventured to say that they were still some eight or nine days from Philadelphia, and if Maelzel continued drinking two bottles per day, he would surely not have enough to last the voyage. To this Maelzel replied quite cheerily, "Oh, I'll not be that long about it." When the steward visited him that evening, however, he was again off his head, addressing him not as Leonard this time, but as someone called Willie. With great agitation he begged Willie to leave off tormenting him. Whimpering and moaning he begged Simpson to protect him from Willie, and said he had heard Willie's voice, Willie talking through the walls.

The steward was alarmed enough to notify Captain Nobre that Maelzel's condition seemed to be declining. The captain reluctantly agreed to visit Maelzel's bedside himself. At first Maelzel seemed partially recovered. He attempted to engage the captain in a conversation about music, making frequent references to Beethoven. Within a few moments, however, he was snarling that Beethoven was a thief whom he would fight through every law court in Europe, and declared that he was surrounded by stupidity. Over and over he asserted that he was surrounded by stupidity, and ended by calling loudly for assistance from Willie. After doing their best to soothe him the captain and the steward departed, leaving a candle burning at his bedside because Maelzel claimed that when he was left alone in the dark Willie talked to him through the walls.

KINGKILL

Late that night Maelzel fell from restless babbling into a deep sleep from which he did not stir, not when his name was called through the knothole separating his stateroom from the galley pantry, and not when his door was silently opened and closed and Schlumberger stood before him with Rouault's cocked dueling pistol pointing down his open mouth and said, "Wake up, you bugger, so I can kill you."

42 | The Faceless Man

IN HIS JOURNAL he called it the faceless man dream. Through the years after the Philadelphia museum fire that destroyed the automaton it recurred often, not always the same in detail but varied within a form strictly governed as a sonnet. Eventually, as you huff in cold air, he gave it a name—to make it visible. "The faceless man again, this time in a railway carriage, sitting across the aisle." The vagueness of the label mimed a certain hazy focus in the dream itself, because the man wasn't actually faceless. It was only that no matter how quickly he glanced up or how elaborately he stalked it, the face would just have dipped into the shadow of a hat brim or behind a rain-streaked windowpane. Sometimes it would hover beyond his left shoulder, so close that a turn of the head would bring him eye to eye with it, but no effort of will or self-beguiling could unfreeze his gaze from some other object: the intricate coils of a sleeping adder, a flame curling a crumpled sheet of paper.

One dream, so vivid he didn't need to check the pages of his journal to call it back image by image, began with the rattle of train wheels over track. The shudder made his whole body tingle. In the compartment where he sat everything had the hallucinatory radiance of flowers caught in sunlight after a shower: the mahogany panels, the upholstery buttons twinkling in the voluptuous leather cushions. The red tassel of a shade cord swayed like a censer across a windowpane, framing trees and dells and cattle ankle-deep in a muddy pond, all wheeling into view and flashing away behind him with a rapidity that quickened his heart, because he knew—by the dreamer's special dispensation to reconcile incongruities—that the train he had boarded that morning in Philadelphia was now flying over the Alsatian countryside to the village where his mother still, after all these decades, lived. Surely she does, she must, though he has not written her in all the years since he left Paris on the Atlantic packet. She must, because his neglectful silence will be atoned if he can burst through the doorway into the kitchen where she will be polishing silver, and spin her in his arms, crying out . . . But what can he say?

What, to equal the pain of his long silence, the pain of having borne him, can he offer? His traveling bag—at his feet on the floor of the train compartment—must contain the gift he has brought. He opens it and roots among the linen, but finds only a black pawn with its round head broken off, and something else, round and dark, which he at first takes for the missing portion of the chesspiece. But it is too large, too heavy: a lead pistol ball. The gift, then, is probably in the pocket of his frock coat. It must be there, and he must find her still alive. He has not come this long journey to lay his life before a stone slab in a field of stones.

To collect his thoughts he looks out the window just as his old schoolhouse glides past, and before he can dart around to catch another glimpse a tree is looming, the oak with the pumpkin-sized gall that marks the lane where he lives—oh, marvelous! And look there: the fork in the road where he watched Bonaparte's regiment pass, and that night she scolded him because he did not come home to supper until the last bluecoat straggler had trudged over the crest of the hill and down into the snows of Russia. Home! He realizes the train will let him off in front of his very door. Quickly: his beaver hat, his gold-handled walking stick—ah, here on the seat at his side. But in the moment he takes to gather them, night has begun to fall and the landscape outside his window has become a wall of storefronts with dark birds swooping from their eaves and flapping heavily back. Was it some other oak? Has the town changed so? To make sure the train has not, in the moment he looked away, passed his mother's house, he peers into the gathering dusk. But gaslights in the compartment have been turned up, and the face of a man sitting across the aisle reflects on the pane, obscuring his vision, floating dim as a daylight moon between Schlumberger and the fields of his home. When he turns to ask the man to move out of his way, just as he begins to recognize a familiar doughy pallor in the cheeks and

The Faceless Man

brow, the candle gutters and the night air blowing in his open window wakes him with a chill.

In his first appearance the faceless man was scarcely noticed, a pale flicker at the border of a more familiar constellation—the fire dream. A recurrence of the fire dream was, I suppose, to be expected following the Turk's actual destruction by fire. After the auction of Maelzel's effects the five crates containing the automaton had fallen into the hands of Dr. John K. Mitchell, who organized a club of Philadelphia chess connoisseurs to finance its purchase and reconstruction. This task took more than a year, thanks to the habitual cunning of Maelzel, who had separately packed and deliberately mislabeled the crucial pantograph device. Mitchell eventually traced it among an odd lot of machinery parts that had found their way into Ohl's warehouse. Like many another beauty, the Turk's chief fascination was its mystery, and once each of the members of Mitchell's club had a turn in the box, emerging stiff-backed and sweating, they looked around for a place to discard it. Peale's Museum accepted the donation. A few exhibition games were arranged, but the Turk was no competition for Peale's Chinese ivories and mastodon bones. When fire broke out in the National Theatre in the early hours of July 5, 1854, leapt an alley and attacked the museum, the Turk was in a large crate under a back stairway. The first newspaper reports of the fire did not mention it among the losses.

To Schlumberger, of course, his eye skipping down the columns of print, the Turk was at the very heart of the inferno, and that night, as if the heat had melted away the sixteen years that separated him from that Havana hotel room, he was there again, in the fire dream, in the museum, petrified among the petrified figurines, the ivory swordsman's blade always about to descend, the warlord's mount reined to an ivory prance. He was there, Lot's wife at his side, her salt stare fixed like his on the one thing in the museum that moved: alive! dancing a necklace round the Turk's head, usurping his turban to make a crown, lapping the cheeks to a radiant blush, transmuting all it touched into rosy life.

In his journal Schlumberger elaborated the dream, suggesting correspondences that are surely accidental, probably invented. Here for the first time the strange chamber full of glass cases and ivory carvings is identified as a museum. It is tempting (and Schlumberger yielded) to

[3 8 9]

claim for this detail an element of prescience. But the heat of the dream's successive incarnations eventually welded the disparate details into an indivisible whole, and if the Turk's first incinerations had taken place in a theatre or a warehouse, in Havana or New Orleans, he would after a time have relocated them all in Mr. Peale's storehouse of the past.

The brilliant chamber inside Schlumberger's skull had, however, only a dim counterfeit in reality. The statuary of Peale's museum was exhibited in another room, and it was not Lot's wife but Euridice. In his tortuous attempts at understanding, Schlumberger at last corrupts the dream into a parable. Each exhibit becomes an artifact in the Turk's twelve-year decline—an obvious literary flourish. Only one new element in the dream rings authentic: "Just beyond the radius of my locked gaze," he writes, "I sensed another presence—solitary, purposeful and evil. It was a greyness—not the amorphous grey of the fire smoke, but fixed; a pallor like the brow of a corpse." The faceless man. And in the months, the years that follow, the fire gradually fades to its ashes, while the faceless man looms from them like a phoenix.

Waking, restless, Schlumberger shuts the window, wraps his body in a dressing gown. Then, as on many other nights, he pokes a few coals to brew tea and takes up his journal, writing, "The faceless man again . . ." Or, if the dream has already cooled to its cinders, he writes of the past, of Louise, of Maelzel. Or Rouault.

It was during the years following the museum fire, the years of the faceless man dream, that Schlumberger commenced his efforts to reconstruct his life as the Turk's brain. He reread his journal, reorganized it, wrote lengthy codas to its entries. Often he was impatient with the journal. It seemed to focus on things of no consequence—elaborate descriptions of his feelings and little information about what caused them. To fill some of its gaps, he hunted down one of the boys who saw him climbing out of the automaton one hot night in Baltimore, and learned that a mysterious man told them where to station themselves for their alley spying. He visited Hiram Walker, and was not surprised to learn that he and his brother were given unexpected assistance in building a duplicate automaton.

His first thought when he began musing on these discoveries was that the faceless man of his dreams had cast a shadow over reality. Before he could even finish the sentence, however, between the drying of his quill and its dipping, he realized the truth was precisely the opposite. He recalled the few minutes he had spent alone with Louise Rouault while he was preparing to gull the old phrenologist, how close she had been to him, swooning on the verge, he felt, of truly loving him—and that very night she had disappeared from his life. Why? And later, just as he was becoming reconciled to winning the Turk's games rather than his own, content with the assurance that he was the essential cogwheel in Maelzel's machine, he found himself pulling strings for the Funambulists, because Maelzel had been frightened into retiring the Turk (a temporary expedient that lasted seven years) by a pair of spying boys and the Walker brothers' automaton. Someone had helped them—who? Through all the years of his association with Maelzel, he had been stalked by a malevolent being, someone powerful enough to nudge a possibility to its most unfortunate fulfillment, yet so impalpable that it was only in these dreams, sixteen years after Maelzel's death, that he became visible.

At this stage in his reflections Schlumberger suffered a nervous attack that kept him to his bed for two months. When he was sufficiently recovered to return to his journal, he began an interminable review of his last conversation with Rouault. At first his reflections centered on himself. Precise and detached as a pathologist noting the magnitude of tremors in a seizure, he detailed the effects of Rouault's successive revelations. When he thought he had each twitching nerve pinned beneath a word, he would snuff the candle and stretch out on his bed. In the comfortable dark, with his eyes beginning to close, it would come to him like the worrying whine of a mosquito that something was still unsaid. One night it occurred to him that what Rouault had told him seemed to have a calculated development, like a piece of formal rhetoric. The next evening he again opened the journal, starting with the heat in the room where they had talked, the yellow walls that seemed to reflect it, the harbor stench pouring through the open window, and at last settling on Rouault himself—the way he would detach his soaking shirt from his ribs, his fingers pinching and drawing the fabric into pointed breasts that he flapped to fan some air along his ribs and armpits.

Thinking of Rouault was hard: what was real about the memory was how Schlumberger felt. Rouault—except for his glistening brow and the constant tugging on his shirt front as if the inside of it were filled with slivers of glass—was invisible; a piece of paper on which the things he said might have been written. A long time before he could say how he knew it, he had decided that what was said that night had a different meaning for Rouault. Then it began to come through: first, a voice. The halts in his speech, the stammers—they came at odd moments. Other things came back as he wrote. Rouault's gestures had been broad and assertive at times when Schlumberger felt he might have expected to be taken for granted. His evasions—those moments Schlumberger recognized as evasions—detoured intricately around the most bland terrain. Then, unblinking, in tones level and dead as the tap of his hammer knocking together a scaffold for Maelzel, he would say things that made Schlumberger cry out as if he had been scalded. Now he could see him clearly, picking at the dead skin on his lip. The hand flicked away, the lips suddenly flattened against the teeth as they did when he knocked back a shot of brandy, and he said, "I only got the letter yesterday." It was grotesque. He said it as if he were owning up to something. It was comic. It was wrong.

He tried to recall Rouault's face as he told him Louise was dead. He was looking for a convulsion, even a tremor. He spent three nights trying to find something to put on paper about Rouault's face, and just as he was about to give up, the face emerged clearly as if it were looking up from the paper under his hand, and he realized there was nothing to put down because there had been nothing there. Less than a day after he got word of his wife's death, Rouault told of it as if it had happened so long ago it could only concern somebody else, someone he had ceased to be. If there was one thing Schlumberger felt he knew about Rouault, it was that no matter how many years had passed since Louise had shared his bed, he would not receive the news of her death stoically. But there it was: he had been sitting in the wicker chair, his eyes lowered, and he looked straight into Schlumberger's eyes and said, "She's where you can't touch her."

Then he described the letter—haltingly, thoroughly, at times using odd, literary turns of speech, as if certain phrases from it had already rooted themselves in his memory, become his own way of thinking about what had happened. As he spoke a bead of sweat trickled through his brow and followed a crease in his eyelid to the corner, where it tracked down his cheek like a tear.

Perhaps he was numb. Shock could do that, he supposed. But it was equally possible that Rouault had lied about the time of her death, or about when he had heard of it. Despite Schlumberger's plea, Rouault had not allowed him to see her last letter. On that point he had maintained a righteous inflexibility. "What she gave me is mine," he had said. And then, in the only moment when the feeling seemed to match the words: "She was, after all, my wife." His throat had tightened around the word. That was genuine. Perhaps too genuine for Schlumberger's taste, since he went over the scene many times before he recollected it. But Rouault might have got the letter years ago. Could it possibly have been only a day that Rouault had kept from him news of Louise's death? Why would he lie? Wrenching the fact into the present could serve but one purpose—to make it more intense for Schlumberger.

Here Schlumberger stopped writing again. He felt giddy. He took a walk along the waterfront and went out to the end of a deserted pier where he would have the ocean on all sides of him. Then he went back to his room and dragged a chair over to the closet so he could reach from a high shelf the wooden case with the red lining in which he kept Rouault's dueling pistols. Inside the case was the message Louise had written the night she disappeared: I'd rather be dead or on the streets than go on like this. That, too, had been addressed to Rouault, but he hadn't seemed to mind that Schlumberger read it. And when he dropped out of sight, the same night he told Schlumberger Louise was dead, he had left it behind. Did he *intend* Schlumberger to find it? The note was scrawled on the last page of a thick manuscript in Rouault's hand. Once Schlumberger had begun, rather nervously and impatiently, to read it. Within a page and a half, however, he decided it was nothing but a religious tract, filled with hysterical pronouncements about judgment and justification. Now for the first time he allowed himself to consider that Rouault's tract might have something to do with Louise's reasons for leaving. Perhaps the idea had once or twice flitted through his mind, but always before he had shied violently from it. His sense of the rightness of things was not flattered by the notion that Louise's only explanation of her flight had been Rouault. As his eyes passed down one yellowed sheet and onto another, he learned of Rouault pressing his ear to the wall not as the cuckolded husband but in the role of God's spy, recording the sinful grunts of Schlumberger's lust and the strange liturgy of Louise's sex with Maelzel. He followed through its intricate course the argument by which for Rouault establishd himself as the savior of his wife's soul and the agent of divine retribution against Maelzel and Schlumberger. Long before he came to the page where the manuscript broke off, he had been shocked at his own naïveté, that he could live side by side with a man for twelve years without realizing how deeply he was hated.

When he had finished he returned to his journal, to the rendering of his last conversation with Rouault, and picked up his quill. The inflections of the sonorous voice, the downcast eyes, the lip-picking grimace, all sharpened into focus like an image under a microscope: they were the symptoms of a man anxious to be believed. With agonizing clarity Schlumberger saw that at the moment Rouault had said, "She's where you can't touch her," his eyes had unhooded in a glare of sinister calculation.

The only thing that surprised him now was why Rouault had waited twelve years. Who can say why? Waiting, like anything else, becomes a habit. Not a matter of patience, only inertia. It is more difficult to make any beginning, however hopeful, than to continue any misery, however endless. Perhaps, so long as the automaton was traveling across the country, drawing headlines wherever it went, he could feel that Louise always knew where to find him if she wanted to return. Why, then, would he have tried to sabotage the automaton's career, destroy the beacon that brilliantly flashed out to her his presence? Moments of despair, perhaps, when a man might be willing to end his suspense by ending his hope. And if it were true after all that he only learned of her death the day before he told Schlumberger of it, that would be reason enough for him to tolerate no longer the ones he so thoroughly hated. Hated still, after all those years? Yes. The departure of Louise might have robbed him of his divine justification, but his hatred remained pure. Through all those years of crating and uncrating the automata, mapping itineraries, fetching fresh bottles for Maelzel and Schlumberger during the long chess dinners and clearing the debris after they had staggered to bed weeping with drunken affection and reviling the woman he loved—through all those years he had kept his hatred in the same corner where he concealed the pistols, and when he unpacked it at last, all he had to do was leave the pistols on the bed for Schlumberger to find. No need at all for God's help. There would be, for Maelzel, a lead ball in the heart, certain but rather unsatisfyingly swift; and for Schlumberger, the full revenge: the torment Rouault himself had endured each of those twelve years and would perhaps bear to his grave—hatred, the worm in the brain.

And then Schlumberger found himself wondering whether Louise had died at all. It was equally possible that what had died was only Rouault's long-starved love for her, or his hope that she would return. He tried to imagine where she might be, how she might be using the life he once thought would belong to him, that she had wrested from his grasp and claimed for herself. He found it much easier to imagine it Rouault's way: the spurning woman spurned in turn, dying outcast, with a final regret for the love she had not valued. A most comforting moral tale. Exactly the stuff on which Rouault would nourish his own hopes, and what he might guess Schlumberger would be most ready to believe.

Her being dead was like having an old wound or a broken bone that never properly healed. He might now and then finger the scar, and a sudden change in the weather would bring pain. The only thing to do was wait for the wind to change. But what if she had not died, were alive today? He waited for the wound to open its lips, the bone to crack in the weak place. Nothing happened. He was an old man. He had outlasted his love and his hatred both. What remained was the need to understand.

Why did she leave? He had always assumed that whatever meaning that fact had was in relation to himself, to his failure. He was not the man to hold her. If she had discovered and read Rouault's manuscript on the night she left, however, perhaps her disappearance was, at least in part, a way of protecting him from Rouault's jealousy. With that thought he felt a soothing benediction, as if he had opened his bedroom window and found the air scented with honeysuckle. But by the same evidence, she might have been protecting Maelzel. He leafed through Rouault's letter till he came to the strange passage in which he confessed that he had knelt at the keyhole outside the door as Maelzel brutalized his wife.

Schlumberger attacked the passage, stripping away the gristle and sinew of its rhetoric until he felt he had reached the spare bone of what Rouault had witnessed. That bone—with its hard alien gleam—he transferred to the pages of his journal, grafting it into his own flesh. Where once he had been tortured at the thought of her loving anyone, yielding to anyone, let alone Maelzel, let alone in the way Rouault had described, he now found that he could reconcile himself to the scene only if he infused her part in it with something like love—or, to be more precise, the need for love. He could not conceive it, even as love, except as something she would need to escape, even as he had escaped. When he thought of Maelzel's hand jamming her core, of the airless shrine Rouault invited her to inhabit, and of his own rampant ardor, he understood that she must have felt she had to escape them all—for her very life.

What else must he come to understand?

I have meditated long over the connection between Schlumberger's fire dream and the fire that consumed the automaton in Peale's Museum. Sixteen years separate that fire from the moment when Schlumberger looked for the last time on the corpse of Maelzel lying in his stateroom berth on board the *Otis*. Can it be that his fear, his hatred, his love were so tenacious that after such a time he was yet compelled to attempt so futile a purgation? And what, then, must those sixteen years have been, what pointless griefs must have filled them, if he could still imagine it required flames blistering the Turk's lips, melting its eyes, cracking and charring the box where he had hunched and sweated so many years—to free him.

The fire didn't free him. For a short while he thought it had. But whatever room he entered still had walls. And the machine he thought to destroy has proved indestructible. Last week I visited the Centennial Exhibition in Philadelphia. A mile of grounds displaying one machine after another, all prisons of wire and steel which the hawkers, echoing Maelzel's grandest fancies, claim will transform the future into a Utopia. And the greatest of them all—pushing the wheels of the others, forking its chill current into each bright glass bulb on the midway—the Corliss Dynamo, relentless heartbeat of the entire Exhibition. As I entered the building housing it my ears were possessed by a hum as if a thousand voices were pitched to the same mindless drone. The floor beneath me vibrated like the deck of the *Delta Belle*.

I was surprised to find that the superintendent who conducted the crowds of gawkers on a tour of the building was a woman, pert and quick and confident, with a voice so rich there was no trouble, even for an old man, hearing her above the dynamo hum as she led the tourists up the ladders and down the ringing steel catwalks of the world to come. Her voice seemed to tame its violence, and she strode along brisk and long-legged, much as I imagine Louise Rouault did the night she closed the door on Maelzel's contempt and Rouault's god and Schlumberger's infantile love, and entered the dawn of a Boston morning owning only her self.

No, the fire didn't free him. Can I imagine that these words, this act of knowing, frees him at last? It may have freed who he was.

Who *was* he then? In his youth he spied insatiably on the cast fragments of himself that were strewn over the multiple mirrors of the Café de la Régence. In later years what took the place of the mirrored walls was the journal, which often seemed to reflect as many vain and shifting facets as the mirrors themselves. Studying its pages, attempting to collate his obsessive rerenderings of the same events, I often felt as Maelzel must have the day he came for Schlumberger and stood at the doors of the grand chess salon in the café wondering which of the images before him was not a reflection. In the end I destroyed the journal, feeding it page by deliberate page into my study fire, and supplanted whatever reality it may have had with this manuscript, my own story. Before yielding to that impulse, which I shall neither explain nor defend, I ripped out this passage, perhaps as near a true reflection as he ever confronted:

". . . don't know why I felt that way, since that's what I'd come for, but when I saw him lying still and grey with his jaw dropped and his eyes staring at what I couldn't see, it was like *Maman* having to comb his hair over again and refold his hands because after they had got him all shaved and combed and his mouth tied shut, they let me into the bedroom for a last look and a prayer, and before they could hold me back I was running to him, throwing myself across him so I could get my arms around his neck and have his beard rasping my cheek just the way it used to before there were rules and he would lift me in his arms and hold me up over his head laughing deep in his throat and bring me down to his face to kiss me with his scratchy beard that I could feel even through the powder on his cheeks until they pulled me away still crying, Oh Papa forgive me.

"Just as if he ever listened."

A moment ago I laid down my quill and looked at the window beyond my writing table. It's been an hour since I trimmed and lit the lamp to stave off the shadows thickening across the page. Old men must protect their eyes. The street outside is invisible. The glass, opaque now, reflects my image. I try to discover if these years of writing have stamped in my own face of the man who was Schlumberger.

My eyes have shrunk deep as they can from the light. The skin across my brow and nose grows tight. Each month the skull emerges more clearly. Creases bracket my mouth, putting whatever I say inside time-hewn parentheses. A few years ago a brown discoloration of skin on my brow began to spread like a hot spring leaking up from some underground fissure of my brain. It is silver-dollar size tonight, and its upper edge swamps the roots of my thinning hair. I pretend that until it covers my skull I cannot die.

The Schlumberger who squandered his mortality on toy kings and queens would never have discovered himself in my disguise. Only when I profile myself to the window, my mirror, do I see something he might recognize: the hump that took a chucker's kicks in a waterfront whorehouse, the hump that Maelzel one day touched for luck.

Who was William Schlumberger?

I turn away from the mirror. Its last lie is less pleasant than the first. The life left me is too short for games.

[3 9 8]

About the Author

THOMAS GAVIN received his B.A. and M.A. degrees from the University of Toledo, Ohio. He has taught in grade schools and high schools and worked as a reporter. For three years he was a member of the English division at Delta College in Michigan. In 1975, he was a Fellow at the Bread Loaf Writers' Conference. Now an Assistant Professor of English at Middlebury College, he lives in Vermont with his wife and children.